Dedicated to the memory of my parents and grandparents,
whose lives and stories were my inspiration.

I

CUSTARD TARTS

Nellie tried not to look up at the clock. She'd checked it not more than a minute ago and knew there was only half an hour till the end of her shift. But the temptation to check again was overwhelming. She looked up at the large white-faced clock hanging on the brick wall between two tall factory windows. The clock had a two-inch-thick coating of pale golden powder over its rim and the square panes in the windows were edged with the same substance, as if a yellow snowstorm had blown through the factory floor, dusting every nook and cranny with a fine powder. But it wasn't snowing. It was high summer and the room was filled with choking custard powder. Albert, the foreman, had gone round earlier with a long pole, pulling open the top windowpanes and letting some air in to alleviate the oppressive heat of the long room. But to Nellie it felt as though the air must be the only thing that wasn't moving in the powder-packing department of Pearce Duff's custard factory.

Nellie had been standing at the bench for almost eleven hours now, filling packet after packet with custard powder, and her calf muscles, thighs and back all screamed as though they'd been stretched on a rack. She shifted continually from one foot to the other in search of momentary relief. Any minute now the hooter would sound, a jarring high-pitched scream, which was nevertheless always welcome. Quickly glancing from the clock back to her best friend Lily, she checked to see if her friend's hands were idle. Lily had stood beside her all day, folding and pasting the filled packets of custard Nellie passed to her. They had to make sure their hands were always moving. Albert constantly prowled between the rows of filling machines, checking on the girls' every movement. He could spot an idle hand from the other end of the factory floor. A pause in the filling, folding or packing procedure was considered the cardinal sin in the powder-packing department. Nothing was ever allowed to be still. She nudged her friend to let her know Albert was approaching and handed her the next packet for pasting.

'Not long now, Lil,' she muttered.

Lily raised her eyes, and without pause shoved the next packet to Maggie Tyrell for loading on to the trolley.

Suddenly a high-pitched screeching noise came keening up from the factory yard below and through the open windows. Nellie and Lily exchanged glances. It was not the welcome sound of the factory hooter sounding the end of their day, but the unmistakable wail of a baby. Instantly Nellie saw Maggie Tyrell freeze. She was a frazzled-looking woman with six children.

'That's my little Lenny!' Maggie darted a look at the clock. 'Me daughter's brought him too early!'

Albert was approaching at a steady pace and Nellie saw panic written on Maggie's face. Ethel Brown, a large woman working at the next machine who had also heard the baby's cry, leaned over to Maggie.

'Ask to go early, Mag,' she suggested.

But Maggie shook her head. 'He'll dock me half hour.'

More and more women became aware of the baby's insistent screaming, shooting quick looks at Maggie to see what she would do, some making gestures for her to go. Only Albert seemed not to hear the cries coming through the high windows as he passed behind their backs, adding up the quantities of packets on each trolley.

Maggie was becoming more and more agitated. 'Oh, poor little bugger, I can't stand much more of this. He's hungry, that's all.'

She fumbled with a packet, dropping it on the floor, its contents spilling out in an accusing golden stream. Nellie quickly kicked the broken packet under the bench.

'Mag, he's coming back, ask him for a toilet break, quick!'

Maggie smoothed her worried features into a placating smile and looked over her shoulder, catching Albert's attention with her raised hand.

'I need to go to the lav, Albert,' she whispered.

'Can't you wait?' Albert said irritably. 'There's only ten minutes to go!'

Maggie crossed her legs and made a face. 'I'm afraid I'll have an accident…'

'Oh, go on then.'

Maggie scuttled off towards the double doors.

'You women drink too much tea, that's your trouble!' he called after her as Ethel Brown waved two fingers behind his back, which set Lily and Nellie giggling.

Soon the sounds of the baby's cries faded away as Maggie fed him at the factory gates, and not long after the scream of the factory hooter sounded their release.

Nellie Clark walked out of Pearce Duff's factory, arm in arm with Lily Bosher. A crowd of women and girls shuffled around them, many linking arms, some laughing, others looking about them. Nellie herself was searching the small crowd of young men who hung about the factory gates, for one special face.

One of the bolder boys took his hands from his pockets and whistled. 'Aye aye, boys, here come the custard tarts!'

More whistles followed and some called out girls' names. Nellie peered over the heads of the crowd as she heard someone call hers. Sam, one of the delivery boys, was seated up on a cart, holding the horse's reins steady.

She pretended not to hear him. Every day he offered to give her a lift on the cart back to her home in Vauban Street, next door to the carter's stables, where he worked with her father.

'He's not bad-looking,' whispered her friend Lily, '*and* he's here, regular as clockwork.'

Nellie shook her head and shushed her friend.

'Leave off, Lily, I'm not getting up on that cart! Anyway, he's such a soppy 'apporth, I'm not givin' him the time of day.'

Nellie, at sixteen, was a fresh-faced girl with bright blue eyes and a sweep of chestnut hair, which she attempted in vain to keep contained in a loose roll, framing her face. She couldn't say why his attentions irritated her so much, but they did.

You're not for me, Sam Gilbie, she thought, as they swept on past the young man with his carefully brushed, wavy dark hair. Undeterred, he jumped down and called after them.

'I was wondering, Nellie—'

'Not interested!' Lily called back as the two girls leaned into one another, their wide flat caps touching, to form a shield against the young man's advances. But after they had passed, another young man detached himself from the crowd and ran to catch up with Lily and Nellie.

'Hang on, girls!'

At the sound of his voice, Nellie tightened her grip on her friend's arm. He was a tall, lithe fellow of about twenty, and as he caught up with them he joined his palms, swimming between them, like a sinuous eel. They parted to allow him in, and he draped an arm over each of their shoulders.

'All set for tonight, you two?' He kissed Lily on the cheek and attempted to do the same to Nellie.

'Get off, you saucy sod.' She jerked her head back, but blushed all the same. Nellie had spotted Lily's brother, Ted, in the crowd and now found herself angry at the rising blush, which she was unable to disguise. He was a head taller than the two girls and wore a flat cap and a white choker, tied around his neck. His clothes, though obviously a docker's, always looked dashing on his long-limbed figure and Nellie found herself noticing the jaunty angle of his cap.

'I told you, we'll be there,' said Lily. 'Don't keep on about it.'

'I'm not sure I can come,' Nellie said. 'My dad's not too keen on me going out on my own at night.'

'Well, tell him you're going to me mum's house.' Ted smiled down at her and squeezed her shoulder. 'It's true enough, it's where I'm meeting you, so you are going there… *first*!'

He broke away, laughing, calling over his shoulder, 'Make sure you come, I want you to meet someone special!'

Nellie's father, George Clark, was a large barrel-chested man with a drooping moustache and a stern manner. He worked as a carman for Wicks, the carter whose stables were next door, delivering grain, foodstuffs or timber to and from the nearby docks. Years of driving a horse and cart, in all weathers, had given him a ruddy, lined complexion and a powerful physique. A man of few words, when he did speak his children made sure they took notice. Nellie tried not to defy him. Growing up, she and her two brothers and sister had learned to fear his anger and, even more, the leather belt he produced when family discipline demanded it. Tonight, he was sitting in his favourite chair as usual, pipe in hand, shirtsleeves rolled up and braces undone.

Nellie thought now would be as good a time as any. Her father was always most amenable after a good dinner and she had obliged by cooking his favourite: boiled bacon and pease pudding. When her mother died two years earlier, she'd found herself the surrogate mother of the whole family. With the help of her younger sister, Alice, she cooked and cleaned and took care of her two little brothers, Bobby and Freddie. Bobby, who'd been six when their mother died, had needed her constant care. For a year he'd clung to Nellie's skirts, burrowing in like some little lost animal. She often felt she was missing out on her own youth, leaping from childhood to motherhood with no preparation, but one look at Bobby's mournful little face, peering up from the folds of her skirt, told her she had no choice. Sometimes an unaccountable sadness would overtake her and for a long time she thought she was simply missing her mother, but lately, as she saw other girls her age launching forward into independence and even the promise of romance, she realized she had been mourning her lost girlhood.

After she and Alice had cleared away the tea things, she determined that she *would* go out that night. In the scullery as they washed and dried the plates she leaned over to whisper to Alice.

'Can you get the boys ready for bed tonight? I don't want to give him,' she nodded towards the kitchen, where her father sat, 'any excuse to stop me going out.'

Eleven-year-old Alice was Nellie's confidante and staunchly loyal. When their mother died, it had been Nellie who'd taken the children into her arms and comforted them. Their father believed in managing grief, as he managed his family, with an iron rod. She couldn't remember him shedding a tear. He'd just seemed to grow more stern, surrounding himself with armour plating. His upright, tight, buttoned-up figure, walking behind the hearse, had never bent or faltered and, as they'd stood sobbing at their mother's grave, his only words had been, 'Control yourselves, you're showing me up.' Sometimes Nellie thought he showed more affection to the horses he drove than he did to his own children.

Alice readily agreed to help with the boys and Nellie went upstairs to change. She dressed with some care, in her best blue skirt, cinched in at the waist with a wide belt, and her frilly white blouse with the leg o'mutton sleeves. Not her absolute best, but she didn't want any awkward questions.

'I'm just popping out to Lily's for an hour, Dad. The boys are in bed.' She leaned down to kiss his cheek. He nodded and carried on picking at his pipe. He let her get to the kitchen door.

'Make sure you're back by ten and don't let that Ted turn your head.'

Nellie raised her eyes, before turning back to him. 'I don't expect Ted'll be there.'

Her father began plugging the pipe with tobacco; he didn't look up. 'Oh, he'll be there all right, don't worry your head about that,' he said impassively. 'And remember what I said, no later 'n ten!'

Nellie sighed, then carefully closed the door behind her and pulled her little blue cape off the peg in the passage. Her sister was there, to see her off.

'Don't talk to no strangers.'

'Oh, Al, there *are* no strangers in Bermondsey!' Nellie laughed at the very idea that their world of poor streets, bounded by the Thames, girdled by docks, stuffed with factories, permeated by smoke, and plagued with noxious smells, should contain anything so unexpected as a stranger. Bermondsey might be situated at the heart of a great metropolis, but for those who lived there it had the familiarity of a village, a soot-covered one made of London brick and slate roofs, but a village none the less, where everyone knew each other and where no one had to face life's trials alone. Nellie reflected that, in Bermondsey, a street was as good as a family. Her real family, at times, felt a little diminished, despite her efforts.

Nellie threw her arms round her sister and kissed her.

'Well, just look after yourself. You look a treat,' Alice said.

'Thanks, Al.' Nellie did not consider herself a great beauty, but her complexion was peachy and her bright blue eyes always drew attention. And this evening she'd spent a while on her glory, her long chestnut hair. But as she closed the door behind her, she found herself musing that tonight Ted would no doubt be far more interested in his important guest than in Nellie Clark from Vauban Street.

The little room at the back of the Labour Institute was full. About two dozen women, seated on rows of hard-backed chairs, filled the small space. In spite of the stiflingly warm night, they kept on their broad, decorated hats and wide capes, their leg o'mutton sleeves alone seeming to fill the room, which buzzed with their high-pitched chatter. Ted and two other dockers were the only men there. Nellie and Lily sat in the front row, waiting for Ted to introduce his guest. He'd been excited on the way round to the institute, and had rushed them all off from the Boshers' house so that Nellie hadn't even had time to say hello to Lily's mum. But then Ted had been excited through all this sizzling summer of 1911; sometimes Nellie wondered if it was the ninety-degree heat that had got him into such a fervour. If the country was being set on fire, then it seemed Ted Bosher was in the middle of it, stoking the flames. She had read the newspaper headlines – the 'Summer of Unrest' they were calling it, and Ted was certainly restless. Every day, for weeks, he had been on at her and Lily to join the union, full of tales of workers striking all over the country. Eventually he'd worn them down and tonight they'd agreed to hear this mystery speaker, for he'd refused to tell them who she was.

'She's important in the movement,' was all he would say. 'Wait till you hear her, she's a bloody inspiration, she is.'

Nellie noticed that his eyes were sparkling and felt a wave of disappointment wash over her that the light in them wasn't for her.

'Oh, the *movement*,' she'd said in mockery and then regretted it when he turned on her.

'It's the likes of you that keep us lot under the thumb. Just listen tonight as though you were a grown-up, that's all I ask.'

Now, looking up at the lady standing next to Ted, she felt tired and irritated. She had no patience with do-gooders who came to improve their lot. A woman sitting next to them leaned over and whispered, 'Looks like the big guns are out tonight!'

'Who is she?' Nellie whispered back.

'It's "Madam Mecklenburgh"!'

When Nellie looked unimpressed, the woman went on, 'Well, that's what we call her behind her back. Her real name's Eliza James, and, speak as you find, she's done a lot for us girls.' The woman nodded in approval. 'She's high up in the NFWW.'

Nellie didn't like to show her ignorance by asking what the NFWW was, so instead she asked, 'Why do you call her Madam Mecklenburgh?'

'Only 'cause she lives in Mecklenburgh Square, that's where the name come from, I reckon.'

'So she's not a proper lady then?' Nellie was rather disappointed.

'Well, she might *act* like one...' The woman looked at her as though she would like to say more, but just then Eliza James moved forward to speak.

To Nellie's eyes, she certainly looked like a proper lady, with her chiffon scarf, wide-brimmed hat and her velvet-trimmed pale grey suit; all very tasteful and not cheap. She had a long face, wavy auburn hair and deep-set dark, almost black eyes. She looked to Nellie vaguely familiar, but a woman like her would not be from Bermondsey. Nellie could tell; it was the clothes. But the voice, when it came, told a different story. It wasn't the cut-glass accent Nellie had been expecting, and the vowels spoke of origins much humbler than Mecklenburgh Square. She could tell that the woman had smoothed out the rougher edges of her accent, carefully sounding her aitches. *No*, Nellie concluded to herself, *if you was born a lady, then I'm the Duchess of Duffs!*

But just as Ted had promised, she was an inspiration. She introduced herself as a leader in the National Federation of Women Workers and then took a long look around the room, as though taking the measure of her audience. Then she launched into a powerful, passionate condemnation of the poor wages and inhuman conditions in the Bermondsey food factories, which soon had the little room full of clapping women. She drew Nellie in and made her feel as if she was the most important person in the room. Three-quarters of the way through her talk, she asked them each to say which factories they worked for.

'Duff's,' shouted Nellie, and the others followed with calls of 'Pink's Jam' and 'Crosse & Blackwell', 'Shuttleworth's', 'Peek Frean's'. Most of the factories mentioned had large numbers of women workers and paid the lowest wages. Lady or not, Madam Mecklenburgh certainly knew what she was talking about, for when each of the factory names were called, she came back straight away with the exact wages paid.

'Pink's? Six shillings a week for you, double for the men.'

Then she pointed at Nellie. 'How old are you, young lady?'

'Sixteen, madam.'

The woman smiled, as though at some secret joke. 'You work eleven hours a day, the same as boys your age, but you only get half the wage, five shillings a week. And that doesn't pay the rent, does it?'

Nellie flushed, but was determined not to be over-awed. 'No, it don't even keep me dad in tobacca!'

The girls around her laughed in sympathy. She was not the only one who handed over all her pay packet on pay day and counted herself lucky to get sixpence back to spend on herself. When Eliza James laughed too, Nellie noticed Ted joining in. But the thought of her father suddenly gripped Nellie with a stab of fear. He would never condone what this woman was suggesting.

She remembered the day, two years earlier, when she'd been taken on at Duff's. She'd considered herself lucky to get a job there, as a powder packer. It was one of hundreds of food factories clustered in Bermondsey – 'London's Larder'. As well as the famous custard powder, Duff's turned out blancmanges, baking powders, sherberts and jellies. She'd known it would be hard work, but nothing had prepared her for the excruciating back pain, after eleven hours standing at her bench, or the monotony of filling and folding custard packets, hour after hour. But the thing she'd learned to hate most was that pervasive custard powder, invading every pore of her skin, seeping into the seams of her clothes, clogging up her lovely chestnut hair with its sticky matt coating. But Nellie's father wasn't interested in her likes and dislikes. For him, it was purely a matter of economics.

'It's a good job and we need that five shilling,' he told her. 'Work hard and don't you dare come back home, one day, and tell me you've been laid off.'

What they had planned tonight was disapproved of by many working men, her father included.

'Lily, what time is it, do you think?' she whispered. 'I can't be late back. Dad'll skin me.'

10

When Lily pointed to the clock at the back of the room, Nellie leaped from her seat and dashed out, without even saying goodbye to Ted. It was gone ten o'clock and she was in all sorts of trouble.

2

GOING HOME

Ernest James had insisted on sending his car to take her to Bermondsey. Eliza James had wanted to take the omnibus from Mecklenburgh Square that afternoon, and she would have enjoyed the ride. Surely the best place to be on yet another fiercely hot day, in this unending furnace of a summer, was sitting on the top deck of a London omnibus. But Ernest wouldn't hear of it, so instead, she had made do with rolling down the window. At least, that way, she could enjoy the delicious breeze as she was driven across London Bridge. The south London streets had been eerily quiet. Normally, they would have been full of traffic: horse and carts delivering to and from the docks, jostling for road space with hansoms and the ever-increasing number of motor taxis and cars. But with the dockers on strike and the wharves all closed, the dockside streets had a dead, dull, aimless air about them. The factories had not yet turned out and those pedestrians who had braved the searing summer heat were visibly wilting; men and boys sweated in thick wool jackets, totally unsuited to the weather. Dockers were hanging around in jovial gangs, holding up placards, engaging any passer-by who showed an interest in their demands in conversation. As the car cruised smoothly along Tooley Street, she had breathed in the Bermondsey air, made more pungent by the heat bouncing off the tar-block roads. It was an odd mixture of horse dung, petrol fumes, old bones from the glue works, leather from the tanneries and the all-pervading spice: cinnamon and ginger drifting up from the spice wharves on the river, mingling with sweet raspberry and vanilla from the jam and biscuit factories. It was the smell of home.

Now, at the end of a long day of planning and meetings, Ernest's driver was waiting at a respectful distance while she said her goodbyes. This evening's meeting had gone better than she'd hoped for and she didn't doubt that the cells of women they'd persuaded, in each of the fifteen factories, would be enough to carry the rest with them. All it would take was a single spark and, in this tinder dry Summer of Unrest as it was being called, a spark was all that was needed. The factory women were burning with a suppressed rage that seemed to have no outlet. They knew it was wrong that they worked the same hours as a man, for half the wage; they knew it was wrong that they worked in unsanitary conditions, for hours on end, with no breaks. Tonight, she'd heard the story of one mother so frightened of losing her position that she had her baby brought to her by one of her own young children, nursed the baby at the factory gates, then went back in to work. There were no concessions made for mothers, or children, come to that. And what enraged Eliza James most was that the men resented their women's presence in the factories anyway. A woman deprived a man of a job, or that was their short-sighted way of thinking.

But not all the men were of that opinion and with the dockers' support, the women's courage had got the final boost it needed. Ted Bosher was a useful man to have on the ground. He understood the women's grievances. His own sister was working all hours as a powder packer, for a few shillings and grateful for it, by all accounts. Eliza was also conscious of the power of his undoubted charms, which he used to good effect, she had noticed, to draw in even the most apathetic of the women workers. That bold little thing, sitting next to his sister, certainly couldn't take her eyes off him. His face had been aglow all evening, though whether that was a result of young Nellie's attentions, or her own, she couldn't be sure.

'We'll have them all out in August, I guarantee it,' Ted Bosher

13

said at the end of the meeting. 'This lot will carry them. After that speech of yours, you've turned them into the firebrands that'll light the fire!'

He had a pleasant voice, and an easy manner, but his eyes had an intensity that Eliza James had grown to recognize in her years as a union activist. Such burning anger as she had seen in them could be as much of a danger to their own cause as it could be to their adversaries. She preferred a more measured approach.

'I hope they've seen the sense in my arguments too. Fifteen thousand women, walking out on one day, has got to make their bosses sit up and take notice. But I know it's going to be hard for the women. They'll get opposition at home, especially the younger ones.'

Ted brushed her misgivings aside. 'It'll be worth it, what's a bit of family upset? The struggle's worth it.'

'Yes,' she said, bristling slightly, 'I wouldn't be here, if I didn't think it was worth it.'

At the door she shook hands with the other two dockers, and Ernest's driver showed her to the waiting car. He opened the back door for her, got in to the front himself and set off towards London Bridge. They had been driving for several minutes, when she leaned forward to tap on the sliding window between her and the driver.

'Simmons, could you turn round? I'd like to take a different route home.'

She gave him instructions, and a puzzled look passed across his young face. But he merely turned the car round, with a nod of his head, and drove towards Rotherhithe as she had asked. The gas lamps along Southwark Park Road were still blazing, but their cheerful glow soon receded. The lamps grew sparser as they skirted the entrance to Brunel's tunnel and moved into the area of docks and wharves strung along the great loop of the river at Rotherhithe. The driver followed her occasional instructions and then stopped when she tapped on the window again. They had come to a street that fronted on to the Thames.

A sign pointed to Globe Stairs, down on the foreshore. The little row of terraced houses was squashed between the wide blackness of the Thames on one side and the square, silent basin of Globe Dock behind. Here and there, the indigo skyline was pierced by the black bows and masts of ships, many of them marooned and still unencumbered of their cargos, while they waited for the dockers' strike to end.

'I won't be long, Simmons.'

She peered at the door numbers as she walked down the dimly lit street, and hesitated before eventually stopping at the last house in the little terrace. She knocked, a weak knock; certainly it seemed less loud than the pounding of her own heart. The door was opened by a young man with dark wavy hair. He didn't smile, just swung the door wide open and stepped to one side.

'Hello, Sam,' Eliza said.

Nellie's lungs burned and she was gulping in painful breaths by the time she arrived at the front door of their terraced house in Vauban Street. A gas lamp hissed and flickered halfway down the street and a few of the houses still had lights in the downstairs windows, but her own home was in darkness, with the shutters closed. She banged on the front door and when no one answered, stooped to call, in a half whisper, through the letterbox.

'Alice, it's Nellie, let me in!'

She heard footsteps on the stairs and, for a moment, was relieved that her sister had heard her. Then she heard her father's voice booming.

'Get back to bed, girl. I told her ten!'

Her sister's muffled, pleading voice floated down to her and Nellie put her ear to the letterbox.

'Please, Dad, she can't stay out all night.'

She heard no reply, just her father's footsteps, thumping down the stairs.

Nellie's face was wet with sweat from her run in the sticky warm night, but now she shivered on the doorstep. She wasn't sure which terrified her more, a night out here on the streets or a confrontation with her father. The front door was flung open and his large figure filled the passageway. He was dressed only in long johns and a hastily donned pair of trousers, baggy at the waist and held up by a pair of braces. He looked faintly ridiculous, but she wasn't going to laugh, not now.

'I'm sorry, Dad, I lost track of—'

'What's it to be?' Her father held up the thick leather belt that he usually wore as well as his braces.

'This, or a night on the streets?'

His voice was quiet and controlled, but his face was even redder than usual and thin spittle had collected at the corners of his mouth. She knew there was nothing George Clark hated more than to be crossed, especially by his children. Nellie avoided looking directly at him.

'I'll come in then.' She knew what was coming.

He took her by the elbow and marched her into the little kitchen. She shot a glance up the stairs, to see her pale-faced sister hovering at the top. Alice shook her head, in a resigned way, that told Nellie she had tried on her sister's behalf and failed. Nellie managed a weak smile, before being pulled into the kitchen. There her father grabbed her hand and administered his usual six smart slaps of the belt.

'You dare defy me again and you'll get more than that, next time!'

His large red nose glowed with exertion and what Nellie guessed was the effect of a drop too much of his favourite tipple. She wanted to grab the belt and strike him back. Images of red welts across his cheek flashed into her mind. But it was useless, then she really would be on the streets. One thing she wouldn't give him was a tear. The bloody big bully could wait till kingdom come for that, she thought, in silent rebellion.

'Get up to bed and don't think you're going out again of a night. And you dare lie to me again! I know it was a barefaced lie, about that Bosher boy being there tonight. You listen to me, girl, him and his Bolshy friends are trouble. Always stirring up people to be discontented with what they've got. Prancing about on soapboxes, telling me I'm hard done by. I can look after me own, and I don't need some jumped-up docker's son telling me different. I don't want you having nothing more to do with them union lot. D'yer hear?'

Now he was shouting. Of course she heard, the whole bloody street could hear. She nodded, longing to get away, and then he let her go. She followed him upstairs and crept into the front bedroom, where, as expected, three heads shot up. The two boys, Freddie and Bobby, sat up in their bed, looking at her expectantly, and Alice jumped out of the bed she shared with Nellie, to put her arm round her.

'Did the old git hurt you, Nell?' she whispered.

'Nah,' Nellie lied, 'he's getting old and soft.' But her palm stung as if a hot poker had been laid across it.

'Gawd, you're shaking, though.'

'It's temper, Al. I'm only shaking 'cause I can't have a go back at the old sod.'

'Come on, love, let me help you get changed,' said Alice, starting to unbutton the back of her blouse.

But Nellie noticed that the two wide-eyed boys were still staring at her. Bobby, especially, looked close to tears. She knew his soft heart would not be able to manage seeing her vulnerable or in pain.

'Go on, boys, back to kip,' she said encouragingly. 'I'm a tough old boot!' She reached down to tickle Bobby and give Freddie a hug, before pulling the little curtain that separated their half of the room from the boys' beds.

'It's so unfair, Al,' she went on in a whisper. 'He treats me like I'm still a child, but if it weren't for me he'd have no one to cook and clean for him, or to look after the boys.'

She was seething as Alice tried to calm her.

'Don't leave us, Nell, will you? He's harder on you than the rest of us and I know it's not fair, but we'd be lost without you.'

When Nellie saw her sister's lip trembling, she forgot her own injuries. It was easy to forget Alice was little more than a child herself.

'Shhh, love, 'course I'm not leaving you, it's just I think he could let me have a bit of a life.'

They didn't dare light the lamp, so in the darkness, Alice helped Nellie out of her blouse and skirt. And when they were in bed, the sisters put their arms round each other, till they had both stopped shaking.

3

A DAY OUT

Fine pale powder hung in clouds above the women, drifting down slowly to cover window sills and walls with a gritty veneer. A blazing August sun glared through the high windows, striping the mote-filled air with light, turning the powder into a fine gold dust. It billowed up in vanilla-scented blooms each time a woman reached to fill a new packet at the delivery chutes, which ran in straight lines down the length of the factory floor. The women stood at a long bench, where one pulled a lever to release custard powder into an empty packet, then passed it on to her neighbour who deftly pasted it closed, while the third in the team stacked filled packets on to a trolley cart. Above the women, a cat's cradle of steam-driven belts chugged and clattered, filling the vast hoppers that fed the delivery chutes. Unending streams of cloying powder chuted down, sending up yet more clouds of choking yellow smoke. Though the women wore rough cotton smocks, all were covered in a fine, sticky coating of custard powder.

Nellie Clark licked her lips, sweet, always sweet. Sometimes she longed for a trickle of sweat to reach her lips, just for the blessed difference of salt. On a day like today, she was likely to get her wish. It was sweltering in the factory and Nellie was suffering, in her voluminous cotton smock. The thought of putting on her best wool jacket made her feel faint. But they had decided to wear their best, and as she only had one good jacket, the woollen one it had to be. At least no one would be able to say that Bermondsey girls didn't look smart. She looked at the clock. Not long now. She licked her lips again and tasted salt. Sweat beaded her upper lip and her face was covered with a sheen of moisture. She brushed her damp brow with the back of her hand, tucking away a strand of chestnut hair, and glanced over at Lily. Lily nodded towards the clock and mouthed, 'Ten minutes.'

'I'm not sure I can last ten more seconds in this oven!' she whispered back.

And when it came to it, could she go through with it? She liked to think she was strong, but even at sixteen years old and a woman earning her own keep, it irked her that her father could still make her quail like a child. The rows over her late arrival home, on the night of the meeting, had lasted for weeks. He would surely throw her out for this.

Nellie raised her blue eyes at the thought and blew out an overheated breath, which lifted another dank lock of hair from her forehead. Her stomach was churning, though whether from fear or excitement, she couldn't tell. Other women around her were getting fidgety. Ethel Brown, a rotund woman in her forties, was turning an ever deeper shade of lobster. Nellie had caught a glimpse of a feather boa under her bench. Maggie Tyrell was rooting around in a bag at her feet and Nellie spotted a black straw hat, with green feathers.

Suddenly she noticed a change in the sounds filtering through the high windows. Distant shouts at first, then snatches of song drifted in. Women's voices sang out, high and excited: *Are we downhearted no, no, NO!* The chanting was coming closer and closer. Then the sound of feet, lots of them, hundreds of feet, boots ringing on the cobbles. The chatter of the women around her ceased, as they registered the noise of the approaching crowd. Just as the clock struck eleven, Nellie found herself standing up. Suddenly she was flooded with the knowledge that she *could* do it! She wasn't on her own. But still her legs felt like jelly and a queasiness lurched in the pit of her stomach.

More than a hundred women rose, as one, from their benches and ran to the windows, craning their heads, looking down on to the street below to see the first of the women marchers. Nellie saw rows and rows of women, filling the street as far back as she could see, some linking arms and singing, others carrying banners. One read: *WE'RE NOT WHITE SLAVES, WE'RE PINK'S!*

The women around her called out excitedly. 'There's Pink's Jam, can you see Crosse & Blackwell's? Where's Peek Frean's? I can see Lipton's. Have they all come? Have Hartley's come?'

Albert, their astonished foreman, was running up and down behind the line of women at the windows. 'Get back to your benches, what d'yer think yer doing!'

They pretended not to hear him and Nellie followed the others as they started to remove their smocks and caps.

'This is it, Nell.' Lily squeezed her hand. 'You coming?'

Nellie paused for a heartbeat, then bent down deliberately and reached into a bag hidden behind a trolley. She pulled out her best wool jacket.

''Course I'm coming, I'm not missing this!'

Other women were putting on their fancy hats and feather boas, as they marched in orderly single file past the open-mouthed foreman. They joined a stream of women workers from higher floors. Jostling down the stone staircase, came the girls from baking powder and blancmange, distinguishable only by the white or pink powder coating them. When they reached the factory yard, Nellie glanced over at the jelly building. The foremen in charge of the great vats of fruit jellies had left the gelatine bubbling, coming out to stare incredulously as the jelly packers joined the other women marching out of the factory gates. They looked as if they were dressed for a day out, but they weren't – they were on strike!

Once Nellie was down among the crowd, she grabbed Lily, feeling overwhelmed by the mass of humanity surrounding her. She had never been in such a vast crowd, not even during the new King George's coronation celebrations, earlier that summer. There must be thousands of women there today, choking the width of Spa Road, holding up carts and trams, drawing shouts from drivers and hoots from the odd motor car desperate to get through the crush. Women poured from side streets, like the tributaries of an unstoppable river. They seemed to Nellie to move in an orchestrated way and yet no one was in charge; they were merely surging forward in a common purpose. Astonished onlookers lined the pavement, unable to negotiate their way through the throng of banner-carrying women. Many of the men and boys stopped, mid-stride, to gawp openly; others, shoving their hands into their pockets, pointedly ignored the women and attempted to barge through them. Some called out as they passed, 'Get back 'ome, and cook yer husbands' dinners!' and other less decorous suggestions. But Nellie felt safe enough, amongst the group of burly dockers who had turned out to march with them. Some of these shouted back at the hecklers.

'Don't I know yer missus, mate? She's here somewhere!'

Nellie pulled Lily in closer, linking arms. 'Look, there's Ted!' She pointed towards the front of the crowd, where Lily's brother and his fellow dockers marched.

Nellie thought Ted looked heroic, with his red-gold hair shining in the bright sunshine, and his strong arms holding one end of the dockers' union banner. At the head of the march she could see the colourful banner of the National Federation of Women Workers, bravely proclaiming that they would 'fight to struggle to right the wrong'. Nellie guided Lily nearer to the banner, which was held aloft by two athletic middle-class young women. Beneath it, marching four abreast with the other strike leaders, was Eliza James, dressed in a long, flowing grey silk coat and a broad straw hat. With her white scarf flying out behind her, she was smiling and urging the women on, calling out to the male onlookers, 'Come and join the struggle, these are your daughters, and your wives!'

She looked magnificent, as bold and brave as Britannia on the face of a penny, and whatever misgivings she might once have had, Nellie felt she would follow Madam Mecklenburgh to the ends of the earth.

Nellie could hardly believe it had only been a few short weeks since she'd first met the woman. Then she hadn't even heard of the NFWW, and she certainly hadn't wanted to attend a meeting, listening to stuffy speeches. At the time, she had gone simply because Ted Bosher asked her to. Since then, she'd avoided her father as much as possible, stayed home in the evenings and attended every one of the trade union's lunchtime meetings at the Fort Road Labour Institute. The more she'd heard the less frightened she'd become, anger and boldness replacing timidity. She and the other women were buoyed up by the dockers' support. Even when the government caved in and gave the dockers their eightpence an hour, they'd pledged to stay out on strike until the women got their eleven shillings a week. Dockers in Hull and Liverpool were striking as well as those in London. The railwaymen had joined them, and her father was livid when even his fellow horse drivers in the carmen's union had voted to support the strike.

'That's the end of it for this country!' he railed at her one teatime. 'Ted Bosher and his friends won't stop till they get their revolution, and who'll pay for it? Their wives and kiddies, that's who!'

Nellie had cleared the tea things away and privately thought her father a blustering coward, too scared to defy his bosses. He was just frightened that his supply of beer and tobacco would dry up! But if he was too weak to make the sacrifice that could change all their lives forever, she wasn't. And anyway, what gave him the right to sneer at Ted? At least he was doing something.

'You think you know it all, girl,' he'd said when she tried to disagree, 'but you don't know what it means. You don't remember the dock strike in eighty-nine. Well, I do. When the strike fund ran out, it was the wives and kids that starved. It was terrible and now it's happening all over again.'

Hard as it was, she had bitten her tongue. She didn't want him getting too suspicious. The rows would have to wait for later, and she shuddered as she thought of what might be in store for her when he finally found out. But she did know enough to acknowledge that striking would mean hardship for her family. Even now, the evidence of the three-week shutdown at the docks was there, in the stagnant, putrid air surrounding the wharves. London's Larder was rotting. After days of fiery ninety-degree temperatures, the scant summer breezes bore only the stink of decaying food, left rotting on the quayside or still in the holds of the warming refrigeration ships, waiting to be unloaded by absent dockers and stevadores. Worst of all, supplies of milk and bread were failing, and even in Vauban Street two children had died of dysentery, some said caused by bad food and milk.

Now, as they approached Southwark Park, the mood of the marching crowd was changing. Gaiety was giving way to anger. Their numbers had swelled to thousands, and scores of nervous policemen were lining Southwark Park Road. Eliza James and the dock union leaders were due to address the marchers in the park. Women streamed through the gates and spread like a rippling tide over the grass, which had been burned to a crisp during the long, rainless weeks of summer. The jaunty songs of the women were being drowned out now by angry shouts and jeers from the dockers, as they spotted rows and rows of khaki-clad guardsmen, with their bayonets fixed. Nellie felt her elbow being grabbed from behind. It was Ted. 'Listen, you two, stay out of the way, there might be trouble.'

'Oh, I wish I was taller,' Nellie said, standing on tiptoe. 'I can't see sod all from here. Can't we get up the front?'

'No,' Ted said sternly, 'those soldiers ain't here for a picnic. They'll *make* trouble if they can't find it. I'm going up to the podium, but you two stay back here!'

With that, he strode off towards the bandstand, where Nellie could make out his tall figure helping Eliza James up the steps. Once she stood on the platform, she called out, above the noise:

'Women of Bermondsey, are you downhearted?'

The refrain went up from thousands of voices.

'No, no, no!'

'Some may say it's the men that run the world, but I say, it's only the women that can change it. Are you ready to change the world?'

And Nellie joined in as the women roared back, 'Yes, yes, yes!' She jumped and waved her makeshift banner, which read *CUSTARD TARTS DON'T COME CHEAP!*

The lines of soldiers seemed to have shuffled closer, forming a ring round the great mass of people. Some union officials walked among the crowd, urging them to stay calm and orderly. The last thing they wanted was rioting; the Riot Act had already been read at rallies elsewhere in the country and the soldiers had orders to shoot, if the strikers turned nasty.

Suddenly a surge in the crowd set it into a slow spiral, and though she fought the momentum, Nellie found herself separated from Lily. The crush of bodies seemed to waltz her round the bandstand, spiralling her closer and closer to the front. She found herself pressed deep into a group of dockers who were shoving and jostling at the line of soldiers. Some of them tried to ease off the crush as her banner bashed them, knocking off someone's cap. Then one of them started haranguing the soldiers.

'Shame on you lot for shooting yer own kind, you're meant to be defending us!'

His fist was curled round a rock. Suddenly he let fly at the nearest guardsman, and soon Nellie found herself tumbled about in a tangle of dockers. The rock had hit its target and now the guardsman, blood streaming from a gash in his forehead, lurched forward with his bayonet extended. She tried to worm her way out, but found she couldn't move her arms as she was tossed between solid muscled bodies, all ducking out of the way of the advancing soldier. The only possible way for her to go seemed to be down, and finally, Nellie was knocked clean off her feet. Frantically pushing up against the crushing weight of bodies, straining on to her hands and knees, she found herself staring into the muzzle of a rifle, the sharp end of a bayonet only inches from her face. She scrabbled to crawl away as shouts and fists exploded about her, punctuated by the sickening crunch of cracking jawbones. A heavy docker thudded down on top of her, pinning her to the dusty earth.

'Get off me, yer big lump!' she gasped, as the air was squeezed from her lungs. Her last thought was that her best wool jacket would now certainly be ruined, ground into the dust.

4

SWEPT OFF HER FEET

When she came round, she was being carried in the arms of a young man who looked familiar. Her head felt sore and her vision was blurred. She was looking up into the strong midday sun, which obscured the young man's features but cast a golden glow around his head. It felt like a romantic dream.

'Ted?' Her voice sounded thick and distant.

He put her down gently and sat her on the bottom step, at the back of the bandstand. 'It's Sam, Nellie. Sam Gilbie.'

'Oh, what are you doing here? Where's Ted?' She put her hand to her forehead and brought it away, sticky with blood. Now she remembered. The terror of the approaching bayonet, the panic as she'd gasped for a breath that she felt would never come. A sharp taste in her mouth told her that she must have bitten her lip as the weight of the docker had slammed into her.

'I'm here with the carmen's union,' Sam explained. 'Ted's still up on the podium, covering himself with glory, by the looks of it.' He glanced up towards the speakers, one of whom was finishing a rousing speech. She thought she could see Ted's tall figure on the bandstand, waiting for his turn.

Nellie had noticed the barb in Sam's tone and remembered that there was no love lost between the two cousins. 'It's my own stupid fault. Don't blame Ted, he told me to stay put.' She straightened up and disengaged herself from Sam's still encircling arm. 'I'm all right now, no need to make a fuss.'

But it was too late and already a small crowd of women was

forming round her. Sam stepped back as they clucked and examined her.

'You'll have a nasty shiner tomorrow, Nell.' Ethel Brown was dabbing at the cut over Nellie's eye with a handkerchief. 'And look at the state of your lovely jacket.'

Just then, the little crowd parted to allow Eliza James through. She was an imposing figure and all the women quietened down, waiting for her to take charge.

'Where's our wounded soldier?' She knelt in front of Nellie and lifted her chin. 'Let's see the damage then.'

'I'm all right, but me jacket's ruined,' said Nellie, holding up her torn cuff.

Eliza laughed. 'Typical Bermondsey priorities. Never mind about the cut head and crushed ribs, eh?'

At that, Nellie realized she would have to explain her state to her father and she groaned.

'Where does it hurt?' Eliza's expression turned to one of concern.

'It's just a bruise, madam. Tell the truth I was thinking of me dad. He didn't want me to strike and now he'll kill me if I go home in this state.'

'Don't worry, love,' said Ethel Brown, poking her head over Eliza's shoulder. 'If an eighteen-stone docker can't kill you, I shouldn't think George Clark would have a chance.'

The other women laughed and even Nellie had to smile.

'I'll take her home... and explain to Mr Clark.' Nellie had forgotten Sam's presence, but now, as he stepped forward, she was shocked at the look he gave Eliza. She had only ever seen him as the pleasant, placid young man she thought of as 'that soppy 'apporth', but now his expression, as he spoke to Eliza, was harder, colder. His normal high colour had paled and his dark eyes were lacking their usual friendly warmth. Eliza stood and turned towards him. Nellie couldn't be sure, but she sensed recognition in Eliza's face. Was it possible they had met before? she wondered. It was unlikely. Sam may have joined the other carmen in the strike, but he wasn't a dyed-in-the-wool union man like Ted. She had never seen him at any of the planning meetings.

Eliza appeared flustered, and as the little group of women wandered back to hear more of the speeches, she turned to Sam. 'That's kind of you and I'm glad you've turned out to support us.'

'I did it for the girls, not for any other reason. Don't think I'd deprive my family of a day's wages for the likes of you and your Bolshie friends.'

Nellie was shocked by his uncharacteristic rudeness, but something about his tone piqued her interest. She'd never seen anything in Sam Gilbie that had interested her much... until now. Nellie had been surprised he was here at all. Her father wouldn't be happy with him either; he wasn't going to do her much good with placating George Clark. No doubt her father had been coping alone all day at the yard.

'No thanks, Sam,' she said, and it came out more curtly than she'd intended. 'Thanks for the offer, but me dad'll be livid with you too. He didn't think you'd turn out today. Anyway, I want to hear Ted's speech.' Just then, Lily came running up, red in the face and puffing.

'What the bloody hell have you done to yourself? I've been looking all over. Someone told me you got shot by a guardsman!'

She flung her arms round her friend and Nellie winced as pain shot through her ribs.

'Quick, Ted's starting his speech!' Lily said as she dragged Nellie round to the front of the bandstand. When Nellie glanced back, Sam was walking towards the park gates and Eliza James was staring after him, looking as if someone had stolen from her all the glory of the triumphant day.

Ted's speech was the last of the day and ended with a roar of approval from the crowds of dockers, who threw their caps into the air. Women waved their banners and little groups started to split away, strolling through the streets, chatting and laughing as though they had been on a beano to Ramsgate. The cooler temperature of the late afternoon brought a welcome breeze and now that any hot-headed dockers had long since cooled off, the carefree atmosphere returned. Nellie felt it was almost like a party.

Ted bounded down from the bandstand and when he saw her black eye and cut head, he joked, 'I bet whoever upset you came off worse!' Then he saw Lily's face.

'Where were you, Sir Galahad?' She rounded on her brother. 'Left us to fend for ourselves, didn't you? She could have been killed!'

'Oh, turn it up, Lily. I told you it wasn't no soddin' picnic.' He turned to Nellie. 'I'm sorry, Nell, does it hurt?'

'No...' She felt Lily prod her in the ribs and drew in her breath. That really had hurt. 'Not if I don't move!'

'Why don't you come with us, over the other side. We've got a camp set up on Tower Hill and there's tea stalls, we can get a bite to eat.'

Nellie desperately wanted to postpone the confrontation with her father, which she knew would have to come. Normally she would have hurried home, but now she wanted the day to go on forever.

'I reckon it's the sun turned my head, or the whack that docker give me, but either way I must be mad.'

Lily looked at her, astonished. 'You're coming?'

Nellie nodded.

The three of them fell in with a crowd of dockers and women strikers heading for the dock union's makeshift HQ at Tower Hill. They passed Butler's Wharf, with its black iron gates still shut and locked. The usual crowds of dockers that hung around street corners were now mobilized into millions of orderly, marching strikers, gathering for their nightly meeting on Tower Hill. The roads were almost traffic-free – the dock strike meant fuel was running out, so fewer and fewer motor taxis and trams were about.

The strikers spread themselves in long leisurely lines across the breadth of Tooley Street, passing under some banners made from sheets, strung across the tenements: *No wages, no dinner!* Some of the dockers' wives were holding a protest of their own *against* the strike.

Ted jumped up, trying to tear them down. But Nellie understood the fear among the women. She pulled him away.

'Leave 'em, Ted. They've got the same right as us to say their piece, haven't they?'

But he'd already grabbed the end of one of the sheets and was ripping it to shreds. 'Yeah, but they won't be complaining when the wages go up, will they?'

'Leave off, you two, stop arguing, you're like cat and dog. Hurry up, I'm gasping.' Lily was impatient to get to the tea stalls at Tower Hill.

They crossed Tower Bridge and waited like excited children in the middle, as a heavy cart and one of the few motors still running caused the bascules to bounce up and down, and them with it. Nellie had one hand on her hat and the other on her sore ribs, as they stood astride the two-inch gap between the bascules, looking down at the river below and laughing like schoolchildren. Then the three of them linked arms as they marched on past the Tower of London.

'Oh, that breeze is lovely!' said Nellie

'Yeah, and so is the stink!' Ted replied. 'Every time that smell gets blown down to Westminster, they know we mean business!' The obnoxious smell, wafting up the river from Butler's Wharf, was indeed overwhelming – a combination of rotting fruit on the quaysides and melting rancid butter, for the refrigeration ships had run out of fuel and the meat was now putrefying in their holds.

'You wouldn't be so pleased with yourself if you had kids to feed, though,' said Nellie. 'My dad says it's criminal to let the food rot and there's people starting to starve now, they say.'

She was thinking of the two dead children in Vauban Street,

and of her own small brothers who had been complaining, only the night before, about tummy aches. She had given them the last of the bread. 'Bread and pull'it, goes a long way!' she'd told them, as though it were some extra-special magic remedy against hunger.

'The union's not going to let them starve, Nell. Eliza James has been writing to the newspapers – she's got thousands of loaves on the way and food coming from all over. She could do with a hand at the Labour Office tomorrow, sorting it all out. Why don't you go over there?'

'I will, if me dad lets me.'

The thought of her father's iron rule caused her to hesitate and she slowed her pace. Perhaps she should just go home now and face the music. Ted had been hurrying them on, elbowing his way through the ambling crowds around the Tower, so that Nellie and Lily were trotting to keep up with his long strides. Now he gave an exasperated sigh and, grasping her hand, almost dragged her past Traitor's Gate. With every half trot, she felt a stab of pain from her bruised ribs, but Ted held her fast and looked in no mood to slow his progress.

'For God's sake, Nellie,' he said fiercely, 'you've got to grow up and start making your own choices. You're taking on the bosses. Don't you think you should start standing up to that bullying father of yours?'

Ted had an infuriating knack of always making her feel like a stupid little girl, and he was one of the few people who could leave her tongue-tied. With anyone else, she gave as good as she got. All she knew was that the excitement she felt when she was with him outweighed the uncomfortable sense of somehow being less than herself.

'How long do you think we'll be on strike, Ted?' Lily asked, diverting Ted's attention. Nellie shot her friend a grateful look. Lily was the only one she'd told about her father's threats to chuck her out.

'As long as it takes! Us dockers will stay out till you get your eleven shillings, and I'm telling you the government's getting desperate to get us back to work. Why else would bully-boy Churchill be sending in troops?'

'I hope it ends soon.' Nellie sighed.

'Well, I don't. I'd like to see Asquith and all his lot beggin' on their knees, and then I'd like to string 'em all up from Big Ben!'

'Well then, you're no better than Churchill, are you?' she snapped.

Nellie was shocked at the vehemence in Ted's voice. What, for her and the other women, was a fight for a few shillings to feed their families, seemed for him a war, and it was one Nellie wasn't sure she wanted to be involved in. The Tower's wooden drawbridge, with its sharp-toothed portcullis, came into view. Nellie shuddered, remembering this was the place they used to put traitors. Ted's talk was sounding perilously traitorous. But when they arrived at Tower Hill, surrounded by other workers, singing songs, gathering round the glowing hot-chestnut carts and tea stalls, the air of camaraderie quietened her unease. There were more speeches and then Nellie felt the fervour around her swell, as someone on a soapbox shouted: 'If they want a war, they'll get a war, and a bloody one at that!'

A roar went up that froze Nellie's heart. She didn't want war; all she wanted was for her family to have to struggle less. Suddenly a deep wave of longing for her family swamped her. She saw the trusting faces of Freddie and little Bobby and stalwart Alice; even her red-faced, perpetually angry father seemed like an anchor, preferable to all the shifting sands and swirling moods around her. Nellie felt as if a new world was coming into being and that everything close to her was changing. A sudden chill wind blew up from the river and Nellie shivered. It was the coldest she had felt all day.

5

DOWN AND OUT

When the speeches were over, they walked back over the bridge to Bermondsey, but their earlier childish mood seemed dampened. Ted had turned sombre, after hearing of two more deaths during a riot in Liverpool. They'd happened at a strike rally and the soldiers hadn't hesitated to open fire, killing two innocent bystanders. Nellie's bruised ribs were hurting at every step and her head was banging. Only now did she fully realize how close she'd come to being one of those fatal statistics. If the crowd in Southwark Park hadn't been so good-natured, that soldier's rifle might have been the last thing she'd seen. When they got to Lily's house, Ted announced he would walk Nellie home. She was shocked; it wasn't something he'd ever done before. She attempted to check her bubbling excitement at the idea of being alone with him. They were always surrounded by other people, and now a half-hour, walking beside him on this balmy night, would make up for all the wounds of the day. But what if he was just feeling sorry for her as a battered casualty of the class war, still with her furious father to face? She decided she didn't care about his motives; she was just happy that it was Ted beside her. When he put his arm round her, she held her breath, not wishing to acknowledge it in case the spell was broken. Linked now, they bumped against each other awkwardly, his long stride outstripping hers. But with a quiet determination she began to match him, and however ungainly their progress might have looked, to Nellie it felt as if she was walking on air. At the corner of Vauban Street, she stopped him reluctantly.

'You'd best not come to the door, in case Dad sees you,' she said quietly.

'I don't care,' he said, pulling her into him more tightly.

'Well, I do. If he sees you with me, that'll be it. He'll be angry enough as it is, when he finds out I've been out on strike today!'

She'd managed to ignore the prospect all day, but now the conflict with her father would have to be faced. George Clark's temper could turn vicious, especially if he thought he'd been made a fool of. Nellie knew her defiance fell into that category and right now she was sick with fear at what her father might do.

'Well, I'm proud of you, Nell. You're definitely grown-up enough for me.'

The words smoothed all Nellie's ruffled feathers from earlier and, as he leaned down to kiss her, she let him. Nellie had sometimes allowed herself to dream of being kissed by Ted, but now the sensation took her by surprise. She felt as though she were floating up to meet him. When he drew his face away, he was smiling.

'I always knew you'd be a good kisser, Nellie Clark.'

She was breathless, but had enough sense to seem unconcerned. 'Well, don't get too used to it, Ted Bosher! I've got to go!'

Nellie ran off to her house without looking back, her feet flying and her heart soaring, knowing that his eyes were following her. She didn't look back until she heard his footsteps ringing on the cobbles, as he turned for home.

Her heart was thumping as she stood before her own front door. Excitement at Ted's kiss and fear of her father had turned her normally sturdy limbs to jelly. Trembling, she waited for the courage to knock on the front door. She felt the cut on her forehead, and pulled the front roll of her hair forward to hide it. Then she buoyed herself up with the knowledge that her father was certainly no bigger than the docker who had squashed her, but before her hand could reach the knocker the door was flung open.

'Git in 'ere!' Nellie was grabbed by the meaty hands of her

father and frogmarched into their kitchen. Alice was still up and sat hunched in a chair by the table, her apron screwed up in her hands as she twisted at it. Nellie was smitten with guilt when she realized her sister's face was red and swollen from crying. At her feet was a laundry bag, tied in a loose bundle, out of which poked the corner of Nellie's blue cape.

'Oh, Nellie, what you done?' her sister wailed. 'He won't listen!'

'You keep yer trap shut, Alice, this is nothing to do with you!' her father shouted.

Suddenly Nellie, who had said nothing so far, found her voice. Being surrounded all day by women who had started sticking up for themselves after lives spent 'keeping their traps shut' had rubbed off, and now she burst out, 'Don't you shout at her, she ain't done nothing!'

Her father raised the back of his hand, but she ducked out of the way, crying out as she cracked her already bruised ribs on the edge of the sideboard.

Her father was breathing heavily. 'No, I'm not wasting me energy chasin' you round the kitchen.'

Alice grabbed at Nellie's skirt and then her hand, squeezing it tighter and tighter as George Clark pronounced sentence on his daughter.

'You don't bring home your wages, then you've got no rent money, have you? So you can sling yer hook!'

He grabbed up the bundle of clothes and threw it at her with such force that she staggered.

Her sister wailed again and she heard crying coming from upstairs. Her brothers had been unseen witnesses to the drama playing out in the kitchen, and now she heard their feet on the stairs. They crept in, white-faced and red-eyed.

'Please, Dad, please,' sobbed little Bobby, the softest-hearted of the two when it came to his adored sister Nellie. He ran to throw himself in supplication round his father's legs.

'Alice, get him off me, before I give him one.' He shook one of his trunk-like legs, as though flinging off an annoying puppy.

Her father's massive physique dominated the little room. They had all edged as far away from him as they could and now he stood isolated, with his back to the fireplace. Nellie felt an iron band tighten round her throat, growing tighter the more she resisted the tears, tears she wouldn't shed in front of her father, or the children for that matter.

'What you waiting for? Go on, sod off and see if yer Bolshie friends'll give you a room for nothing! Bosher'd make you pay, but not in shillings!'

She thrust out her chin and clenched her fists, mirroring her father's pose; they looked more like two prize-fighters than father and daughter. Nellie burned at the humiliation. She knew she should try to placate him, if only for the sake of the children. Who would look after them? Alice couldn't have the burden, and they'd get no tenderness from George Clark, but his insinuation rankled too much.

'Well, if that's what you think of me, I'm off!' Nellie battled to control her voice. She snatched up the bundle, ran to her sister and kissed her, whispering, 'Don't worry,' in her ear. She hugged the little ones and kissed them in turn.

'Don't cry, kids, Nellie'll make sure you're all right. I'll come back and see you!' And she gave them a brave smile as she turned her back on her father and walked out of the kitchen. Giving the front door a good slam so that the frame rattled and the window shook, she turned to face the night alone.

She marched to the end of the street and then stopped, realizing she had nowhere to go. The night was still warm; the intense heat of the day had permeated the tar-block roads and a smell of melting pitch wafted up to her. The previous evening, in their tiny airless bedroom, she had cursed the stifling heat, but now she blessed it. At least she wouldn't freeze, if she had to sleep in a doorway. But where could she go? Ted's? She dismissed that option. Her father's disturbing suggestion about Ted had made that impossible, but in any case he lived in lodgings with his brother Ginger, so there'd be no way of decently putting up a sixteen-year-old girl for the night.

She considered going to Lily's mum's, but Lily Bosher and her parents lived in just two basement rooms of a house. Nellie knew that, if there was no room for Lily's brothers, then there'd certainly be no place for her. Lily's mother Betty was a decent woman, but always hard up. Anyway, she'd have to walk under the railway arches to get there and she didn't fancy that, at this time of night. She looked up and down Spa Road. The pubs would be turning out soon and the last thing she wanted was the attention of any drunks, staggering home. She walked back down Vauban Street, passing her own front door again. She stared at the shuttered windows and they seemed to stare back at her like the eyes of a stranger.

I've got no home now, she thought, and the realization was enough to start the dammed-up tears flowing. With no one to see her, Nellie allowed herself to weep. She dropped her little bundle on to the cobbles, sat down upon it and sobbed, chokingly, still trying to stifle the sounds of her misery in case her father should hear.

In the stillness of the deserted street, she became aware of a dull, rhythmic thumping, coming from Wicks's carter's stable yard, next door to her house. It must be old Thumper, the biggest of the dray horses. The Clarks' scullery wall was the only thing between them and the horse stalls in the stable next door, and when the big horse was restless he would kick the wall of his stall and make their scullery shake. The heat was obviously keeping Thumper awake tonight. Nellie realized there *was* somewhere she could go. It would be warm, it would be dry and she wouldn't have to face anyone at all. She could slip out early tomorrow morning and no one would be any the wiser! All she had to do was get inside the bloody place.

She stood up, wiping her tears with the sleeve of her jacket. The double wooden gates to the carter's yard were locked with an iron chain, but her little brothers had a favourite way of circumventing the rudimentary security. Bobby had demonstrated one day how leaning on the ill-fitting gates, just where they met, allowed enough space for a body to squeeze through. Nellie reckoned she might just make it. She pushed hard at the middle of the gates till she could force her shoulders through, then, wincing with pain, she squeezed her bruised ribcage through. Half in and half out of the yard, she had the uncomfortable image of herself stuck there till old man Wicks came to unlock in the morning. She sucked in her breath and crammed the rest of her body through, then, like a cork popping out of a bottle, she tumbled to her knees on the cobbles inside the yard. She was in! She tugged at the bundle of clothes until that followed her too. Creeping quietly up the yard between the double row of horse stalls, she came to the end building where the hay and carts were kept.

'Shhhh, quiet, you bugger!' she hissed as old Thumper stirred at her presence and gave his stall a kick.

She tried the hayloft door and it opened with a creak, revealing the bales of hay stacked in a bay at the far end. Suddenly weariness washed over her. The day had been the most eventful of her short life. She had defied her father and been on strike. She had marched with thousands of people through the street, been caught up in a near riot, looked down the barrel of a gun, been virtually squashed to death by a docker and then kissed by a man, and now, at the end of this remarkable day, she was homeless, alone, and with no idea what the future would bring. The temptation to lie down and weep came with the fatigue, but Nellie refused.

No, she thought, *I've had me cry. Crying's not going to help me now.*

So, instead, she burrowed into the sweet-smelling hay bales, creating a little nest for herself. Alice always teased Nellie that she could fall asleep standing up in a snowstorm. Now, within minutes, she had fallen into a deep, exhausted sleep.

6

PENNY-FARTHING PROMISE

Nellie had been dreaming of Ted Bosher. He was galloping over Tower Bridge, on Thumper. Ted was shouting a warning that she couldn't quite make out, then he halted in the middle of the bridge, where she stood, straddling the gap between the two halves. He leaned down to scoop her up, but the bascules started to rise and they both tumbled through the gap down to the murky Thames below. She was falling, falling, and could hear Thumper neighing as the inky water rushed up to engulf her, but, at the moment of impact, she woke. Sitting bolt upright, she found herself looking at a dark figure who was bending down, scrabbling at something in the hay. She screamed and then he screamed.

'What are *you* doing here?' His mouth was open in shock.

'None of your business, Sam Gilbie. What are *you* doing here?'

'I *work* here!'

'Oh, my Gawd, is it morning already?' Nellie jumped up, plucking at straw.

'No, no, it's not morning. It's nine o'clock at night! I've just come to see to the horses. Your dad had to cope on his own today, with the rest of us all out.'

Nellie sat back down in relief, then she saw the object Sam had been searching for among the hay bales.

'What's that?'

'If you tell me what you're doing here, I'll tell you what it is.' He was shielding the object with his body, but she caught sight of a metal frame and a brass plate with the word *Ariel* stamped on it.

'*I'm* here, because me dad chucked me out.' For some reason, admitting this to Sam threatened a return of the tears she had tried so hard to keep at bay. She struggled to control her trembling lips.

'Oh, Nellie, I'm sorry! I know he's against the union, but I never thought he'd do something like this to his own daughter. What'll you do?'

Nellie shrugged. 'I'll manage somehow.' She didn't want to talk about it with Sam. She didn't want him to think badly of her father, which was puzzling to her, as she didn't care a hoot what Lily or Ted thought of him. Why should Sam Gilbie's opinion matter?

'Anyway, I've done my bit. Now you tell me what that is.' She craned her neck, trying to look at what was behind his back.

He stepped aside and pulled out from the straw an old penny-farthing bicycle.

She didn't know what she'd expected, but this was the last thing she'd imagined he'd be hiding. 'Oh, Sam, you don't see many of them these days. Where on earth did you get it?'

Sam carefully brushed off the straw, revealing the large front wheel first, then pushed it out to the centre of the floor so she could see the whole frame and the smaller back wheel.

'It was me dad's,' he said proudly. 'He rode it all the way from Hull to London, long before I was born. If he hadn't done it, I'd have been a northern lad instead of a Bermondsey boy!'

For the first time, Nellie noticed his smile. It gave his face a sweet expression she'd never noticed before. Not that she'd spent much time in his company. She had a few vague childhood memories of him. There had been some precious country outings, organized for children by the Bermondsey Settlement, where his parents had sometimes helped out. She remembered how the brake, decked with paper garlands and drawn by two massive dray horses, had trundled up to the settlement, where they were all ready in their Sunday best for a day out in Kent. It had been like a day in heaven, the first time she'd seen fields and, more mysterious still, cows! She remembered a dark-haired young Sam, sitting up at the front, eager to hold the horses' reins. She remembered too his spirited mother and his father, who seemed much more fun than her own. Sam, at sixteen, had got his wish to become a horse driver himself. He was a favourite of her father's, who thought him a decent hard-working boy. He often praised the way Sam had shouldered the burden of supporting his family, after his father had died. When she encountered him going in and out of Wicks's yard, he would always have a ready smile and it felt natural to stop and chat. Only at Pearce Duff's gates did she find herself being irritated by him. His face then was always either too hopeful or too disappointed, depending on whether it was before or after she'd refused his offer of a lift in the cart.

'Dad made me promise to keep it.' He turned his face away, looking down at the machine. 'We lost the bike shed when we had to move out of Globe Buildings – it was a tied place, from Wright's seed mill. I've been storing it here and doing it up in me spare time.'

'I wonder why he made you promise to keep it?'

Sam sat down in the straw, laying the penny-farthing down between them. His voice took on a wistful tone as he remembered his father.

'It was a lucky charm for him. He always said it changed his life. They didn't have much up north, nearly ended up in the workhouse, but the bike got him down here and he finished up foreman at Wright's Mill. It was a good job.' Sam fell silent.

'How long's he been dead now, Sam?' Nellie asked gently. She had guessed this was the reason for the family losing their tied accommodation.

'Only last year. It was the job did it in the end. All those years in the seed mill – chaff and dust ruined his lungs. Still, he was just glad he'd made something of his life, and he thought this old thing would bring me luck.'

Sam spun the wheel between them and Nellie absently let her fingers trail over the spokes, filling the hay barn with a sad harp-like thrumming.

'Can you ride it?' she asked suddenly.

Sam smiled again. This time, there was more mischief in it than melancholy, and without a word he righted the penny-farthing and scooted it towards the open door.

Nellie followed, in time to see him hopping on to the back mounting bar. He hooked his leg over the saddle and was off, in a smooth roll, down to the end of the yard, where he executed a tight turn, wobbled, and, to Nellie's delight, was back with her in two pedal strokes. He hopped off, looking very pleased with himself.

She was seized with an overwhelming urge to try it herself. 'Can I have a go?'

Sam looked doubtful. 'Oh, I dunno about that!'

Nellie, disappointed, wondered at the irony of Sam Gilbie saying no to her!

'Come on, Sam, I need cheering up. I've just been chucked out of me home!'

Sam soon relented and helped her up. He kept a tight hold of the saddle as she mounted inelegantly and then wobbled her way down the yard. After a circuit with Sam trotting at her side she was getting more confident.

'Let go, let go!' she hissed, as quietly as she could. 'I can do it on me own!'

Sam looked worried but Nellie showed no signs of getting down, so he released his hold on the saddle and soon she was pedalling for all she was worth, back towards the double doors.

'Brake, Nellie, brake!' Sam warned in a stage-whisper. If she hit the double doors, the whole of Vauban Street would be awake soon enough.

'The brake! Where's the bloody brake?' she hissed back. She fumbled about, around her skirt, and just in time found the lever for the spoon brake. Coming to a juddering halt, she almost toppled over the handlebars but recovered, just as Sam leaped forward to grab the teetering machine.

'Are you laughing at me?'

Sam shook his head, smiling. 'There's not many people would celebrate being homeless with a penny-farthing ride. But then again, there's not many people like you, Nellie Clark.'

She got flustered by his admiration and jumped off the bike. 'Let's hope I'm as good at finding somewhere to live, eh?'

'Well, you can't sleep here. You'd best come home with me for tonight.'

Nellie shook her head vigorously. 'No, no, no, I'm not going anywhere with you. I'm staying put.'

'Well, it would only be for tonight. We haven't got much room, and anyway...' He hesitated. 'Mum's not so good at the moment. You can share with my sister, Matty. I'm not leaving you here on your own.'

Nellie could tell he wouldn't budge and in the end she agreed. Sam put the penny-farthing back in its hiding place behind the straw bales and they set off towards Rotherhithe, where he lived. As they walked along the riverbank, he carried her bundle of clothing and proudly related more tales of his father's bicycling exploits. He'd won many trophies for the Bermondsey Bicycle Club, but when shortness of breath put an end to his cycling days, he'd refused to get rid of the penny-farthing.

'Mum used to go off alarmin' at him 'cause we had to pay for the bike shed as well, but he wouldn't part with it. *That's my fortune*, he used to say, *and it'll be Sam's one day too*. Poor Dad, he never did earn a fortune, and if I stay a carman I don't suppose I shall either.'

Nellie had begun to warm to the boy, who had for so long been an irritant, and in spite of her own sorry situation she wanted to encourage him. 'Well, there's more churches than Christ Church and there's more than one sort of good fortune. He had a loving son, like you, one that's kept his promise, and that's something to be proud of, eh?'

Sam nodded silently, the dark river gliding on beside them as they made their way round the winding peninsula of Rotherhithe.

When they finally reached the little house in Beatson Street, Nellie could barely walk straight, she was so tired. Sam lived in a two-up, two-down between the river and Globe Dock, with his mother, Lizzie, his younger brother, Charlie, and his little sister, Matty. A lamp was burning in the window and the end-of-terrace door was opened so quickly, it was obvious someone had been looking out for him. A dark-haired boy, of about ten, ushered them in; Nellie was surprised he wasn't already in bed.

'Nellie, this is my brother, Charlie. The little boy smiled briefly at Nellie, accepting her unknown presence without question.

Turning worried, dark eyes to Sam, he whispered, 'She's been terrible bad today.'

Sam ruffled his dark, wavy hair and led the way into the little front room.

In spite of the warmth of the night, a fire was burning in the grate and a pale-faced woman was sitting next to it, wrapped in a shawl, with a blanket covering her legs. She looked up weakly and smiled at Sam. Then her face suddenly came to life with curiosity as she spotted Nellie following.

She attempted to rise a little, but the effort proved too much for her and she sank back. 'Sam, you should have told me you were bringing company. Introduce me to your friend.'

She smiled encouragingly, and Sam half pushed Nellie forward, quickly explaining the situation.

Just then a little girl, of about eight or nine, came in from the back kitchen and flung herself at Sam. He lifted her up, planting a kiss on her cheek, but when she spotted Nellie her pretty face scowled.

'Who's that?' she said baldly.

'Matty, remember your manners.' Her mother's weak voice still had enough steel in it to bring the little girl to book.

She blushed. 'Sorry,' she said, looking appealingly for rescue to Sam, who now put her down and placed a hand on top of her soft auburn curls. She was an exceptionally pretty child, with large dark eyes, filled with a restless curiosity.

'Nellie, this is my little sister Mathilda, but we all call her Matty.'

'Sorry, but there's only enough dinner for Sam,' Matty addressed Nellie, with a worried frown, 'and I've been keeping it hot for him, ain't I, Mum?'

The weary woman sitting by the fire nodded proudly.

Nellie felt her heart go out to the anxious child. She knew, only too well, the situation she was in. Crouching down to Matty's level, she took her hand and apologized for spoiling all her well-laid plans.

'I don't want to be any trouble. Anyway,' she lied, 'don't you worry about me, Matty, I've already had me dinner ages ago!'

If she was going to be sharing the child's bed, Nellie thought it best to make friends. She was keen to avoid the sharp elbows and knees of a disgruntled eight-year-old digging into her all night. But as soon as the child realized her beloved brother would not be robbed of his tea, she smiled and trotted back to the scullery. Nellie felt awkward, standing there with her bundle at her feet. She wished Sam would see how exhausted she was and ask Matty to take her to the bedroom. But, instead, he followed Matty into the scullery, where Nellie heard him scrubbing his hands and talking to the two children. She heard much whispering, which she judged to be about the possibility of dividing Sam's tea between two plates.

Mrs Gilbie beckoned Nellie to sit next to her. Nellie had kept a distance from the fire, but now she slipped off her jacket and went to the hard-backed chair next to Mrs Gilbie.

'I'm very grateful, Mrs Gilbie. I won't trouble you no more than tonight. I'll find somewhere tomorrow.'

'It's no trouble, love, and you're welcome to stay as long as you like. Don't I remember you from the girls' club, at the Settlement?'

Nellie nodded.

'I thought I recognized that chestnut hair of yours. You've grown into a lovely young woman, Nellie.' She smiled. 'Always with the little 'uns, you was, always carrying a baby around, I remember now.' And it was true, for Nellie's mother had given birth to two babies between her and Alice. Nellie had loved both the frail little things, who had stayed for such a short while in the world.

Mrs Gilbie unexpectedly took her hand. She had been a handsome woman in her day. There were still streaks of a fiery auburn in amongst her grey hair, and her face, though worn with hard work and illness, was still pleasant to look at. But it was her eyes that drew Nellie in: there was an intelligence there, which seemed to take in more than the bare facts told her by Sam.

'I didn't know my Sam was walking out with someone,' she said in a weak voice, which came in gasps between laboured breaths. 'I'm glad it's you.'

Nellie tried to explain but struggled to find words. How could she tell this proud mother that Sam was the last person she was thinking of walking out with?

'He's… very kind,' she finished lamely.

'He's a good boy. He's been the breadwinner since his father passed away and he's never once complained. But you know that already. He doesn't make a show of things, but his feelings go very deep, Nellie. What I mean is, I hope you'll be good to him, won't you? And if ever the day comes…' she took in a wheezing breath '… then be good to my children as well.' Here she paused, while she struggled with a bout of breathlessness that Nellie thought had ended the conversation. She thought the woman, who had closed her eyes, had drifted off into sleep. But then she stirred and, still with her eyes closed, went on in a barely audible voice. 'Look after Sam and the children… when the time comes. I can see you're the one for him, Nellie. I can see it in his eyes.' Her voice had faded away almost to nothing and now there was only a silence, waiting for Nellie to fill it.

All Nellie could think of was her dream, how she had been

falling with Ted, through the gap in Tower Bridge, to the engulfing water below. And now it felt to her as if another gap was opening up to swallow her, here, in this little cosy room, where the dying woman was extracting from her a promise she could never keep. How could she promise such a thing? How could she not?

7

BREAD

Nellie inhaled the tantalizing aroma of the freshly baked crusty loaves. There were thousands of them, stacked on trestle tables in the large lecture hall of the Labour Institute. She had left Sam Gilbie's home, without breakfast, not wishing to deprive the children or his sick mother of their last bit of bread and jam. She'd last eaten the evening before, sharing a scant half of Sam's mutton stew. Matty had ladled out the supper, giving Nellie mostly cabbage. Nellie admired her fierce protectiveness towards her older brother. She would have done the same. In fact, it hadn't been long before Nellie was bewitched by the child. She had a way of singing to herself as she undertook the grown-up tasks of the kitchen, and when she finally took herself off to bed she was still singing. While Nellie washed up plates, she could hear Matty's voice, clear and pure and bright, receding up the stairs.

'We call her our little canary,' Sam explained. 'She keeps the place bright and it reminds us of Dad. He had a good voice.'

She and Matty had shared the bed in the top back bedroom. The other room was occupied by Sam and his brother, while their mother, who was too weak to climb stairs, had a truckle bed in the kitchen. The little girl was still awake when Nellie finally crept into the bedroom. She snuggled up in the bed, next to Nellie, and now seemed to view her visit as a great adventure. What was left of the night was almost all used up listening to the little canary's chattering and childish confidences, until finally Nellie fell into a fitful sleep, full of dreams of little caged birds, singing, singing, singing.

Now, standing behind this trestle table loaded with bread felt like torture. Her hollow stomach gurgled and she wanted nothing more than to tear into one of those warm, enticing loaves. Instead, she went to find Eliza James. She found her out in the back yard, supervising the deliveries of food pouring in from well-wishers and strike supporters. The woman had an energetic air about her, as though the act of standing still was only ever a launching pad for another activity. Now she was moving down a line of packing cases, list in hand, ticking off each delivery.

'Perishables over there in the brick outhouse. They need to be distributed first.' She addressed some volunteer dockers, who immediately started to heave off crates of fish, stacked in ice.

Eliza James turned and noticed Nellie waiting patiently for instructions.

'I've come to help with the loaves, madam,' Nellie said quietly.

Eliza smiled broadly, obviously remembering her from the day before. 'Ah, it's Nellie, isn't it? I see you survived your father's wrath!'

'I'm afraid he chucked me out when I got back, madam.'

'You don't mean to say you spent the night on the streets?' Eliza's shock was obvious, and Nellie felt acute shame on behalf of her father.

'No, madam, I stayed with… a friend.' She hardly knew how to describe Sam now his kindness had subtly shifted their relationship. 'Sam, the young feller that helped me yesterday, Sam Gilbie.'

Nellie immediately became conscious of an uncharacteristic stillness about Eliza. Once more, she felt she'd stumbled upon a feeling of connection between Eliza and Sam. Nellie's curiosity needed to be sated. 'You met him yesterday,' she probed. 'Do you know him?'

For the first time, Nellie saw that Eliza's habitual poise had left her, and she actually stuttered. 'I… no… not well. I don't know Sam well.'

Nellie waited in silence as Eliza James, a woman who could command thousands from atop a tea crate, stumbled and blushed, but she said no more. Instead, Eliza hastily turned to address a query from one of the young lady volunteers about the queue of noisy women forming at the door of the institute.

'Yes, let them in now, if you will, Sarah.'

When she turned back to Nellie, she was more composed. The smooth veneer, which had cracked briefly, was once again in place and she was every inch the Madam Mecklenburgh of the podium.

'But look, Nellie, we must help you find somewhere. You've lost your home for the cause and the least we can do is help you find somewhere permanent.'

Nellie just had time to thank Eliza for the offer of help before Sarah came back to marshal her away to the work station. She led Nellie back into the lecture hall, full of the fragrant loaves, and immediately Nellie's growling stomach protested. Once she was engaged in making up parcels of bread and tea for strikers' families, she slipped a loaf under the trestle table. Digging her fingers into the end, Nellie pulled out a hunk of the soft white bread, surreptitiously stuffing it into her mouth. She was starving and it was delicious.

The doors opened at eight o'clock, and after three hours the stream of women and children showed no sign of slacking. The hall was all confusion, full of chatter, laughter and screaming babies, but as soon as Ted came through the door Nellie spotted him. She was so disconcerted that she handed out an extra food parcel to a woman and her children, who trotted off quickly with their windfall. Ted walked boldly up to the trestle table, leaned over and filched a loaf.

'Oi, keep your hands off, Ted Bosher!' She went to slap his hand, but he simply laughed at her,

'While I'm at it, I'll have one of these an' all.' And he leaned across the table and stole a kiss for good measure.

'How did you get on with the old man last night?'

When Nellie told him, Ted's face hardened. 'Why d'you go with Gilbie? Me mum would've taken you in!'

Nellie shook her head. 'No, Ted, she's got enough on her plate, without me turning up on her doorstep.'

Ted seemed unconvinced and turned his anger on her father. 'I tell you what, Nell, you've got more guts than your old man will ever have, turning his back on his own! Don't worry, he'll get his, we're going to start cracking down on the scabs.'

Nellie grew frightened. Hard as he was, her father's explanation of his behaviour had made a kind of sense. 'No, don't say that, Ted. He's only doing what he thinks is best for the family. You can't bully people into going along. I've made me bed—'

'And now we'll just have to find you another one to lie in...' His green eyes twinkled mischievously and Nellie caught his meaning. She flushed.

'Don't you come the old acid, Ted Bosher. You may call us the custard tarts but that don't mean you can take advantage!'

Nellie shoved another parcel into a woman's hands and beckoned to Sarah. Her bruised ribs ached, her legs were trembling with tiredness, and her heart was thudding with what felt like fear. She felt caged behind the table, cornered by Ted and suddenly overwhelmed. Like a hunted animal, her instinct told her to head for home, and yet she had no home, not now.

'Can I take a break now, Sarah? Is there anyone to fill in?'

The young woman smiled over at her. 'I can do that, Nellie. You go off and have a bite to eat. You look tired out. There's a little canteen set up in the basement.'

Nellie hugged Sarah gratefully and swept past the young man, feeling a fool as she remembered her father's warnings. Ted followed her, with the loaf of bread still clutched in his hand.

'I didn't mean anything by it, Nell. Listen—'

But she let the double doors swing back in his face and was already clattering down the stone steps to the basement kitchen.

'What a stupid, stupid fool! He's only interested in what he can get,' she berated herself.

It was mortifying to her to think her father had been right, probably knowing a young chap like Ted could get his pick of the girls. She sat at a round wooden table, with a mug of tea and a bowl of soup. Eliza James and her helpers had thought of everything, even down to feeding their own workers. She'd heard Eliza had written to all the newspapers, asking for handouts and funds to support the strike. The woman must have worked round the clock to get so much organized; Nellie doubted Eliza would ever find time to solve her personal predicament.

She was beginning to wonder if the estrangement from her family hadn't been a huge mistake, even for such a good cause. She'd faced the rift with her father because she wanted to show herself, more than anyone else, that she wasn't just a wage slave. But now the memory of Bobby's tears and her sister's anguish made her realize what was really important to her. Who would be a mother to the family, if not her? She was no Madam Mecklenburgh, she knew that much – a woman with seemingly no other life, or family, or purpose, but the struggle. Nellie had taken on the mothering of Bobby, Freddie and Alice without complaint, and whatever her father had done to her, she couldn't desert them. Now she wondered how they would be coping without her. Still, she told herself, Alice was a good girl; she would manage for the time being.

She dipped some bread into the soup, but a lump of it stuck in her throat and the tears welled up, like an unstoppable spring. Eliza James might be able to find her a room, but the thought of another night away from her family was more than she could bear. She put up her hand, to shield her face and her tears. She heard chair legs scrape as someone came to sit beside her. Quickly brushing her wet cheeks, she looked up into Lily's worried face.

'Ted's just told me! Oh, Nellie, why didn't you come to me?'

Nellie fell gratefully into her friend's arms, unable to stop her tears. 'It was too late and your poor mum's got no room, and then Sam came along. He was so kind, but, oh, Lil, I don't think I can stay there again. I've promised his mother something stupid!'

Nellie felt entirely safe confiding in her friend, for she knew Lily would not judge her, and now all her troubles and worries came tumbling out between sobs. 'Mrs Gilbie's so ill, I didn't have the heart to say no. Now I've gone and promised I'll take on her kids if she dies!' She buried her face on her friend's shoulder, with another heaving sob. 'Oh, Lily, what am I going to do? I've got enough on my hands, with looking after me own family!' She went on, in a choking whisper, 'And I must've given her the wrong idea about me and Sam... I'm sure she wouldn't have asked, unless she thought he was my feller!'

'Oh you soppy 'apporth, Nellie Clark, that won't never come back on you!' Lily said, cutting through Nellie's confusion with her own certainty. 'And it's not *your* fault she got the wrong end of the stick. You must've been in a right two an' eight, poor thing. Now, I don't want to hear no arguments. You're staying with me tonight!'

Nellie's objections were stifled by another hug from her friend. There was no one she would rather stay with, even though it would mean sleeping on the floor.

'We'll make you up a cosy little bed next to mine, Nell, and at least you'll be close to the kids.' Lily herself slept in a cot bed, made up each night in the kitchen.

'Thanks, Lily, the poor little things were heartbroken. I've promised them I'll go and see them, but I've got to pick the right time.'

Lily nodded understandingly. 'Don't you worry about that. I'll let Alice know where you are and she can bring the boys round later on.'

A wave of gratitude overwhelmed Nellie, and the two girls linked arms as they went back upstairs to dole out more food parcels to the seemingly unending line of hungry strikers' families.

It was almost like being at Pearce Duff's, the two of them working together as they reached for the food, wrapped it, and handed it out. And when Lily took her home at the end of the day, Nellie was glad she at least had her own strike-fund pay and a food parcel, to contribute to the Bosher household.

When they entered the kitchen, Betty and Billy Bosher were sitting down to a meagre tea of bread and dripping, but Betty took Nellie's presence in her stride.

''Course you're staying here, where else?' was Betty's immediate response. 'That's so long as you can put up with this big bugger's snoring all night. The walls is paper thin!'

Billy Bosher's large pug-nosed face creased into laughter as he got up from the table and grabbed his coat from the back of the kitchen chair. 'I'm off. I'd rather be on the bloody picket line at Butler's Wharf than in a houseful of women. I'm outnumbered good and proper now!'

As he was leaving, Nellie glimpsed through the kitchen window three familiar figures, trooping down the basement steps. She ran to the front door and immediately swung Bobby up into her arms. Even the usually undemonstrative Freddie hugged her, as Betty called from the kitchen for Nellie to bring them all in. She plonked an enormous enamel teapot on the table and an assortment of mismatched cups. 'They're all welcome to sleep in the kitchen too, but we'll have to put 'em top and tail!' she added cheerily. Once the three Clark children were seated around the Boshers' kitchen table, drinking Betty's dark sweet brew, Alice quickly unburdened herself. She said their father had forbidden all mention of Nellie's name, but oddly he seemed to have lost interest in the rest of them.

'We ain't seen nothing of him today, didn't come home for his dinner, and I've been so worried about you, Nell!'

'Don't worry, Al,' Nellie said, squeezing her little sister's hand, 'we'll be together again soon, I know we will.'

'We can't stop long, I'm scared in case he comes home and finds us gone,' Alice said, gulping the rest of her tea.

Nellie saw them out and, at the top of the basement steps, gave Alice some hurried instructions about looking after her brothers and father. Alice left with promises to bring the boys back to see her when she could.

'And you two boys do as Alice tells you while I'm gone!' Nellie called after them as they turned the corner.

The following evening, after another long day at the Labour Institute, she and Lily were sitting outside on the wall at the top of the Boshers' basement steps, trying to cool off in what passed for an evening breeze. The temperatures had reached a hundred degrees that day and the two girls barely had enough energy to chat. Nellie saw Alice first, being followed two steps behind by the boys, who both had sorrowful hangdog expressions. She was surprised to see them again so soon; she'd expected her father to monitor their comings and goings more closely. But as Alice sat herself on the wall beside them, Nellie knew immediately that all was not well.

'What's the matter with you two?' Nellie asked the glum-looking boys.

'Dad give us a walloping!' Freddie shouted at her, his face swollen and red with tears.

Before Nellie had a chance to blame her father, Alice jumped in. 'He found out they've been swimming in the river.'

Bobby and Freddie, like all the boys who lived anywhere near the Thames, made it their playground during the summer. They would regularly sneak down the river stairs, leap across the moored barges tied up in rows that reached almost to the middle of the river, and then dive into the treacherous currents. The great wide sweep of the Thames, which wound through Bermondsey and Rotherhithe, was perilous and polluted and their father had quite rightly forbidden them from swimming in its waters. But Nellie could understand how the overwhelming heat had won out over her father's warnings: the water might be filthy, but at least it was cool.

'Well, don't come looking for sympathy, it's your own fault!' she said, as Bobby came to lean on Nellie's knees. She kissed the top of his head, nonetheless, belying her stern tone.

'He don't care about us, anyway,' said Freddie, banging his

boot against the bottom of the wall. 'He never even speaks to us, just belts us.'

Whatever Nellie felt about her father, it hurt her to think his sons thought this way about him. 'Well, he just doesn't want you to end up like your friend Michael McIlvoy, does he?'

One of their neighbour's children, nine-year-old Michael McIlvoy, had swum out to a notorious current in the centre of the Thames known as the Fountain. Boys would let themselves be dragged under and sucked along beneath the water by the undertow and, if they were lucky, they were shot clean out of the river by a water spout. It was deadly fun, but Michael McIlvoy was not lucky: he had missed the water jet and the undercurrent took him all the way down to Greenwich, where his body was found the next day.

'But we didn't go anywhere near the Fountain!' Freddie protested.

'It doesn't matter! If you slip between the barges, you drown anyway. How many times do we have to tell you!' Bobby's head felt hot in her lap and she lifted him up. 'You two have got to be good while I'm away. Just keep Dad happy, all right? Now promise me you won't go down the foreshore tomorrow?'

When Bobby nodded and Freddie gave her a grudging promise, Nellie dug into her apron pocket. One of the more eccentric philanthropists had responded to Eliza James's appeal for food with six jars of humbugs and a barrel of sardines. The boys' faces lit up at the sight of the bag of humbugs that Nellie now dangled in front of them.

'You only get 'em if you're good for Alice!' she said as Freddie whipped them out of her hand and immediately stuffed a black-and-white striped sweet into his mouth.

''Course we'll be good, we're always good, ain't we, Bob?'

With their cheeks bulging, they looked like two grinning hamsters, and Nellie was glad she'd at least managed to send them home happier than when they'd arrived.

*

Nellie worked for the next few days at the Labour Institute, leaving the Boshers' house early, with Lily, to start assembling food parcels and then doling them out all day. Sometimes she found it more exhausting than working in the factory; the constant press of people, with their worried faces and their hungry children, was draining her. She was grateful for a ten-minute break in the little basement canteen and was just enjoying her first cup of tea of the day when she saw Eliza James approaching.

'Nellie, dear, you'd best come with me. Someone wants to talk to you.'

'Who?'

But Eliza simply took her by the arm, leading her out to another small basement room. Nellie asked again, 'Who wants me?'

Eliza pushed open the door and stood back to reveal Sam Gilbie, standing with his cap in his hand. Nellie was confused and looked at each of them in turn, wondering what on earth was going on. For a moment, she thought it was something to do with finding a room for her. But Eliza didn't look as though she was about to impart good news and Sam's face was grim.

'What is it, Sam?' Nellie felt fear ripple through her. Had his mother died?

'Nellie, your father sent me to fetch you…'

There was a moment's relief, first that it wasn't Lizzie and then at the thought that her father had relented. She could go home again! But then she saw Sam shake his head.

'It's Bobby, it looks like he's got the dysentery…'

Nellie's hand covered her mouth as she tried to stifle the cry, remembering the two little coffins she'd seen pass along Vauban Street only a few days ago.

'Oh, no, Sam, not Bobby. Is it bad? Oh, no.' Her knees buckled and he sprang to catch her. Eliza had her under the other arm and the two of them half carried her up the stairs out to the back yard and the waiting cart.

'Get me there quick, Sam. Bobby needs me, get me there quick.' Panic had fallen over her like a chill, icy covering, which no summer heat could penetrate. Her mouth was dry, but a cold sheen of sweat enveloped her. Her breath came in shallow, harsh rasps. They helped her up on to the front seat and, as though from a great distance, she heard Eliza say, 'I'm so sorry, Nellie. I would come with you, but I can't leave things as they are here...'

'No, of course you can't,' Sam replied, and his tone was steel.

'Thank you, madam, thank you. Could someone let Lily know?' Nellie asked, just as Sam slapped the reins and manoeuvred the cart out of the yard. The streets were a blur as the horse clipped along, and Nellie found herself gripping the side board till her knuckles were white. She thought of all the times Sam Gilbie had asked her to ride in this cart, feeling she would give anything if only it could be one of those times now. And then she found herself making a stupid bargain with God. If you spare Bobby, I'll be kinder to Sam. I promise I'll ride in the bloody cart whenever he wants me to. Spare Bobby, she prayed silently and fervently, and I'll keep the promise I made his mum, I will, just let Bobby be all right...

Sam pulled up the cart in Vauban Street and helped her down. 'He's a strong little 'un, Nellie. Try not to worry too much, he'll get through it,' he said quietly.

She wished she could believe him. If the other two children in the street had been carried off by dysentery, what was there to save Bobby? People were blaming the dock strike for the lack of fresh food and milk. Hungry children had to be fed and, like other families, they'd been forced to buy the 'specks' of rotting fruit and whatever ends of meat were left over at the market. She knew too well how hungry boys would eat whatever was to hand; she'd never forgive herself if Bobby had eaten bad food, just because she wasn't there to supervise.

Alice must have heard the cart draw up and in seconds she was at the front door, flinging her arms round Nellie. 'Oh, Nell, he's bad. Come quick, he's been asking for you.'

Her father was slumped in his chair, staring at the empty grate. She didn't think he saw her as they passed through the kitchen and up the stairs to the bedroom, where Bobby was lying alone in the bed he normally shared with Freddie. A white-faced Freddie, all the bravado knocked out of him, now knelt beside the bed and she rushed over to join him.

'Bobby,' she said, gently stroking the little boy's damp hair, 'it's Nellie come back to see you.'

His eyes flickered open and he gave her a weak smile. 'Dad let you come home! I kept asking him. I didn't give up, even when he got angry.'

Nellie swallowed the tears. ''Course I'm home, I wouldn't leave you, would I?' She held the little boy's hand and it was icy cold. She felt down to his feet and, though the room was stifling, they were frozen too. Her sister's fearful look told her everything.

'Stay with me now, Nellie, don't go away again,' the boy pleaded weakly.

She looked at Alice, who nodded. 'Dad's taking it bad, Nell. I don't think he even noticed you come in.'

'I'm here, Bobby. I'm staying here.'

And she kept her word, kneeling at the little boy's side, hour after hour, as the window darkened and the stars came out. Periodically she got up and tried to make him drink. Alice had been dozing in the other bed, comforting Freddie, but now she got up and asked anxiously, 'Can't we call the doctor out, Nell?'

She shook her head. 'There's no money for the doctor, Al, but everyone says the best thing is to keep putting the fluid back in them.'

She got up to fetch Bobby another drink, but Alice caught her arm. 'Come on, Nell, let me take a turn watching.'

But Nellie would not leave him. With the dawn came a change. His shivering increased and his breathing became shallow. And then she felt all the strength leave her and she fell sobbing on to the bed. 'What good's a promise to you,' she shouted at God, 'if you're going to take him anyway!'

She must have been screaming, for her father came running up the stairs and, kneeling down beside her, gathered her into his arms.

'It's my fault, Dad, I'm so sorry. It's the strike did it, it's the bad milk and food. We caused it, it should be me there.'

Her stern father's face melted with tears. 'You can't blame yourself, Nell. He could have caught anything, swimming in that filthy river, and I found out they've been eating food from the wharf side. It's been rotting there for days. That could've caused it.'

She was stunned. She had expected blame, abuse, rage, but not this vulnerable, weeping old man. She had never seen him like it, not even when her mother died.

'If anyone's to blame it's me,' he went on. 'Oh, God, Nellie, my poor little boy. The last thing I did to him was beat him, till he begged me to stop.'

They stayed locked in each other's arms for a long time, united, for once, in a common bond of guilt and grief.

8

AND ROSES

Nellie woke with a start, then realized she was in her own bed, though how she got there she couldn't for the moment recall. The bright morning sun was already piercing the thin curtains and then she remembered. Bobby! How could she have left him? She instinctively turned over to shake Alice, but found she was alone in the bed. A cold panic rose like a paralysis and she was held fast by the fear of what she would find if she left the bed. If she stayed where she was, she needn't find out. If she stayed still, here and now Bobby could still be alive. Now a memory surfaced of waking in the early morning light in the arms of her father as he carried her to her own bed. She must have fallen asleep at Bobby's bedside.

'He's still the same, Nell,' her father had whispered. 'You sleep, I'll watch him.'

Too tired then to protest, she had sunk into a deep sleep. How many times she'd fended off wakefulness she couldn't be sure, but each time she felt herself rising out of sleep a sickening fear that her beloved brother had gone overwhelmed her, and she clutched at unconsciousness once more.

But Nellie knew she couldn't run away from the dreadful news forever. Forcing herself to get up, she walked barefoot across the room. Pulling aside the curtain, she saw him. His pale face looked so peaceful, she even thought there was the trace of a smile. Why was no one here with him? Why had they left him to grow cold all on his own? She felt a surge of anger at the old grey blanket covering him to the neck. He had always hated its scratchiness. He should have been wrapped in something soft. She reached to turn down the blanket and was startled by a movement. Had the blanket risen with a breath or was it her imagination giving her what she so desperately wanted? Placing her hand lightly on Bobby's chest, she felt it again, an almost imperceptible rise and fall. He was breathing! But so shallow, light as a baby's breaths and with so many agonizing seconds between them. She sat quietly on the bed, counting each breath till she assured herself the next one would come. She remembered her mother's favourite saying: 'Just remember, Nellie, when you open your eyes in the morning and you're still breathing, you know you've already had a bloody good day!' Bobby's eyes might not be open, but he *was* still breathing.

'Oh, Bobby,' she whispered, leaning closely over him, 'Mum says you're having a bloody good day.' She let the tears fall as she stroked his smooth childish cheek.

Just then she heard the voices of Alice and her father downstairs, speaking in low tones. What were they keeping from her? She flung her coat round her shoulders and hurried down. Freddie was sitting silently by the fire.

'What's going on?' she asked him, but he shook his head.

She ran out of the room to be met by a white-faced Alice, alone in the passage.

'Where's Dad gone?' Nellie asked.

'He wouldn't say, Nell, just said the waiting was driving him mad and he had to get out of the house.'

Nellie understood. She felt just as helpless, yet she wished her father had been brave enough to stay at home with them. His absence meant that it would be up to her to keep Alice and Freddie's spirits up, and she didn't know if she had the strength. She took her sister's hand as Alice began to weep, and drew her back into the kitchen. 'Come on, love, we've got to be grateful our Bobby's still with us. I'm sure he's through the worst of it,' she lied. 'Tell you what, let's put the kettle on and I'll see about some breakfast. God knows what we've got left, though.'

Her face clouded with worry as her thoughts turned to the problem of feeding the family; without her wage she knew her father had been struggling. Alice and Freddie watched her go to the larder. When she opened the cupboard door, the astonished look on her face made Alice smile through her tears.

'Where did all this lot come from?' Nellie gasped. The larder was fuller than she'd seen it in weeks.

'We got a parcel of food from the neighbours, they've all been so good,' said her sister, 'and Sam Gilbie even brought some eggs from his mother.'

Tears pricked Nellie's eyes as she imagined the sick woman sending Sam off with his precious gift. 'Oh, Alice, his own little ones could do with 'em, you shouldn't have taken them.'

'I tried to tell him that!' Alice protested. 'But Sam said no, his mother was adamant, the eggs was for Nellie's family. Kind of her, eh?'

Nellie nodded, wondering how Lizzie Gilbie was. 'And she's not well herself either.'

Full of gratitude, she set about making them a breakfast of toast and dripping, and tea sweetened with condensed milk. They ate mostly in silence and though she tried to cheer them up, her own thoughts were with the little boy upstairs. As soon as Freddie had finished eating, she sent him up to sit with Bobby.

While she and Alice were washing up the breakfast plates in the scullery, Nellie heard the front door open. 'Let me speak to him first.' She shot a look at her sister. 'You stay here.'

She wanted to make sure her father knew how much the younger ones needed him now. The prospect of losing Bobby had seemed to weaken his spirit to the point of inaction. She couldn't get through this without him and she hoped that after their shared grief of the night before, he would listen to her.

She was astonished to see him walk into the kitchen with a domed-headed, bespectacled man who carried a leather bag. His face looked familiar. Her father said nothing to Nellie, but the look he gave her begged her not to show surprise. She had no idea how he'd found money for a doctor, but she certainly wasn't going to question him about it now.

'Follow me, Doctor, he's upstairs,' her father said meekly.

She walked back into the scullery where Alice was waiting patiently.

'Well, where's he been?' Alice whispered.

'He's been to fetch the doctor, but how he's paying for it I don't know.'

Realization dawned on Alice's face and she explained that her father had gone out carrying a bundle. 'He's been to the pawnshop!'

If anything could have persuaded Nellie that her father was changed this was it. Though she and her mother were regulars at the pawn shop, her father's pride would never allow him to step into the place or even acknowledge how his income was supplemented each week. His Sunday suit was available to wear every weekend, and what happened to it during the rest of the week he pretended not to know.

'Then it's just as well he never joined the strike, otherwise they'd have refused him!'

In an attempt to break the strike, the government had ordered all pawnbrokers to close their doors to strikers, and Nellie wondered now at the irony that her stubborn father's anti-union stance might actually be the saving of Bobby. When the doctor finally left, George Clark returned to the kitchen. 'He wouldn't take a penny! What d'ye make of that?' her father said with a puzzled look on his face.

Now Nellie remembered where she'd seen the doctor. He'd been a great supporter of the strike, speaking at all the rallies. 'That's Dr Salter,' she said. 'He's a strike supporter... he knows how tight things are, Dad.'

Her father grunted, repeating almost to himself, 'Well, give him his due, he wouldn't take a penny!'

'So what did he say about Bobby? Will he be all right?' Nellie asked anxiously.

'He's given the boy something to help him.' Her father looked at her pityingly. 'But he couldn't promise nothing, we'll just have to wait.'

They sat together in the little kitchen, besieged by worry and fear for the rest of the day, each taking it in turn to sit with the little boy. Towards evening Nellie was with Bobby, trying to drip water into his parched mouth, when suddenly he took a shuddering breath and opened his eyes.

She sank down and sobbed, 'Oh, thank God!' Then she covered her mouth, stifling her cries, in case she should frighten him. Running to the stairs, she called down as quietly as she could. 'He's awake!'

Her father was first up the stairs, followed by Freddie and Alice. They gathered round Bobby's bed, tears of joy streaming down each face. As their father leaned over to kiss his son, Bobby lifted his head to ask in a hoarse whisper, 'Can Nellie stay?'

Choking back his tears, her father answered, 'I've got one child back, now I'll make bloody sure I don't lose another. She can stay, son.'

Bobby let his head fall back on the pillow, closed his eyes, and smiled.

Later, when she was assured of his returning strength, Nellie left her father and Freddie tending to him while she went to rest. Sitting with Alice in the quiet kitchen, flooded with relief at Bobby's survival and joy in her own return home, she finally told her sister where she'd spent her first homeless night. From the light in the young girl's eyes, Nellie gathered she had jumped to the same conclusion about her and Sam as Lizzie Gilbie had.

Oh, why did life have to be such a tangle? But she hadn't the heart to be cross at either her sister or Mrs Gilbie, not with her sweet Bobby safe upstairs. All she knew was that her prayers had been answered and that now she must keep her side of the bargain. Her promise to Lizzie had been compounded by a promise to God and, however burdensome they felt, she knew that whatever life brought her and however far down the road, these were promises she must keep.

All the following week Nellie remained on strike. Volunteering at the Fort Road Labour Office every day had its compensations: she brought home precious food parcels each evening, which made the children's faces light up, to say nothing of her father's. He no longer gave any hint of opposition. It seemed Bobby's illness really had changed him and now all his powerful anger had melted into an awkward carefulness. His once overpowering physical presence in the house was muted and he haunted the upstairs bedroom like a hulking spirit. Soon he was able to carry Bobby downstairs and deposited the frail boy in his own chair. Nellie shook her head and whispered into Alice's ear, 'Leopard's changed his spots!', causing Alice to giggle and her father to look up placidly and ask her to share the joke.

It was another long hard week. Every day Nellie would see Eliza, with her coterie of union workers, gathered in huddles in the Labour Office, before returning to negotiations with the factory owners the next morning. On Friday she and Lily were put to work wrapping parcels in the main hall.

'Aye aye,' whispered Lily, 'Madam Mecklenburgh is back!'

'And it's the first time I've seen her crack her face with a smile all week,' Nellie replied. 'Oh, Lily, do you think we could've won?'

'Please God. Me poor mother's getting thinner by the day and Dad can't tighten his bloody belt any further. I can't see us managing another week of it, Nell, not with Dad out as well as me.' Lily sighed. Billy Bosher, like his sons, had already been on strike for weeks, and Ted had told them the strike fund was running perilously low.

Suddenly Eliza James came to the front of the hall and called for attention. Volunteers were summoned from the basement and the back yard and soon the hall was crowded with expectant faces. Eliza paused, her face flushed with excitement, and she paced up and down until everyone had been hushed.

'I have an announcement!' There were further shushes as

murmuring started up again. Once they were quiet, Eliza continued. 'Today we have met with the fifteen largest factory owners in Bermondsey and I am pleased to let you be the first to know they have all agreed to our terms!'

A shout went up and 'Hooray for Madam Mecklenburgh!' echoed tumultuously around the room. Eliza James laughed like a girl as Ted and another docker hoisted her up on their shoulders and paraded her round the hall.

'Put me down! I have more to say!' she shrieked.

Reluctantly they deposited her at the front of the hall again.

'You'll have eleven shillings a week!'

There was another cheer. Nellie and Lily hugged each other, jumping up and down in a little dance, Nellie's heart bursting. Wait till she told her dad. No more worrying about the rent, no more pawning his Sunday suit every week! They drew other women into their victory dance, linking arms to form a chain that spilled out of the hall and into the street. Nellie noticed that Eliza James had retreated a little from the crowd, standing apart, a look of pride on her face as well as what Nellie took to be a hint of sadness. It looked almost as though she was saying a silent goodbye.

Nellie disengaged herself from Lily and went back to Eliza.

'I just wanted to say thank you, madam. We could never have done it without you.'

Eliza smiled and took Nellie's hands in her own. 'Nellie, don't give me the credit, take it for yourselves, you and the other girls. You've been so brave. What with your father and your poor brother. You've kept as steady as a rock, Nellie, and you've made me so proud.' Suddenly Nellie was surprised to find herself enveloped in a warm, perfumed embrace. The powerful, hard-headed Madam Mecklenburgh really did have a heart after all.

Everyone wanted to celebrate, and the crowds of women joined the dockers on the pavements at the end of the day. That night the Land of Green Ginger public house was packed with jubilant dockers and factory women. Nellie and Lily had come with Ted to join the celebrations and they pushed through the crowd that had spilled out on to the pavement. The doors were open to let some air into the stifling pub, but a fug of heat and smoke hit them as they made their way towards the bar, where Ted's uncle, George Gilbie, the landlord, was presiding.

'Not that we can expect any free rounds from that tight old geezer,' Ted had warned them. 'I'm just glad we can rub his nose in it. He'll be livid we won the strike.'

There was no love lost between their Uncle George and the Boshers, Lily had told Nellie as they'd walked towards the pub. 'He always thought me mum let down the Gilbie family name by marrying a docker.'

'What's wrong with being a docker?' asked Nellie. 'As if owning a pub's anything special. Your dad would make two of him.' Nellie was ready to leap to the Boshers' defence. Betty and Billy were the most generous of people when they got a chance, as she had good reason to know; it was just they never had much of anything to share round. Now the girls found a table and waited for Ted to bring their drinks. It was then that Nellie noticed Sam Gilbie drinking with a group of carters by the bar. Of course, he was related to George as well.

'You looking at that Sam?' Lily asked, amused.

'No, I am not!' Nellie lied. 'I was just wondering what relation he is to you. Are you cousins?'

'His dad and me mum were cousins. He was lovely, Sam's dad.'

Nellie nodded. 'Yes, I remember his dad from the Bermondsey Settlement outings when we was kids. Do you remember the time we went to Eynsford and got half drowned when the brake went through the ford? Sam's dad jumping up and down, telling *us* not to panic!'

Lily laughed at the memory. 'But didn't his mother get herself in a two an' eight, shouting her orders at the driver?'

'She's still got some spirit in her, but she's fading, Lil.' Nellie shot another look over to Sam at the bar. 'Do you know why Sam and Ted don't get on?'

Lily gawped at her. 'Oh, gawd knows, could it be jealousy over someone they both like?'

Nellie blushed. 'Don't be stupid, Lil, I hardly know Sam.'

'Except you slept at his house the other week.'

'There was nothing in that. He was just being kind.'

Lily rolled her eyes, but their conversation was cut short by Ted coming back with their drinks. 'Told ya, not a penny off!'

'Oh, give it a rest, Ted, you've just got yourself a pay rise, haven't you?' Nellie replied, with a sharpness that had nothing to do with the price of drinks.

This so-called rivalry between Ted and Sam was unsettling her, and what was more, her own stubborn attraction to Ted was making her angry. She had always thought herself such a sensible person, especially since her mother died. But sense had nothing to do with what she felt when she looked at Ted, at those long lashes framing the sea-green eyes; at the way his burnt-gold hair fell across his forehead... Dear God, she believed she'd just let out an audible sigh and wanted to slap herself! *All that glistens is not gold, Nellie girl, remember that.* She heard her dead mother's voice coming back to her and knew she would not heed it. Sneaking a look over at Sam now, she almost wished it *was* him she liked – there was certainly much in his character to admire. But, instead, her predominant feeling was one of obligation. Those damn promises to his mum, even to God, seemed to have obscured any true vision she might have of him. She felt robbed of choice, tied to him, whether she liked it or not. She didn't even want to catch his eye, and yet she knew one of them had to stop pretending they hadn't seen the other. She'd promised God, the Fates, herself, that she would be kind to him, and that, at least, she was determined to do. She made an excuse to go to the Ladies and as she passed the group of carters, she stopped, waiting for Sam to look at her. His mate gave him a shove, causing the beer to slop over the glass he was holding to his lips. Sam looked up, lip covered in beer foam and beer trickling down his chin. He quickly wiped it with his cuff, his face suffused with a smile.

'Nellie!'

'Hello, Sam. I never got a chance to thank you properly for all your help and I wanted to thank you for the eggs. It was so kind.'

He blushed and his slight stammer reasserted itself. 'It was M-Mum's idea.'

'How is she, Sam?' Nellie steeled herself. She had never asked Sam exactly what was wrong with Lizzie, but the poor woman had looked on her last legs.

'She rallied!'

'She rallied?'

Sam nodded. 'She rallied,' he repeated.

'Oh, thank God for that!' she blurted out.

Nellie felt immediate shame at her relief, which she knew was more for herself than for Sam's mother. But even though she felt mean, she couldn't help being grateful that Mrs Gilbie's children still had a mother and wouldn't be needing a substitute one yet a while. While Mrs Gilbie lived, so could Nellie Clark. In spite of all her own responsibilities, she felt a sudden surge of freedom, a desire for life and excitement so strong that she threw her arms round Sam and kissed him on the cheek.

'Oh, Sam, I'm so pleased for you. Give her my best and don't forget to thank her for the eggs!'

She practically skipped back to their table. Ted sat morosely staring into his beer and Lily was looking fixedly into her glass. 'What's the matter with you two? It's meant to be a celebration, not a wake!'

'What you kissing that drip for?' asked Ted.

'If you must know, his poor mother was at death's door and she's a bit better. I was just being kind.'

'Well, you should save your kindness for me.' His petulant, full lips reminded her of Freddie's when he couldn't get his own way.

'You've got no claim on my kindness, Ted Bosher. We're not even walking out.'

'Well, then, perhaps we should be.'

Lily's head snapped up. 'Oh, look, there's Ethel Brown and the girls, I'll just go and have a word.' And she darted off, leaving them alone.

'What do you say, Nellie? Will you be my girl?'

Nellie smiled nervously at first, then excitement began to wind about her heart like an ever-tightening spring. She felt triumphant. If life was a war, she had won the first battle. She had fought the most powerful people in her life: her bosses and her father. She had looked down the barrel of a rifle and stared out death, she had willed Bobby back to life, and now she had won her prize, her fiery hero: the future opened before her in a vision of unending golden days.

9

'OVER THE OTHER SIDE'

Eliza James smelled like a field of strawberries. It came of spending most of the day in the boiling heat of the jam factory. At times she had felt just like one of those soft fruits, boiled to a pink pulp and sealed into the airtight jar that was the factory owner's office. Bending her head to the sleeve of her grey jacket, she inhaled deeply as she stood in the black-and-white tiled hallway of the house in Mecklenburgh Square, enjoying the cool, light space, the marble floor and pale stone staircase. So triumph felt like this? She smiled to herself at the irony of the phrase that came to mind. For once, just for once, it actually wasn't a case of 'jam tomorrow'. They had wrested binding agreements from the management; had won the women their eleven shillings a week and improved conditions; and she had come home smelling of sweet summer fruit. She looked up the stairs to the first floor. The oak door of Ernest's office was shut. All was quiet in the house and Eliza found herself hoping that Ernest wasn't at home. She wanted a small space in the day to enjoy what she'd achieved. God knows, the sacrifices had been great enough, and not just over the past weeks of the strike. From the day she'd left her home in Rotherhithe, almost fifteen years ago, it seemed she'd had to forgo everything that was precious in her past, in order to forge a new, better future, not just for herself but for others like her. That sweet little Nellie Clark for one, who knew no more of life outside Bermondsey than she had herself when she'd come to work for Ernest as his housemaid. Eliza pulled a face. What a sight she'd been then, a gawky fifteen-year-old, with auburn hair that refused to be tamed under that hideous white pleated cap. Yet Ernest had seen something in her and sometimes Eliza fervently wished he had not.

She wondered what her life would have been if she'd stayed as that anonymous little housemaid. She had not been to see her mother again since that last painful, unannounced visit after the planning meeting. What had made her turn the car round and why had she allowed herself to face young Sam's stony disapproval? Perhaps some bonds just couldn't be broken, not by class or station or temperament, and in the end she had simply wanted to see her mother before she died. Lizzie Gilbie's weakness had shocked her, but Eliza was not surprised to find her mother still had that same old touch of fire sparking through her. It was clear from the start she would not let Eliza get away with years of neglect, without saying something. Her mother's emotions had always been very near the surface, and ill health had done nothing to diminish that.

That night had taken more courage for Eliza than addressing a fifteen-thousand-strong crowd from her soapbox in Southwark Park. She could face a boardroom full of hard-nosed industrialists or politicians with relish, but to look into her mother's eyes, after almost nine years' absence, took all her courage. Her legs had trembled when Sam left them alone. He'd taken the wide-eyed Matty and his younger brother Charlie up to their beds. She'd heard Matty's inquisitive 'Who is she?', and Sam replying, 'That's your sister Eliza.' Did they never speak of her then? Suddenly Eliza's limbs had turned to water and she knew she would have to sit down, or risk falling down. Her mother's weak blue eyes had followed her as she walked towards the chair by the fire. Only her eyes had moved, everything else about her was very still and she'd uttered no word. Finally, Eliza broke the silence.

'Hello, Mum... I've come to see you.'

'You took your time,' Lizzie replied, in an oddly familiar way, just as if Eliza were a child sent on an errand who had loitered on the way home, not a woman who hadn't been home for nine years. 'You'd better sit down.'

Lizzie didn't smile. She closed her eyes, shifting in her chair, and, as she did so, Eliza spotted her swollen legs beneath the blankets that swaddled her. The rest of her was stick thin, her skin clammy and pale. Sam had not exaggerated; she should be glad at least that she'd come in time. 'Sam wrote and told me you've not been well, Mum. I didn't know.'

Lizzie opened her eyes. 'No, well, you wouldn't, would you?' Again, so matter-of-factly no one could argue with the truth of that.

How *could* Eliza know the state of her mother, or that of any other member of her family, when she had been as cut off from them as if she'd lived in Timbuktu and not just 'over the other side', as Lizzie called Mecklenburgh Square?

'Over the other side' of the Thames was a whole world away from Rotherhithe and, after she'd gone there, she'd left behind family, friends, social acceptance, everything that had made her who she was. If she had lost her place in her own world, then she was determined she would carve out a new one.

What could she say now? *Sorry?* That would never erase the last nine years. And anyway, she wasn't sorry for the work she'd done since meeting Ernest. He was the one who'd made her the woman she was; given her an education and a purpose in life. The girl Eliza Gilbie had simply disappeared when she'd gone to work for him 'over the other side'. Ernest had remade her. Eliza James was her name now, though there never had been and never would be a marriage between them. Still, he had asked her to take the name and she'd done it for love and gratitude. But that night, sitting beside her failing mother, had brought home fiercely to her all that she had lost, abandoned, allowed to flow down and away from her on the stream of time.

'There was nothing stopping you visiting, Eliza.' Lizzie spoke with effort and took a laboured breath after each utterance.

'You know Dad never approved of... Ernest.' Eliza felt awkward saying his name in this house, where so many rows had erupted around it in the past.

'He was only so angry because he thought you'd chucked away your chance of a happy life, but he wanted to make his peace with you... before the end. You could have come, if not for him then to see... the little ones.'

Eliza bent her head then and the tears fell in fat drops into the lap of her skirt. 'No, Mum, I couldn't, it would have been too painful. I had to make a new life. I thought it would be for the best, for... for everyone, if I was out of the picture.'

Lizzie pushed herself to sit up in the chair, trembling with the effort, and looked her daughter in the eyes. 'Well, it wasn't for the best, Eliza. It's never for the best when a child doesn't see their parents.' She was gasping for breath now, but resisted Eliza's attempt to quieten her. 'And I'm not saying it was all your fault, no... don't stop me.' She paused for a moment, struggling, but found her strength again. 'I want to tell you that I'm truly sorry if I made you feel you couldn't come home.' Lizzie paused again for breath. 'I want you to know that I never stopped being your mother, never, and whatever might be the opinion in Mecklenburgh Square, you never stopped being my daughter.'

Now, as Eliza trailed wearily up the stone staircase to her room, she wondered if there was really any way she could be Lizzie's daughter again. Madam Mecklenburgh they called her behind her back – her own people, women she might have been at school with, played with in the streets and around the wharves. She shook her head. If only they knew that she was as trapped in her life as they were in theirs. She walked softly past Ernest's office door, but had not reached the end of the landing before she heard his voice.

'Eliza? Is that you, my dear?'

The door opened and he poked his head out, like an alert spider on the margins of his web. He was middle-aged, with thick dark brown hair and a rather drooping moustache, and wore round spectacles. His frame, beneath the tight-fitting brown tweed suit, was surprisingly muscular for an academic and politician who spent his days behind a desk, or in meetings. He'd been a great rower at Cambridge and still liked to keep fit.

'I didn't want to disturb you,' she called back. 'Did you finish writing your speech?'

'Yes, almost. But what about you? Are your Bermondsey gels 'appy?'

She hated it when he spoke mock cockney; she knew it wasn't as affectionate as he liked her to think. Sadly, she had learned too late that at heart Ernest James, prominent Fabian and member of the Independent Labour Party, was a hopeless snob and the tragedy was that he didn't even know it. Self-knowledge was not his strong point, but in all other respects he was far cleverer than she could ever hope to be, and that was her tragedy. His clever words and fanciful phrases were what had seduced her, far more of an attraction than his athletic physique, although that had certainly played its part in the early days of their relationship.

She blushed to think of her naivety, falling into the clichéd trap of an innocent housemaid being seduced by her employer. But as time went on, he'd begun to take her more seriously, listened to her opinions, had real conversations with her and for the first time in her life she'd felt 'attended to'. That was the nearest she could come to explaining her feelings. She had felt the world opening out before her, but later Ernest had made it clear she would always be a mistress and never a wife. He made his free-thinking, progressive attitudes his excuse, but now she knew better. She could be mistress in his bedroom and mistress of his house, and no more. She had become his housekeeper, a screen for the sensibilities of the more conventional members of his family. She had even joined him in his trade union work, but as for being his social equal, well, even nine years' separation from her family couldn't quite erase the Bermondsey girl in his eyes. She knew all this, and yet she stayed – trapped by her own choices and by Ernest's indomitable will.

'Come and tell me all about your triumphs. Did you have old Duff shaking like one of his own pink blancmanges?'

She had to laugh at the image. It so perfectly summed up the rotund owner of Pearce Duff's, who had grown more and more agitated as the negotiations progressed. 'Let me change first. You wouldn't like me, I smell of the factory.'

He sniffed the air. 'Ah, that's what I can smell! I'm sure I shouldn't mind a spoonful of that particular confection!' He raised an eyebrow, but she knew his penchant for cleanliness.

She was already halfway up the next flight of stairs. 'I'll come down and talk later, before dinner!' she called, anxious to be away. It wasn't just the stickiness of the jam factory and the heat she wanted to wash off. Too many memories and associations overwhelmed her. Being so near to her old home had brought her weeks of uneasiness and anxiety and guilt, and now all she wanted was to shut herself away alone. The only place she truly felt at home these days was in her own company. The two worlds she had been inhabiting over the past weeks felt as though they were tearing her apart; she'd been overcome by a sense of her own rootlessness and now there was nowhere she could settle. But whatever her personal feelings, she knew she had done some good today, and if Ernest himself had proved a personal disappointment to her, the work had not. It *had* been worth the sacrifices... or so she had thought, until now.

After washing off the scent of strawberries and changing her clothes, she felt herself settling once again into her own life. She found Cook and arranged for a simple supper to be laid out for them in the dining room. When she came down, Ernest already had drinks poured. He handed her a glass of wine and they began to talk about the wage settlement while they drank. He freely praised her efforts.

'You've done more for them, Eliza, than you ever could if you'd stayed one of them,' he said finally. 'You do realize that?'

She blushed, realizing he'd seen through her false cheeriness and hit at the very heart of her sombre unease. 'Perhaps, Ernest, but you can't know what it's like to be an exile.'

He snorted at that. 'For God's sake, Eliza, you of all people should know I'm the family black sheep!'

'Yes.' She bit her lip, so that he shouldn't see it trembling. 'But at least you still see your family.'

That he could not argue with. But he paused, as though weighing up what he was about to tell her. Ernest never said anything without thinking it through ten steps ahead.

'Perhaps not for long, though. In fact, I may well be launching into a new world myself, far from the clutches of my dear relations.'

'What do you mean?' Suddenly alert, a wave of fear pulsed through her body. Whatever she might think of her life with Ernest, he gave her a certain protection in society, and without him she would be vulnerable. She moved to the sideboard and selected cheese and fruit, pouring them each another glass of wine.

'Well, my dear, a wonderful opportunity has arisen... I've been invited to work with the Australian Labour Party!'

'In *Australia*?'

'Even my organizational skills couldn't achieve the job from here, my dear,' he said dryly. 'Yes, in Australia.'

A million questions presented themselves.

'Don't look so worried, me little cockney sparrer, you're coming with me!'

She flushed, caught between the sideboard and the table with the plates of food in her hand. Turning back to get the glasses, she spilled wine on the walnut veneer, and dabbed at it with a napkin. Frantic for time to think, she could feel Ernest's impatience.

'Leave it, you're not *really* my housekeeper, for God's sake. Just sit down and tell me what you think!'

An hour before she had wanted nothing more than another chance to choose the course of her own life, and now, presented with it on a plate, she felt unable to act. She cast about in her mind for something both reasonable and delaying to say.

'What I think is that you might have asked me first before deciding to drag me halfway round the world!' she said quickly.

He reached out his hand, the back of which was covered in thick dark hair, and placed it over her own. 'But where else would you go, my dear?'

She felt herself struggling for a way to demand her freedom, hopelessly ensnared by her own fear and Ernest's paralysing logic. And then she gave in, suddenly feeling the relief of the idea of flight, of leaving the two worlds warring inside her far behind. Australia would be new to both of them; perhaps there he would forget her origins and the scales of their relationship could even out into a kind of balance? A brave adventure, that's what their friends in the movement would call it. She tried to hold on to the exhilarating rush of imagining her new life in Australia, but at the back of her mind was her own voice, calling herself a coward. She smothered it and focused on what might await her so many thousands of miles away from Bermondsey and Mecklenburgh Square.

'Australia?' she mused. 'Then I really would be "over the other side", wouldn't I?'

10

SHIFTING SANDS

The custard tarts went back to Pearce Duff's in jubilant mood after the strike was settled, and to show that their newfound strength was no passing thing, they orchestrated a mass return. It was every bit as carnival-like as the day they had walked out, and though they didn't wear Sunday best, since they had a day's work to do, they were happy to at least be returning triumphant. The extra shillings in their pocket each week meant life was changing for all of them. But Nellie felt their mood had far less bravado in it. Every woman now knew the cost of striking. For herself it had been the loss of her home, for a while, and nearly the loss of her brother; for others, the faces of their hungry children had been almost too much to bear. Nellie suspected that a few weeks more of privation might have seen even the strongest of them cave in for the want of a loaf of bread or a week's rent. Still, Nellie joined the buoyant women as they trooped through the factory gates four abreast, with her own happiness boosted by the thought that she was now Ted Bosher's girl. As she smiled at Lily and the other women, she felt an unexpected surge of love, and somewhere inside she knew it was connected to her own sense of being singled out by Ted. Now she knew for certain that he liked her too, it felt safe to let all those feelings of warmth and attraction bubble to the surface, and like an unstoppable spring they seemed to be spreading out to include whoever crossed her path.

Lily grabbed her round the waist. 'Look at you! You're like the cat that got the cream! Smile any more and you'll split yer face!'

Nellie giggled. She didn't mind the teasing; she knew she

would get more when the other custard tarts heard her news. Anyway, it was news she was proud of. Who wouldn't be proud to have Ted as their chap? The hero of the hour, he was now known by every factory girl in Bermondsey and there were quite a few in Duff's would be envious of her handsome firebrand.

'What d'yer mean, got the cream – what cream?'

Maggie Tyrell had overheard; there wasn't a secret she couldn't worm out of anyone and she could be relied on not to keep it once she'd found out.

'Well, you might as well know,' Nellie admitted, trying desperately to make her smile a little smaller. 'At least you'll save me the trouble of telling all the others. Ted asked me to walk out with him and I said yes.'

Maggie let out a squeal of delight – marriage and six children hadn't dampened her thirst for romance – and she hugged Nellie.

'I'm so pleased for you, love, you deserve a bit of life, and don't forget if you need any advice about *anything*…' and she finished the sentence in a dumb show that horrified Nellie. 'You just ask me, gel, I've got lots of experience of that, haven't I, Ethel?'

Ethel's raucous laughter joined Maggie's and Nellie blushed to the roots of her hair. And this, she knew, was only the beginning!

Albert, the foreman, was waiting for them at the double doors of the packing room as they trooped to their workbenches. He gave each of them a long hard stare as they passed, making Nellie feel like a naughty schoolchild.

'He'll make our lives a bloody misery now, you wait,' she whispered to Lily.

'Nothing new in that,' Lily replied.

The factory floor looked darker to Nellie, dingier and more closed in than she remembered it. Normally, when they changed shifts, everything was already in motion and there was barely a pause in the ceaseless activity of the factory. But now the web of machine belts was still and the whole floor had an abandoned feel to it. Without the army of packers to keep the work flowing out, all of the factory's production had ceased during the strike.

The minute an agreement was reached, the boiler men had been called in to stoke up the furnaces in the basement, the filling machines were made ready, and the hoppers filled with custard powder. As they slipped into their accustomed places, Nellie was struck by the unusual silence; it was like waiting for the orchestra to strike up from the pit. As soon as the hundreds of women were settled by their machines, Albert stood on a packing crate and launched into his speech, no doubt one that was being repeated in various forms by foremen in blancmange, jelly, and the print works.

'All right, settle down!' he hushed their chatter. 'Now you've had your little revolution and you've got your eleven bob a week, you'll be pleased to hear that the management has kindly agreed to take no action!' He appeared to be waiting for a grateful response from the custard tarts; instead he was met by blank faces and stony stares.

'Bloody too right an' all!' bellowed Ethel Brown. Fondly known by the custard tarts as Mouth Almighty, Ethel was always willing to be their spokeswoman. She looked round at Nellie, grinning.

Albert tugged at his shirt collar, holding up his hand for silence, but there were more rebellious comments from around the floor. They might be back at work, but Nellie could feel there had been a shift in power. She'd felt it immediately she'd got back in front of that delivery chute. She was still just a pair of hands, another human cog in the machine, but at least now she and all the other women knew the result of removing those cogs: nothing worked without them.

'What's more,' Albert went on, trying to ignore the catcalls, 'the owners have responded to demands for better working conditions and you've been given a room in the basement to hang your coats and eat your sandwiches!'

'That's bloody big of 'em,' Ethel shouted fearlessly. 'Still no canteen, though! Hartley's have got one, so why can't we?'

She was backed up by shouts of agreement.

'All right, that's enough, Ethel, you're not on your soapbox now!' Albert shot back.

'No, but you are!' The comment had come from Annie, a normally timid girl who worked opposite Nellie.

Albert quickly jumped off the crate. 'All right, they're not paying you to stand here gassing. Let's get back to work!'

With that, he signalled to a group of boys who'd been waiting patiently by the lifts. They flung open the gates, pulled out the trolleys and began trundling them along the packing room, leaving one at each packing team. Albert picked up a speaking tube, giving the instruction for the great hoppers on the floor above to be opened. Nellie heard a clanging and then a whooshing as the tide of yellow powder chuted down. Machine belts started whirring, custard powder flowing, and Nellie grabbed her first bag of the day.

It was a long hard morning. Unused to their repetitive tasks, Nellie's muscles began protesting after a couple of hours and she was glad when the noon hooter sounded, allowing them to inspect their new cloakroom in the basement. It was a low-ceilinged room next to the boilers and the hot pipes ran through it, making it only a little cooler than the furnace itself. Rows of wooden railings with coat hooks screwed to them ran the length of the room, and round the edge benches had been attached to the distempered walls.

'Shall we go outside, Nell?' a shiny-faced Lily asked. 'I don't fancy roasting in this oven, do you?'

Nellie agreed and as they hung up their smocks and caps, Lily gave her a mischievous smile and asked, 'So where's that brother of mine taking you? Make sure it's somewhere nice!'

In fact, Nellie had no idea where they would go. They had left it that he would call for her one night after work, and meanwhile she had the job of smoothing the way with her father. It was a task she knew she had to tackle that evening. Her father might have mellowed, but not enough to accept an unannounced visit from Ted Bosher without protest.

She waited until after tea, when her father was comfortably seated in his favourite chair with a pipe and a drop of his favourite brandy, which he took from a little flask he kept tucked behind a shelf. Of course he had been pleased with the extra money she was bringing in, but he had avoided any praise of the strike or its organizers.

'Nice you can have a tipple now 'n again and not have to worry, eh, Dad?' she began.

'If a man can't have a bit of comfort after a hard day's work it's a poor show.'

Nellie nodded. She would have to steer in another direction. 'It'll be lovely not to have to worry about new boots for the boys an' all.'

He nodded, drawing on his pipe. 'If you want me to say I agree with what was done, I won't, but I'm not going to chuck the money back at 'em either. If they've given you more, so be it.' He paused. 'And I was thinking, Nellie, you deserve a bit more pocket money out of it as well.'

'Oh, thanks, Dad!' Nellie was genuinely surprised, but relieved as well. She would need a new dress if she was walking out, especially with Ted, he took such care with his clothes. If she went out in the same old skirt she'd look like a rag doll on his arm.

'It *would* come in handy… I was thinking I'll be needing a new dress now…'

Her father looked at her enquiringly and she was conscious of twisting at her skirt. She laughed nervously, wishing his fierce blue eyes were a little less piercing.

'I mean, look at this skirt, it's more darn than anything!' she gulped, then decided *in for a penny*… 'But the thing is, Dad, I'll need something a bit nicer when I'm walking out with my young man.'

Her father inhaled a little too deeply and choked on his own pipe smoke. 'What young man?' he coughed out finally.

Here it comes, she thought, and launched in. 'I know you

won't like it, but Ted Bosher wants to come and call for me and I really want to go, Dad!'

She hadn't asked her father for anything in a long time; any generosity of heart that he might have had seemed to have vanished with her mother's last breath. But his simple offer of a few pennies more pocket money gave her a little hope. Perhaps he really had changed? She waited. He took another nip of brandy and this time, when he looked at her, his eyes were different. She knew it wasn't possible, but their colour had changed. The blue had softened, darkened, it seemed to her, and in their smokiness she saw something that surprised her; she saw sadness. He simply shook his head. 'Well, Nellie, gel, you know what I think. He's trouble and I hate to think of you hooked up with the likes of him. But I'll say no more on the subject. If he's really what you want I won't forbid it, just don't bring him in this house.'

Nellie's heart quailed before this softening of her father. For some reason, it made her even more scared than his threats and bullying. His resigned tone disturbed her more than all his shouting ever had. For half a second she wondered if he might be right, but then her heart lurched with excitement. Her father had said yes!

Next day she had much discussion with Lily about what she should wear, for Ted was calling that evening and there had been no time to buy the new dress.

'What about your Sunday best?' Lily suggested. 'You could always wear that.'

'I could... but it's only best 'cause everything else is so much worse!'

In the end Lily had the idea that Nellie should wear a beautiful kingfisher-blue shawl of her mother's over her dress. It was a little old-fashioned, but Nellie loved it and Lily told her it brought out the blue of her eyes.

'Our Ted will be drowning in those eyes soon enough, mark my words!' she joked.

Nellie privately thought that the only drowning going on would be hers, in those sea-green eyes she hadn't been able to get out of her mind for days.

When the time finally came and she heard Ted's knock, she was ready at the door. She was a little embarrassed not to ask him in, but as she slipped out she whispered, 'He said it's all right.'

Ted looked pleased, but then hesitated. 'Shouldn't I come in and let him tell me to behave myself?'

'He doesn't want you coming in.'

Ted's face hardened, but he said nothing. Then, solemnly, he held up his arm and she took it. She gave him a sidelong look. She was right; he looked immaculate. He hadn't just put on a clean collar, as many boys would have; he had on his best suit with a new cap, and proper shoes, not his work boots. His copper-gold hair had been brushed till it shone. Nellie thought she would burst with pride and she squeezed his arm just so that he would look down at her and she could begin to drown, as she knew she would.

However, as it was, walking out with Ted meant exactly that, walking. For in spite of his new cap and his good suit, Ted was as short of money as any other docker after the long strike.

'Sorry, Nell, it'll have to be just a trot round Southwark Park, but I promise I'll make it up to you, soon as the next ship comes in.' Ted was a casual at the docks and his wages would always depend on which ships were at Surrey Docks, or Butlers Wharf, and on whether or not the dock foreman favoured him on that particular day.

'Oh, Ted, I'm not bothered about where we go! The park is lovely.' Nellie meant it. For her, it was the perfect destination. She didn't want the distraction of a show or a pub, and anyway she didn't feel as though she were walking at all: she might as well have been floating. Her senses seemed to have narrowed. She was conscious of her hand on Ted's arm, the feel of good cloth, and the hard muscle beneath it. She felt the heat of his body where it touched hers, and when he spoke he looked down and she felt his breath on her cheek. His breath was sweet, all mixed with the scent of roses, as they walked through the rose garden towards the pond.

They found a secluded bench by the pond and Ted put his arm round her, pulling her in close. 'Now I've got you!' he said mischievously. 'I've had my eye on you for a long time, Nellie Clark!'

And I've had my eye on you! thought Nellie, though she wasn't going to admit it to Ted. Instead she feigned mock surprise.

He laughed. 'Obvious, was it?'

'I should say so.'

'Well, I'm a lucky man, you're as sweet as a peach!'

Nellie blushed, but Ted lifted her chin and kissed her. It was a more lingering kiss than their first, but his mouth felt harder. His kiss became more insistent, more probing, and a fluttering of panic rose in her as she looked into his eyes. It was like the sea closing over her head and she breathed into Ted's mouth like a dying woman.

Nellie barely noticed dusk gradually turning to night, and it was Ted who suggested he should walk her home by ten. Nellie hoped this would make a good impression on her father. But he only grunted over his pipe when she stuck her head round the door to say goodnight. In bed as she drifted off to sleep, she felt rocked by a sea as green as the colour of Ted's eyes and when she woke next morning she felt the previous evening must have been a dream. But as soon as she met up with Lily in Duff's cloakroom before work, her friend brought her back down to earth.

Lily was full of questions and when Nellie told her they had walked round Southwark Park, she shook her head. 'You've got to keep your head, Nellie, where my brother's concerned. And if he can afford new shoes, then he can afford to take you to a show! Next time don't let him get away with it!'

But all through the rest of that summer they walked. Arm in arm, they walked around Southwark Park and sometimes across

Tower Bridge to look at the boats and listen to the barrel organ at Tower Hill. It was on their walks that Nellie learned of Ted's hopes and dreams of a better future. One day, as they strolled in Southwark Park, Ted drew her towards the empty bandstand. As they sat together on the steps she seemed to see the swirling crowd of strikers, felt again the power of their numbers driving her towards the waiting soldiers. Perhaps he was remembering that day too, for suddenly he grabbed her hand.

'I'm not staying a docker all me life,' he said vehemently. 'I tell you what, Nell, I think it's high time working people had a bigger share of the cake.'

He had plans to become a union leader, like Eliza and Ernest James.

'Might even be a politician!'

Nellie laughed and his face grew serious.

'Why not? I can go to night school. I've been in negotiations with them bosses and I tell you, they're no cleverer 'n us, they just got a better start!'

What he said had its appeal. She only had to remember the difference those extra six shillings a week made to her to see the value, and then when she imagined Bobby and Freddie living a different life from hers, perhaps not having to work till they dropped, it made her admire Ted and his big plans all the more. Her dreams, in comparison, felt small, unimportant even. When he asked her what she wanted out of life, she told him, 'I want to bring up the boys and keep the family together. I'm their mum now, you see, Ted, and you know how Dad is...'

'You don't have to tell me about your old man, he's a mean old sod to you and to them. But don't you want nothing more, Nell?' And his face seemed to quiver with the intensity of his question. She hesitated, but why should she be embarrassed to admit it?

'Well, I should like a husband and family of me own one day, 'course I would.'

Ted went quiet. He seemed disappointed. Nellie stood up,

hastily pulling Ted to his feet in an attempt to dispel the awkwardness she felt.

'Let's go over to the pond,' she suggested quickly, knowing it would please him. 'Their bench', as they now referred to it, was tucked away in a little arbour near the water, where they were hardly ever disturbed. Linking arms, Ted grinned at her, but Nellie regretted sharing her true desires. Why hadn't she bitten her tongue? Of course he wouldn't be thinking of settling down with anyone like her. A couple of kiddies would soon put paid to his plans of changing the world!

Nellie's romance was now counted as common property among the custard tarts, spicing up their breaks, and Nellie was no longer offended by their unsubtle questioning about first kisses and favourite rendezvous. Instead she felt pleased to be initiated into this new world of courting. It was the sort of talk she'd never been party to, but now she drank it all in as if her very life depended on it. The strike had won them the right to a ten-minute break in the morning and the afternoon, which they were allowed to take in the new cloakroom. In spite of the stifling heat, no one would turn down the chance of ten minutes off their feet and it had quickly become the place where all the gossip of the factory was exchanged. Even the hot pipes had their advantages, the bottles of cold tea the women brought with them could be warmed on the pipes, and some even brought pies to heat up on them. It was a warm cave that smelled oddly of gravy, vanilla from the custard, and coal from the furnace room.

During one morning break, as Nellie shared a bottle of tea with Lily, the talk turned to the custard tarts' favourite topic.

'How's that Bosher treating you?' Maggie nudged Nellie. 'Any hanky-panky going on?' Nellie blushed as the other girls leaned forward to hear the details.

'Go on, gel,' urged Ethel, 'don't be shy, even little timid mouse Annie here's admitted her feller's getting a bit handy, ain't he,

Annie?' she said, turning to the shy girl who giggled, covering her face with her hands.

'Come on, tell us, Nell, we ain't got all day,' Maggie persisted. 'Albert'll be sending a boy down after us in a minute.'

Eventually Nellie confessed that Ted might be getting a little impatient with a kiss and cuddle on their favourite bench. Maggie, true to her word, gave her the benefit of her unsophisticated but sound advice. 'What you got to remember, Nellie, love, specially with 'andsome gits like Bosher, is that he can always get another once he's got what he wants from you, so if you want to keep him, gel, just keep yer legs crossed!' This had been followed by a chorus of approval from all the custard tarts.

One Sunday not long after this she and Ted walked all the way to Greenwich Park, where they strolled up to the observatory to view the sweeping Thames snaking away into a haze-filled London. They found a secluded ancient oak and lay under its shade. There Ted's hands first wandered from her waist and she sat up abruptly.

'Ted Bosher, you keep yer hands to yourself!' she snapped. 'I'm not yer fancy woman!'

He leaned back on his elbows and laughed at her. The sun was behind him, obscuring his expression in shadow, but she was surprised not to see the expected anger. Instead she saw something worse: the flash of his teeth and the tilt of his head spoke only of scorn.

'All right, all right, little girl!' he soothed infuriatingly.

She was tempted to prove him wrong, but instead she thumped him on the arm. It would be so easy to let him have whatever he wanted, but she wasn't so much a fool as to go that way. She knew what happened to girls who got into trouble and, with Maggie Tyrell's advice ringing in her ears, she pulled herself away from Ted, marching off down the steep hill towards the park gates.

'Don't be like that, Nellie!' he called after her, but she began trotting, picking up speed till she reached the bottom of the hill, breathless and dishevelled. Determined not to look back, she heard rather than saw him careering down the hill after her, his feet slapping the hard-baked earth as he halted behind her. She paused to tuck her hair up, allowing him time to amble up to her.

'I didn't mean nothing by it, Nell,' he said placatingly. Triumphant, she took his proffered arm, feeling far more of a woman than she'd ever done before.

The summer did not want to end. By September an oppressive heat still turned the factory into an oven and the Bermondsey streets into furnaces, so when Ted suggested a day out to Ramsgate, Nellie was overjoyed. She felt bad about leaving Alice and the boys at home, but Ted had been clear he didn't want them along, so she promised them each a stick of rock, and she and Ted took the horse tram up to London Bridge, where they boarded the train to Ramsgate Sands. She wore her new summer dress of pale lilac and white stripes with a straw hat and little parasol. Alice had made her walk up and down in the kitchen so she could get the full effect and pronounced her 'just like a proper lady!'.

Even her father had grunted, 'I hope he knows he's a lucky man!', which she took as his seal of grudging approval.

London Bridge Station was a heaving bustle of excitement and movement, and the noise of the chugging steam trains entering and leaving was overwhelming. Nellie grabbed Ted's hand as they dashed to catch the Ramsgate train, which was packed full of other Londoners hoping to escape the city's heat. Families with huge amounts of luggage and day trippers like themselves filled every carriage. They were lucky to find two seats next to the window in a carriage already full of a family of five. Nellie could tell Ted would have preferred a carriage to themselves, but Nellie wasn't bothered; she was used to the noise of children and nothing would spoil this perfect day. As the tightly packed roofs and smoky chimneys eventually gave way to fields, Nellie's sense of excitement grew. Life, she felt, was moving forward finally, opening out for her with each engine whistle and spurt of steam; it made her feel expansive and generous and soon she had the little girl next to her sitting on her lap, craning to see the first cow or sheep. The boy wanted to sit on Ted's lap too, but the pin-sharp crease in Ted's trousers won out and the little boy had to make do with taking turns on Nellie's knee.

When they arrived at the Ramsgate Sands Station, the hordes of people seemed to tip off the train straight on to the beach. There was hardly a patch of sand to be seen; all was covered by rows of deckchairs and little encampments of families, by children making sandcastles or enjoying donkey rides, and people queueing at ice-cream sellers. The water's edge was a smudge of paddling children. Nellie clung tightly to Ted's arm until they were safely on the promenade. They walked a leisurely length of it and then out on to the pier.

'Oh, Ted, it's beautiful, feel that breeze!' Nellie tipped her head back and smelt the sea wind on her face. It was fresh and clean, billowing out her blouse and whipping her skirt around her ankles. She wished with all her heart she had the children with her.

'It's bloody crowded, though!' said Ted, and, in fact, they were almost tripping up over the feet of the couple in front of them.

When they reached the end of the pier, Ted stopped to read an advertisement for trips to Goodwin Sands.

'There won't be any crowds out there, that's for sure!' he pronounced, and explained that the Goodwins were sandbanks a few miles offshore. They were treacherous to shipping and many wrecked boats mouldered there, but at low tide miles of the sands were uncovered and you could sail out and stroll about, while the sea completely encircled you.

'Do you fancy a trip out there on a boat, Nellie?'

In fact, she didn't. His tales of wrecks and tides had terrified her, and she wondered what would happen if the tide turned while they were out there. But he looked so excited that she agreed.

'Oh, all right, then, but don't you get me drowned, Ted Bosher!' She didn't want to seem like a child to him, and why should her fears dampen the joy of the day?

Grabbing her hand, he led her to the side where the boats were leaving for Goodwin Sands. They boarded the little flat-bottomed steamer and Ted paid the captain. There were others on the boat with them, but Nellie hardly noticed them. Ted seemed to fill her vision like the brightest of suns, obscuring everything else from her sight. The voyage out was not as frightening as she had expected, the sea calm as a silver disc, beaten down by the sun, and the blue sky unrelieved by any cloud. They stood at the front rail, watching the golden bar of sand slowly approaching. The breeze was delicious, but Nellie felt her face getting hotter and redder under the burning sun. When Ted looked down at her, all smiles and excitement, she could barely make out his features for the glare of sunlight. She squinted and suddenly he grabbed her parasol, put it up and, shielding both of them from the other passengers, kissed her passionately till she struggled for breath.

'Ted!' She pushed at his chest, mortified, excited and scared all at once.

'What do I care what they think?' he said defiantly.

'But what about what I think?' She pretended to be angry, keeping her voice down.

'You're a good kisser, Nellie.' He smiled, disarmingly.

'You said that before.'

'Yes, and it's like anything else, if you're good at something, you like to practise it.' He flashed her his brightest grin, and then pointed towards where the Goodwin Sands now stood, miles of them, like a golden island surrounded by the silvery sea.

Once they got there, the descent from the boat was precarious. Nellie was beginning to wish they hadn't come. She was hot, flustered by Ted's uncontrollable boldness, and now she wondered if she really wanted to be standing on a sandbank with the deep sea all around her.

'What if the tide changes, Ted?' she asked anxiously.

'It won't. The old captain knows his job, we'll be right as rain. Come on!'

He had descended the wooden duckboard that had been laid from boat to sand and was standing at the bottom, waiting for her. So that she didn't have to walk through the pools of water in their path, he picked her up and carried her to the firm beach.

Nellie caught her breath and looked around her. She was astonished. The sand was not flat; the tide had sculpted it into long rippling mounds which looked like the ridges on the back of some slumbering sea beast.

'What a sight!' Ted exclaimed. 'This is something to tell our kids about, eh, Nellie?'

Time seemed to stand still for Nellie – had she heard right? Did he really think that much of her? She'd told herself he was a long way from any such commitments, probably always would be.

'Alice and the kids will never believe it!' was all she said.

They looked back and could just make out Ramsgate seafront, but Ted did not want to stand still; he was off, pulling Nellie along with him. She had only ever seen him look as excited when he was up on a soapbox during the strike.

'Let's see how far it goes, there's miles!'

Nellie was having trouble keeping up and she half trotted beside him, trying to keep the parasol between her and the sun, which was burning her fair skin. Thinking that by now she must look as attractive as a boiled lobster, she doubted he'd want to be kissing her on the voyage back.

Soon they had outstripped the other day trippers and Ted put out his hand, helping her to leap over the increasingly frequent pools of water in their path. Nellie looked nervously back at the others, now just white smudges, standing in groups near the boat. 'I think we should go back, Ted, we don't want to get cut off.'

But he wouldn't listen; he pushed on and her anxiety grew. Finally she stopped still, digging her heels in to the soft sand. 'I'm not going any further!' she called to his back, and he turned his sunburned face to her, his green eyes clouded with incomprehension.

'Come on, it's safe as houses. Don't be such a baby.'

But, no, Nellie was sure of it, the texture of the sand had

changed. Whereas the long ridges had been hard and compacted, this sand was sucking and jelly-like.

'Ted, come back now!' she almost screamed at him. 'I'm sure the tide's coming in, you'll get stuck!'

Still he trudged on and she knew she wouldn't follow. She heard the long shrill hoot from the steamer, the signal for them to get back on the boat, and she turned and began walking back on her own, dimly aware that Ted had at least stopped his advance. She had never felt such fear in her life. Every pool seemed to be filling rapidly, the sand sucking at her feet and slowing her progress. Panic had overtaken her, she didn't care if Ted was behind her or not, and when she finally reached firmer sand she picked up her skirts and sprinted back to the steamer. Now she could see clearly how much danger Ted had put her in, for the sea had encroached upon the sand alarmingly. Ted's distant figure was at least now moving towards the boat, but two claws of bright water were closing around him like pincers. The passengers were all aboard and the captain ushered her up the duckboard. 'What's that young idiot up to? Was he trying to drown you both?' he growled.

Nellie tried to apologize, but the captain was furiously pulling on the hooter and gesturing for Ted to get a move on. She could see him coming closer, walking swiftly now but still not running. The other passengers were getting restive and shame turned Nellie's sunburned face a deeper red as he finally made it on board. With the merest tip of his cap he gave his apologies to the captain, who was now furiously pulling in the duckboard, while shouting at Ted, 'Help me with this, you young fool. If this boat gets stuck in the sand, she'll sink.'

She felt the boat lurch as the tide lifted it and the steam engine chugged into life. They swung out, they were clear!

Ted joined her at the back of the boat and tried to take her hand. She snatched it away. 'If you ever do something like that to me again, Ted Bosher, we're finished! You might not care about your own life, but I've got kids depending on me!'

She was livid, blaming herself for forgetting that her life was not her own. Ted Bosher had not just jeopardized her life, he'd threatened theirs. But if she'd insisted Al and the boys come with them, this would never have happened. Was it so selfish of her to have wanted this day alone with Ted? For any other girl her age, perhaps not, but now Nellie knew that the claims of her heart would always have to take second place to the welfare of her family. She turned her face away from Ted and gazed steadily back at the Goodwin Sands. All she could make out were the spars and ribs of some ancient wreck and soon the last of the sands were covered by the deep green sea.

II

FIRE AND ICE

Their day at Goodwin Sands marked the end of that fierce summer. For the first time in months the sun no longer shone, and by October the temperatures began to cool. Ted's ardour did not cool, however, and he continued to court her into the shorter, misty days of autumn. But her early feelings of girlish elation had suffered a blow that day at Ramsgate. She had taken an instinctive step back. A preservation instinct had been born in her the day her mother died, but not just for herself. The day she became a motherless child, she'd stepped into the role of childless mother, and she would protect Alice and Bobby and Freddie as if she'd given birth to them herself. Ted's actions had nearly deprived her siblings of their second mother and that she could not forgive. So little by little she began to shield her heart.

She was glad of this defence when the day came, as she knew it would, that Ted finally lost patience and demanded more than just kisses and cuddles. If she had only herself to think about she might have given him what he wanted for, in spite of his faults, he could still make her heart lurch just by the way his hair fell across his forehead. She might have ignored all Maggie's advice if it hadn't been for the two little boys she still tucked up in bed every night. She felt the irony of it, but had to admit that another firm anchor to her home was her changed father. The prospect of losing his youngest son had forcibly ejected him from his prison of grief. For a time it seemed he felt physical pain just being separated from the little boy; he would come home at odd times throughout the day to check on him, calling out, 'Where's my brave boy, are you staying out of trouble?' At first it seemed as if he would only have enough love to spare for Bobby and this contented Nellie, for it made him a much pleasanter presence in the house. Then, gradually, that love spread like honey from the broken comb of her father's heart, first to Freddie who, not wanting to be left out, would make sure he was present whenever his father started fussing over Bobby. Being the practical boy that he was, he ran for drinks or blankets at his father's command and basked in the few words of praise he received. Then Alice was pulled into the charmed circle. Still Nellie wanted nothing for herself; it was enough to have a peaceful home and a father who let her come and go as she pleased, with no questions. But over the weeks she noticed a change in his treatment of her. It felt as though Bobby had formed a bridge from her father's heart to her own, she caring for the boy on one side, her father caring for him on the other, and across that bridge finally she saw him looking at her with a warmth she longed desperately to call love.

She and Ted still walked but their destinations altered with the season. Often now they went through the misty evenings to London Bridge Station, just for somewhere to go. Wreathed in smoke and steam, there was life and bustle and warmth there, which Nellie preferred to the chilly streets. Ted liked to watch the trains chuffing and screaming into the platforms, and would make Nellie wait till the engine-room doors opened and they could catch a glimpse of the stokers feeding the flames. Nellie preferred to stroll around the station, watching the travellers and imagining their destinations. On their way home one night, Nellie suggested stopping at the Green Ginger.

'I'm skint, Nell,' he admitted.

'What, didn't you get called on today?' she asked.

'Not today, there's nothing on,' he said, and looked at her steadily. She wouldn't question him but she risked embarrassing him. 'It's my treat,' she offered. She was missing her friend and guessed Lily might be in the Green Ginger with some of the other custard tarts.

She was right and it felt a relief to be enveloped by their warm, welcoming chatter. She slipped Ted some coins to get a drink and he made a grateful retreat to the bar. But Maggie Tyrell had missed nothing.

'Oh, your chap's very free, ain't he?' she called out, loud enough for the whole pub to hear. Nellie shushed her and Ted looked back. Lit by the gas lamp, his face flared with a fierce annoyance. Lily leaned over and whispered, 'What's he cadging off you for? Dad worked all day, then did an all-nighter, he said the boats was queueing up for unloading!'

Ted came back, but seemed uncomfortable with the boisterous familiarity of the custard tarts. Nellie was thinking of leaving when Sam Gilbie, who sometimes drank there after work, walked in. Nellie always made a point of acknowledging Sam, stopping for a chat and asking after his mother and the children. She knew this would make Ted even more morose and testy.

Oh, sod him, she thought, annoyed that he'd taken money and dismayed that he'd lied about his work. She turned her smile towards Sam, who had stopped at their table. Ignoring Ted, she asked after Sam's family. 'Mum went into Guy's for a week.'

Her heart lurched at the news, evidence that her promise to Lizzie had the power to wrench her out of her own life at any moment. Try as she might to ignore it, a part of her was always on alert that one day the Fates would ask her to redeem her pledge and then the whole of her youth would be used up in looking after other people's children. Sam, seeing her face, hastily reassured her.

'Don't look so worried, it seemed to do her good! And our Matty was a little diamond, running the house. She's old before her time, that one. Did I tell you she went in for a singing competition at the Star?' This got the attention of Lily and the other girls.

'What did she sing?'

'Charlie says she brought the house down with "Last Rose of Summer" and she come first!'

Nellie was delighted, and joined in the chorus of congratulations. Looking round for Ted, she saw he'd left the table and was back up at the bar. It wouldn't have hurt him, she thought, to be pleasant for once. Sam went off to join his mates and when Ted came back, she quickly got up and said her goodbyes. She kissed Lily, who whispered, 'Give bear's breath his marching orders and stay with us!' Nellie shook her head and, as she followed Ted out of the pub, she wondered if it might not be easier if they kept to their solitary walks in future.

They were, in any case, beginning to spend more time outside Bermondsey, venturing over the other side to a café, or if they had money to a show in the West End. But it became obvious over the following weeks that Ted was increasingly short of money, and it was often she who paid for their outings. These days when he came to meet Nellie at Duff's gates after work, her initial delight was too often tempered with the suspicion that his main interest was in cadging the odd shilling from her. 'Just a sub until the next boat comes in,' he would say, and she would dig uneasily into her purse, knowing deep down that the boat would never arrive.

The momentous year of 1911 turned, as a freezing December gave way to grey January skies damp with perpetual drizzle. Nellie found herself longing for those sunbaked eventful days of the previous summer. The new year also seemed to bring a change in Ted. Perhaps the excitement of the strike victory and his new romance with her had begun to wane, but she noticed an increasing number of absences through those early months of 1912 and by the beginning of summer he seemed to be away more often than at home. When she questioned him about where he'd been, his stock reply was, 'Union work.'

She told herself she had no reason to doubt him. The unrest of 1911 had carried over into this year, erupting into more strikes; the coal miners came out in March and the London dockers again by May. Ted always wanted to be in the thick of it, at rallies in Wales or meetings in Poplar. But sometimes the details of his trips away were so sketchy that Nellie began to feel uneasy. Perhaps he'd finally got fed up with her and found himself another girl, one who wouldn't be so prudish with him.

Then one day towards the end of July, Lily came to her in a panic. 'Nellie, I've got to talk to you about our Ted. Mum's worried sick about him!'

Nellie was immediately alert. 'Why, what's he done?'

'Nothing... I hope, not yet. But Mum found some pamphlets in a jacket she was mending for him. Nell, I'm scared, they were full of anarchist talk about revolution, there was pictures of men with guns and bombs!'

Nellie tried to calm her friend. 'You know Ted! Sometimes it's all talk, Lil.'

But secretly Nellie was worried about what Ted might have got himself involved with. She remembered how angry he'd been when the soldiers turned their bayonets on strikers last year. The deaths of innocent bystanders in Liverpool and Wales had incensed him. Afterwards, when the soldiers got off scot-free, he'd gone on and on for days about it, saying it was murder and they weren't even in the strike, just putting up shop shutters or standing in their gardens. He took it so personally, nothing she could say would make him let it go. Nellie had learned to look out anxiously now for a liquid fire in those green eyes; it was like something burning under the sea and some days it frightened her.

During the latest dock strike this summer, she'd stopped asking him where he disappeared to for days on end, but her talk with Lily convinced her that she had to confront him. Even so, she waited more than a fortnight, looking for the right moment to face him, frightened of the truths she might uncover. When he asked her to go with him to a meeting at the Labour Institute she agreed with an enthusiasm that seemed to please him. She hoped that if she entered a bit more into his world, he would be less guarded with her. The meeting turned out to be a victory celebration of the latest fourteen-week dock strike, which had ended two weeks earlier with an agreement for a shorter working week. After the meeting, people clustered in groups, chatting and drinking tea. Ted drew her into the centre of one group discussing the latest politicians' warnings of war with Germany.

'War!' he cut in. 'They shouldn't be worrying about the Germans. Don't they know we're already at war, with *them*, the rich bastards that take the food from our mouths. Time for them to sit up and take notice! They'll know all about war then.'

She was glad when it was time to leave, and as he walked her home after the meeting he was in high spirits at their victory. Putting his arm round her, he said casually, 'I'll be away most of next week.'

Now was her moment and she steeled herself to take it. 'What's going on, Ted? Why do you have to be away so often? You've not got yerself a fancy woman, have you?' She tried to sound light-hearted.

Immediately his good humour vanished and he rounded on her. 'There's more things in life than courting, you know! I've told you time and again, it's union work!'

'You say it's union work, but the strike's over now!'

He dropped his arm from her waist, jamming his hands into his pockets. 'I don't know why I bother with you,' he sneered. 'Didn't you understand anything I was saying tonight? The strike may be over but the struggle's not!' He stalked away from her, brushing off her hand on his arm as she tried to hold him back. Ignoring his jibe, she persevered.

'Well, just don't do anything stupid, Ted Bosher,' she said as firmly as she could. 'You've got family to think of and you've got me, and...' her voice broke. 'If you get put away, it'll break my heart.'

He stopped her tears flowing with kisses and pretended not to know what she meant. When they passed a small alleyway just before Vauban Street, he drew her into the unlit byway. Putting his arms round her, he tilted her chin up towards him,

'I'm not getting put away,' he reassured her. 'Anyway, they'd have to catch me first, and there's only one person ever caught me…' The sneer was gone from his beautiful mouth and for now all her questions seemed to have vanished.

It was at such tender moments that Nellie hoped he might talk about settling down with her. When his voice turned soft, she saw a gentleness that belied all his violent rantings. Sometimes he would talk about a better world for 'our children' and then Nellie dreamed there might be a future for her and Ted. But increasingly she was losing patience and whenever his musings turned into a rant, she came back at him.

'Oh, put a sock in it, Ted, any kids you have would be bored to death, poor little buggers, before they starved to death. You can't *live* on a soapbox, you know!'

Then that soft glimpse of him would harden, the fire would ignite in his eyes, and she'd know she'd lost him.

This was a year when summer simply refused to arrive; the damp spring had heralded long months of cool, wet days which now froze into winter. The excitement of the previous summer had all but faded from her memory, and though now most of the girls were union members there had been no more strikes for the custard tarts. That one glorious victory had won them a hard-earned pay rise and a cloakroom, but they had soon settled back into the inevitable routine of long days of back-breaking work. The only bright spot on their horizon was the Christmas 'do' at the Green Ginger, which Ethel Brown was organizing. She took up her station every Saturday lunchtime at the payroll office, black book and pencil in hand. It was the one time of the week the girls would be certain of having their money for the Christmas club. One Saturday morning, as Nellie and Lily were walking away from the office with their brown envelopes, Ethel stopped them.

'Come on, you two, pay up – no sub, no pub! Nellie, I haven't got you down for last week!'

Nellie raised her eyes. 'You don't miss a trick, do you? I was a bit short last week.' She ripped open her pay packet. 'Here, two weeks!' She pushed the coins into Ethel's plump outstretched palm.

'It's that brother of yours,' Ethel addressed Lily. 'He's skinting her, treats him like her little prince, don't she?'

'Don't blame me for my brother, Ethel, it's not my fault if he's poncing off Nellie.'

'Don't talk about him like that!' Nellie rounded on her friend a little more vehemently than she might have done if her own feelings of loyalty to Ted weren't being tested so much.

'All right, don't be so touchy.' Lily grabbed Nellie's arm. 'Come on, I'll walk back up to Vauban Street with you.' Lily linked arms with her as they walked, pulling her in close for warmth against the chill wind that blew up Spa Road.

'You don't seem very happy these days, Nell. Is it our Ted?' she asked quietly.

Nellie sighed. It seemed that since the chill dark nights had set in, her walks with Ted had grown less easy. She supposed she must be grateful that he still asked her to go with him to his meetings. At least she knew where he was, but she had grown bored with them and now confided to Lily.

'His idea of a night out these days is a talk at the Labour Institute! I know the strike did us a favour, and I wouldn't chuck the eleven shillings back. But I'm only seventeen, I'm still young! I get little enough time to myself as it is. When I do get a night off, it's not my idea of a good time to spend it listening to Ted going on about the evils of poverty and the class struggle. I'm bloody living the evils of poverty, nobody needs to give me a lecture on it!'

It struck her as odd, when she thought about it, that she felt the necessity to remind her friend that she was young. Perhaps it was because, these days, she felt as though she was becoming old before her time. The truth was that her father had become far more reliant on her since Bobby's illness, and another year on her age had confirmed her as mother of their family. It was taken for granted that, after a day's work at Pearce Duff's, she would come home to clean and cook and bring up the children. It was only because of Alice's staunch support that she could even contemplate the luxury of a night off to spend with Ted.

'Well, you're not going to change him now, Nellie,' was Lily's response, 'not if he won't listen to Mum and Dad. Even our Ginger's had a go at him, told him he's getting in too deep.'

But still, once Nellie was alone with Ted, her misgivings always melted away. He was so handsome and it made her dizzy sometimes, when he came strolling along with that loose-limbed stride, smiling at her, singling her out from all the other 'custard tarts' at the factory gates. Walking along the street with him, she felt she could be on the arm of a prince and it couldn't have felt better.

But now, on this freezing afternoon in December, she was cursing her pauper prince. Ted was late. If she was his girl, then why didn't he want to spend time with her? It was a question she could no longer suppress. She needed answers: why was he always away? Liverpool, Manchester, Hull. Everywhere but Bermondsey. Nellie's early dream of how wonderful it would be walking out with Ted now seemed worlds away from the reality. Ted was late and it wouldn't be the first time he'd let her down. Today she'd made arrangements for Alice to watch the boys and see to her father's tea, so she could have this day free. Ted had promised her they'd go for a walk in the snow-trimmed park and then for tea in the café, before they went on to the music hall. This was to have been her Christmas treat and she'd been quietly excited all week. Nellie had so wanted to walk arm in arm with Ted under the park's snow-laden trees and round the frozen pond, which looked magical, like a picture postcard, but after hanging around the park gates for an hour, she had lost hope and come to the Star, hoping to meet him here.

It was so bloody cold! She stuffed her hands deeper into her fur muff and breathed into the scarf she had wrapped round her collar, trying to generate some warmth. She had worn her new dark blue coat with the silver-grey fur cuffs and had on the matching hat with fur trim. She had been paying into the clothes club all year for the outfit, and this was its first outing. Ted always took such care with his appearance. He had to have the best clothes and his suit never saw the inside of the pawnshop. She'd set her heart on this coat, so that she didn't show him up. Her father was still suspicious of Ted, so he never came to the house, which was why she was now pacing up and down outside the Star Music Hall in Abbey Street, waiting for him to turn up. She stopped and stamped her small booted feet on the snow-caked pavement, but she could no longer feel her toes. Snow lay thick over the road, and the cobbles looked like tiny pillows outlined in black stitching. Looking up at the leaden sky, she judged more snow was on the way. She found herself wishing that Lily were home, so she could unload her feelings of disappointment; her best friend was always ready to hear complaints about her brother. But Lily and her parents were away, visiting family up north.

Now she was losing patience. The crowd outside the music hall slowly diminished, and as groups and couples met up and went inside, she grew increasingly forlorn. It seemed certain she was being stood up. She had grown used to Ted's sudden cancellations. They usually came with no warning and no explanations, but this was the last straw. She waited until the last of the crowd outside had shuffled eagerly into the Star's lamplit warmth, then she gave up on him and started walking home.

He's just not worth it, she thought bitterly, and if he's lost interest, he only has to say. I'm not going to shed any tears over Ted Bosher!

But even as she thought it, a lump formed in her throat and she proved the emptiness of her promise by angrily brushing away a tear. Night was falling and the gas lamps lit up the snow with their hissing, flickering flames. For some reason, she remembered the anarchist pamphlet Ted's mother had found and her blood turned colder than the icy flakes that began to fall on to her cheeks.

It was as she neared the end of Spa Road that he jumped out on her, grabbing her from behind and putting his hand over her mouth to stifle her cry of surprise.

'Shh, shhh, Nellie, it's me,' he hissed as he dragged her back into the alley where he'd been hidden. She knew he'd done something terrible when she saw his torn jacket. *And he's always so particular about his clothes*, she found herself thinking stupidly. But now they were ripped, the arm of his jacket was shredded, and his leg was showing through a rent in his trousers.

'Ted, what have you done? Look at the state of you, yer as black as Newgate's knocker!' He looked almost like a sweep, with his face and hands blackened. 'Where've you been? I was waiting and I got so cold. Ted, tell me, for God's sake!'

Her voice was rising in an attempt to make sense of what she was seeing, but in her heart she knew exactly what had happened.

'Shhh, Nellie, it's all gone wrong. It was a bomb, an incendiary. I was only carrying it, it wasn't meant to go off yet!' His eyes were wild, whites stark against his blackened face. 'Nellie, the police'll be after me. You've got to help me!'

His hands were shaking, but as she attempted to grasp them, he winced. They were both burned raw. Then she noticed his lovely gold hair all singed and blackened, an ugly burn shining red across his soot-caked temple.

'Hide me, Nell, somewhere, anywhere, just till me mates can get to me.'

'Where? Where can I hide you? Wait, Ted, I've got to think. Oh, look at your hands!' They were trembling with pain and shock as he held them out to her. She took off her scarf and scooped up some snow, binding the icy cloth around his hands. It was all she could think to do. He looked almost as though he were handcuffed as she led him to the end of the alley. All the fire seemed to have gone out of him and he was as pliable and obedient as a child.

'Come on, I know somewhere I can take you.'

'The bomb was for a protest over at Westminster,' he explained, sounding exhausted as they scuttled along in the snow-lit shadows. 'I was just taking it to load on to a boat up by Tower Bridge and it exploded.' They darted from gas lamp to gas lamp, afraid of being seen, until they reached the corner of Vauban Street.

'We've been planning it for months, making the bombs in a lock-up under one of the railway arches,' he gasped as he paused for breath, his back to the wall of the corner house.

'Well, thank God you never got there, you could've killed someone!' She rounded on him angrily. 'Don't you care about anyone else? And didn't you even *think* of what this would do to your mum, or Lily, or me?'

He grabbed her then and pulled her close. She tried to push him off, but he spun her round, shielding himself behind her. Then she heard the footsteps, muffled in the snow, but slow and deliberate, on the other side of the street.

'Copper!' he whispered into her ear, and she stayed very still until the footsteps retreated. Glancing over her shoulder, she checked the policeman had gone.

She looked him full in the face, despairingly. 'Oh, Ted, what's this got to do with our life? You can't think anything of me, not to drag me into this.'

'It's only for tonight, Nellie. Once they know what's happened, the others will help me lie low. Please, Nell.'

With a feeling of dreadful certainty that she would pay for her folly, she relented and led him quietly down Vauban Street to her old hiding place, Wicks's carter's yard. She helped him squeeze through the locked gates, just as she'd done the night her father threw her out. She crept with him past the stable blocks and, leading him into the cart shed, she helped him lie down by the hay bales, covering him over with straw. She felt his whole body shaking as she tucked the straw round him as though he were a sick child, but when she went to leave, he clung to her.

'Don't leave me, Nellie. I'm sorry but I had to do it, there's more at stake than our little lives. We'll always be ground into the shit if we don't fight back. Don't you see?'

She stood above him, pity and anger mingling in her heart. She looked around the shed and inhaled the acrid smell coming from the horse dung in the yard.

'Well, you've certainly landed yourself in the shit now, Ted Bosher, haven't you? I'll be back when they're all asleep. Stay quiet and I'll bring some stuff to clean you up.'

'Get me a drink of something if you can, Nell, I'm right shook up.'

He held up his burned hands, which were still trembling, and she heard his teeth chattering. She nodded and made her way back to her house. She was considered old enough now to have a key of her own and as she eased open the front door, she cursed him to herself, 'You stupid bloody fool, Ted Bosher, you've ruined me, I reckon, and everyone else that ever cared about you too.'

She attempted to sneak upstairs without alerting her sister and father, who were still up, but as her foot creaked on the stair, Alice called out.

'That you, Nellie?' She came out of the kitchen. 'You're back early.'

Taking in Nellie's tear-stained face, her sister simply shook her head. 'He upset you again? He's not worth it, love.' And this time Nellie agreed with her.

Later when all was quiet in the house she eased herself out of bed, trying hard not to disturb Alice. She put on her old work coat in the passage and crept out with a bottle of her dad's brandy and some clean rags from the kitchen for bandages. Ted was in the stable where she'd left him. His whole body was still shivering and she made him sip the brandy slowly through his chattering teeth. Then she cleaned up his face and hands and bound his burns. She stayed with him till near dawn, lying on the straw and holding him tightly, with the growing fear that she would never again hold him like this. He slept fitfully, but she was wide awake and in the false light that the snow cast through the window she saw the glint of metal at the back of the stall. It was Sam Gilbie's old penny-farthing. She remembered that night she'd ridden it across the yard and later made that fateful promise to look after Lizzie Gilbie's children when she was gone. It seemed a lifetime ago. Did she really make that promise? She often saw Sam delivering at Duff's or at Wicks's yard after work. They always spoke in a friendly way to each other, but there was never a suggestion of anything more. Though there certainly had been nights when she'd lain awake worrying about how she would manage if she were ever called upon to take care of another family, her life had been too full of her own responsibilities and her heart too full of her own dreams to leave much room for Sam or old promises.

And right now she had other more pressing burdens to bear. Shifting her attention from the penny-farthing back to Ted's sleeping form, heavy in her arms, she felt numb with cold and the weight of him. Looking down at his troubled face, she knew she couldn't abandon him and it was loyalty to her own first love which kept her here, holding him so tightly.

About an hour before dawn, Ted reckoned he should make his move. Slightly calmer and warmed by the effect of the brandy, he'd told her he had been transporting the bomb in a handcart full of tea crates. It was meant to look as though he was making a collection from the docks, and he had got as far as St Thomas's stairs on the riverbank near Tower Bridge, when the bomb exploded. The cart and crates had taken most of the blast, otherwise he would have been floating in bits down the Thames. He reckoned the area would be crawling with police by now. The anarchist cell's lock-up was in one of the many workshops housed in the arches beneath the railway viaduct that bisected Bermondsey on its way up to London Bridge.

'We agreed to meet back there if anything went wrong,' he explained.

Nellie shook her head, appalled. 'Listen, don't tell me any more about it, I just don't want to know. I'll help you this once, not for you,' she lied. 'It's for your poor mother's sake. What she's done to deserve a son like you, I don't know.'

'Oh, don't be so hard on me, Nellie,' he said. 'I know you love me.'

'More fool me,' she said, but silently wondered whether she really could love a man who would blow innocent people to kingdom come. He might be beautiful on the outside, but as Nellie looked back into his long-lashed eyes she could see only ugliness and pain reflected in their green depths. He tried to kiss her, but she turned her face and began to help him to his feet. The streets would be deserted by now and she had a chance of getting him to the arches unseen. From there, his friends could get him to a doctor and then out of London to lie low, he said.

'Here, lean on me,' she ordered. She knelt down beside him; he smelled of soot and charred flesh. Hooking his arm over her shoulder, he staggered as she struggled to ease him up. He groaned with the pain in his arm and leg, and tried to muffle his cries in her hair. They staggered forward across the icy cobbled yard, with the snow falling around them. Ted was dragging his injured leg behind him, with Nellie taking his weight on her shoulder, but the pain was too great. Suddenly Ted howled and Nellie fell to her knees, tumbling Ted over into the deepening snow.

'Shhh, try to be quiet, Ted!' She clamped a hand over his mouth to stifle his groans.

Then she heard a sound up by the yard gate. She looked up. The gate was being unlocked and as it swung open she saw a figure, silhouetted against the pewter dawn sky. He was muffled in a scarf and had a cap pulled down over his face. He had spotted them.

12

ALIBI

The figure at the yard door sprang, launching himself across the icy cobbles to where Nellie knelt by Ted. He skidded to a stop.

'What's going on here?'

She recognized the startled voice. 'Oh, thank God it's you. Sam!'

Sam Gilbie looked straight past her at Ted and the two men stared at each other. 'What the bloody hell have you got her involved in now, Bosher?'

Ted was silent, apart from his breath coming in short gasps.

'Sam, he's in trouble bad and he's hurt, you can blame him all you like later on, but he's still your family, ain't he?'

Sam looked at Nellie. His fists were clenched and she could see the muscle in his jaw tightening. 'Frightened to tell me what you've been up to, Ted?'

'What do you know?' Ted's voice rasped.

'Oh, I can guess most of it. Your anarchist friends have been round trying to recruit us all at one time or another, but there's not many of us fool enough to agree to what they had in mind.'

Ted's voice came dry and croaky between hoarse breaths.

'Someone's got to make the sacrifice. You two, you're both the same, blinkered. You don't see where the real evil is, the bosses that want it all for themselves and dare to shoot us, dare...' his voice was rising in anger '... when all we ask is our due...'

'Oh, Ted, just shut up,' Nellie cut in. She'd had enough of his rhetoric for one night. 'Yes, it's a hard bloody life,' she snapped, 'and don't I know it, and doesn't your mother know it. But you're talking about murder, however you try to pretty it up, murder of some mother's son, so just shut up about it.'

She looked at Sam. 'I know it's a terrible thing to ask you, Sam, but can you help me get him down to the arches? Once he's there, he says his friends can help him. I wouldn't ask, only he is your family.'

Sam was silent for what seemed an age and then he seemed to decide. 'If it was up to me, I'd shop him tonight, but it's you I'm thinking of.'

He moved swiftly then, with a strength that surprised her. He lifted Ted over his back in a fireman's carry and took him to one of the carts.

'Nellie, help me.'

She ran to help him lower Ted on to the back board of the cart.

'Cover him over with this sacking and I'll take him out now, as though it's me early morning round. We've got to be quick, though, before old Wicks gets in.'

She grasped Sam's hand as he went to harness the horse. 'Thank you for this, Sam. I'm so grateful, you're forever helping me out.'

'I don't want you to feel beholden, Nell,' Sam said in a low voice. 'I just want to make sure you're all right and then we'll say no more about it.'

She reached up and kissed him on the cheek. 'I won't forget it, Sam.'

He put his hand up to rest on the spot she had kissed. 'Nellie, why did you agree to help him in the first place?'

She didn't see judgement on his face, only puzzlement and anxiety.

'He didn't give me much choice, Sam. We were supposed to be having a lovely day together, walking in the park, then going to the Star, but of course he never turned up, which to be honest is not that unusual. Then he just jumped out on me and in this state – what else could I do, leave him on the street?'

Sam looked at her as though that might have been the more sensible option, but he seemed satisfied by her explanation and began leading the horse back to the cart, where Ted lay groaning.

'You best get back indoors, Nellie, before they wake up and miss you.'

She nodded and left with a backward look at Ted's shrouded form. She was sick with anxiety for him, yet there was a puzzling hollow in her heart as well. It felt cold as the icy dawn air. She wondered at how suddenly love could freeze and how when it did, it burned the heart that had once held it. She felt powerfully all the glamour of attraction surrounding him and yet, now it had the quality of a memory, she saw it evaporating among the violent images that had assailed her that night.

An anxious week passed and she heard nothing from Ted. Sam had quietly let her know that he'd safely delivered Ted to the lock-up under the arches, but other than that she had no idea what had happened to him. She went to work as usual, cooked, cleaned, looked after the children, and tried to avoid her sister's questions. Alice obviously noticed that her sister was staying home at night and her father looked pleased every time he received a negative answer to his repeated, 'Not out tonight, Nellie?' It helped that Ted's name had rarely been mentioned in the Clark house, but from the anxious looks her sister gave her, it was obvious she thought that Nellie had been thrown over for someone else. Nellie let her believe what she wanted to; at least it meant she didn't have to explain anything.

It was strange to her that after more than a year of thinking of no other person but Ted Bosher, Nellie should suddenly find herself imagining a life without him. When Lily came home from visiting her family in Hull, Nellie risked asking her.

'Have you heard anything from your Ted?' She pulled Lily aside, as they were donning their white smocks and caps at the beginning of the working day.

Lily looked over her shoulder, but all the other women were

chatting in little gaggles or making their way on to the factory floor. She put her finger to her mouth. 'I'll tell you about it dinner time,' she whispered.

At least he had been in touch with his family. In the packing room Lily took up her place at the filling machine. Nellie was glad that today she would be the folder and paster in their little team; it required more concentration than either filling or packing. You had to be quick to avoid filled packets piling up on the bench, and God forbid that Albert should see she'd kept Maggie Tyrell waiting for a packet to load. At least this morning she would be distracted a little as she waited impatiently for the noonday hooter. When it finally came she and Lily walked quickly through the freezing streets to the coffee shop. They linked arms but said not a word. Anxiety was written on Lily's face, so Nellie feared the news would not be good. As they sat in the steamy warmth of the coffee shop, divesting themselves of hats, gloves and mufflers, Nellie could no longer contain herself. 'For God's sake, Lily, tell me what's happened to him, what have you heard?'

'Oh, Nellie, me mum's nearly died of grief over it. He turned up at me aunt's house in Hull where we were staying. When he walked in, with his hands all bandaged and his hair singed off, I nearly fainted. There was such a row over it. Dad was for sending him packing, but Mum said to give him a chance. Not that he deserves a chance in my opinion, he's broke her heart... and your'n too, by the looks of you.'

Nellie shook her head, looking down into her lap. The truth was she hardly knew what state her heart was in.

'I've been so worried about him, not hearing a thing. Did he tell you what happened?'

Lily nodded. 'Most of it.'

'But how did he get up north?'

'His friends got him on a boat going up to Hull from Surrey Docks. The story we've got to put about is that he had the chance of work on the boats up there, over two weeks ago, all right?

Ginger's warned his workmates what to say if any questions are asked.'

'But what if someone asks the dock foreman at Butler's Wharf? He'll know Ted's been working there for the past two weeks.'

Lily looked shocked. 'Didn't Ted tell you? He's hardly been getting any work at all, at most two days a week. The foreman's not been calling him on, not since the strike. They pay you back one way or another, Ted says. But I can't believe he's not told you.'

'Not a word.' Understanding dawned gradually. 'No wonder he was always cadging money off me!' Nellie began to wonder what else Ted hadn't told her. His frequent absences on 'union' business were obviously covers for whatever more sinister activities he'd become involved with. Lily took her hand across the table.

'He told us, Nell, what you did for him, not that he deserved it, selfish git that he is.'

'Oh, Lil, it's done now. I only hope he's learned his lesson.' She paused. 'Did he say anything else about me? Only, I would have thought he'd try to get word to me.'

Lily shook her head. 'I think he's just concentrating on keeping his head down at the moment. I expect he'll write when he's settled.' Lily paused, a pitying look on her face. 'Nell, I think you've got to give up on him, love. He may have already got a deckhand job. He could be halfway to Russia on a cargo ship by now!'

'Russia!' Nellie sighed. 'Well, at least he'll feel at home, with all those Bolsheviks.'

'I don't care where he ends up, Nell, just so long as he's not causing trouble for the family here.'

The waitress had brought them steaming cups of coffee and plates of toast, and they were silent for a while as they ate. Nellie put her hands round the hot mug and sipped her coffee.

'Don't you think he'll ever come back?'

''Course he'll come back some time. This is his home, after all.'

But Nellie wasn't convinced and perversely, now that she knew he was alive and well but seemingly out of reach, she started to feel the old tug upon her emotions. It was like a prison door swinging shut and she sat up with a start as the door of the coffee shop banged open in a gust of icy wind. Both girls looked up as the large, blue-uniformed figure filled the doorway and quickly shut it behind him. The young constable scanned the room and then walked over to their table. 'Either of you two young ladies Nellie Clark?'

Terror slammed into her heart like an icy fist and she gripped the mug so tightly that it shook as she placed it back on the table. 'That's me,' she stammered.

The policeman looked pleased with his own detective work. 'Thought it was one of you two, you can't disguise that Duff's coating!' He pointed to the light dusting of yellow powder that clung to their shoes and the fringes of hair that hadn't been covered by their work caps.

'What's it about?'

Nellie heard Lily's voice, strangely thick. If her own face were as white, they must look like a pair of ghosts, she thought.

'We need to ask Miss Clark some questions about a very serious crime, an incendiary blast near Tower Bridge last week.' He paused to see her response, but, now she'd pulled herself together after the initial shock, she managed to keep her face a blank. She'd had years of masking her feelings under her father's deep scrutiny.

'We believe we have the perpetrator, miss, and he seems to think you can give him an alibi.'

Nellie saw Lily about to open her mouth and quickly kicked her under the table. The less they said the better. Whatever plan Ted and his friends had made to get him away had obviously gone horribly wrong. But how had the police tracked him down in Hull?

'Well, I'm sure we can clear this up quickly, but I'd like you to come down to the station, miss.'

Nellie's legs were like water, so she was grateful that the policeman saw fit to put a hand under her elbow. Above all she was desperate to keep Lily out of it. So long as the bobby didn't know who she was, Lily might escape questioning. It would be better for Ted if she could at least get home and warn her parents to expect a policeman's knock themselves.

'Lil, will you tell the foreman what's happened and if I'm not back by clocking-off time, tell me dad too?'

Lily nodded and hurried off through the snow flurries, back in the direction of Pearce Duff's. Nellie prayed she would have the sense to go straight home and warn her parents first.

Oh, Ted Bosher, she thought, *I knew you'd ruin me; if only you* had *been halfway to Russia.*

She felt sick as she walked up the stone steps of the newly built Tower Bridge Police Station. She had never been in such a place, and was filled with shame and fear that she'd be spotted going in by someone who knew her. She probably feared her father finding out more than the grilling she anticipated from the police. Although Nellie's family were considered respectable among their own class, they shared the deep Bermondsey distrust of the 'Old Bill'. So much of their life was lived just outside the confines of the law, and even those who thought themselves respectable were too poor to turn down the odd crate of foodstuffs that 'fell off the back of a cart' down at the docks. But underground transactions between friends were one thing; bringing the family into the line of fire was another. Nellie was only too aware that her head was poking well above the parapet and she was about to become a visible target. After the kindly desk sergeant with the droopy moustache had taken her details, she was shown to a back office to await her interrogator. The detective, who introduced himself as Stone when he came in, was a clean-shaven, chubby-faced, middle-aged man in a suit, who looked more like a grocer than an officer of the law.

Nellie felt heartened; he didn't look too mean. But as soon as he began his questions, she understood that he was sharper than he looked.

'Now, Miss Clark, don't look so frightened. You're not in any trouble,' he said kindly. 'Just answer my questions as best you can and you'll be home by teatime. Talking of which...' He made a drinking gesture to the bobby standing at the back of the room, who nipped out and was soon back with two cups of strong tea, the sweetness of which helped to steady Nellie's nerves. Her mouth felt as dry as dust and she gulped her tea down, as Detective Stone continued.

'Now, the constable told you this is in connection with a bomb blast on the eighth? Well, your friend was witnessed on the night of the incident, in the vicinity of what we believe was the bomb workshop.' Here Inspector Stone paused for what seemed to Nellie an awkwardly long time, scrutinizing her intently, then he smiled abruptly and went on. 'But *he* insists he was with you at the time of the explosion. Can you confirm where you were on the night of eighth December, Miss Clark?' He smiled again, this time more encouragingly.

She'd had the presence of mind, during her walk to the police station, to work out her story. She'd heard the best lies were those based in truth, so she launched in with a show of confidence she hoped would be more convincing than it felt to her.

'The eighth, was that a Sunday?'

The policeman nodded but said nothing.

'Well, I think I do remember that night, because I went for a walk with my chap in the park, before we went to the Star.'

The detective nodded and looked at his notebook. 'And afterwards?'

'Well, we walked home and then...'

'Go on, Miss Clark, don't be shy,' he encouraged her.

'Then we went into Wicks's stables.'

'And the purpose of your visit?' Stone looked as if he was enjoying her blushes.

'It was snowing and the stables are warm... well, truth is we never get a chance to be on our own...'

'So you went there for a bit of canoodling, is that what you're telling me?'

Nellie nodded; her reputation was the least of her worries. The detective smirked. 'Well, that seems to corroborate your friend's statement. I won't keep you any further, Miss Clark.'

He shut up the notebook and showed her out of the office. Nellie felt like sprinting out of there like a hare at the greyhound track, but she purposely slowed her steps to match the inspector's leisurely gait.

'He didn't seem like the type to me, as it happens,' he remarked as they walked towards the entrance hall. 'Respectable fresh-faced lad like him, good steady worker, it seems, no record. Anyway, thanks for your help, Miss Clark. You and Mr Gilbie can go now.'

Nellie looked at him, bewildered. What did he mean? Surely Ted hadn't been stupid enough to give a false name, and did he hate Sam so much he would try to set him up? Nellie was about to correct him, but just then, from an office opposite, emerged the familiar figure of Sam Gilbie.

'Sam!' His eyes met hers and with an almost imperceptible shake of his head she knew to say no more as he walked up to her and took her hand.

'You're free to go, Mr Gilbie,' said the detective. 'Sorry for the inconvenience, but we have to follow every lead.'

Sam nodded and said it was no trouble and he was pleased to have been a help. He still held fast to Nellie's hands and she could feel him trembling. They made a show of walking slowly out together and down the station steps.

'Let's walk over the other side,' Sam said as they got free of the station. He led her towards Tower Bridge and they walked northward across it, towards the Tower of London, not stopping until the full width of the Thames was between them and Tower Bridge Police Station.

13

TO THE TOWER

They descended an icy flight of stone steps beside the bridge, Sam holding her arm as he led her to the embankment in front of the Tower. A row of pitted old black cannons, each capped with a mound of snow, stood sentinel before the silent walls of London's old fortress. A Beefeater stood with a pike by a little drawbridge, his scarlet coat bright against the carpet of snow. Nellie wondered why they called it the White Tower, when it was black with soot and grime: the only white she could see was in the snowdrifts, blocking crenellations and arrow slits. They said nothing until they reached Traitor's Gate, a desiccated reminder of all the ghostly prisoners who had passed beneath its portcullis. Nellie shivered and turned back to the wide open Thames, where a pewter sky rested heavily on its slate-grey waters. She walked to the railing and gazed up at the bridge, as its arms rose to let a red-sailed Thames barge pass beneath, on its way downriver.

'It's a wonderful sight.' Sam spoke her thoughts. He leaned his elbows on the railing and they watched in silence as the arms descended again.

Finally, she spoke. 'Sam, why did you give me as your alibi, why didn't you just tell them you were at home?'

She turned to look at him. His face was grey and strained. 'Because I wasn't *at* home.'

'You weren't? Well, wherever you were, surely someone saw you?'

'No, nobody saw me, Nell. I didn't *have* an alibi, you see.'

Nellie's mouth went dry and she felt the silence of snow all around them, like a heavy presence. She tried to quell the horrible suspicion that Sam could be involved in the whole thing too. Had he just been playing a charade with Ted that night? Wasn't there anyone she could trust?

'Well, where were you, then?'

'Mum's bad again, and I needed to get out. It upsets me sometimes, Nell, to see her like that. So I reckon, at the time Ted was blowing himself up, I was in the stable working on the old penny-farthing and the only witnesses were old Thumper and his mates.'

Nellie realized she hadn't been breathing. She took in a gulp of the freezing air, surprised at her own relief. When had it started to become important to her, this feeling that she could trust Sam, that he was like a solid hub in all the turning world? But she wouldn't reveal a feeling to him that was still so new to her. 'Well, why didn't you just tell them that, you stupid sod?' she snapped. 'And what if my story had been different? They would have put you down as a suspect straight away!'

'I suppose I panicked. I wasn't entirely innocent, remember. I helped Bosher, we both did, and that made me think you could do with an alibi as well...'

Nellie hadn't thought of that.

'But anyway, knowing you, I guessed you'd be clever enough to tell them as near the truth as you could. I remembered you were going to walk in the park and then go to the Star, so I told the same story and made out I was your sweetheart.'

Sam swallowed the last word and she saw his familiar blush rising, but now, instead of scorning it, she felt an urge to cup his burning face with her cold hands. She resisted and said instead, 'You're a kind-hearted fool, Sam Gilbie, and I don't think I've deserved your friendship. Thank you.'

'I'll always be a friend to you, Nellie,' he said quietly, and before she could reply he went on, 'and don't think I mean more than that, will you? I'd hate to think we couldn't be friends.'

Their shared jeopardy seemed to have broken down a barrier between them and loosened Sam's tongue. 'And another thing, Nellie, that night you came home with me, remember?'

'Of course I remember.'

'I know Mum got the wrong end of the stick about us, and you're to take no notice of anything she said... or might have made *you* say... D'ye get me drift?'

This was even more of a shock. How much did Sam see, how could he know about her promise? He'd said 'knowing you as I do' – how did he know her? And how did he see what she felt? For all the time she had spent with Ted, she never once felt that he *knew* her; it was all about what she felt for *him*, nothing more, she realized that now. She sighed.

'I get your drift, Sam, but that's something between me and your mum.'

He stared hard at her and seemed to decide not to pursue it. 'Come on, you're perishing. Let's keep walking,' he said finally.

They walked briskly along the river front, passing a few other well-wrapped Londoners, heads down, immune to the glories of history surrounding them – a couple of delivery boys trundling handcarts along the cobbles; a noisy group of sailors coming from St Katherine's Dock, no doubt in search of the nearest pub. The normal hordes of Baedeker-carrying tourists were absent, though, and they skirted the Tower largely undisturbed. A few late white roses were blooming at the foot of the curtain wall, drooping under their extra petals of snow.

'Who do you think spotted you at the arches?' Nellie said, as they paused at Tower Pier to watch a paddle steamer swing out into the tugging tide, steam pluming from its white funnel.

'They said it was an anonymous tip-off.' He frowned. 'But I don't know how anyone saw me – there was no one about and I was careful when I moved Ted. Have you heard from him?'

Nellie shook her head. 'No, but Lily says he made it up north and they're telling everyone he's been up there a fortnight. He's trying for a job on the boats, getting out of the country.'

'Good riddance an' all! If he's out of the way, the coppers won't be coming after you, will they?'

Nellie felt a pang of disloyalty to Ted, in spite of his silence and apparent abandonment of her. Sam must have seen it in her face. He took her elbow, guiding her back towards the moat.

'Sorry, Nell, it's just I don't think he's been good to you, that's all.'

'No, he hasn't been good to me, Sam, but I made my choices, didn't I? So you could say I haven't been good to myself.'

They had made an almost full circuit of the Tower and were now heading towards Tower Hill. The moat and front drawbridge fell into view and, with the gas lamps beginning to be lit, the castle took on a sparkling fairy-tale look, their light flaring off icicles dripping from the battlements. By now she was shivering. They stopped at a tea stall and Sam ordered two glasses of steaming-hot sarsaparilla. On a bench nearby Nellie spotted what looked like a huddled bundle of rags. As she stared, the bundle moved and a haggard white face peered out from under a worn docker's cap. The old man was gazing at her drink.

'Sam, look, I think he needs this more than I do,' she said, and strode over to the bench, holding out her sarsaparilla to the man.

'Thanks, miss, you're very kind,' he rasped. Cupping the glass in both hands for warmth, he gulped at the steaming liquid.

'Have you got a bed for tonight?' she asked. The bundle of belongings on the floor beside him showed he was obviously tramping.

The man shook his head. 'Nah, no room in the Limehouse doss house, so I'm making me way over to the Sally Army in Bermondsey, but me legs give out.' He lifted up from the bench two misshapen limbs, one foot twisted inwards. 'Got these in an accident at the docks ten year ago. Finished me for heavy work and I couldn't get no other work, so it's tramping for me now.'

Sam had joined them and was looking worriedly at Nellie. But she prided herself on being a good judge of character. 'He's all right,' she whispered to Sam. 'Will you get into the Sally Army?' she asked the man. 'It's a bit late.' She was familiar with the long queues outside the doss house in Spa Road. They'd sometimes start at lunchtime, both men and women, trying to make sure of a bed that night.

The man shrugged. 'It's worth a try. Better than settling down here for the night. This old bench'll make a cold bed.'

'We're walking that way, you can lean on Sam, can't he, Sam?'

Sam didn't look too pleased to be offered as a crutch, especially as the man had obviously gone a while without a wash. When the bundle of rags extended itself to its full height, it was obvious he had once been a bull of a man, and the twisted legs gave him an odd rolling gait that made Sam's job even harder. As they walked over the bridge, the man, whose name was Jim, pointed down to Butler's Wharf on the south side. 'I've worked bloody hard down there in my time,' he said.

The wharf, in contrast with the idleness of this summer's strike, was now back to business. Barges packed the dockside and dockers and stevedores were scurrying to finish unloading the vessels before the light failed.

'All back to work now, eh?' Jim remarked. 'Much good striking ever did me. I was one of the first to go out in eighty-nine, a right firebrand I was, but look at me now. I read me Marx and Engels, oh, yes. Got the docker's tanner, thought I was so clever and still ended up on the scrapheap. I tell you they always win…' he concluded morosely.

Looking at the wreck of a man walking beside them, Nellie's mind was filled with the memory of Ted's fiery hair and flashing eyes that day of the women's strike last year. His lithe, youthful figure striding up and down the podium had been a picture of passion and purpose as he gave his speech. Was it possible he could one day end up like this? Who knew how any of them would finish – a day's work was all that kept them from a life on the streets, like this poor soul. Once they'd crossed the bridge, Nellie turned to Sam.

'I'd best go straight to Lily's, to let them know… Will you go on with Jim?'

Sam nodded. 'I'm going back that way to the yard. Old Wicks'll be wondering why I never turned up for work today.'

'Let me know how you get on.' Nellie squeezed his hand and watched as he made his way up Tower Bridge Road, his rolling charge leaning on his arm, swaying out and then banging into him as if they were a pair of barges on the Thames.

Nellie knocked at the Boshers' basement door and Betty answered at the first knock. Her face bore the evidence of a few sleepless nights and her eyes were red-rimmed. She had clearly shed as many tears over Ted as Nellie had herself. 'Come in, love, quick before nosey parker upstairs sees you.'

Betty led her past the stairs, across the dark passage into the kitchen. Noises from the family who lived above drifted down – a child crying, and the raised voices of its parents arguing. 'The noise of it! Still, if they're at each other's throats at least she's not getting her nose into my business.'

When the kitchen door was closed, Betty turned her searching eyes to Nellie. 'Nell, tell me he's all right. Did they let you see him?'

'Sit down, Mrs B., and let me make you a cuppa,' Nellie said, for the poor woman looked exhausted with worry. 'You can stop worrying. It wasn't him, they'd got the wrong feller!'

Betty's hands flew to her mouth. 'Oh, thank God!' She collapsed on to a chair and Nellie saw she was crying. 'Oh, but I don't mean that. Who was it, the poor soul?'

'Sam Gilbie!'

Betty groaned. 'Sam! But how?'

'Someone spotted him near the arches… well, did Lily tell you Sam helped him?'

Betty nodded. 'He's his father's son. Michael was my cousin, you know, always did a turn for anyone. Sam wouldn't turn his back on his family.'

Nellie didn't think it was the time to let her know Sam's true opinion of Ted. 'You're right there, he's got a heart of gold, Sam. It was lucky for him I could give him an alibi, though.'

She handed Betty the tea and sat down to drink her own. 'Mrs B., have you heard anything from Ted?'

Just then there was a knock on the front door and Betty hurried out. She came back, holding a telegram. Putting it on the table in front of Nellie, she slumped back into her chair.

'Read it,' she ordered shortly, for she couldn't.

Nellie picked up the telegram. '"Took ship for St Petersburg, am well."' Her voice faltered. 'At least he's safe,' she said weakly.

Betty was not stupid enough to be taken in, however. Looking at Nellie as though she were an idiot, she shook her head sorrowfully. 'Oh, Nellie, *safe*? On a ship sailing through *icebergs*! You have *heard* of the *Titanic*, haven't you? And *Russia*? If I know my Ted, he won't rest till he joins them Bolsheviks and ends up dead!'

14

CHRISTMAS CONTRASTS

She breathed deep. It was a warm, balmy June morning of
unbelievable freshness. Even the air of Australia felt expansive,
and on such days Eliza James had no doubt that her choice
to come with Ernest had been the right one. Freedom! It
was the reason she had come here. They had taken the white
weatherboard villa shortly after arriving in Melbourne, and she
loved it. On fine mornings she drank her tea on the wraparound
verandah, looking over the well-tended garden. It was a world
away from the huddled streets of Bermondsey where she could
have spent her whole life, and every day she let herself appreciate
that difference. She breathed deeply again and caught the scent
of sun-warmed eucalyptus, the smell of freedom. The instinct
that had driven her to this new world might have been flight,
but her choices in life had always aimed at self-improvement,
and this one was no exception: life in Australia was definitely
an improvement.

Her greatest relief was to drop the pretence of being Ernest's
housekeeper. In a country that easily swallowed the secret pasts
of those arriving on its shores, no one openly questioned her
marital status. So, too, the balance of her relationship with Ernest
had changed for the better. Even he had to acknowledge that her
work among the women's trade unions was proving of equal
value to his own. The working women she met had the same
no-nonsense earthiness of Bermondsey women and she'd thrown
herself into improving their lot, making a name for herself as
someone who could break the will of the most intransigent of

factory owners. Ernest seemed to have found a new respect for her: no longer his token cockney sparrow, she felt herself a falcon soaring. In London she had chafed at his iron grip on her life, but here it had relaxed somewhat, perhaps because he was happier in his own work. Whatever the reason, he seemed content to allow her more freedom to come and go as she pleased and to choose her own companions.

But sometimes, on dark nights, when Ernest was working in his study, she would sit on this verandah, looking up at the unfamiliar stars, and she'd hear troubling echoes. She heard her mother's sad voice during that last meeting, apologizing for doing anything that might have kept her daughter away. At such times, the deep flame of her own self-knowledge would spark into an unwanted life. She knew it was never her mother or father who'd kept her away. It had been her own choice, her own drive for freedom, her own desire for more in life than the lot of a domestic servant. Servitude of any kind was repulsive to her, whether it was the everyday servitude of a wife and mother, or the institutionalized servitude of the wage slave. It was the act of submission that she wished to evade, to smash and to conquer.

But on this particular June morning, something had happened that threatened all her newfound liberty. She found she was expecting Ernest's child and now the discovery was filling her with dread. The doctor who confirmed her suspicion had seemed shocked at her reaction.

'No, no, I can't have a child! It will kill me!' she'd cried out in horror.

The tall, composed woman before him had suddenly crumpled and he left his desk to come and put his arm round her heaving shoulders.

'But there is really no danger, my dear, you are a strong healthy woman. You're what, thirty-one now? Your age should cause no problems, and we will give you the best of care. So there is no reason why you should lose your life in childbirth!'

He was a kindly man, but she became irrationally angry that

he should so misunderstand her and shouted into his concerned face, 'I mean, it'll kill me to lose my child. I can't lose another!'

The doctor nodded; he thought he understood now. 'There's no reason why you should not deliver this child,' he said softly. 'We'll take special care of your baby, Mrs James. Never fear, you will not lose this one.'

But Eliza left his office and walked in a dream through the Melbourne suburbs, unconvinced by all the doctor's reassurances. He hadn't understood at all and now she must speak to Ernest; he had to be told. But first she needed to think and calm herself. She took a tram to the Labour Office and cancelled her meeting for that evening, then walked to the riverside. It was a world away from the Thames, but she had always felt soothed by wide stretches of water. As she walked, she pondered. Was there any way she could be a mother to a child this time round? Her thoughts went back nine years to the other baby, the cause of so much heartache and regret.

The child had been a girl. Eliza was surprised a pregnancy hadn't happened before, but they had been careful. She was twenty-two at the time and had believed that the baby's arrival would be the end of her life in Mecklenburgh Square. She and Ernest had been carrying on their affair for over five years, at first in secret, but then the situation had become obvious to most of the household and also to Ernest's friends. But, still, an illegitimate child by his housekeeper? How could that be contained within his life? Even with his radical views, Eliza had expected that she and the child would be packed off and never spoken of again. In the years since, she had sometimes wished it had happened that way, but it seemed she had become essential to Ernest.

She was never quite certain why. She doubted it was still passion. She liked to think he might value her for the work she had begun with the Anti Sweated Labour League, but in her darker moments she feared she might simply be his pet 'cockney sparrer', a trophy, to prove his radical credentials to his Bohemian friends and colleagues in the Labour movement. If she *had* left with the child her union work would have been over. Thousands of women, she could say for a certainty, would have been the poorer, but would she have been the richer? Instead, she had followed Ernest's baldly stated wishes.

'Eliza, you must give the child up,' was all he had said and she had taken care of it. He did not wish to know the arrangements, had merely given her an allowance to be used for the child's upbringing. It had broken her heart and it was then she'd thrown herself into union work, as distraction and a consolation: if she had lost her child, she would make it count for something. And for many years she had worked to that end, but this new baby forced her to admit that, on the scales of her heart, all that she'd achieved had never once outweighed all that she'd lost. Knowing that, how could she allow herself to make the same disastrous choice again?

By the time she got back to their villa that afternoon, her decision was made and she had prepared herself to do battle with Ernest. This one she would not give up! He was home early and after supper they walked on to the verandah. Ernest smoked while leaning on the railing and Eliza joined him there, in the cool of the evening, wrapping a shawl around her shoulders and settling into one of the cane chairs in the corner.

'Ernest, come and sit down, I want to talk to you.'

He strolled over to her. 'You seem rather pensive this evening, my dear. Is there something troubling you?'

She shifted in her seat, the sounds of the night seeming exaggerated; insects clicking, frogs croaking and the wind soughing in the trees, all competed with the thudding of her own heart. 'Ernest, I'm going to have a child.'

At first he did not answer. He carefully put out his cigarette and then he sat down beside her. He reached out with his hand to cover hers. She sat rigidly, waiting for his reply.

'Is this why you cancelled your meeting?'

She nodded, still waiting.

'Well, my dear, I suggest you cancel all meetings for the foreseeable future. Your life will be much changed. But not forever, you must remember that.'

And he turned to her a face of inscrutable politeness.

Her heart sank; now she knew she would have to fight. 'Ernest, I wish to keep this child.'

'And what of your work... our work?'

'There is no reason this time to give up the child!'

He interrupted her with a peremptory gesture. They had never spoken of their firstborn, not since the day Eliza took her away. But she would not spare his guilty heart, not now.

'I'm sorry, Ernest, but we must speak about it. I know it wasn't an easy choice for either of us, and we both agreed our lives would not allow for a child... not then. But this time is entirely different. We are in a new age now and a different world! Is it a scandal you're worried about? No one here has ever questioned that we live as man and wife! They're only too happy to have a man of your stature helping them, they don't dare ostracize you!' She would flatter and plead shamelessly, if it meant getting him to agree.

He took away his heavy hand from hers and stared into her frightened eyes. 'I'm sorry, my dear, it may well be that the mores of the old country haven't the same grip on society here, but I thought I made it clear the last time. You must understand that my life will not allow for a child. Really, my dear, the last thing I wish to do is give you pain. Make whatever arrangements you need to and I will see to it you have the very best of care.'

He smiled at her and as his hand closed around hers again, in what might have been clumsy reassurance, it felt to her like a shackle. He got up and went silently to his study, leaving her to mourn the choices that had brought her back to this place. The bird had taken flight and delighted in riding the wind for a while, but then had come the familiar tug on the jesses, calling her back. She might fly halfway across the world but she could never escape this particular falconer. Underneath all their newfound freedom, the unequal alliance persisted. She was, after all they had shared, still his scullery maid.

Christmas Eve found Eliza strolling along a wide Melbourne street, arm in arm with Ernest James. Even though this was her second in Australia, she still hadn't got used to celebrating Christmas in summer time. The heat was oppressive and she held the pale blue parasol at an angle, grateful for its meagre shade. She tried to imagine a London Christmas, replacing in her imagination the unbroken blue skies above her with foggy streets lit by small circles of gaslight. She saw, in her mind's eye, the great dark river at the heart of her childhood, the crowding wharves and teeming streets. But then, as though her memory were a moving picture, a black screen cut in and the scenes of home vanished. She came back to herself as Ernest pointed out their destination. They had been invited to attend a luncheon at the impressive villa of a prominent Labour politician. Their work had brought them into contact not only with grass-roots union members but also a number of influential socialists and reformers.

Ernest turned towards her; he leaned his head under the blue shade of her parasol and kissed her perspiring cheek.

'Are you quite sure you are up to this, my dear? The afternoon is abominably hot and Edward McMahon's chairs are dreadfully over-stuffed. Why people who live in a hot climate should adopt the furnishings of a castle in Ireland, I can't imagine!'

Eliza outwardly smiled at his accurate description of the McMahon residence, while inwardly grimacing at his overprotectiveness. The child she was expecting had brought out the worst in his controlling nature.

'I'm perfectly fine, Ernest, you must stop fussing. You forget, I've done this before.'

It was out before she realized it and though she regretted her thoughtlessness, she did wonder if she might have done it half on purpose. Sometimes like a bird in a snare she would flail and peck – too bad if his hand were on the net and got stabbed by her beak.

His concerned expression changed to tight-lipped disapproval and he ducked his head back out into the blazing sunshine.

'At least Mrs McMahon always keeps a good table,' Eliza said. 'She tells me the latest sensation from her cook is an ice-cream Christmas pudding melba, with a nod to Dame Nellie. Thank God it hasn't been boiling in a pan for eight hours!'

Ernest laughed; she had deflected him. She would enjoy this Christmas and be thankful it wasn't like the bleak festivities of her childhood when an orange emerging from a stocking was like a magical sunburst into the world of sooty walls and slate roofs.

After dinner, Eliza joined the other women gathered on the wide wraparound verandah, while they left the men to smoke. A cool breeze tugged at her white skirts and she leaned on the wooden railing with one hand. She felt the baby kick and gasped. She felt it again and looked around for someone to tell, but the others were deep in conversation.

Eliza found herself caressing the swell of her belly beneath the voluminous flowing garments she had taken to wearing. Unease gripped her. Justice, fairness, equality – these were all the things that she and Ernest had worked towards. But how were they served by the treatment meted out to these two children of hers? The child she was carrying seemed to protest and kick even more, but soon Eliza realized it was not so much a protest as a demand to be born. Surely it couldn't be happening now; her baby wasn't due for another fortnight! But she was almost certain these were contractions!

She cried out, doubling up in pain, and was immediately surrounded by a bevy of clucking, dipping women, ineffectual hands flapping and plucking at her. Eliza James screamed and was saved by the arrival of the McMahons' maid, a middle-aged Irish woman who had fortunately delivered many more babies than she had served ice-cream Christmas pudding melbas. Eliza's eyes locked on to the deep, calm eyes of Mary Donovan and felt a rush of confidence sweeping away the bolt of fear that had seized her. Mercy's directions were soft susurrations but full of authority, and Eliza simply did as she was told. It was impossible that Eliza should return through the dining room, where the men still sat drinking their brandy, so with Mercy's strong arms around her she was helped round the verandah to the side entrance. A flustered Mrs McMahon led them to a spare ground-floor bedroom. Eliza, apologizing uselessly to her hostess who had catered so thoughtfully for everything except this early birth, gratefully allowed Mercy to help her to the bed. She was aware of a screen being erected round her and heard orders for towels and hot water. This child was in a hurry, her contractions were deep and violent, and she imagined the angry infant surging out into the world, demanding to be valued. At the stroke of midnight, under Antipodean stars, her son was born. He announced his arrival with an ear-splitting cry and as she looked down at his red face and clenched fists, Eliza knew she had given birth to a fighter. She prayed she would do a better job of motherhood this time round. She whispered to him as she drew the child up to rest its cheek against hers.

'You're going to need all that rage, little one. Hold on to it and I will hold on to you.'

The Christmas of 1912 was an anxious one for Nellie, Sam and Lily. Lily and her family waited for news of Ted, or for a policeman to knock on the door; Sam waited for his mother's illness to reach its natural conclusion and Nellie waited for all three. Sam had become a hero in the Bosher household and it was Lily who suggested he join them for a Christmas drink in the Land of Green Ginger pub. When they all met up after work to walk to the pub, Nellie was surprised to see that Sam had brought his best friend Jock McBride along, a lively round-faced young man who'd known Sam since their schooldays.

Jock was full of embarrassing stories about their escapades. 'What about the time the choir master caught us lighting up? Sam stuffed the dog end under the choir pew and nearly set the church alight!'

'Sam! A choirboy? I always said he'd got an innocent face, eh, Nell?' Lily was showing off a bit for Jock, but Nellie didn't mind. It had been a bleak enough few weeks for them all – they deserved a bit of fun and, besides, Sam was laughing too as he and Jock launched forth in falsettos with a verse of *'Lead Kindly Light amid the encircling gloom, the night is dark and I am far from home, lead thou me on!'*

Nellie had a sudden vivid sense of the two fresh-faced boys they must have been and she found herself being moved by the mournful tune. But then Lily jumped in with, 'Gawd's sake, give us something a bit more cheerful, you two!' and they immediately started up a mock hymnal version of 'Oh, You Beautiful Doll,' with Sam doing the harmonies.

'If you ever leave me how my heart would ache, I want to hug you but I fear you'd break, oh, oh, oh, oh, ohhhh you beeauuutifulll dollll!'

The two girls applauded loudly and passers-by stared and smiled at them as they walked four abreast down Southwark Park Road. They still called this new wide thoroughfare 'the Blue' because it had once been the narrow, winding Blue Anchor Lane. Now it was a fine shopping street lined with shops, all of them still open, every shop front illuminated by pools of gaslight, showing off their Christmas wares. Shoppers were still milling about, buying last-minute groceries and cheap poultry. It was Christmas Eve and there were bargains to be had at the butchers and the fruit-and-veg stalls that lined 'the Blue'.

'Come and get yer cheap turkeys! Half price a lovely bit of brawn, if you ain't made none yerself, yer lazy cows!' The stallholders sang out their good-natured insults to the harassed housewives, who clutched their purses and counted out the pennies of every purchase.

'Times is hard but you won't get none cheaper'n 'at! E'are 'alf price the oranges, don't disappoint yer kiddies, what did you say, madam, yer 'usband got ten knocked off from the docks. Where's the Old Bill?' There was never a pause in the patter, they sang out as though their lives depended on it, and indeed often they did.

But Nellie, at least for this night, wanted to feel above domestic constraints like the price of veg. She was young! Or so she kept reminding herself, but as they strode past the stalls she felt a desperation in their light-heartedness, as though time were running out for their youth. If all the talk of war and the thought of Ted's life in ruins wasn't enough, there was still the nagging remembrance of her promise to Lizzie Gilbie. When the poor woman finally died, fate would come knocking on Nellie's door, to call her to account. She wished Sam's mother a long life, but she felt mean every time she did so, because she suspected it was more for her own protection than for Lizzie's preservation that she prayed.

Oh, give over, you gloomy old stick, she thought to herself sternly and decided not to care if her joy were forced or not. She was seventeen years old and it was Christmas Eve and who knew what the future held for them all?

As they pushed through the door of the pub she felt her spirits lift, the Green Ginger was full of the 'custard tarts'.

"'Ello girls, over 'ere!' Ethel Brown stood up and beckoned to them. 'We've been saving you a place, but we didn't know you was bringing yer new chaps!'

Nellie blushed, but Lily swaggered over to the table where Ethel sat taking up the width of two chairs with her wide girth and voluminous feather boa. Maggie Tyrell had squashed her skinny frame in beside her.

'Well, you should've known we'd be in demand, Ethel,' Lily said brightly.

The women shoved up along the plush-covered bench and Sam found another stool. Nellie noticed he placed it at the end of the table nearest her.

'You heard anything from your Ted, Lily?' asked Ethel, but her currant-bun eyes flicked towards Nellie. The girls all knew that Ted had left suddenly and she'd heard them whispering about her being left in the lurch.

'He's found a job on the boats, but we ain't heard no more.'

Nellie hoped no questions would be directed at her, but admired her friend's composure.

'Shame for your poor mother, she'll miss him,' said Ethel, sipping her stout.

Nellie felt the sympathetic eyes of Maggie and her workmates resting on her.

Sam got to his feet. 'What you drinking, ladies?'

Nellie was grateful to him for the distraction as the girls gave full attention to their orders, but she wished he hadn't offered. He wasn't old enough to get a full carter's wage yet and she knew only too well how his family depended on him. She didn't want to feel responsible for depriving the Gilbie children of their Christmas treats, so she was relieved when Jock followed Sam to the bar. He was a good friend and he knew Sam's situation as well as she did.

They drank Sam's round and then Jock got in another, and the pub filled to bursting, the air thick with smoke and chatter and good-natured laughter. The landlady, Katie Gilbie, a short buxom woman in her forties with a frothy halo of fair hair, famed for belting out the latest songs, struck up a tune on the piano. Then Ethel Brown planted her impressive bulk precariously on top of a bentwood chair to give her own tear-jerking rendition of 'Silver Threads amongst the Gold'.

For some it was too early in the evening for such maudlin sentiment and someone shouted from the bar, 'Liven it up, for gawd's sake, it's Christmas!'

Ethel's ample bosom gave her a precarious centre of gravity at the best of times, but determined to finish and lifting her arms to emphasize the chorus, she toppled forward like a sack of coal, burying Maggie Tyrell beneath her black-coated bulk. Nellie leaped forward, pulling a breathless, laughing Maggie from the tangle of hats and feather boas.

'It was me "shelf" done it, not the drink!' Ethel protested.

In all the confusion, Nellie saw Sam and Jock go over to the piano, whispering to Katie. When they burst into their own version of 'Beautiful Doll' the whole pub joined in. Nellie found herself smiling, and she realized she hadn't really smiled since the moment Ted left. Her cheeks felt almost stiff as the grin spread across her face and what had become perpetual furrows in her brow eased. The grin turned to a giggle as the two boys hammed it up at the piano, gazing cow-eyed at plump Katie, their 'beautiful doll'. Nellie relaxed back into her chair. Yes, she was having fun.

The whole night went by in a blur of ease and banter; she felt a world away from the anxious fears of the last few weeks. Perhaps she really had escaped the consequences of that dreadful night when Ted had come to her burned and smoking and broken. For a moment she pictured him wrapped in furs with a Cossack hat at a jaunty angle instead of his flat cap, saw him waving a red flag on a barricade, and then the image faded. It was a fantasy – perhaps all her feelings for him had been as phantom-like as that image; insubstantial, just a girlish dream that had turned into a nightmare. She consciously turned away, putting her face to the real world around her: the warmth of the people she had grown up with, short on material goods but full of human sympathy and decency. She allowed herself to feel safe, to feel hopeful.

The boys came back to the table and shortly afterwards Lily leaned over to whisper in her ear, 'Jock's walking me home tonight, is that all right?'

Nellie exchanged a mischievous look with her friend. 'You're a fast worker, Lily Bosher! Of course it's all right. I'll have to be getting home now anyway, there's things to do for tomorrow's dinner.'

When she announced she would be leaving, Sam got up naturally and offered to walk her home. They left the pub amid a chorus of 'Night, love, Happy Christmas!' from her fellow custard tarts. They emerged from the heat and fug into a still, crystalline night. Nellie shivered – even her ears were tingling and her breath formed a frosty plume in the air. She flung her boa around her neck and she and Sam set off side by side, back to Vauban Street. They chatted easily about the plans they each had for the following day and although Sam's voice was tinged with sadness when he spoke about his mother, his face brightened as he told Nellie his plans to surprise Matty with a little doll and Charlie with a cricket bat, both of which he'd made himself from offcuts of wood he'd found in the yard. It made her laugh to hear about Matty's bustling bossiness over the Christmas dinner. 'She's only nine, but I swear that child could organize an army, she's already got me lined up to peel the spuds!'

But as they approached Nellie's door, her laughter died. They hurried their steps as they approached Nellie's house, for the front door was already open and Alice stood on the step with a policeman, her anxious face signalling that something was wrong. Thoughts of Ted sped through Nellie's mind, but this time the law had nothing to say about Ted Bosher.

15

A GAME OLD BIRD

'Alice, what's the matter?' Nellie asked, taking her hand and looking from her to the policeman. The young girl burst into tears.

'Oh, Nell, I'm so glad you've come home. It's Dad.'

The policeman, having delivered his message, seemed glad to take his leave. Alice had all but collapsed on the doorstep and Nellie asked Sam to help her. They half carried her into the kitchen, sitting her in front of the range. Nellie knelt before her.

'What's happened, Al? For God's sake, tell me.'

'He's been in a terrible accident...' Alice sobbed, her voice thick with tears.

'Where is he now?' Sam asked her.

'He's in Guy's Hospital, they took him straight there.'

'Was he driving the cart?' asked Sam.

Alice nodded and slowly, as the normally stoical twelve-year-old tried desperately to control her sobs, the story emerged. Their father, although stern and unyielding in matters of family discipline, had always tried to give his family a good Christmas. All year he saved into a Christmas club and on Christmas Eve, when the club paid out, he would take the cart down to 'the Blue' market. There he would spend the Christmas money on treats for the family. If it had been a bad year and he'd had to borrow out of the club for new shoes or clothes, then the treats would be few, but Nellie's wage increase had made all the difference and this had been a good year. He'd told Nellie he'd buy a goose and vegetables for Christmas dinner and bring home oranges, nuts and a few sugar mice. There was no money left over for toys, but the young ones would each get a stocking filled with an orange, sugar mouse and a silver sixpence, which for them was a fortune. Her father's morose temper had certainly softened and Nellie remembered, as he'd told her the plans for his Christmas shopping that morning, feeling a warmth towards him she hadn't felt in years, not since those long-gone days when she would skip along beside him and swing from his strong hand, singing *oops a lala, oops a lala, lost the leg of her drawers!* The silly song came back to her now as she heard what had happened to the strong man with the firm hand who had ruled her childhood.

'There was a cart in front of him, some kids were larking about, holding on to the back board and skidding along behind it.' Nellie and Sam nodded. It was a common but dangerous game for the local children to grab the back board, scrunch down on their boots and let themselves be pulled along the cobbles. At times sparks would fly from their boot studs and often the driver would crack his whip behind him to dissuade them, and sometimes they tumbled to the ground. Alice explained that this was what had happened.

'A kiddie fell off into the road right in front of Dad's cart and he had to pull up sharp or old Thumper would have gone right over him. Thumper reared up and Dad's cart tipped over and he got pinned underneath it. Old Thumper was still in the harness and thrashing about. Oh, Nell...' Here Alice broke down again and they waited for her sobs to subside. 'The policeman says Thumper caught him in the head and his skull is broken and his legs got smashed under the cart.'

'Alice, he's still alive, isn't he?' Nellie's voice sounded to her like a croak; her lips were dry and her throat constricted.

Alice put her hands to her tear-stained face. She nodded. 'Yes, but, Nell, they've had to take his legs off!'

Nellie didn't know where the strength came from; she just knew that it would be down to her. Three children were depending on her decisions now and she focused on making the right ones.

'Now, Al, you've got to be strong and grown up for me. All right?'

Her sister straightened her shoulders and wiped her wet face with the cuff of her sleeve.

'You stay here and look after the boys, while I go up Guy's. If they wake up you'll have to tell them what's happened, but you can't cry in front of 'em, do you hear me?'

'Nell, what about their Christmas stockings?' Alice pointed to a bundle by the door. 'The policeman brought it, said everything had tipped out over the road, that was all they could save.'

Sam picked up the sack and tipped the contents on to the table. Nellie felt an overwhelming sadness as she saw the battered remnants of her father's Christmas cheer. The goose, covered in dust, tumbled out along with the oranges, some squashed to pulp. A few of the sugar mice had survived, but the nuts must have rolled all over the road and a few brazil nuts were all that was left. In an instant Nellie forgave all the past beatings and harsh words and remembered him at his best, when their mother had been alive. His heart simply hadn't had enough room for all the grief at her loss and his children had suffered for it. She understood this for the first time and the sight of his renewed attempts to be a loving father broke her heart.

She lifted her pale sad face to Sam and before she could ask, he offered. 'You can't go up there on your own this time of night. I'll take you up there.'

'Thanks, Sam, but what about your mum, won't she be worried?'

'No, she knew I was out for the night, come on.'

They hurried to catch the bus to Guy's Hospital, passing rowdy crowds of Christmas Eve revellers piling out of the closing pubs. Sam deftly weaved his way through an overly friendly crowd of dockers who wanted to include Nellie in a lively waltz they were enjoying among themselves. They might have been lumbering prancing giants from another world for Nellie. In her world now there was no Christmas, there was no dancing, there was no night or day; there was perhaps the shadow of Sam at her side, but everything else was half-formed. She was on the fringes of a nightmare and round every corner she seemed to see the vision of the old tramp with the crushed legs that she and Sam had befriended on their way back from the Tower. But the old tramp now had the face of her father, and the terror of the workhouse was hers alone. For even if her father survived, he might never work again and then it would be up to her to feed, clothe and house her family.

She felt herself being shaken.

'Nellie, it's our stop next.'

They were on the top deck of the bus and she followed Sam down the stairs. They hopped off at the end of Tooley Street and made their way across the colonnaded courtyard into Guy's Hospital. Two nurses were crossing the black-and-white tiled entrance hall and Sam stopped one of them.

'We're looking for a man brought in from a cart accident today.' He lowered his voice, Nellie thought, in a kind though futile attempt to protect her. 'He's had his legs amputated. Do you know which ward he might be in?'

Nellie had an aversion to nurses; when her mother was dying, the fierce old matron had guarded her like a fire-breathing dragon. Although it was probably unjustified, Nellie had always blamed the matron for robbing her of those precious last moments with her mother. She was ready for a fight now; nothing would keep her from her father.

But this young nurse turned round with a pleasant smile. She looked briefly at Nellie and then spoke softly to Sam. 'If it only happened today, he probably won't be in a fit state to see you.'

Nellie took a half step forward, a surge of adrenalin making her clench her fists, but the nurse went on. 'Still, it *is* Christmas Eve, Matron might take pity on the young lady and let you see him.'

She gave them directions to the ward and with a sympathetic smile hurried off to catch up with her friend.

It took them what seemed like hours to find the ward. Long green and cream corridors smelling of carbolic all looked the same and Nellie found herself half running along them, her footsteps echoing on the tiles. Sam put a restraining hand on her arm as she dashed past the last staircase.

'Hold up, Nell, it's this way.'

She turned on her heel, Sam keeping pace with her as they sped up the flight of stairs. All her thoughts had narrowed to a single focus, a point of light that was her father's survival.

The young nurse was right; some Christmas spirit had invaded Matron's regimen. The ward was dimly lit, but the stern-faced woman softened as she saw Nellie's ashen face. She led them with a soft swish of her blue matron's dress between two rows of sleeping patients to a curtained-off cubicle at the end of the ward. Through the tall, iron-framed window Nellie caught a sight of the moon and a single bright star. Flecks of newly falling snow were caught in the moonlight and by its silvery glow she saw her father's bandaged head. She saw the rise and fall of the blanket that swaddled him and relief trembled through her. At least he was alive. She forced her gaze to move down to where his legs should have been: a cage had been placed under the blankets. She was glad – she could imagine that underneath his legs were still there; she could let herself believe he was still whole. The damage to his skull was another matter. Although he looked to her like a turbaned Indian with his head swathed in thick white bandages, even these could not disguise the terrible change to his features. His nose had been crushed and one cheek had sunk, and his face looked as though someone had smashed a flat iron into it. He didn't look like her father at all, and that she wasn't prepared for.

'You can have five minutes with him, then you'll have to leave,' said Matron. She laid a hand on Nellie's arm. 'You've got to be a brave girl now.' Nellie looked from the matron to Sam and saw, in both faces, pity and resignation.

'He's not going to die!' she said, with a conviction she didn't really feel, but saying it helped and her trembling limbs quieted themselves as she approached the bed.

'Dad, can you hear me? It's Nellie. What've you been doing to yourself?'

The great shattered frame of her father breathed on, but there was no flicker of recognition in his ruined face. She pulled the single chair closer to the bed. 'The doctors are going to sort you out, don't worry about the kids, I'll make sure they're all right. Dad?' She took his hand. The fingers were coarse as an iron file and his palm the hardest leather, but she felt a twitch, a tap against her own palm. 'Do you know me, Dad? It's Nellie.'

Then came a series of weak taps, almost a rhythm, as though her father were keeping time to a tune. His lips formed a word and as Nellie leaned forward she heard '*oops a la la*'. She leaned forward over the bed with a great heaving sob. 'Yes, I remember, Dad, I remember *oops a la la, oops a la la, lost the leg of 'er drawers*. We used to sing it when I was little, didn't we?' A ghost of a smile played on her father's lips and he nodded.

'My little Nellie.' His voice was a hoarse whisper. 'Sorry, duck, sorry about Christmas and everything else, sorry.'

He gasped and let out a cry of pain. Nellie heard the swishing approach of Matron's skirts and leaned forward, urgently. She felt as though she held in her hand the fragile, sweet, short time of her childhood, when she was beloved and life was still a dream.

'Oh, Dad, don't worry about that. I only want you to get better and come home to us.'

He mustered strength with a huge effort, which she felt in his trembling hand. Pulling her close, he whispered a few words into her ear and then fell back into the light of the moon that still shone across his pillow. She held fast to his hand, and it was only when she felt Sam uncurling her fingers that she realized the matron had come back. She heard her talking to Sam, but the voices came from far away and though she knew she must urge her limbs to motion, she found she could not walk.

'Nellie, listen, I'm going to take you home now.'

'What about Dad?' she knew it was a stupid question, but her normally quick mind was focusing in all the wrong places.

'Nellie, Matron says we have to go and there's nothing we can do for your dad. They'll look after him here tonight.'

She nodded. 'Yes, it's Christmas.' She felt proud of herself, surely that was a sensible thing to say. Sam put his arm round her and led her gently out of the ward. They walked back the way they'd come, slowly now, out through the deserted black-and-white tiled colonnade and into St Thomas's Street. With each step came the realization, firstly that her father had always loved her and secondly that she hoped she hadn't found this out too late. She looked up at Sam.

'What am I going to do if he...?'

'Don't think about that. He's still here, isn't he? What did he whisper to you?' Sam must have seen the puzzling exchange and heard the little childhood song.

Nellie spoke softly. 'He said he was sorry, and then he said, "Don't let the goose go to waste."'

'Trust your dad,' said Sam, shaking his head, and they smiled at each other through their tears.

They walked up to London Bridge Station where Sam insisted they get a hansom cab back to Spa Road.

'Two bob for a cab! You don't think I'm going to let you pay that, do you?' Nellie objected.

'Don't argue with me, Nell, you've had a shock and you can't be out in this weather.' The snow was falling more thickly now, coating the pavements and sitting in fluffy shelves along the window ledges. But Nellie stubbornly refused, as Sam pulled out some silver from his pocket and began hailing a cab. She closed her own hand over his, surprised at its warmth.

'Is that what's left of your Christmas club money?'

Sam hesitated.

'Honest, Sam, I'll be all right, we'll just get a tram back. That money's for your family's Christmas and Dad didn't want to spoil Christmas.' Her lower lip trembled and she realized she had not let go of Sam's hand.

'All right, Nell, if you're sure, come on.' He led her to the stop outside the station where a horse-drawn tram, covered in adverts for Pears' soap and Nestlé's milk, was waiting to leave for Southwark Park Road. The horse's breath plumed and he stamped his hooves, impatient to be off. Nellie was glad of the warmth inside and was even gladder for Sam's company. Although they didn't speak and she often turned her face to the window to hide her tears, she felt comforted by his steady presence all the way home.

Christmas Day dawned, with a sky heavy with the threat of more snow. Nellie and Alice had spent a sleepless night, huddled together in the bed in a hopeless bid for warmth and comfort, neither of which had come to them. Eventually they'd crept down to the kitchen as first light broke.

In their whispered conferences of the night, Nellie had related her father's words to Alice.

'I think we should follow his wishes, Al. If it's the last thing we do, we'll bloody cook that goose and eat it, even if we choke on it!' Her sister had nodded her assent, burying her tear-stained face into Nellie's breast.

'Shhh, shhh, Alice, he's a game old bird himself. He won't leave us, not if he's got anything to do with it.'

Nellie allowed herself to think of nothing else but giving her brothers the Christmas their father had wanted. They hadn't woken the boys and she'd decided to keep as much of the accident from them as she could. After she'd arrived home the night before, she and Alice had salvaged an orange and sugar mouse each from the sad remnants of her father's purchases and put them in stockings for the boys, along with silver sixpences. Then they'd washed the goose till every trace of dust and grit was gone, and found potatoes in the sack, and cabbages. Now Nellie set Alice the task of preparing vegetables as she knelt to light the range. The little kitchen felt so cheerless and empty. Even though their father's presence had so often been a threatening one, she still missed it. The house only seemed half its true self without him. Her sister's face looked as grey and bleak as the cold grate. Nellie lit the curled-up newspaper and watched the flames, yellow and orange, dance into life.

'Come on, Al, love,' she said, 'once we've got the fire going and the range on, we'll feel more cheerful, eh?'

Alice nodded and began peeling the potatoes.

Warmth and steam began to fill the kitchen; light crept in through the sash window. Soon tantalizing smells of goose skin crisping and the spicy aroma of Christmas pudding boiling in the copper announced that Christmas Day had arrived, and it wasn't long before they heard the thud of the boys tumbling out of bed and thundering down the stairs. They burst excitedly into the kitchen, holding their stockings aloft, as Nellie poured tea for them all. Bread and hot sausages were ready for their Christmas breakfast and it wasn't until they were all seated round the kitchen table that the boys noticed their father's absence. Nellie forced her face into the false expression of cheer that must last all day.

'Dad's a little bit poorly, boys, and he had to go to the hospital, but he says we must have our Christmas all the same. He was very particular about that.' She smiled encouragingly.

'Have another sausage each.' If she could feed their ignorance with food all day she would be happy to, and they accepted her explanation readily – perhaps, she thought, a little too readily. It saddened her to think how her broken father had robbed himself of their love over the years. It could have been so different, if only he'd let them in a bit earlier. She knew they could have formed the closest of bonds, all of them, after her mother died. They could have huddled, like bereft ducklings, around him; instead he had retreated and blamed the world for his loss.

But while her father was in the hospital, she was head of the house, and she would try to do things differently. She would need all the children's help and was determined that they would be her allies, never her enemies.

'Listen, boys, you're going to have to be the men of the house while Dad's not here.' She hesitated. 'He might not be able to come home straight away. Do you think you can help me and Al with the coal and the firewood?'

Bobby nodded eagerly, biting a chunk out of his sausage. 'An' I'll help you with the laundry, Nell. I can turn the mangle.'

'An' I can fill the copper!' Freddie piped up, not willing to be outdone.

Smiling, she went to each of them, gathering them into her arms and pulling Alice close too.

'We'll be all right, us lot, won't we? We just have to stick together.'

She hoped her sister and brothers did not catch the quiver in her voice, or the trembling of her body, as the comforting lie rose from her lips and hung above them in the steam-filled room.

It was a long day, but Nellie waited until the boys had thoroughly tired themselves out before putting them to bed. She didn't want them giving her sister any trouble. She pulled on her good woollen coat and twined her scarf around her neck. She would walk to the hospital. She had already started to do sums in her head; whatever money her dad had squirrelled away for Christmas was all they had to live on till her next pay day. She would try to see old man Wicks tomorrow; he might see her, even though it was Boxing Day. She would milk as much Christmas kindness from him as she could, though there was no guarantee he would be forthcoming with injury money. Knowing him, he'd be docking money for damage to the cart from her father's wages. She was just thankful that old Thumper had emerged unscathed, otherwise Wicks would be docking the vet bill as well. No, she would be taking no more trams.

'You be all right here with the boys?' Nell asked her sister, who nodded. 'You're a good girl.' She hugged Alice goodbye. 'I don't know what I'd do without you. Please God he'll be all right and we'll just have to get through it till he's home again. Now don't forget to wrap the rest of the goose and put it out in the safe, and we can have bubble and squeak with it tomorrow. We'll have to make do and mend for a while.'

Alice, though still only twelve, knew as well as Nellie did what it meant for her father to be off work. Nellie's wages alone wouldn't be enough to feed them and pay the rent.

'Don't look so worried. I'm going to see Wicks tomorrow, we might get a sub.'

Nellie gave her another squeeze and went out, catching her breath as the biting cold invaded her lungs. She put her head down and started off down the Neckinger till she got to Druid Street arch. She had always hated the arches beneath the railway viaduct; as a child she had run through them to escape their darkness and the thunderous rumbling of the trains overhead that filled them. This particular arch brought back memories of Ted Bosher: it was around here that he'd spent his days making bombs, while pretending to her he was working at the docks. She shook her head; she'd heard nothing from him and neither had Lily. The weeks had gradually drained her of any longing she might have felt for his voice or his touch, but loyalty ran through her like a strong vein of precious metal and it wasn't easy for her to abandon his memory. Now this latest trouble brought into clear focus that he simply wasn't there. His choices had robbed her of her girlish romantic notions and whatever troubles she had to face, Ted Bosher would certainly not be around to support her. She inhaled the freezing air and let its scarifying sharpness scrub all those tender dreams she had for Ted clean away. It felt as if she were cleaning her heart, clearing the decks, getting ready for God knew what almighty battle. She walked quickly through the arch and hurried on down Druid Street, which ran parallel to the viaduct, almost all the way to Guy's. After twenty minutes' fast walking she arrived panting and pink-cheeked. Visiting hours had been relaxed for Christmas Day and so she walked freely on to the ward, passing the rows of patients, some with family members who had obviously brought in Christmas treats. The carbolic smell was overlaid with tints of orange and spice and some effort had been made to decorate the ward. She looked nervously around for Matron, but she made it to the end of the ward unchallenged. Her father's bed was still screened off and she pulled aside one of the screens. The freshly made bed, with its tight-as-a-drum sheets and blankets, was quite empty. She looked over her shoulder in panic, to see Matron approaching. The look of sympathy on her face told Nellie everything.

'I'm sorry, my dear,' was all she said. And she put her arm round Nellie, who, in spite of her resolve to be strong, broke down, sobbing. Matron guided her out of the ward past the rows of patients and visitors, each of whose eyes were lit by a common relief that this time the tragedy was not theirs to weep over.

16

SIX BOB SHORT

No matter how many times she did the sums, the result was always the same: six shillings short. For the want of six shillings a week they might all end up in the workhouse, or if she chose to pay the rent, instead of buying food, they might simply starve. Her choices were becoming terrifyingly simple and every mathematical effort brought her back to the same dead end: she could find no way to make the figures add up to more. Nellie turned over the piece of paper and began again. Sitting at the kitchen table by the light of a candle end she fought her lonely battle with shillings and pence. She worked out their outlays to the last farthing. Eight shillings for rent; twelve and six for a very little meat, potatoes, bread, jam, sugar, tea and milk; two and six for coals, wood and soap: twenty-three shillings was the very least it would take to keep the four of them. This was six shillings more than their income and even so it didn't include a penny for new clothes, or boots for the boys, who seemed to be growing like bean plants. God forbid she ever got ill and couldn't work; in that event any choices would be taken completely out of her hands. Dad's penny policy had buried him and had given them the breathing space they needed, while the remainder had paid January's rent. At least 1913 had brought one good thing with it – Alice had turned thirteen and could start work at Pearce Duff's, for the girl's wage of six shillings a week. Nellie's wage was now eleven shillings and she blessed the memory of Eliza James every day for that. But she banged the table in frustration; seventeen shillings a week was still not enough.

Something had to be done and done quickly, or they'd all end up on the streets; she would not even contemplate the workhouse, which loomed like an ogre at the edges of her imagination and filled her dreams with nightmare visions of the boys being torn from her arms. So, for the moment, her only choice was to pay the rent next week and if she had to live on bread and tea, so be it, at least the others would be fed. A knock on the door interrupted her brooding. It was past ten o'clock and late-night callers were not usual. Alice and the boys were in bed, so she crept to the front door and called softly through the letterbox.

'Who's that?'

'It's me, Lily!' came the unexpected reply.

Nellie opened the door quickly. 'What you doing here this time of night? I thought you were going out with Jock.'

Lily bustled in, bringing the cold night air, which hung damply to her coat. She was buzzing with an almost tangible excitement. 'I was – but I had to come and tell you first, love, he wants us to get married!'

Her friend did a little pirouette in the passage and Nellie dragged her into the kitchen.

'Gawd, Nell, it's like the black hole o'Calcutta in here. Why are you sitting in the dark?'

Nellie quickly went to light the gas lamp. She didn't want to dampen Lily's excitement with tales of her own troubles, but her friend was quick enough to register the paper covered in sums on the kitchen table.

'Oh, Nellie, don't tell me things are so tight you can only afford candlelight? Didn't Wicks help you out?'

Nellie shook her head. 'Not a penny from him, but Dad's workmates had a whip-round, and then there was the penny policy come out, but that's gone now. But listen...' she scooped her workings off the table and scrunched it into a ball '...we're not talking about my troubles now. Tell me all about it, start to finish!'

'He only asked me tonight, but to be honest it wasn't a surprise. Well, I knew he was keen, Nell, right from that first night we met, it was on the Christmas Eve . . .' Lily hesitated, as if unsure whether to go on or not.

'Is that why you've said nothing?' Nellie reached out and hugged Lily across the table. 'Life has to go on, Lil.'

'I know, but it didn't seem right to be talking about my happiness when you've been going through it like this.'

Nellie was secretly grateful for her friend's delicacy, not because she wouldn't have been pleased for her but because she might not have been able to show it. Now, as the details emerged of Jock and Lily's whirlwind courtship, Nellie remembered her own dreams. Suddenly she felt a resurgence of the young girl she'd been only the year before. The flush of romance Lily had brought in with her and the excitement in her bright eyes took Nellie out of her dire situation, and with that relief came the inner assurance that everything would be all right – she would find a way.

'Now I must go and tell me mum,' said Lily, getting up and throwing on her coat.

'Give her my love,' Nellie said as she saw her friend to the door.

'Who knows, Nell, might be you next, eh?'

But as she looked into her friend's eyes Nellie saw a shadow dim their brightness and without being told knew Lily was thinking of Ted and what might have been. But she felt impervious to his memory; whatever power he had to dazzle her had been largely driven by her own long-vanished naivety. Ted might have robbed her of trust, but he certainly hadn't dented her hope, her strength or her resolve. She felt bold enough to ask, 'Have you heard from him?'

Lily nodded and then concentrated on buttoning her coat. 'We did get a letter.'

'You don't have to pussyfoot around me, Lil. I'm not under any illusions where Ted's concerned, not any more.'

'He told Mum not to worry, then went into one of his rants, says there's work to be done out there, and I don't think he was talking about the sort that brings in any money. He's staying with friends, Bolshies by the sound of it, and...' She paused, then went on. 'Well, you might as well hear it from me, he's taken up with some Russian tart called Tatyana or something, so I don't think he'll be coming home soon, love.'

Nellie shrugged. 'I feel sorry for your mum,' was all she said, but in her mind she heard the click of a door quietly shutting. When Lily was gone she turned off the gas lamp and wearily climbed the stairs to bed. Her sums could wait till morning; all she wanted now was a night of dreamless sleep.

Old Wicks was a wiry, weasel-faced man in his late sixties. He had a receding chin and a protruding forehead, and squashed between the two was a face permanently screwed into suspicious defensiveness. Her father had always said Wicks feared being cheated more than anything in the world. 'And that's only because he's such a bloody cheat himself!' Her father complained how Wicks would dock them half a day's pay if they were even a few minutes late in the morning.

'By *his* watch, though!' Her father would tap his own watch vigorously to illustrate the point. 'Mine is always on time, but he keeps his running five minutes fast, just to trip us up, thinks we're all bloody idiots.'

The run-ins between her father and Wicks were explosive, but George was his most experienced carter and there was no one, apart from Sam, who was half so good with the horses. Wicks was a man of means and property: he owned not only the stable yard but the houses either side, one of which had always been Nellie's home. She knew Wicks would like nothing more than for her to fall into rent arrears, now her father was gone: he could get more if he rented the place out to two families. They'd been lucky to have the whole house to themselves – it wasn't uncommon to have a family of four occupy one bedroom, sharing the kitchen or scullery with another family living in the other bedroom. Wicks could almost double his rent at a stroke.

There he stood, as he did each Monday evening, hand held out. Nellie carefully counted out the eight shillings and then he counted it again, keeping her waiting on the doorstep, a bitter wind catching at her skirt and leeching all the precious heat out of the house. The few sparse strands of sandy hair on his balding head lifted and flicked like little whips and she hated the sight of his cherry-red lips, moving silently as he counted the last farthing. He nodded and she loathed his nodding head with its liver spots and scabs.

He had offered not a word of sympathy since the death of her father and had only alluded to it once. That was on the day of the funeral, when George's fellow drivers lined up at the yard gate to see him off. Sam Gilbie and the other men had stood with caps in hands, while the neighbours came to their doors in respectful silence. Nellie saw Wicks pushing his way through them to where she and the children were standing in their mourning black. They were about to set off, walking behind the hearse, but she stopped and turned, meaning to thank Wicks for coming. She had been hoping he would turn up with her father's last pay packet, for he was owed a week's money.

Instead Wicks nodded curtly and launched into a complaint. 'Your father had no right using that cart on his own time. Do you know how much it's costing to put the thing back on the road? I'm docking his last pay for it, so don't expect anything from me.'

With that he turned abruptly away, ignoring the looks of disgust from his drivers and the disapproving mutterings of the neighbours. Nellie was too shocked to reply, but Sam was at her side.

'Don't worry about that heartless bastard, Nellie.' She had never heard him swear before, but she could see now his face was red with suppressed rage, his knuckles white, as he clenched his fists. He was holding an envelope, which he handed to her. 'Here, take this, me and the boys had a whip-round.'

The tears, which she'd held back successfully so far, now

brimmed over, staining the black silk dress with round damp splotches.

'Thanks, Sam, I'm so grateful. Thank the other men for me, will you?'

He nodded and put a hand on her arm. 'If you need anything, let me know. Don't try doing it all on your own, will you?'

She covered his hand with her own and swallowed her tears. How well he knew her.

'Come on, Dolly Daydream, you're holding up the line. You've filled one packet in ten minutes!'

Nellie, startled out of her musings, dropped the packet, spilling custard powder all over her shoes. 'Bugger!' She hopped back. It was bad enough trying to get the yellow dust out of her hair each evening, without filling her boots with it. Lily, who'd been waiting patiently for the packet for pasting, gave Nellie a sympathetic look. None of them liked attracting the attention of the foreman. A martinet who rarely gave the girls an inch, Albert was proud of the custard tarts' output and if they were behind quota would often refuse them toilet breaks with a smirking instruction to 'Cross your legs!'. How long he'd been standing behind her, she hadn't a clue. She wanted to yell into his round, stupid face that it was his fault, but she must do nothing to jeopardize this job, and, anyway, today she had to ask him a favour, so instead she speeded up and tried hard to focus on the monotonous task before her.

As Albert walked away, Maggie Tyrell caught Nellie's eye and mouthed, 'Tin soldier! Take no notice.'

Nellie smiled. Her friends at Duff's had helped get her through the awful Christmas and New Year. Maggie had organized a collection and those that had no money to spare turned up at her door with rice puddings and egg custards, or a loaf of bread. Some sent bits of clothing for the boys, anything to let her know she was not alone. But what they could not do was to take the worry away – it ate at her night and day. The penny policy money was gone and next week the rent and food would be coming out of her and Alice's wages. She had to find extra money from somewhere.

When the time came for their team's ten-minute morning break she told Lily to go on without her and nervously approached Albert, who was inspecting a machine that had clogged up. He was lying on his back with his nose virtually stuck up a delivery chute.

'Get us a spanner!' For a moment she thought he'd addressed her. She looked around for the spanner, at a loss, but just then one of the young boys who ran errands jumped up from behind the machine and ran off in search of the spanner.

Nellie coughed. 'Albert, could I have a word, please?' she asked, hating the fact that he'd ignored her presence. He might be under the machine, but he could bloody well see her legs. She resisted the urge to put the toe of her boot into the paunch poking out from his waistcoat and instead waited patiently for a response.

'Not the best time.' Albert wriggled further under.

'It's me break.' She hunkered down and looked under the machine. He was red-faced and trying to pry off a plate. 'I was just wondering, Albert, if I could have a couple of hours' overtime?'

Just then the boy returned with the spanner.

'No, you dozy little sod, this is a socket wrench. I want an open spanner!' Albert flung the wrench at the little boy's ankles, Leaping out of the way, he dashed off again without a word.

'I could really do with a couple of hours' evening shift, if there's any, Albert,' Nellie persisted.

Now he deigned to pull himself out from under the machine.

'You've got the kids now, haven't you?' he asked, wiping off his greasy hands with a cloth.

She nodded.

'You women with kids are always letting us down on the evening shifts,' he mumbled, almost to himself. 'Any rate, I've got no overtime, Nell. All the shifts are full. Where's that lazy little sod with the spanner?' He could barely look at her. She knew very well that there were spaces on the evening shift, but Albert was notorious for giving any spare overtime to his favourites.

'Well, I'd be very grateful if anything did come up.' Still she had to be polite, deferential, pretend not to know the way the system worked, but she would get nowhere with Albert.

Nellie returned disconsolately to her bench just as the girls were coming back from their break. Before she started up the machine again she leaned over to Maggie. 'I've got to get some more money coming in, Mag.'

'Is that what you've been worrying about all morning?'

Nellie nodded. 'Albert says I can't have any more hours.'

Maggie raised her eyes. 'Make you beg, did he?'

Nellie pulled a face, trying to replace the humiliation she felt with an appearance of defiance.

'What about home work?' Maggie asked. 'Me and the kids get a bit extra making matchboxes – your boys could help you.'

It was a possibility that had occurred to her, but she'd dismissed it, mainly because her father had always looked down on families that took in home work. But could she afford to carry the burden of her dead father's pride? She could also hear the echo of Madam Mecklenburgh's voice, attacking those who took advantage of women and children forced to do 'sweated work'. 'White slavers', she'd called them. She had worked with the Anti Sweated Labour League and had even urged the factory women to boycott any home work they were doing on the side. But to Nellie all that seemed a long time ago and the temptation to find at least some of those missing six shillings in a pile of matchboxes was too great.

'How much do they pay?' she asked Maggie.

'Tuppence 'apenny the gross.'

'Is that all! What's that? Twelve dozen matchboxes? And how long does that take you?'

'Well, you might do six dozen an hour, but if the kids are working with you, you could treble that. I'll take you down the depot, if you want.'

Nellie said she would think about it. Eliza James had been right, though, they would certainly be slaving away. As she stood packing the custard powder, she did the sums in her head. If the four of them worked every evening for three hours, they might make three shillings a week. Still three bob short of what she needed, but it would be better than nothing. As they left the factory that evening, she ran to catch up with Maggie, who had her arms full of screaming baby. Maggie's youngest daughter, Amy, had brought little Lenny to the factory gates, glad to hand over her burden.

Maggie looked up apologetically, indicating the infant. 'This one's teething. Poor Amy's had a day of it, haven't you, love?'

Nellie spared a smile for Amy. The ten-year-old's dirty face was framed with a tangle of fair hair and her short pinafore hung well above what looked like a pair of her brother's cast-off boots. Nellie remembered how, at that age, she'd been in charge of the babies. School wasn't considered a priority when there was childminding to be done.

'You're a good helper for your mum, aren't you?' The child nodded vigorously.

'Maggie, I've decided to do the home work. When are you going to the Bryant & May depot?'

'Tonight, after this one's fed. I'll come and knock you up, all right, love?' And she was off at a near run, rushing home to get the tea and settle the youngest of her six children before work started for the evening.

Now all Nellie had to do was convince the boys to join in this new game, what Eliza James would certainly call the 'child slave' game.

But it wasn't easy. Alice was doubtful. 'Dad wouldn't have liked it.' She looked exhausted; an eleven-hour day at Duff's had come as a shock to her. She was much frailer than Nellie, who had inherited George Clark's strong bones, and since their father's death she and Nellie had tacitly agreed to eat less, so the boys would not go hungry. Nellie hated to put more work on her young shoulders. She handed Alice another plate to wash up.

'Listen, Al, I don't want to frighten you, love, but it's either this or the streets, and it's still not enough.' The tremor in her voice seemed to steel Alice. Carefully sliding the last of the plates into the rack above the wooden draining board, she pulled the plug from the stone sink and turned a determined face to Nellie.

'Well, it won't be too bad. What else we going to do with our time, eh?'

'Good girl!'

Together the sisters finished drying the blue and white crockery, Alice stacked it away in the scullery cupboard, while Nellie explained her plan. 'I'm going with Maggie tonight, to get the stuff. Will you be all right with the boys till I get back?'

Alice nodded, a smile lighting her pale face as she turned towards the broom cupboard. ''Course I will, you go and get yourself ready.' Nellie looked on doubtfully as her sister began vigorously sweeping the red-tiled scullery floor, all traces of her earlier weariness banished in her eagerness to support the new venture. 'Go on!' Alice urged. 'Maggie'll be here soon. I'll be fine!'

When Maggie knocked, Nellie was surprised that she had four of her six children with her.

'These are me little donkeys!' Maggie explained. 'They help me lug all the sides and the glue back.' They were soon ready and set off like a small tribe on a foraging trip, up to the matchbox depot at London Bridge to collect the raw materials for the boxes. Nellie almost threw the glue pot at the warehouseman when he told her she had to purchase it herself. She was given the rudimentary instructions to assemble the matchbox and paste on the label, and then hefted the material in a hessian sack on to her back. There was a strap of leather designed to go over her head and she supported the weight of it by cupping her hands behind her back.

It was a long, neck-wrenching, back-aching walk back to Spa Road. She ignored the looks of passers-by. Maggie's bravado enrobed them all in a brash cloak of protection. 'Had your penn'orth?' she would fling at anyone who stared too hard.

'Only trying to make a living, so what's it to you?'

Her little ones joined in, capering and laughing, shouting: 'Made yer look, made yer stare, made the barber cut yer 'air!' at the gawpers, till they were forced to retreat. By the time Nellie arrived home, exhausted, Alice had put the boys to bed. Nellie dumped the sack in the kitchen.

'We'll have to work out a better way of getting the boxes back up to London Bridge, once we've made them. Maggie's got a little army of her kids to help her, but I don't want to drag you and the boys up there every week, if I can help it.'

Alice put a cup of tea in front of her and as Nellie sipped thoughtfully, she had the beginnings of an idea as to where she might find the help she needed.

17

A MATTER OF TRUST

'Please come, Nellie!' Lily pleaded. 'It's only a drink and a few sandwiches, and Jock's paying.' Nellie and Alice were walking home after work with Lily, who'd been waging a campaign all day. She was determined that they'd both be there at the Green Ginger that night, to celebrate her engagement.

'Lil, I can't just leave the boys on their own at night, and anyway, we've got to get our quota of boxes done for next week,' Nellie reasoned wearily.

'Well, the boys can come too. We'll send them out some ginger beer and a pint of winkles. Surely they deserve a little bit of a treat. They've been so good.'

Lily had hit just the right note. Nellie felt guilty every time she looked at her brothers' eager, bright faces and nimble fingers as they played the 'game' of assembling the matchboxes. Bobby was a painfully careful worker, holding up every box for inspection with a 'Will this do, Nell?' She'd had to tell him that the boxes weren't intended for the queen and no one was going to send them back because of a crooked label, so he could afford to go a little faster.

Every evening, for weeks, they had gathered round the kitchen table, with the glue pot and brush in the middle, Nellie pasting the label and putting on the sides, Bobby and Freddy forming them into boxes. Alice made the drawers and stuck on the striking edge. Nellie was glad of the boys' enthusiasm – for them it was fun to feel grown up and of use. For the first couple of hours each night they chattered and laughed, producing astonishing amounts of boxes between them, but later in the evening their heads began to droop and their eyes to close. They worked till they dropped and then Alice would take them upstairs while Nellie carried on.

Soon they couldn't move for matchboxes: there were piles under the stairs, then in the coal hole, and finally they were tripping over them in the bedrooms. But worse than the nightly toil, had been the weekly trip up to the depot. Walking to London Bridge and back with their burdens of matchboxes was proving so exhausting for the boys that they were falling asleep at school. Poor Alice felt the shame of it keenly, and had pleaded with Nellie to be let off the trek, but the stark fact was that the more boxes they could carry to the depot, the more they were paid. There was no doubt that, at the end of the week, they could all do with a rest.

'Oh, all right, Lil, I'm so sick of matchboxes I'm likely to strike a lucifer and send the lot of us up in flames! We'll all come then, but just for an hour!'

Lily jumped up and down excitedly. 'Sam will be there too,' she said. 'He's going to be Jock's best man, did I tell you?'

Nellie nodded in approval. 'I'm not surprised and he couldn't have picked a better one.'

'He's still holding a torch for you, I think,' Lily said, a mischievous light playing in her eyes.

Nellie sighed impatiently. 'Do you think I've got time for that sort of thing these days?' But she had her own reasons for being pleased that Sam would be there, which she didn't divulge to Lily.

'There's always time for *that sort of thing*, Nellie Clark!' Her friend winked at her and Nellie found herself caught up by Lily's infectious humour. By the time Lily left them, they were all giggling.

And as Lily walked on towards her house with a jaunty step, she called back. 'Be there at seven. I'll save a place for you... next to Sam!'

Nellie and Alice hurried on towards Vauban Street. Nellie had noticed her sister's eyes light up the minute she'd agreed to the outing and now she was eager to get home and tell the boys. But as soon as they heard the news they became so over-excited they were hardly able to eat their tea. Nellie was adamant – not a scrap was going into the dustbin in this house. 'If you don't finish your bread and jam, we ain't going and that's that!'

That settled it and they were as quiet as lambs as they went off to wipe their faces and damp down unruly hair.

Now they were wrapped up in warm jackets and scarves, sitting on a wall outside the Green Ginger with the other children. Nellie handed them a pin and the pewter pot of black winkles.

'Sit here and don't move, Alice will be out to check in a minute.'

They nodded obediently. At the pub door she looked back and saw, by the light of the gas lamp, that Bobby had already planted a black beauty spot from the top of the shellfish on to one little girl's cheek. She smiled, relieved. They didn't look like child slaves; they were having fun, just as children should.

Lily had been as good as her word and Nellie sat in the place saved for her next to Sam. They talked for a while about his mother. And there it was again – Nellie could feel that invisible thread of a promise tugging anxiously at her heart. She listened quietly as he told Nellie that Lizzie's liver disease, brought on, so the doctors had said, by years of hard toil and poverty, couldn't be cured. But in spite of her slow decline, she was still managing to rule the house from her truckle bed. Nellie noticed that talking about his mother seemed to drain the joy from Sam's face. Suddenly she came to a decision. She pulled out from her bag a drawing she had made on the back of an old envelope and spread it out on the table in front of them. Making herself heard above the din and laughter surrounding them, she leaned forward to explain her plan to him.

'I know it's a big favour to ask, Sam, it being a family heirloom, but I wouldn't ask if I wasn't desperate. I can't go on dragging the kids up to London Bridge every week.'

'Of course you can use it, Nell. Me dad would be only too pleased to think of it being put to good use, but...'

She held her breath as he silently appraised her plan.

'Please say it will work!' she burst out, and startled Sam, who could only laugh at Nellie's resolve. He seemed to relax.

'Well, I'd say it all depends on the quality of the workmanship, which of course will be of the very finest; *and...*' he went on before she could interrupt him, 'the skill of the driver, which is the risky bit!'

'Are you saying I can't do it?' Nellie bristled at the suggestion, even though she had her own doubts. Sam held his hands up in mock defence.

'I'm not saying that, I'm just thinking you'll need a bit more practice, you've only done it once!'

The plan had come to her, while thinking about her brothers' truncated childhoods. One of their favourite street games, before matchbox-making took over their lives, had been to trundle around the cobbled streets on a box cart, made from an orange crate mounted on to old pram wheels. One would push and the other would sit in the crate, steering the thing with a piece of rope attached to the front wheels. It had struck her as an ideal sort of conveyance for the completed matchboxes, but she needed something bigger and faster. The butcher's boy, making deliveries with a basket attached to his bicycle, had furnished the other part of the design she'd presented to Sam.

'The trailer's got to attach to the back of the penny-farthing, so that when you go round a corner, the box goes round too, something like this...' he said, sketching in a curved bar, designed to attach the proposed trailer to the penny-farthing frame. 'See, if we put in greased pins at each end of this bar, the crate should follow the bike wherever it turns!'

Nellie nodded. 'That looks just the ticket. I'm not keen on coming a cropper with twelve gross of matchboxes on the back! I could practise this Sunday... that's if you think you can make the cart by then?'

'I'll go down the docks tomorrow and sort out a nice deep crate, but it's got to be light enough for you too.'

By this time, Jock had wandered over and was peering at the sketch on the table. He moved Sam's pint out of the way, intrigued. 'I reckon we've got an old crate just the right size at the shop,' he offered. Jock worked at his father's ship chandlers in Rotherhithe Street. 'There's all sorts of odd bits of iron in the back yard that might come in handy. Bring the bike in tomorrow, and I'll help you if you like.'

Sam grinned at his friend. 'Another pair of hands won't come amiss, even a south paw's like yours! The only problem is getting hold of two pram wheels... unless we could borrow some...' Sam glanced towards the pub door, where sounds of Bobby and Freddie's laughter drifted in from outside.

Nellie got his meaning straight away. 'Well, I'll have to promise we'll give them back... one day! Besides, I've got the two of them so busy making boxes, they don't have time to play carting any more.' Her voice trailed off and her sadness made its impression on Sam.

'Nell, they're good boys,' he said gently. 'They understand everything's changed now, playtime's over.'

She looked at him thoughtfully. 'You must have felt the same when your dad died, Sam. Was it all down to you?'

He nodded. 'Well, there was no one else could take on the kids and Mum's been so ill since, so I just got on with it.'

She felt strangely strengthened, knowing that here was someone who knew exactly what she was going through. Sam had become the family breadwinner at an even earlier age; he had managed and, with his help, so would she.

That night as she fell wearily into bed, she found herself feeling more hopeful than she had for a long time. And her dreams were full of penny-farthing bicycles with wheels made from shiny shillings and silver sixpences.

The next day was Saturday. Sam and Nellie both worked in the morning and had agreed to meet at Wicks's stables that afternoon. Nellie stood watch behind the lace curtain of her kitchen, waiting till she saw Wicks leave the stable yard. She made a face at him from her hiding place: it was childish but satisfying, and made her grin to herself. The old man often left Sam in the stables to finish feeding the horses; but it wouldn't do to draw Wicks's attention to the penny-farthing, still hidden there. Knowing him, he'd want to charge Sam rent on it!

Once Wicks was out of sight, she left her house and ran to the yard gates, a sack over her shoulder, containing the two pram wheels liberated from the boy's box cart. Sam was waiting for her at the gates with the old penny-farthing.

'How did you get on?' He cast a conspiratorial glance towards Nellie's house.

'They weren't too happy about it. Freddie says he wants a treat out of the home-work money, as he's providing the wheels, cheeky little git!'

Sam laughed. 'I don't reckon he's destined to stay poor all his life, do you, Nell?'

She smiled ruefully, handing over the sack to Sam. He tied it over his shoulder and mounted the penny-farthing.

'I'll bring it back tomorrow afternoon. Make sure you're fighting fit – I'll be putting you through your paces!' With a wave, Sam was off, wheeling over the cobblestones with the sack bouncing on his back.

'Good luck!' Nellie called out to him, and hurried back to boil potatoes for dinner, before marshalling Alice and the boys for their afternoon's work.

'Oh, you've already done it, good girl!' she said, smiling, as she walked in the front door.

In the kitchen, Alice was busy peeling potatoes and had already sliced the little bit of mutton they had been able to afford. The young girl had stepped into her role as Nellie's helpmeet without complaint, but she seemed subdued today. 'What's the matter, love? You look worn out.'

Alice did not find the long hours of custard-powder packing easy, especially when it was her turn to load the trolleys – trundling the heavy carts of completed packages to the loading lifts had taken its toll on her back. Nellie had begged her to transfer over to the print shop, where all the Duff's packaging was produced. As a bag maker, at least she'd be sitting down all day, but Alice had refused to be parted from her sister. She would stay on custard, however hard the work.

'It's not that I'm worn out, Nell. I don't mind the work, it's just I'm a bit worried.'

Nellie took the saucepan of potatoes from her sister and put it on the range to boil. 'We'll be all right, Al. We're staying together and we're stopping in this house, Wicks or no Wicks. I'm going to make bloody sure of that.'

Alice shook her head. 'That's you all over, Nell. I know you'll do it, but what I'm worried about is you'll kill yourself trying!'

Nellie was shocked. She hadn't imagined the girl's worries were about her. 'What do you mean?'

Alice sat at the table, turning mournful eyes to her sister. 'I mean that contraption! You can't ride it up to London Bridge with all this stuff in it.' She spread her arms to indicate the piles of matchboxes. 'The first cart comes round the corner'll tip you over and if the same thing happens to you as happened to Dad, what will we do then?'

Alice brushed away the tears trickling down her cheeks.

'Oh, love, is that what you think?' Nellie went to her side and put her arm round Alice's shoulders. 'Listen, I promise I'll be careful, and Sam's going to make me practise and practise, he says, before he'll let me on the road.'

Alice looked up. 'Is that what he said?'

Nellie nodded and Alice seemed satisfied. 'That's all right, then, you can trust Sam. He'll look after you.'

Nellie had no doubt what her sister meant: if Ted had proved himself untrustworthy, then Sam was of a completely different breed. 'You can trust Sam,' she had said, and suddenly for Nellie the world turned. She looked down at her young sister, knowing she had spoken a truth that had been silently growing like a hidden wildflower between the cracks of her heart. Silently she mashed the potatoes, ladled them on to the plates and called the boys, listening to their chatter as they ate, but all the while with a litany echoing in her mind: *Sam will look after you.*

Her one concern had been to look after others for so long she had forgotten entirely that she might need looking after herself, and if she ever had admitted the possibility she'd dismissed it, in the certain knowledge that there *was* no one in her life who could look after her, not now. But Alice's words had shown her how wrong that was. For months it had been Sam, quietly there when she needed someone the most. When Ted was putting her in utmost danger, Sam had been there to divert that danger from her path; when her father had been struck down, Sam's steady presence by her side had made her feel she was not alone, and now here he was again, making sure she had exactly what she needed. It might only be an old bicycle and a box cart, but it was her means of keeping the family in one piece and it was as precious to her as any golden chariot. As she joined her family round their work table to begin the monotonous labour of assembling hundreds more matchboxes, finally, to her own astonishment, she believed it herself. She could trust Sam.

But Nellie soon found out that even Sam could not protect her from the bumps and grazes she earned during the hours of practice that he put her through. He turned up on Sunday afternoon, proudly showing off the fruits of his labour.

'It works a treat!' he said, demonstrating how the trailer cart obediently swung round behind the penny-farthing.

'You and Jock should be proud of yourselves!' Nellie said, delighted. 'It's plenty big enough. Now get off and let me have a go!'

Nellie practically pushed Sam off the bicycle, in her eagerness to try for herself. She was annoyed that her first attempts were much less impressive than her first secret midnight ride around Wicks's stable yard. After her fourth tumble she began to despair.

'It's the bloody cart. I could ride it fine without,' she said, dusting off her skirt and examining the graze on her elbow. It didn't help that her training was taking place in front of the entire street. She was proving to be excellent Sunday afternoon entertainment for the assembled children. They were voluble in their encouragement and equally exultant every time Nellie toppled off. She was getting fed up.

'Can't we go somewhere else to practise, Sam? What about the park?' she begged, in desperation.

He looked round at the eager faces of the children, all waiting to see the next part of the show, then shook his head. 'They'll only follow us, now they're on the scent. Anyway, you'll be in full public view down Tooley Street, so you might as well get used to an audience.'

Resignedly, Nellie got back on and, after another hour, was able to perfect a figure of eight without upending either the trailer or herself. She blew out a sigh of relief, when Sam finally announced, 'All right, that's enough for today. You'll do.'

But she knew there would be a price to pay for her gruelling training session and when she woke on Monday morning the bruises she had earned were ripening and her muscles felt as if they'd been stretched through the mangle one by one.

At work, she even had the foreman's sympathy when she gave up pushing a full cartload of custard powder and slumped over in exhaustion. 'Crikey, Nellie, what's happened to your strength?' Albert asked as he gave her a rare helping hand.

'Oh, I'll be all right, Albert. It's just I was up early, doing the laundry, that's all.' It was a convincing enough half-lie. She had indeed been boiling the boys' shirts in the copper before work. But Albert didn't have to know she had put herself through the wringer on Sunday.

On Tuesday evening, the boys and Alice helped her carry the carefully wrapped parcels of matchboxes out to their small back yard, where the penny-farthing was now to be kept. They loaded the cart up, packing it to the limit with the precious fruits of their labour, finally covering it all with a piece of old tarpaulin. Nellie strapped it down securely and opened the gate leading to the back alley.

'All right, boys, be good for Alice while I'm gone. Straight to bed now.' She kissed them all. 'Go on,' she shooed them in, 'don't look at me, or I'll wobble!'

They obediently closed the gate. Nellie mounted the penny-farthing, unaware that three anxious pairs of eyes were peering through the slats in the gate at her unsteady progress along the alley. She concentrated hard to get the rhythm of the wheels going, before reaching the end of the alley and turning into the street. The full cart responded well to the turn and she blessed Sam and Jock's idea of a lock that prevented the thing from swinging round too far and knocking her off. She eased into a faster rhythm at the top of Spa Road. It was a still, warm March evening, almost spring-like, and couples were out walking. Some stopped to stare, others waved and shouted encouragement, but she daren't take her eyes off the road.

Soon her trepidation turned to exhilaration. She ventured some more speed as she turned down Grange Road and into Bermondsey Street, the power of propelling herself forward transforming itself from hard work into an unexpected joy that rose from her feet to her heart, and for the first time since her father's death she felt truly light-hearted. Her skirt whipped away and the breeze caught in the sleeves of her jacket, her hair lifted, and the cobwebs of her mourning and struggle seemed swept away. She smiled to think she could drop off the boxes, get paid and load up with material for the next week's work in a fraction of the time it would otherwise have taken her. And what's more, the boys hadn't been dragged through the streets to be objects of derision; they were safe in bed, and for once she'd be in bed herself before midnight. She would be there and back in no time!

Later she would put it down to vanity and a hatpin. If she had worn her old wide flat cap, it would never have happened, but she'd chosen to wear her pretty little straw hat. The hatpin had never been long enough to secure that hat to her abundant chestnut hair, so when her increased speed lifted the hat from her head, it flew off, causing Nellie to make a grab for it; but riding one-handed wasn't something she'd practised. The big wheel wobbled, the little cart responded, and when Nellie leaned over to compensate she found herself flying through the air. She landed safely but ignominiously on her backside, not far from her hat.

'Bloody hat!' she addressed the offending article of clothing, and snatched it up. Fortunately, she had reached the less busy area of Crucifix Lane running alongside the railway arches, so no one had witnessed her tumble. She brushed off her skirt and attended to the penny-farthing. The trailer was on its side, still attached to the cycle, and luckily, the tarpaulin and ropes had held fast, so the matchboxes were intact.

'Thank Gawd for that!' she whispered in relief. The thought of all their hard work being ruined was too sickening to contemplate.

But by the time she had struggled to right the bicycle and trailer, she was cursing her over-confidence. The accident had delayed her badly and she only made it to the depot in the nick of time. Then the storeman insisted on tallying each gross before he paid her out, so by the time she had loaded up the materials for the next week, darkness was falling.

She got back on to the bicycle, angry at the tears that caught in her throat. 'You turn on the water taps too quick!' she told herself, in her father's stern voice. Whether it was the fault of the hatpin or the tardy storeman, the result was that she was cycling home much later than she had expected, and as she rode by London Bridge Station she spotted a couple standing just beyond the light of a gas lamp. From a distance it looked like a touching family scene, perhaps one of farewell, as the woman was holding a bag over one arm and an infant in the other. The young man, presumably the father, leaned over to kiss the baby gently on the forehead, before the woman and child disappeared into the train station. A cold sickness seemed to descend over Nellie's heart, for although she could not see the woman clearly by the time she'd passed them, she was certain that the male figure, now turning back to the dimly lit street, had been that of Sam Gilbie.

18

CHOICES, MISTAKES AND PROMISES

I couldn't care tuppence, she thought. If he's got a fancy woman, good luck to him. What's it to me?

But words which once might have been true, carelessly tripping off her tongue, now turned round to bite her. She simply could not rid herself of the sick feeling lodged in her stomach, the churning disorientation of seeing Sam there, with a woman and child he had never mentioned. She thought she knew him; even more foolishly, she believed he knew her. Perhaps he did, and perhaps he had used that knowledge to manipulate her feelings, just as Ted had. But Sam – could she really believe it of him? And even if it were true, why should she care? It was nothing to her.

The endless cycle of questions whirled round and round in her head, till she was sick of them. Eventually a small voice inside her insisted on giving the answer: she cared because she cared, and it wasn't nothing, it was definitely something.

Even so, the next time she saw Sam Gilbie she prepared herself to give him a cooler reception than she usually did. But when he knocked at the door after work a few days later, his fresh open face made her thoughts of deception and manipulation seem absurd. Still, she told herself, she knew what she had seen.

'Well, did you manage all right?' he asked.

'Fine!' she lied brightly. She saw him glance doubtfully at her grazed knuckles.

'You might as well tell me what happened. I thought it was funny you never came and told me all about it.'

She shook her head dismissively. 'Don't look so worried.

I'm all right, but you might need to give the bike the once-over, though.'

She opened the door and led him through the passage to the back yard. On the way, he put his head round the kitchen door. 'I'm just borrowing your foreman – no slacking, you lot!'

The boys laughed at his mock sternness.

'I'll keep them at it, don't worry about that!' Alice said.

The penny-farthing was propped against the back wall of the yard and Sam bent down to inspect the damage.

'How did you know I'd come a cropper?' she asked.

'Little bird.' He was already tightening the bolt on the cart axle and didn't look up.

'That Alice! I'll kill her, I told her not to say anything.'

She looked on as he methodically checked each bolt and screw and lined up the wheels to make sure they were still true.

'It's nothing to be ashamed of, Nell. These things ain't easy to control, even without a cart behind you.'

'I wouldn't have forgiven myself if I'd broke the bike, though.'

'Oh, Nell, the bike don't matter! So long as you're in one piece, that's all I'm worried about.' He got up, wiping his hands on a handkerchief.

'You seem a bit down in the mouth, though. I thought you'd be happier now your deliveries are easier… Don't worry about the tumble, you'll get better at it,' he said encouragingly.

Her face was revealing more of her doubts than she had realized and she could see he was puzzled by the change in her demeanour. They had reached an easy sort of friendship, one that tonight she felt incapable of.

'Perhaps I'm just tired.'

'You work all the hours God sends, you've got every right to be tired, but I'm getting the feeling I've done something wrong.'

She sighed. She had no right to make him feel awkward; he'd been nothing but kindness. She wanted to take a step back, but her heart, like the penny-farthing, seemed to have no reverse gear. She leaned against the wall and gazed up, beyond the crowded rooftops and chimneys, to a patch of sky, now suffused with a deep orange glow. Soon it would be too dark and they would go inside. If she was going to say anything, this was as private a place as they would get.

'You're not in trouble, Sam, and anyway, it's nothing to do with me.'

'Th-there you are, I knew there was something wrong!' His stammer had returned and he looked flustered.

He obviously wouldn't let her get away with saying nothing, and not knowing was clearly upsetting him. She took a deep breath. 'Oh, well, it's been playing on me mind so I might as well have my say.'

He looked worried. Was it guilt? 'What is it? Tell me, Nellie.'

'It's just that I saw you, at least I think it was you... Tuesday night, up at London Bridge, with a woman and a baby.' There, it was out, and before she could change her mind, she rushed on. 'And that's your business, but I was just surprised you'd never said a word about it. I thought we were friends,' she ended lamely.

His face reddened immediately and then she knew she had not been mistaken. 'We *are* friends!' he said, looking her in the eyes, in spite of his blushes.

Just then the door from the scullery opened and Alice poked out her head.

'Me and the boys are going up to bed, they're dead tired.' She hesitated; perhaps she'd heard Sam's last words. 'You two carry on chatting, though!'

She smiled at them, a puzzled look on her face. Nellie hoped the tension in the air wasn't that obvious, but Sam certainly looked even more flustered now. Nellie felt he'd wanted to say more, but the moment had passed.

'No, it's all right, Alice,' Sam said, putting on his cap. 'I'd best be going now. I'll go out the back way.' Glancing briefly at Nellie, he let himself out of the back gate and was gone before she could even say goodnight.

*

Next morning, as she hurried along Spa Road to the factory, she was still confused and at odds with herself. She had been going over her conversation with Sam all night, and there was only one meaning she could attach to those guilty blushes of his. She turned in through the factory gates, jostling a crowd of other women all eager to clock on. Nellie simply couldn't afford to be docked half an hour's money for only a few minutes' tardiness, but waiting her turn to clock on, she grew more and more anxious. If only she hadn't stopped to do the ironing this morning. The chores had to be fitted in somehow, but now she cursed herself for cutting it so fine. She wondered what her father would have said; stickler for punctuality that he was, their lives had once run by his old watch. These days the watch served a completely different purpose: it sat in the pawnshop all week, helping keep the family afloat. *Dad would be turning in his grave*, she thought.

'Get a move on! We ain't got all day!' came a cry from further back down the line. She punched her time card and groaned: five minutes late! She flew towards the main building, but halfway across the yard noticed Sam's cart, loaded with sacks of sugar, outside the jelly building. Although he'd been constantly in her thoughts this morning, she hadn't expected to see him so soon. He must have been out early at the docks, picking up the sugar. Now he was standing on the back board, tying sacks to a rope, then guiding them as they were hoisted to the top-floor loading bay. Slowing her pace, she half raised her hand to get his attention. But the unspoken greeting caught in her throat and she rushed on, glad that he was occupied and that she was hidden three deep in a crowd of scurrying latecomers.

She tried to slip into the packing room unnoticed, hoping Albert would be busy at the other end. Dodging along the rows of machines, she slipped into position as Lily raised a questioning eyebrow. 'Where've you been?' Lily said under her breath. 'We've been covering best we could!'

Lily was filling packets while at the same time sharing pasting and loading with Maggie Tyrell. Now Maggie shoved up, letting Nellie take her place at the trolley. Today it was Nellie's turn to load.

'I got carried away with the ironing!' Nellie blew up a strand of hair from her forehead and tucked it up under her cap. Maggie gave her a sympathetic look. With six children to get ready in the morning, Maggie was always incurring late fines. Just as Nellie started loading the pile of waiting packets, Albert pounced like a stalking cat. She might have known it – he had a sixth sense where latecomers were concerned.

'I'd about given up on you, Nellie Clark! You've been holding up the line! I can't have you coming in late, Nellie, I won't stand for it, d'ye hear me?'

Lily and Maggie dipped their heads and carried on working. Neither did Nellie pause; she carried on methodically loading and tamping down the packets. It wouldn't do to stand idle, not even for a reprimand.

'Sorry, Albert, it won't happen again,' she said, blushing with shame.

'See it don't!' And he stalked off down the line, arms behind his back, stopping to pick up packets, checking chutes, while hands flew and bodies bent to their work under his scrutiny.

Ethel, who was filling at the next team, bent round to offer her opinion. 'Bastard, ain't he? I think it's cos he's so short, meself.'

'Shhh, Ethel! Mouth Almighty!' said Nellie. 'I can't afford to get on the wrong side of him!'

'Sorry, love, I know I've got a gate on me, but I don't like to see him bullying you. You've got enough on your plate with them poor children.'

Nellie was sorry now for speaking sharply to Ethel. She might be loud-mouthed, but she was large-hearted and always ready to defend the underdog. Ethel placed an empty packet under her chute, asking, 'How's things at home?' The woman's broad face was creased with concern. Pulling three packets off the bench, Nellie dumped them on to the trolley; it was nearly full.

'Oh, we're coping, Ethel.' She couldn't even manage a smile this morning; her brave face eluded her. She felt bone-tired and heavy-hearted.

Determined to push through her weariness, she hauled the trolley on to the tramlines that ran on a gradient the length of the room towards the lifts. She put all her weight behind it and shoved. Nothing happened. The gradient normally helped generate the necessary momentum to move the heavy trolleys. But today, however hard she pushed, she couldn't get the thing moving.

'Bugger it! Bloody trolley's stuck,' she blurted out, near to tears with the effort. In an instant Ethel was by her side.

'Mind out.' She almost lifted Nellie off her feet. 'Let's have a go.' And with what seemed like the lightest of pushes, Ethel's massive hands had the trolley rolling forward in seconds. Nellie took over with a grateful 'Thanks, Ethel', trundling the trolley the rest of the way herself. Once she'd returned to the bench, Lily moved aside.

'Let's swap. I'll load today, eh?' Lily offered.

'But that's not fair on you,' Nellie protested, for they always split the various jobs equally over the week.

'Don't be stupid, Nell. You're worn out already. You won't last the day at this rate. Now get filling quick before he notices.' Lily shot a look at Albert, standing further down the aisle of machines.

Nellie gave in; she had no energy to argue. As the morning progressed she hardly registered the banter around her, or the concerned looks from Lily. Her legs felt like water and she was beginning to doubt she'd have the strength to stand for another five hours. Perhaps she'd caught a chill while out on the penny-farthing? Soon she found herself back in the same loop of unanswerable questions about what she'd seen at London Bridge the other night. She wished to God she'd seen nothing at all.

She and Lily were making their way out at dinner time when Albert called her over. 'You go on, Lil,' she whispered. 'I'm for it.'

Albert was studying a leather ledger, tallying up a list of figures. He stuck the pen behind his ear and lifted his round face to her. He didn't look happy.

'Do you know your team's not done even half their quota this morning?'

She shook her head.

'Well, it's down to you.'

Her heart lurched. *Please God, don't let him sack me*, she prayed silently.

'And don't think I haven't noticed what's been going on. You come in late, the girls are having to cover for you, and you've got the cheek to ask me for overtime!'

'I'm sorry, Albert. I think I'm a bit under the weather.'

'Well, under the weather or not, it's not good enough. There's plenty more'll do the job if you can't!'

She felt her legs trembling. 'I really need the job, Albert. I'll make sure our team catches up, I promise.' Her hands were clasped behind her back, nails digging into her palms.

Suddenly he flung the ledger back on to the shelf in disgust. 'Well, pull your socks up or you're out.'

She took this as a dismissal, turned away, and walked as steadily as she could towards the double doors. Outside she practically fell over Lily and Ethel, who were both waiting for her. They had been eavesdropping.

'Bastard!' Ethel said, but this time Nellie didn't tell her to be quiet.

For the rest of the week Nellie was preoccupied with keeping her job, and thoughts of Sam were relegated to those few drowsy minutes before falling into exhausted sleep at night. She was therefore surprised when he turned up at her door late on Saturday afternoon. He said he'd noticed the penny-farthing was missing a bolt, which he'd come to replace. She led him out to the yard, where he bent over the bike, quickly tightening the new bolt into position.

183

His face averted, still inspecting his work, he stammered, 'It's b-been playing on my mind, Nell, you know, what you saw the other night.' He stood up to face her. 'You said that it's my business, and it is… but not the sort of business you think.'

Nellie sat down on the cart and motioned Sam to sit next to her. 'Not your fancy woman, then?' she said with a placating smile. But if not, then what had his guilty blushes meant the other night?

'I've done nothing to be ashamed of, but there's things I might not want known around here. People talk and I've still got a mother alive can be hurt by talk.'

When Nellie still looked puzzled, he went on. 'Dirty laundry; you know what they're like round here. If the front step's not scrubbed, you're a fallen woman. So what about having a sister who's had two kids out of wedlock? How would that go down in Beatson Street, especially one that flaunts it.'

'Your *sister*?'

As far as she knew, Sam had only one sister, and Matty was nowhere near childbearing age.

'Matty's not my only sister,' he explained, interpreting her confusion. 'The woman you saw me with at London Bridge was my elder sister. She goes by the name of James now, Eliza James.'

'Madam Mecklenburgh's your sister!' Nellie had jumped up so suddenly that the trailer tipped up and Sam tumbled off the end. She offered him her hand and, brushing off his trouser seat, he shook his head.

'I'm not proud of it, and to be honest I'm glad she changed her name to James. She broke my dad's heart and I can't forgive that. Don't matter how much good work she's done for others, she's not done much good for her own family, Nell, I can tell you that.'

The revelation had stunned her, but so much of what she'd witnessed between Sam and Eliza now made sense. More than that, she now regretted letting Sam see how much she cared about his possible other attachment.

'I'm sorry, Sam, about your dad, but we all make mistakes.'

For Nellie, Eliza James was still firmly on a pedestal and she couldn't reconcile her heroine with this picture of a fallen woman and heartless sister, but Sam was immovable.

'Mistakes? Once might have been a mistake, but twice! And it wouldn't be so bad if she hadn't palmed off her child. She had more important things to do, saving the world, didn't she?' he said bitterly.

'She give it away?'

'The first one, yeah, she give it away.'

He stopped abruptly and Nellie filled the awkward silence. 'But the child I saw was just a babe in arms. Is she keeping it?'

Nellie was alarmed to see tears brimming in his eyes. He shook his head and sighed.

'I'm not sure what she'll do. She usually ends up doing whatever James wants, so I reckon it'll be up to him.'

'Ernest James is the father, then?'

Sam nodded, and Nellie had a flash of insight into her idol's life as that man's mistress. Ernest James had a reputation for being a tough champion of workers' rights but a ferocious enemy. A man you would want on your side but never on the opposition.

'He's the type that usually gets his own way, I should think,' she commented.

'Eliza was only young when she went into service at Mecklenburgh Square. Dad always said she was James's "project". He was sure she'd come back to her family one day, but she never did. The strike was the first I'd seen of her in eight or nine years.'

'But what's she doing here? I thought they'd gone to Australia after the strike.'

'She says she wanted to see us, but it's a long way to come, seeing as she couldn't cross the river to see us before! He's not come back with her and reading between the lines, I don't think he was pleased. But Mum looked on her last legs when Eliza last saw her; I think she wanted her to see the baby, in case…'

'Anything should happen?' Nellie finished for him.

'That's about it, yes.'

'Is she going back to him?'

'She never told me what her plans were, but now she's seen Mum and the kids, I don't expect we'll see her for another nine years!'

'So how did your poor mother take it?'

'The thing you've got to remember about me mum is that she's a lot stronger than she looks. I mean her health is bad, but her spirit, my God, Nell, she's kept us going through everything and she'll always speak her mind. You know what she said to Eliza, when she walked in? She said, *Oh, it's you, I must be dying!*'

Nellie laughed. 'Eliza probably gets her spirit from your mum, you know.'

'I never thought of that before, but you're right, she is like Mum in lots of ways. That's probably why Dad idolized Eliza.'

'Oh, Sam, I feel a bit sorry for your sister. It's like she got herself caught in another world and couldn't come back.'

Sam's face hardened. 'No, don't make excuses for her. We all make our choices, don't we?'

'Yes, we do, and we all make our mistakes as well...'

Perhaps his thoughts now turned to her own big mistake, for he asked, 'So have you heard from him – Bosher?'

'No... but Lily has. You know he went to work on a Russian boat? Looks like he's taken up with the Bolshies... and some Russian woman as well.' Nellie felt that Sam was holding his breath, perhaps unsure what she wanted him to say, so she saved him the discomfort. 'She's welcome to him.' And Nellie probed her heart to see if that were true. If she felt a twinge, she put it down to the memory of a feeling that would one day fade to nothing. But she had other mistakes on her mind. She paused. 'Sam, you know Ted wasn't the only mistake I made that year.'

'No?'

'I'm not talking about another feller. I wanted to talk to you about it when it happened, but there were so many things going on. Anyway, it wasn't so much a mistake, more a promise...'

Her face was half-hidden in the twilight and she felt that made it easier to be honest. As dusk settled over the back yard, she uncovered the part of her heart that had been carrying the burden of that promise for almost two years. He listened quietly, till she had finished telling him how she'd been unable to disappoint his mother when she'd thought they were a couple, and had rashly made a promise to look after the children when Lizzie Gilbie was gone. How almost immediately she'd felt her mistake – that she would never be able to take on another family, without sacrificing her own – and how guilt had taken hold of her. When she fell silent, he lifted her chin and looked into her eyes.

'You're a good girl, Nellie Clark,' he said, 'and I want you to remember what I said about Mum, how strong she is really. Nellie, I'm telling you, I gave her no reason to think we were walking out. I think she just had you pegged the minute you walked in our house for someone with a good heart. Her family comes first with her, Nell, never forget that. You walked in and she saw a way to make sure they'd be all right when she's gone. She might be ill and frail, but she'll use whatever comes to hand when it comes to her family. Listen, Nellie, make *me* a promise now, will you? You just get on with your life and be happy. You're under no obligation. It's my family and when Mum goes, I'll be Mum, Dad, brother… everything to Matty and Charlie. You can trust me on that.'

He was letting her off! She waited for relief to flood her, yet all she felt was a sense of loss. It didn't make any sense. Sam had given her back her future, handed it to her on a plate; all she had to do was reach out and take it.

19

DOING THE ROUNDS

All that spring of 1913 and on into early summer, Nellie's life was a round of constant toil. She and Alice woke at dawn to a couple of hours' cleaning or laundry, before leaving for an eleven-hour day at Pearce Duff's. The boys had learned to get themselves ready and off to school, but Nellie rushed home at midday to give them their dinner. In the evenings, after a tea of bread and dripping, they would all gather at the kitchen table, making matchboxes. Both girls worked on till late into the night, long after the boys were in bed. The future that Sam had handed back to Nellie was on hold, while she concentrated solely on their survival. But each week ended with the sickening knowledge that she was still three shillings short.

By now, she had sold or pawned everything of any value: her father's best suit, her mother's wedding ring, her own best woollen coat. She dreaded the inevitable day when Wicks would come knocking and there would be nothing to put into his loathsome outstretched hand. She could feel her strength draining away. Each week it got harder to cycle up to London Bridge and back with the matchboxes. Her clothes were starting to embarrass her. Not only were they old and darned, but they were much too big; she had been forced to cinch them in and sew in tucks. When she caught her reflection in the kitchen mirror, or passing a shop window, she now quickly looked away. She thought she looked a fright.

She also tried not to notice how Alice's naturally bird-like frame seemed to be diminishing even further. Her only consolation came from the two sturdy little boys, healthy and clean, and still each with a pair of boots with soles intact. It was the best she could do, but she burned to do better for them.

The only bright spot on the horizon was Lily's wedding and her friend had talked of nothing else for months. Although her parents could not afford to contribute much, Jock had a good job working in his father's chandlery shop and he had told Lily she was to have everything just as she wanted it.

'He's been so thoughtful about everything, Nell. I can't believe my luck,' she confided to Nellie one dinner time as they sat on a wall outside the factory. 'We're putting away every penny, and his father's giving us some as well. We should have enough by next year, but Jock wants it sooner. He says there's a war coming and gawd knows where we'll all be this time next year.'

There had been so much talk of war over the past few years that Nellie had ceased to take it seriously. 'War? We've heard it all before.'

'Well, he says this time it's coming and he wants us married first.' She leaned in conspiratorially and whispered, 'He don't want to die a virgin, but I've told him I don't want to die a whore, so he's to keep Tommy out!'

Nellie blushed crimson. 'Lily!'

'Well, you've got to put them straight, Nell, otherwise they'll take advantage, no matter how nice a feller. Anyway, talking of nice fellers, I've told him that if he's having Sam as best man, then I've got to have my best friend for bridesmaid!' She beamed at Nellie. But when the expected excitement was not forthcoming, her face dropped. 'Don't you want to?' she asked. Nellie picked at a thread in her already threadbare skirt. Her face was pale and drawn and her hands red raw.

''Course I want to,' she said quietly. 'You're my best friend. But, Lil, I could never afford a good enough dress and I'm certainly not going to show you up, coming to your wedding in this old tat!' She scrunched up the skirt in her fist and slumped even lower on the wall.

'Oh, Nellie, don't worry about that. Jock's paying for the dresses! Your'n and mine!'

Nellie was shaking her head vigorously, but Lily ignored her. 'You can't say no because I've already bought the material!'

Nellie looked up at her friend. 'Are you telling me a pork pie, Lily Bosher?'

'Antique lace for me and satin for you!' She scooped Nellie off the wall and swung her round in her excitement, but after one spin she stopped abruptly with her hands encircling her friend's waist and squeezed hard.

'Get off!' yelled Nellie playfully, but not before Lily had registered her lightness and lack of flesh.

'Good gawd, Nellie, you're fadin' away. There's nothing of you!'

Nellie blushed and her friend became more serious.

'Nell, you've got to eat more. You can't keep feeding up those two boys and starving yourself!'

'Tell the truth, Lil, I've got no choice. I just can't make enough to keep us – I'm always three bloody bob short!'

She put her face in her hands and had no strength to stop the sobs that suddenly racked her. Lily put her arms round her friend.

'Shhh, Nell, this is not like you. Where's your fighting irons? Listen, we'll find a way, even if you all have to come and live with me and Jock above the shop. You're not going into no workhouse.'

Nellie let herself rest on Lily's shoulder for a moment. When the hooter went for the afternoon shift the girls joined the other women returning through the factory gates. They held hands as they went and Nellie, though unconvinced by her optimism, was grateful at least for Lily's strong grip and her even stronger friendship.

In the following days, Lily launched an undisguised campaign to keep Nellie's spirits up, making her laugh with rude comments behind Albert's back and doing more than her share of the heavy work of loading the trolley. She even tried to pay for her dinner one day at the coffee shop, which Nellie refused, insisting she wasn't a charity case just yet.

Then, later that week, Lily suggested they take Bobby and Freddie for an outing to Southwark Park. 'You all need to get out of that house and do something different!' she'd insisted, and Nellie hadn't taken much convincing. It was free and the boys could run around in the open air all day. The warming summer was making them restless. She could feel a mutiny coming; her brothers wouldn't want to be making matchboxes all summer long. But when she met Lily at the park gates on Sunday, Nellie was surprised to see she was not alone.

'You don't mind me bringing my chap, do you, Nell?' Lily said, laughingly grabbing Jock's arm. 'And we thought this little lot could do with an outing too!'

Sam, who was walking behind them, alongside Matty and Charlie, smiled at Nellie. The Gilbie children immediately ran ahead, with Nellie's brothers. 'We're going to the pond!' they called back, and Alice followed to make sure none of them fell in.

The four friends walked together behind them and as they strolled along the wide avenue of oak trees, Nellie realized she was glad of Sam's presence. Since their talk about her promise to Lizzie, she had been shy of seeking him out. She would chat to him as he left the stables, but time off was so rare she had little chance to be in his company. They walked past the bandstand and she thought back to when he had carried her out of the stampede of dockers and soldiers; she had been so ungrateful, feeling only disappointment that it wasn't Ted. Now, walking by his side on that very spot, she realized, given the choice, there was no one else she'd rather be with.

Jock had brought a blanket and spread it beneath some trees in view of the pond. Lily and Nellie sat on the blanket, while Jock and Sam lounged on either side. It seemed like heaven to Nellie to be sitting there, warmed by the early summer sun, watching the children play around the pond. Alice was helping them make boats from odd twigs and bits of reed, and their splashing and laughter sounded to Nellie like the lost music of childhood. Sun dappled through the trees where she sat and painted her faded cotton skirt with splashes of lemon light. She let out a long sigh and leaned back on her hands. Sam was lying on one elbow next to her.

'What was that for?' he asked.

'Oh, it's just nice to see them running around, being kids.'

'I know. Our Matty's taken on most of the cleaning and laundry now. Poor little mite, she can hardly reach the scrubbing board, she has to stand on a crate! Charlie's got his jobs, but he won't help with the laundry. Says it's women's work, the little bugger.'

Nellie smiled ruefully. 'You do your best, Sam, it's all we can do.'

Lily was rooting around in a large bag. Finally, she lifted out a huge wrapped parcel of jam sandwiches and some bottles of ginger beer.

'Grub!' she declared triumphantly. 'Come on, Jock, let's go and feed the hungry hordes!' She dragged him up and Sam and Nellie laughed, watching her dole out the sandwiches with strict fairness. 'Hang on, Freddie, you gannet,' Lily shouted. 'You took two, give one back!'

Sam sipped from a bottle of beer, while they looked on at the children, sitting with their legs dangling over the edge of the pond, each of them now in a competition to cram as large a slab of bread into their mouth as possible.

'Anyone would think they're starving!' Sam joked.

For some reason this seemed like a criticism to Nellie, who responded sharply. 'Well, they're not, they're just greedy little gits.' She called over to her brothers, 'You two, remember your manners. It's not a race, you know!'

Sam smiled. 'Oh, they're just growing boys.' He looked across at her warily. 'I didn't mean anything by it, Nell. You're a bit touchy.'

But Sam had hit on the very subject that did make her feel defensive. It was embarrassing enough to be on the breadline, without her brothers acting as though she didn't put food on the table for them.

'Listen, Nell, don't take this the wrong way, but if you should need an extra few bob at any time—'

'I'm not taking handouts!' she cut him off.

'Give us a chance! I wasn't suggesting a handout. I just heard that the Labour Institute is looking for delivery boys for the Co-op groceries, and I thought, well, you've got the cart on the penny-farthing and why not a delivery *girl*?'

'Oh!' This stopped Nellie in her tracks. She had to admit it was a tempting idea. 'But when would I find the time?'

'You could do the Saturday afternoon round, if you think you'd be up to it?'

''Course I'd be up to it!' She wasn't going to admit how exhausted she was feeling. 'But do you think they'd take me on?'

'Well, I was down there last week and I did mention it to Frank, the Co-op manager.' He paused, as if fearing a prickly reaction. When it didn't come, he went on. 'Anyway, he said he knew you were reliable, from when you volunteered during the strike, so I reckon you've got a good chance... another three bob a week wouldn't go amiss, eh?'

Finally, Nellie smiled. Three bob: how did he know the exact amount she needed? 'Has Lily been talking to you, by any chance?'

He dipped his head and smiled into his beer.

The Labour Institute Co-op was a popular way of saving money on foodstuffs. Most people could only afford to buy tea, sugar and other staples in the smallest of quantities, which meant they paid a high premium from the corner shop. But the Co-op bought in bulk and passed the savings on to their members, a simple way to help them evade one of the traps of poverty. On Monday evening, Nellie presented herself at the Labour Institute and was sent round to the back yard. She recognized the Co-op manager from the strike days, a rather serious-looking, youngish man with round glasses and thinning fair hair. The Co-op had been his brainchild and she remembered at the time thinking he worked as hard as any docker, dashing about all day, stacking crates and organizing deliveries.

'Frank Morgan,' he introduced himself, and shook her hand. 'You must be Nellie. Sam Gilbie said you might be interested.'

Nellie liked him immediately, for the way he listened carefully, as she told him the hours she could manage and described her unusual form of transport.

'A penny-farthing! And why not? If the bogey cart works as well as you say, then it's better than the handcarts some of our boys use. You might raise some eyebrows, but so long as the job gets done, I'm not fussed about that.'

So it was that Nellie became a familiar sight flying through the streets of Bermondsey on the old penny-farthing, with a cartload of groceries swinging out behind her and an extra three shillings a week in her pocket.

Lily's wedding day had finally been set for late September. In the previous weeks, every spare hour of Nellie's had been commandeered by her friend. They went to the dressmaker to have fittings for their dresses, and to the Mayflower pub on the river where the wedding breakfast was to be held, Lily seeming to need her advice on everything from the sandwiches to the cake. One evening, after returning from London Bridge with her matchbox delivery, she came upon Lily knocking at her door. Scooting to a halt, she wearily dismounted the penny-farthing.

'Come on, Nell,' Lily said impatiently. 'I need you to come and help me pick out the carriage.'

'Pick out the carriage! What, at this time of night? It's nearly nine o'clock! Anyway, where's Jock when he's needed?'

Lily looked hurt and immediately Nellie regretted her irritable jibe at Jock.

'He does what he can to help me, but his father's such a slave driver he's working all the hours God sends in that shop. I wouldn't ask, only you are me best friend ...'

'Oh, Lil, don't mind me, I'm just tired. 'Course I'll help you pick out the carriage. Just let me put this away,' she said, patting the saddle of the bike. Lily followed her as she trudged round to the back gate. After stowing the penny-farthing and checking on Alice and the boys, they set off briskly through the darkening streets.

'I'm sorry to drag you out, Nell,' Lily said apologetically. 'I know Jock's not been able to help much… looks like the most he's doing is picking out his suit!'

Nellie nodded sympathetically. 'That's men, but you could do a lot worse than him. At least he's not out pissing money up the wall, like some!'

Lily seemed cheered by this faint praise of Jock and Nellie suddenly realized that it mattered to her friend what she thought of him. Perhaps it was this glimpse of her usually confident friend's vulnerability that prompted Nellie to ask, 'Do you really love him, Lil?'

Her friend considered the question silently, before answering.

'He's a decent bloke and I know he'll be good to me.' Looking sharply at Nellie, she went on, 'There's all different sorts of love, Nell. I might not be all moon-eyed over him, like you was with our Ted, but, yes, I do love him.'

Nellie felt her heart contract. Suddenly the image of Ted striding towards her, with his bright hair falling across his forehead, came back to her.

'Sometimes, when I was with Ted, I couldn't even breathe properly, like I was holding my breath, waiting for something to happen.' Her voice was almost a whisper.

'What?' her friend asked,

Nellie shook her head sadly. 'I think I was waiting for him to leave me. I always thought he would because he didn't really love me back, Lil.'

'Oh, you got that wrong, Nell. Give me credit for knowing something about me own brother. I've seen him with plenty of girls, but he was different with you.'

'Well, then, he didn't love me enough, did he? 'Cause in the end, he sodded off, just like I expected he would!'

They were silent for a while, weaving their way through the

back streets towards the carriage hire yard in Grange Road.

'I thought you'd got over him,' Lily said suddenly. She looked so sad that Nellie drew her in reassuringly and linked arms as they walked.

'Oh, I have, I don't think about him hardly at all now. It's just with the wedding... it's bound to bring up old feelings.'

'Nellie, I wish you could find someone as decent as Jock! I know I shouldn't say it, but Sam Gilbie is twice the man my brother will ever be. You do know that, don't you?'

Nellie sighed. 'Lily, I've told you, we're just friends. If he ever had any interest in me, that bloody promise his mother wheedled out of me put paid to it. It's like a brick wall between us. We're always skirting around it, and even after he let me off it!'

'You've talked about it?'

Nellie nodded and explained Sam's response, though not what had prompted their conversation.

'See what I mean!' exclaimed her friend. 'He's a bloody diamond, and if there's a brick wall between you two, my advice is to get out yer sledgehammer, gel!'

Both girls were laughing so loudly as they arrived at the carriage yard that the sound brought the proprietor to the double gates.

'Ah, now you two ladies both look so happy,' he said, smiling as he swung open one of the gates, 'I really couldn't pick out the one in love!' He was rewarded with another burst of laughter from the two friends.

The open, shiny black carriage, decorated with gold-painted curlicues, looked splendid, and Nellie thought Lily looked every inch the princess, in her antique lace and short veil, as she arrived at St Mary's, Rotherhithe, on a September day of late summer warmth. Nellie rushed forward to help arrange her friend's dress, as she stepped down out of the carriage. Nellie was wearing the dress of pale blue satin, which she loved, not least because it would do very nicely for Sunday best after the wedding. As she walked down the aisle behind Lily and her father, Nellie saw

Jock look round, rather red in the face, nervously pulling at his collar and smoothing down his new suit. When they reached the altar, Nellie privately thought that of the two men standing there Sam Gilbie looked by far the more handsome, but, then, she wasn't the one getting married, as she told herself when Lily handed over her bouquet. Her heart was bursting with happiness for her friend, but Nellie knew things would never be the same again. Growing up together had forged a bond that she was certain would never break, but from the moment Lily walked out a married woman, the balance would shift and Jock would be the first in her life. In the last two painful years it had always been Lily she could rely upon to raise her spirits when she despaired, or to give her no-nonsense advice when she ran out of her own resources. Of course they'd still see each other at work, but Nellie knew there was a part of her friend that would disappear and she would miss her. As Nellie took Lily's bouquet, she whispered, 'Good luck, love, no turning back now!'

Lily squeezed her hand and, as if divining Nellie's thoughts, whispered, 'Friends forever, Nell.'

20

A STORM BREAKS

Nellie pulled aside the kitchen curtain and looked up at the dark bank of gathering clouds. The rooftops either side of Vauban Street already shone black with rain and though only a narrow strip of sky was visible between them, its solid gunmetal grey foretold a coming storm.

'Bloody weather!' Nellie complained to Alice. 'I'll get soaked again.'

It was Saturday afternoon and Nellie was due to set off on her Co-op round. By now she was used to coping with most weather on the penny-farthing. Riding through the previous winter months had been hard, but now she decided she preferred the perils of snow-packed streets and icy cobbles to this incessant drenching rain. The heavens had opened at the beginning of March and had poured out their watery bounty all month long. The rain was insistent and inescapable. Even being indoors afforded no relief – the earth was so sodden, that damp wafted up through the floorboards and sometimes Nellie felt she was dwelling in a dank cave. Trudging through downpours on her way to the factory, she spent days with sopping shoes and was kept awake at nights by drumming rain on roof and windows. Gutters overflowed, shooting like waterfalls down algae-covered brick walls, and the Bermondsey streets ran like streams towards a bursting Thames.

The sky this afternoon was like a grey winding sheet, swaddling the street with gloom. It was only just after one o'clock but dark as dusk. She sighed, pulling on the old mackintosh of her father's that she had taken to wearing on all her bicycle trips. Alice handed her a rain bonnet.

'Very fetching, I'm sure!' Nellie said ironically as she tied it over her wide flat cap.

Her brothers were morosely pasting matchbox labels at the kitchen table. They were fractious from being kept indoors and would gladly have gone splashing about in the rain, but Nellie feared pneumonia more than their moaning.

'You two behave yourselves while I'm out, and don't give Alice no cheek!' she warned. 'And you're not going out, so don't even ask,' she got in quickly. Now they were growing older, the boys had started to try their strength against her authority. Twelve-year-old Freddie, convinced he was the man of the house, had begun to defy her few rules, which were lenient enough. She didn't want to replicate her father's heavy-handed regime and preferred to use Freddie's budding manliness to her own advantage by giving him all the heaviest jobs for, like her father, he was built like a bull.

'I'm not sitting in doing matchboxes any more. It's girls' work!' he complained, just as she was dashing for the door.

'I haven't got time to argue about it now, Freddie. I've got to go out in this lot and earn some money to put food on the table! I said when Dad went that we've all got to pull together, and you promised you'd help me, didn't you?'

Freddie's defiant scowl crumpled a little at the mention of her father; she understood the nagging guilt the boy had. He'd hated their father's tyranny and had never quite been won over by his later softening. She went over to him, the mackintosh crackling, the rain bonnet slipping, and gave him a hug in spite of her irritation.

'I know it's hard, Fred, but we've got to keep the money coming in, if we all want to stay together. If you're fed up of the home work, perhaps there's something else you could do to earn a few bob, eh?'

'I already have. I asked Wicks for a part-time job at the yard!' he declared proudly.

'And what did he say about that?'

'He said yes, so long as I didn't mind shovelling shit, and I said I'd rather be doing that than pasting matchboxes.'

Nellie gazed at him, impressed. 'Well, that's a turn up. What's he paying you?'

'Two bob and all the horse shit I can carry away. I'll make a packet selling it round the allotments, Nell, and it won't interfere with school, I promise. Can I do it?'

'Can you do it? 'Course you can bloody do it!'

She planted a kiss on her resourceful brother's cheek. It was agreed the extra money would go straight into the housekeeping tin, but Nellie promised her brother he could have sixpence back for himself. Sam had predicted this boy wouldn't stay poor all his life and now she didn't doubt it.

By now she was terribly late. She jumped on the penny-farthing and cycled as quickly as she dared through the stinging rain. Tyres hissing on the wet roads, she felt herself skidding dangerously and made herself slow down. When she arrived at the Labour Institute, Frank Morgan was fretting in the yard. She dismounted as nimbly as she could in the voluminous mackintosh.

'I was getting worried, Nellie! Thought you might have come a cropper. Sure you can manage your round in this weather?'

'Don't worry about me, Frank, I'll go steady. Anyway, I think it's easing off now.'

She eyed the heavens and held out her hand. Frank looked doubtful but Nellie was determined to do her round, and, in fact, it did feel as though the fat raindrops had given way to a stinging drizzle.

Frank loaded up the penny-farthing's trailer with groceries; each parcel wrapped in oiled paper was labelled with an address. Scanning the delivery sheet, she noticed an order for Beatson Street.

'Oh, is this one for Mrs Gilbie? Sam not collecting it today?'

Frank shook his head. 'Wicks made him work this afternoon. He's down at Surrey Docks, collecting a load of grain.'

Some Saturday afternoons on his way home Sam collected his mother's Co-op groceries, but when he had to work, Nellie would make the Gilbies' delivery. Beatson Street was the last in her round and she usually stopped for a cup of tea with Lizzie Gilbie whenever she delivered there. The first time she'd delivered to Lizzie, she'd expected to hand over the groceries at the door and be on her way, but she'd reckoned without Matty, who called out to her mother, 'Look who's come with the groceries!'

It had been one of Lizzie's good days and she'd walked on painfully swollen legs to the front door. Her face showed both astonishment and, to Nellie's surprise, delight. She'd spotted the penny-farthing.

'That's never Michael's infernal machine!' she'd exclaimed. 'Sam told me you were using it for your matchbox deliveries, but look how spruce he's made it, and what a clever little cart!'

Leaning heavily on the front door frame, she'd seemed suddenly overcome with weariness. It was a natural thing for Nellie to help her inside. She'd settled her gently back into her chair by the fire in the kitchen.

Lizzie had smiled gratefully. 'My husband would have been so pleased to see his old Ariel getting such good use.' She patted Nellie's hand and wouldn't hear of her leaving without a cup of tea. 'Charlie, go and watch the penny-farthing!' she called to her son.

'Shall I get Dad's old padlock and chain it to the lamp post, Mum?' asked Charlie.

Lizzie nodded and then sent Matty off into the back kitchen to make their tea. Lizzie, though ill, was obviously still the matriarch, and her will clearly kept the home running. Nellie thought it touching the way the younger children were so gentle around her.

So it had become a habit for Nellie to stop and chat to Mrs Gilbie at the end of her Saturday round, and when the woman was strong enough, Nellie enjoyed her bright mind and sharp wit. She entertained Nellie with tales of her old life in Hull, before her husband brought the family to London. Sometimes Nellie would still be there when Sam came home and then they would carry on chatting together, till Sam became embarrassed by the tales of his childhood.

'Oh, he was a terror for swimming in that river! Do you know, I think he's swallowed more Thames water than he's had cups of tea! Used to swim all the way across to Wapping and back again, little mudlark. And the colour of his shirt when he come home, it was dandy grey russet!'

Nellie noticed how indulgently Sam let his mother rattle on. Sometimes he would cleverly deflect the conversation to one of the other children. 'What about a tune, Matty?' he would call to his little sister, and without any hesitation or shyness the child would take her place on the hearthrug to perform her latest song.

'Now, take a deep breath, and sing from down here!' Lizzie would instruct, patting her stomach.

Nellie never failed to be moved by the strength and sweetness of their little canary's voice. She was glad of this new easiness with Sam's mother. Never once did they refer to the night of Nellie's promise, or to Lizzie's misunderstanding about her friendship with Sam. The little kitchen in Beatson Street became simply a warm haven for Nellie at the end of a long gruelling Saturday, and she was grateful for the respite from her endless round of responsibilities.

So, on this rain-soaked March Saturday, she was looking forward to the end of her round and a quiet spell, drying off in the Gilbies' warm kitchen. The little cart was empty but for the one parcel and was much less of a drag on her as she wove in and out of the carts that splashed and hissed along Rotherhithe Street. Saturday traffic was always busy and crowds of shoppers on their afternoon off added to the menace as they ambled along the street, stepping out in front of her as though she were invisible. At least today the rain had kept many people at home and Nellie made good progress. She passed Jock's father's chandlery, waving to Jock, who happened to be standing in the doorway. Gratefully, she turned into Beatson Street. Sam had given her his dad's padlock and now she chained the bike to the lamp post outside his house.

When Matty opened the door, her face was clouded by anxiety and she frowned at Nellie, hesitating. 'Nellie, I'm not sure if Mum can see you. She's ever so bad today, and I don't know what to do 'cause Sam and Charlie's not here and I'm all on me own!'

The little girl's lower lip trembled and her sobs broke. Nellie was too wet to take her in her arms.

'Do you want me to come in and just sit with you for a bit? We won't wake your mum up if she's sleeping.'

Matty nodded, wiping her tears with her pinafore, and Nellie stepped into the passage. Hanging up her wet mackintosh and hat, she followed Matty into the kitchen, where Mrs Gilbie lay in her truckle bed beside the fire. Her hoarse, laboured breathing filled the little room. Nellie ushered Matty into the scullery.

'Has she been like this all day, love?' she asked gently.

Matty nodded, fingering a bowl of porridge on the scullery table. 'I tried to get her to eat it, I did try!'

Nellie's heart went out to Matty. 'It's not your fault if she doesn't eat, love. It's just she didn't fancy it, that's all. Did she have anything to drink?'

'Tea and condensed milk, she likes it strong.'

'And when did she go to sleep?'

'All day.'

Twelve-year-old Matty had been forced to grow up early but, still, Nellie knew it must have been a terrible ordeal for the poor girl, alone in this house all day, watching anxiously over the insensible woman, longing for her to wake. She hoped she was wrong, but Nellie feared that Lizzie might not wake again, not in this life anyway.

'Did Sam say when he'd be home, Matty?'

The young girl shook her head. She seemed frightened even to open her mouth in case the tears came again. Even though she had seen Lizzie in every state of illness, perhaps she too sensed that this time it was different. Lizzie's harsh breathing penetrated the thin scullery wall, but apart from that, a strange stillness filled the house. Nellie felt she couldn't leave Matty here alone and was wondering what best to do when she heard the front door open.

'Sam!' she said in relief. 'Thank goodness he's home!' But then she heard Charlie's voice calling.

'Matty, where are you? What's wrong with Mum?'

His loud boy's voice roused the sleeping woman and Nellie heard her croaking voice calling. 'Michael! Is that my Michael?'

Nellie rushed in from the scullery and knelt beside the truckle bed. 'It's Nellie, Mrs Gilbie. That's just your Charlie come home.'

For an instant she thought Lizzie didn't understand. Her glassy eyes looked past Nellie, seemingly searching for someone who was not there. Then she fell back.

'No, I remember now, not Michael. What a fool I am,' she said weakly. Then, recognizing Nellie, she asked, 'Have you seen my Sam?'

'No, but I'm sure he'll be home soon, Mrs Gilbie.' Nellie stroked the woman's hair from her face.

'I don't think I can wait, love.' The large liquid-blue eyes were now full of her usual intelligence and she looked at Nellie, in full understanding. 'I think you'd better get him. I'll hang on. Can you get my Sam for me?'

Nellie was galvanized. 'I'll get him, Mrs Gilbie. Charlie and Matty are here.'

She pulled the two children closer. 'Stay with Mum. I won't be long, don't worry.'

As she looked back from the door, Mrs Gilbie was reaching out to the two children, so that they were half on the tiny bed with her. Nellie threw on her mackintosh and hat, then dashed out and fumbled with the wet padlock. She had to find Sam in time, but where to look first? She knew he was picking up grain somewhere in Surrey Docks, but the docks and basins covered a vast area and it was getting towards evening now. What if he'd already made his collection and she missed him?

Out in the street, it was much colder now. The rain had stopped, but dark skies still threatened. She threw herself on to the penny-farthing and sped, heedless of anything but finding Sam, back down Rotherhithe Street, the great loop of the river always on her right-hand side. Pedalling hard, the first icy drops of hail stung her face and hands. When she got to the familiar frontage of Jock's shop, she pulled hard on the spoon brake. Letting the bike fall, she dashed into the dark tar-smelling interior of the chandler's. Jock was tidying coils of rope and looked up, startled.

'Nellie, whatever's the matter? Have you come from Sam's?'

Shivering now and breathless, she nodded, only able to manage staccato bursts. 'His mum, she's bad, asking for him. Do you know where he'd be picking up grain?'

Jock took her hands. 'Nellie, you're freezing, you can't get back on that bike. I'll go.'

But Nellie wouldn't have it. 'No, I'll be quicker on the bike. Just tell me where, there's not much time.'

Jock reluctantly gave her directions to the huge grain warehouse near the Surrey Canal. 'Go down towards Stave Dock and it's right by the entrance. You can't miss it. Be careful!' he called after her, but she was already out of the door.

Now she pedalled like the wind, her breath coming in burning gasps. Huge hailstones the size of pigeon's eggs began to beat down. She'd never seen hail like it! With her vision obscured, she pushed on through the icy piles of hail collecting in the road. At last she saw the entrance to the canal. Dismounting at the warehouse, she searched out the loading bay.

Please God be here, Sam, she prayed silently, every muscle aching and screaming. She'd pushed herself so hard to get here she hardly knew how she would get back. But none of that mattered, so long as Sam saw his beloved mother before she died. Then she spotted him. His cart was in a covered loading bay, fully loaded. He was covering the grain sacks with tarpaulin to keep them dry.

'Sam!' she called to him. He looked over at her, hail-battered, dripping and bedraggled as she was, and his face registered fear. He knew.

'Mum?' was all he said.

She felt a pain shoot through her, knowing what he would have to face, but she kept her voice calm. 'She's waiting for you, Sam, but go now, there might not be much time!'

He nodded grimly, looking at the cart. 'I can't leave the load here...'

He looked so hesitant and vulnerable she made the decision for him. 'Take the cart home, then.'

'Will you come with me, Nellie?'

'Of course I will, Sam, if you want me there. You go on, I'll follow on this. Go on, go quickly!'

She cycled back more slowly. Mercifully, the hail was easing, though the streets and rooftops were now so deep in ice they looked coated in snow. She stopped off at Jock's to let him know what had happened, then made her way back to Sam's. She dreaded what she would find, but she steeled herself to be as strong for Sam as he'd been for her when her father had died. Charlie opened the door without a word and she followed silently. Sam, seated beside his mother's bed, looked up at her as she entered the room. Had he been in time? She looked down at Lizzie, whose eyes were closed, but her breath still came, weak and erratic now. Lizzie Gilbie's children had formed a protective circle round her bed; now they made a space for Nellie and it didn't seem to her like an intrusion. Lizzie's eyes opened, resting on each of her children in turn and then upon Nellie. She smiled, as though to herself, and said, 'Ah, she's here, they'll be all right now. I'm ready to go and see my Michael.'

Then she closed her eyes and, still smiling, drifted away.

21

ORPHANS OF THE STORM

It seemed natural for the children to melt into Nellie's arms, and for Sam to join the circle to enclose them all. This was how Jock and Lily found them when they walked in through the unlocked front door. Jock immediately went to Sam, offering his hand and whispering a quiet condolence. Nellie was relieved to see her friend, for there was no one she'd rather have beside her in a crisis than Lily. Straight away, Lily saw Sam would need someone with him to attend to his mother and to the children. She drew Nellie into the scullery.

'If you want to stay with Sam for a bit, me and Jock'll go and tell Alice where you are.'

'Oh, thanks, Lil, I was beginning to worry about her. She'll be wondering where I've got to.'

'Well, you're not to worry. Sam needs you here for now. We'll come back later and stay with this lot while Sam takes you home. How's that?'

Nellie kissed Lily and the young couple left quietly for Vauban Street, letting themselves out.

After the grief of the children had subsided, Nellie tucked them up into bed and left Sam comforting them, while she went to the kitchen where Lizzie lay. She did what she had done for her own mother at far too young an age. Death for her no longer held any horror. She had seen her two baby brothers die while still in their cots, then her mother fade away under the burden of hard work and her father cruelly crushed by the weight of his own grief. Now she treated death as what it was, another part of life.

She washed the woman, carefully combed her once fiery hair, and pulled the sheet up to her chin. Lizzie looked peaceful, contented even, all the marks of woe and worry lifted forever.

'I can't believe she's gone.'

It was Sam's voice behind her. He slumped down into the chair next to his mother and held his head in his hands, raking his fingers through his hair. His shoulders began to shake and Nellie could tell he was trying to stifle his sobs.

'Sorry, Nell, sorry,' he said, apologizing for the tears, wiping them away. 'It's not like I'm the first to go through it. I should be stronger, got to be, for the kids.'

Going to his side, she put her arm round his shoulders. 'Time enough for strength, Sam. You let yourself go now, it's only me.' She was comforted that he trusted her enough to let the heaving sobs take him and the tears run down freely. When he was able to speak, he looked up and said, 'I thought I was prepared, oh, but, Nell, I never thought it would hurt so much.'

Then Nellie's heart broke for him and they both cried quietly, while Lizzie lay serenely beside them. When eventually his crying ebbed, Nellie went to make them tea. She came back with two cups of brown, steaming, sweet tea and he took his, gratefully.

'Thanks, Nell, for coming to get me and for staying. I'm glad I wasn't here on me own.'

'You didn't leave me on *my* own when Dad died, did you?'

'Well, I'm grateful, that's all. I don't know why this is such a shock for me, Nellie. I suppose it's all these years she's kept going and I can't understand why now, why now?'

'When did she first get ill, Sam?'

His eyes wandered to his mother and he seemed to think back.

'She was always living on her nerves, never really strong, but she had a will of iron and that's what kept her going. Lost two little babies and then had the worry of my simple brother. He died before I was born and I know it broke her heart. The doctors always said it was her liver packed up, 'cause of years of hard work and worry. But you know what I think took the life out of her?'

Nellie shook her head.

'When me dad died; that's when she took to her bed and she's never been the same since.'

'Did she manage to talk to you before I got here?'

Nellie knew it was important to fix Lizzie's last words and looks in his mind. She herself had fed upon the last words of her father like a starving woman, and they had made up for so much that sometimes she simply forgot the harshness of former years.

'She did say something. She said I was to keep the family together and she said I was to…' He hesitated, seeming unsure whether to go on. 'Well, she said I was to look after you.'

'Me? Look after me? I don't need looking after!' Nellie said, bewildered.

'Don't you?' he asked.

Nellie was surprised for the second time in her life by Lizzie Gilbie's assessment of her. She was flustered. 'Well, I'm blowed, your mother! First she wants me to look after her kids when she's gone, then she's asking you to look after me!'

Sam actually laughed and shook his head. 'You can never second-guess my mum, she's always making her plans. Don't mean to say any of us ever take much notice of them, though!'

Nellie laughed with him, glad he could speak of Lizzie as though she were still with him.

'One other thing she did, though, I think that's what's made me so upset. She got Matty to sing for her. One of Dad's favourites. His people came from around Loch Lomond years back and he loved the old Scottish songs. Matty picked them up so quick.'

'Which one did she want?'

'"My Love is Like a Red, Red Rose". Matty sang it all the way through, not a note wrong, what a little trouper.'

Here Sam had to blow his nose again and dab at his eyes. Nellie knew the old air and she thought she understood why

Lizzie Gilbie had chosen to die now. She whispered the last verse almost without thinking.

> 'And fare thee well my only love,
> And fare thee well a while
> And I will come again my love
> Though twer ten thousand mile.'

'You wanted to know why she went now, Sam. Don't you remember her last words?'

He nodded, understanding dawning. 'She said she was ready to go and see her Michael now.'

'She missed him, Sam, she just missed him.'

All this time the horse and cart had been tied up outside. Sam had checked on Blackie once, but the horse had stood patiently, waiting for the human drama to play itself out in the house. When Lily and Jock returned, Sam hefted the penny-farthing up on to the grain sacks in the cart, roping it on firmly. The rain still lashed down in sheets as they clambered up on to the cart. It was as if the storm was reluctant to let them go and they hunkered down, submitting to it. Sam looked across at Nellie, swathed in her father's mackintosh with the rain bonnet covering her frizzled hair, and as rain streamed down his face, he smiled.

'You do look a bit funny.'

'I always try to look me best,' she replied tartly, glad to give him some amusement.

'Ge'up!' he called to Blackie and the cart lurched forward. Clattering along through the rain-painted streets, they talked about what Sam would do now. He had to shout above the pummelling rain. 'I'll leave the cart in the yard and explain to Wicks; better go and see him tonight, or I won't have a job on Monday!'

She didn't envy Sam his interview. 'Best not to expect any sympathy from that old git, but you'll need time off to see the undertaker and the vicar.'

'I'll go Monday; he'll have to find someone else to deliver this load.'

'What will you do about the kids?'

'That's not for you to worry about, Nell.'

She sighed, exasperated at his pride. 'I wasn't *worrying*, I'm just asking, and anyway, we're both orphans now.' She let that sink in. 'And I want to help… if you need it.'

'Sorry, Nellie, 'course I'll be grateful for your help, but you know that damn promise makes me feel awkward. Any rate, they're not such kids any more. Charlie's thirteen and Matty's twelve, and, to be honest, she learned how to run the house years ago. I reckon I can manage with 'em till they start work.'

'Well, I suppose yer mum knew that as well, eh?'

Lizzie Gilbie had waited as long as she could, but now that it came to it, Nellie felt almost robbed. After all, she had promised to look after them. Still, she offered what she could.

'It might be harder for Matty. Twelve's not an easy age for a girl, Sam. We'll have her over to us, me and Alice. There's things she won't want to talk to her big brother about.'

Nellie could see Sam blushing by the light of the cart lamp. He coughed and thanked her.

'Tell you what, Nell, there is something you could do.'

'What's that?'

'You could give her a few cooking lessons. She might be able to sing, but she can't bloody cook for toffee!'

They laughed together and then fell into silence, broken only by the beating rain on the tarpaulin and Blackie's hooves striking the cobbles. Just as they turned into Spa Road, the rain stopped.

'Look, Sam!' Nellie exclaimed.

The full moon rode high above the black jumble of roofs and chimneys, just as the clouds parted, allowing an inky window of sky to reveal its shining face, almost too bright to bear after the gloom of the day.

*

Lizzie's funeral was a small affair, just her children and Sam's friends. Sam's second cousins, Betty Bosher and George Gilbie of the Green Ginger, came too. Nellie was pleased for Sam that at least a few relatives were there. George Gilbie, not famed for his generosity, even offered to put on drinks and sandwiches at the Green Ginger after the funeral.

'Cousin George wasn't close to me dad, but he respected him for trying to make something of his life,' Sam explained to Nellie as they sat in the bar of the Green Ginger after the funeral. George spotted them and came over to their table.

'Do you two want a top up?' he asked, pointing to their glasses, and when they declined he sat down. He was a red-faced, tightly wound man, who gave off a chill that Nellie didn't find appealing. She wondered why he would choose such a social job when he seemed to find small talk so hard. He sighed and looked round.

'Me and your dad had such a ding-dong once in this pub,' he said to Sam. 'We give each other such a pasting, there was blood everywhere!'

'He never said!' Sam was astonished.

'Oh, yes, but it was jealousy, pure jealousy on my part, if you want to know the truth. See, he already had the love of his life, and I was still trying to catch mine.' He jerked his head over to the stout little woman serving at the bar. She didn't look too much of a catch to Nellie, but Katie Gilbie was known to have been a stunner in her time and could have been a music hall star, so people said.

'I got her in the end, though. But your dad, he would have done anything for your mum, idolized Lizzie. That's why he come all this way on his penny-farthing, you know? She gave him merry hell for it, but he thought she deserved better than what she had up north. Can't say I disagree with him, she was one in a million, your mum. Wouldn't have hurt that Bolshie sister of yours to have turned up, though.'

And with that, George Gilbie got up and walked off, loosening his tie and offering pints to anyone who needed one.

'Well, he's deep,' Sam said, under his breath. 'Hardly says two words to me all me life and now he comes out with that.'

Nellie had wondered if Sam had been in touch with his older sister. 'Did you let Eliza know, Sam?'

He shrugged. 'I tried, wrote to Mecklenburgh Square, but didn't hear a dicky bird from her. Either she didn't want to come or she's gone back to him in Australia.'

'I can't see her missing her own mother's funeral!'

'Oh, Nell, you've got no idea what Eliza would miss.' He shook his head, sipping his beer.

She hated the bitterness that entered his voice whenever he spoke of Eliza. The very thought of his sister seemed to mar his kind face. But Nellie knew enough not to press him. This was the only subject that seemed closed between them and she was relieved when the children came running in from the pub yard, seeking more drinks.

After the funeral, life for Nellie returned to normal. Sam made good on his word to his mother and kept Matty and Charlie with him, but he was often at Nellie's house with them and they began turning to her for comfort and advice. Matty, especially, relied on her and as the two orphan families became intertwined, Nellie's connection with Sam grew deeper. She didn't know what to call it. To say it was *only* a friendship would no longer be true for her, and yet it was not a simple matter of attraction and romance. It wasn't what she'd hoped to find with Ted, but with Ted nothing was what she'd hoped for, so she felt ill equipped to judge the difference. Her bond with Sam seemed forged of necessity and fate; it hardly felt like a choice.

'But do I care?' she asked herself one day in July. 'Do I care if I never chose him?'

She was learning that not all choices were wise ones, anyway. Look at Eliza. Nellie often thought about the woman who'd deliberately chosen to move out of her own world, to improve her life, and where had her deliberate choices landed her? Judging by what Sam said of his sister, she was trapped in an exile she bitterly regretted. It seemed that life itself had chosen Sam for Nellie. Their shared experience of Ted's betrayal, her father's death, her promise to Lizzie and caring for their siblings were all links in a chain that had become stronger over the past three years. At nineteen, she could now no longer imagine life without Sam.

It was a subject that occupied her friend Lily very much – she worried at it like a little terrier. One Saturday evening, towards the end of July, Lily paid Nellie an unexpected visit. Always a ray of sunshine, today her smile was even broader. Nellie hugged her and drew her in. 'Come in, love, I've got a houseful, but there's always room for you.'

Lily stopped short at the kitchen door. 'Good gawd, how many kids have you got now?' she exclaimed.

Crammed round the table sat Alice, Bobby, Charlie and Matty. They were supposed to be pasting matchboxes together, but Charlie and Bobby were into a glue fight and Alice had stopped to tie ribbons in Matty's hair. Freddie counted himself exempt since he'd started mucking out at Wicks's; the most he now deigned to do was wrap parcels and load the penny-farthing. He was standing at the head of the table, tying bundles and criticizing the quality of their workmanship.

'Well, love,' Nellie replied, surveying the scene, 'I'm thinking of starting me own factory, but this lot spend more time gassing than us custard tarts do!'

Lily laughed as Nellie took the glue pot from Charlie's hands and planted it firmly in the middle of the table. The two friends went into the scullery.

'Tell you what, Nell, with all those kids, I reckon you must be the purest unmarried mother since the Virgin Mary... unless there's something you ain't told me!' She poked Nellie, till she giggled like a girl.

'Shut up, Lily Bosher – sorry, *Mrs McBride* – I might as well be a nun.'

Lily sighed. 'Well, if you're not a nun, you're a bloody saint.

Seems to me you get all the worry of being a mother and none of the fun.' She winked saucily at her friend. 'I think he should make an honest woman of you.'

'Who?'

'You know.' And she nodded towards the kitchen. 'Why's he left the kids here?'

'Wicks sent him on a late delivery out in Sussex somewhere. He can't get back till tomorrow, so he asked me to have them overnight. Wicks is such a mean bastard. He knows Sam's got the kids to think of, but he don't give an inch.'

Lily shook her head in disgust, absent-mindedly spooning more condensed milk into her tea. 'Ugh, Lil, you never usually like it as sweet as that! Anyway, tell me what's brought you over this way today?'

'I've been to see me mum.' Lily sipped her tea, smiling over the cup. 'There's a reason I can't get enough sugar. Some people want pickles and sour stuff – me, I can't get enough jam and biscuits... Can't you guess, Nell?'

Nellie choked on her own tea. 'You're not?'

Lily nodded her head. 'I am!'

'Oh, Lily, I'm so happy for you, no wonder you was going on about all my kids!'

'Well, you're the first to know, apart from our mums and dads.'

Nellie hugged her friend. 'At least you know who to come to when you need advice on bringing up kids!' she said matter-of-factly. But Lily might have it easier with a husband to help, she thought. Not just for the extra money but for all the endless small decisions that bringing up children demanded. Perhaps Lily was right and it was her lot to be ever the virgin mother. But listening to the escalating laughter and excited giggles from next door, it didn't seem such a hardship to have a houseful of other people's children.

'You lot shut yer cake'oles, you're making more noise than old Thumper!' She banged on the scullery wall and the laughter

215

was stifled for a while. 'Lesson one, that's the way you keep 'em in order!'

Lily laughed and put down her cup on the draining board. 'Best be getting back to me husband!' she said, still proud to show off the novelty of her married status to Nellie.

'Is he happy about it, Lil?' Nellie asked.

'Oh, he's not stopped grinning since we found out, but he's a bit scared.'

'What, of being a dad?'

'Not so much that. He's worried he won't be here when the baby's born.' Lily's smile faded.

'What do you mean?'

'He thinks we're in for a war soon.'

Nellie had heard rumours of war with Germany ever since the days of the strike and she had discounted the latest news stories. 'Oh, they've been saying that for years. It won't happen, love, and anyway, you silly mare, it'll be soldiers that go away to war, not the likes of Jock McBride!'

'Jock's been following it in the paper and he says it'll be our boys that fight this one.'

Nellie could not believe that an army would want the services of Jock McBride, chandler's assistant, or Sam Gilbie, carman, for that matter, but Lily would not be persuaded. It saddened Nellie that Lily's wonderful news was tarnished by such a terrible fear, that of losing her young husband to war.

Nellie and Alice spent Sunday morning in the kitchen, teaching Matty how to cook an edible meal. Sam was expected back from Sussex by dinner time and their idea was to surprise him with a meat pudding, made by his little sister. A warm July day was not an ideal time to steam a pudding for hours, but Matty said it was Sam's favourite meal and insisted this was what they should cook.

'Mine never turns out very good, Nellie,' the young girl confessed. 'The pudding goes all white and gluey. That's not right, is it?'

216

'Well, it's better if it's golden and light, Matty,' Nellie answered, trying not to smile. 'Me and Alice'll show you how.'

Matty proved an eager pupil, as Nellie showed her the right measure of flour and suet, and how to seal all the meat in so that none of the thick, dark gravy escaped.

'See, you tie it up tight like this with the pudding cloth.' Alice demonstrated, tying the muslin top over the basin.

'And be careful not to let the pan boil dry. Do you remember the time I did that, Alice, and nearly burned the house down?' Nellie chuckled. 'Poor Mum took the blame when Dad come home, rather than let me get a belt for it.'

'Poor old Mum,' echoed Alice.

Nellie looked over at Matty and saw her lower lip trembling. She wiped her floury hands on her pinafore and put her arm round the young girl. 'It's only natural you miss your mum, Matty. Me and Alice know what it's like, don't we, Al? It's early days, love. It will get better, I promise.'

'I just wish she was still here.' Matty's small wail pierced Nellie's heart.

'Well, she is here, in a way. I think about my mum every day and when you remember them, they're with you. I mean, who do you think taught me to make meat pudding just this way?'

'Your mum?'

'Yes, and every time I do it, you can be bloody sure she's with me, looking over me shoulder saying, *Don't do it that way, do it like this!*' Nellie mimicked her mother's voice so well that Alice had to laugh, and that brought a smile to Matty's face too.

'Well, I wish my mum had taught me to cook better, but I suppose she was too ill by the time I was old enough. I want to make sure Sam will like this dinner, though.'

Matty looked at the pudding, simmering on the range, and gave a determined nod of her head, shaking her auburn curls and lifting her chin as though ready for battle. Nellie had the feeling Matty would be all right.

The pudding steamed for several hours and the table was set.

Nellie sent Alice to call the boys, shouting at her to make sure they scraped their boots before they came in. They had spent the morning at Wicks's yard, helping Freddie with his part-time job, mucking out and tending to the horses. Almost as soon as he'd started at the stables, Freddie had dragooned Bobby into what he called his 'shit shovelling' business, sending the younger boy out with a shovel and sack and instructions to scrape up as much horse dung off the Bermondsey streets as he could carry home. Nellie was astounded by how much the allotment owners would pay for a sackload of manure and she was proud of her brothers' efforts to keep the family afloat. Now, as the boys all trooped in from the stables, Nellie pushed them towards the scullery.

'Wash those hands first, before you come near this table!' she ordered.

Freddie waved his mucky hands at her threateningly and the others followed suit. She hopped back. 'You terrors, no dinner for you!'

But the boys hooted with laughter at her empty threat. Suddenly Matty rushed to the window. Her quick hearing had caught the clopping of hooves on the cobbles.

'It's Sam, back from the country!'

She ran to open the door, just as he pulled up in the cart. He didn't get down, but the young girl leaped up on to the cart seat and hugged him.

'Oh, I should go away more often, if that's the welcome I get!' said a smiling Sam.

Nellie pushed up the sash window and leaned out. 'You must have smelled the dinner cooking. You're just in time!'

His dark brown eyes locked on to hers for a moment longer than was usual between them. He was still shy enough to look away or down at his feet when they met, but now she noticed an unguarded warmth in their dark depths and she smiled back broadly. 'Move yourself, then. I've got a houseful of starving boys here and they won't wait much longer!'

Matty jumped down from the cart, while Freddie helped Sam

unharness Blackie. When Sam came in, he was carefully balancing a tray of eggs and Freddie was carrying a huge sack of potatoes.

'Look what Sam's brought us!' he said excitedly.

'I was delivering near a farm,' Sam explained. 'Every little helps, eh?'

'Oh, Sam, there's no need for that,' she said.

'I'm not letting you feed us all for nothing,' he told her. 'Besides, I couldn't have done the job if it weren't for you, Nell.' His tone brooked no argument, so she took the tray of eggs and thanked him. She thought Sam looked weary, and not just from a long couple of days' work. It had only been four months since Lizzie's death and the lines of grief were still plain to see, but there was something more: a heaviness hung about him lately and two new vertical worry lines had appeared on his brow. As she and Alice busied themselves with dishing up the dinner, she found herself glad to be doing something for Sam. The children squeezed themselves round the table and Sam joined them.

'How do you like Matty's meat pudding?' Nellie asked him.

'Matty cooked it?' he said, in surprise.

Matty nodded, bursting with pride.

'You're a good little cook, Matty. It's the tastiest meat pudding I've ever had!' He looked over at Nellie and winked. 'Do you think you could teach her boiled bacon and pease pudding next?'

After dinner, the children wanted Sam to go with them to Southwark Park, but he hesitated.

'Sam's worn out, kids,' Nellie jumped in. 'He probably needs a kip, don't you?'

'I'll go with 'em,' offered Alice, and the boys rushed to the door before anyone could change their mind.

'Thanks, Alice,' Sam said, looking relieved, 'but don't let them keep you out too long.'

When they were alone, Nellie offered him her father's chair. She liked the way he relaxed there, with his legs stretched out, getting in her way, so that she had to step over them to get to the scullery.

'I'll make us some tea,' she offered, and when she came back with their cups Sam was leaning back, resting his head on the antimacassar, his eyes closed, those two vertical worry lines creasing his forehead. His face was bronzed from being out on the cart in all weathers, and the heat of the steamy kitchen had forced him to take off his jacket so he was in his rolled-up shirtsleeves. She noticed that his sinewy nut-brown arms were those of a man now, not a boy. His strong expressive hands, which he usually kept jammed into his pockets, rested lightly on his thighs.

'Sam,' she called softly.

He roused. 'I'm not asleep!' he said groggily.

She handed him the tea. 'What were you thinking about? You looked so worried.'

'Not worried, just whacked out, I suppose.'

'It was a hard job, then?'

He rubbed his face, trying to erase the tiredness, and groaned. 'It was a long old haul and a lot of shifting to be done once I got there. Wicks loves giving me the worst jobs these days. Anyone's got kids, he's the same. I think it's 'cause he's got none of his own, he won't make it easy for those that have.'

'So you're not worried about nothing, then?' she persisted.

'Well... I've been talking to Jock...'

Nellie's hands flew to her mouth. 'Oh, gawd, I forgot to tell you! Lily came round last night with some news!'

Sam looked uncertain. '*Good* news?'

'She's expecting!'

Sam grinned. 'Good for Jock!'

'Good for Jock? Lily's got something to do with it too, I should think.'

'Well, that's what I meant, good for both of them,' he said, flustered. 'Good news might be in short supply, as far as Jock's concerned.'

Nellie's face fell. 'Why? And what did you mean before when you said you'd been talking to Jock?'

She got up to open the scullery door into the yard. 'I need to let some air in,' she said, fearing to hear the answer to her question.

As she watched the steamy windows streaming with moisture, she felt sweat trickle down her spine. It pooled in the hollow of her back, like fear. Her legs turned to water as the comforting solid foundation of a day spent with a tired man and a houseful of children suddenly shifted beneath her. When she returned to the kitchen, she had already prepared herself for his answer.

'We've been talking about the war,' he said.

22

A FEATHER ON THE WIND

The threatened war, which had stalked their lives for so many months, had finally, by August of 1914, become a reality. Every day now she passed the growing line of eager recruits snaking halfway down Spa Road. Sometimes men four deep crowded the pavement, jostling each other, laughing and joking, as though they were lining up for a pub beano. Not one face looked worried; not one was sad. Nellie would be forced into the road to get round them and she would think, *I wonder if your wife or your mother looks so happy today?*

But it seemed not all women felt like her. She was saddened to find that some good women – mothers, wives and sweethearts – were vociferous in calling for their men to enlist and now, even at the factory, Nellie found she had to run the gauntlet of the White Feather League, an organization of women who thought it their patriotic duty to hand out feathers to any young man not in uniform. One dinner time, as Nellie was hurrying out, her way was barred by a group of women gathering at the factory gates. Nellie recognized a few from the jelly building, others from the print works and the packing room. A few held placards reading '*Serve your country or wear a white feather!*' Others were dashing into the dinner-time crowd of workers, shoving white feathers into men's hands. Many men seemed so astonished they instinctively held out their hands for the feathers, as though they were gifts. Nellie felt pity for the younger boys, who blushed and stammered that they were only sixteen.

But it wasn't just men being targeted. She was pushing her

way through the press of people, some of whom had simply come to gawp, when she heard raised voices. She was astonished to see of all people shy Annie being berated by Sally, another custard tart who'd recently joined the White Feather League. Sally was a hard-faced, opinionated girl, who Nellie had always instinctively steered clear of. Now she was pushing a feather into Annie's hands.

'Here, take this home for that coward brother of your'n!' Annie tried to dodge round her, but Sally barred her way. 'Don't go without this one, that's for your chap. You tell 'em to enlist and be men!'

Before she knew it Nellie had jumped to Annie's defence. The poor girl could barely hold a normal conversation, she was so timid, and this smacked of bullying.

'What's it got to do with you?' Nellie prised the woman's hand off Annie's arm.

'What's it to do with me? Only that I sent my two brothers off last week *and* my feller Alf!'

But poor Annie, too mortified to answer back, simply grabbed the proffered white feather and scuttled off. Nellie was about to run after her when Sally caught her by the arm.

'Same goes for you, Nellie Clark! What d'ye want with that Sam Gilbie? He must be nineteen now, old enough to enlist! You should be ashamed of yourself walking out with a man not wearing uniform.'

The crowd at the gates was growing rowdy, with the more hot-tempered men beginning to shout back at the feather-wielding women.

Nellie turned furiously on the woman. 'Whether I'm walking out with Sam is none of your bloody business, so keep yer big nose out of it! And if you're so bleedin' keen, why don't you get out there yerself? Go and nurse some poor sod you've sent to get blown up!'

Not expecting to be crossed, Sally was taken off guard. Not all of the girls had Nellie's spirit; most, like Annie, were too shamed by such insinuations to protest, and were often cowed into pressurizing their men to enlist. There was no way Nellie was going to be one of those. She wanted Sam to keep safe for her and the kids as long as he could. Grabbing a handful of feathers from Sally, she flung them into her face.

'And *that's* what I think of you and your white feathers!'

In the end, it was Mrs Arnold, one of Nellie's neighbours in Vauban Street, who gave Sam the white feather. He was leaving the yard one evening after work and the woman, who had obviously been waiting for him, darted out of her door. She thrust the feather into his hand before he knew what was happening. Nellie knew that the woman had sent off two of her sons, dressed in khaki, only the week before.

Sam had come straight to her, holding the feather like a love offering, tears of shame pooling in his eyes. She took the feather from him gently, held it up, blew it on the wind and as it floated up towards the grimy rooftops, she knew she loved him.

'I shall have to join up, Nellie. I'm not a coward, and I won't have them talking about me – or you!'

She drew him into her empty kitchen. The house was still for once. Alice was at the late shift and the boys were out, delivering to the allotments. Looking at Sam's white face, she understood the wretched humiliation he was feeling, but her need to stop him was overpowering. She would use every subterfuge, every argument, to dissuade him from signing up. Perhaps it was her patriotic duty to encourage him, perhaps his king and country did need him, but she needed him more and so did his family.

'People who know you don't think any the worse of you for not volunteering; you're only thinking of the kids,' she said, in a voice tight with urgency.

'I know that, Nell, but you don't have to face them day in, day out, with their snarky comments. One of 'em even stuck white feathers in Blackie's harness while I was delivering. The thing is,

I *want* to go! I want to go so badly!' he said, with a vehemence she'd rarely seen.

'No! Don't say that...' She found herself clinging to his arm. His gaze travelled from her hand as it lay on his sleeve and he looked into her frightened blue eyes.

'Jock's definitely going.'

Nellie groaned. 'Oh, no, I knew he was thinking about it. Poor Lily.'

'Nell, you don't understand what it's like for us men. All our old school pals, all our workmates, they're all going. How can we watch them go off and do their duty and us stay safe at home? It's not right, Nell. It's not fair.'

'Well, Jock's not being fair to Lily! Leaving her when she's having a baby – what if he dies out there and she's got to bring it up by herself?'

Sam threw himself into her father's old chair and ran his hands through his hair.

'I wish I could explain it, Nellie. He doesn't want to shame her, no woman deserves to be hooked up to a man who won't protect what's his.' His tone was almost pleading. Was he asking her permission to do the same as Jock? When she gave him only the stoniest of stares, he went on. 'Any rate, the war'll be over by Christmas, before the baby's even born!'

Nellie shook her head, exasperated. Why was he being so dense about this? Yet Sam wasn't a stupid man, she'd discovered, quite the opposite. He was a regular at the Spa Road library. She often met him coming back in his dinner break to Wicks's yard with an armful of books. She always inspected his selection and noted he was partial to adventure novels. Now, thinking of his reading tastes, she thought she had an insight into his motives. It infuriated her.

'Sam Gilbie, you're talking a load of old codswallop!' she shouted at him. 'Why don't you just be honest? You think it'll be an adventure, like one of your stupid books!'

She slumped down in the chair opposite him and her yelling

turned to quiet weeping. He jumped to her side.

'Don't get upset, Nell, please don't think badly of me. I know the difference between a story and real life. I just want to do the right thing.'

His strong hand was light on her arm. He must be able to feel her trembling and she tried desperately to control herself, but the hollow pain was too great to bear. She had thought she knew the pain of love after Ted's betrayal, but that was the merest paper cut, compared to the deep, wrenching agony she felt now. She felt bewildered, unprepared for her own reaction.

'I don't think badly of you. You're the most decent feller I've ever met and whatever you decide... well, it'll be the right decision.' She grasped the hand that still lay on her arm. 'And remember if you need any help, I'm here.'

'You're a rock, Nellie, you always seem to say the thing that'll make me feel better. Whatever's coming, I'm just glad I've got you for a friend.' He got up from where he'd been crouching at her side and picked up his cap. Slapping it against his thigh, he seemed reluctant to go, as if he had more that he would like to say.

'Best be going, duck, kids will be expecting me,' was all he managed, leaving Nellie to ponder her own deepest feelings and the unexpected nature of a love that could steal up so lightly on a person, floating past all her defences into the very fortress of her heart. For it had come to her, light as that white feather on the wind, that she loved Sam. All the pain of it ripped through her at once; and now, with the long-rumoured war finally here, she feared she'd realized how she felt too late. He would enlist for certain, next week or next month, and sooner or later he'd go away to war and he would never know she loved him. From now on she knew she would live her days in an agony of dread, waiting for the day when he'd come to her with his army papers and those feverish, unnaturally bright eyes she'd seen shining from so many young men's faces as they queued outside the recruiting office in Bermondsey town hall.

When Alice came home an hour later, she found Nellie still sitting as Sam had left her. It was so unusual to see her sister unoccupied that Alice's face clouded immediately with worry.

'What's the matter, love, don't you feel the ticket?' she asked.

Nellie shook her head. 'I'm all right. I was just sitting here, thinking about the war.'

'Oh, all the chaps at Duff's are volunteering, did you hear? They're saying the women'll have to do their jobs.' She sank wearily into the chair next to Nellie. 'Soon they'll have us mending machines and boiling up the jellies. Bet they won't be giving us men's money, though.'

'Sam's thinking of volunteering.'

Alice looked at her, understanding dawning. There was not much that quiet, loyal Alice did not notice about her sister. Sleeping in the same bed gave them opportunity for many a late-night confidence and although Nellie had only just realized her love for Sam, Alice seemed to comprehend immediately.

'You'd better say something before he goes, then,' Alice said softly. 'No good regretting it once he's over there.'

Nellie blushed. 'Say what?'

'Oh, Nellie,' her sister chided, 'he's been sweet on you for years and now, if you feel the same, what's to stop you saying something?'

'He's not sweet on me any more, Al,' Nellie said morosely. 'We had it all out ages ago. It's just friendship, that's all he wants, and I *will* be a good friend to him, whether he stays or goes.'

'Not sweet on you! Do me a favour, Nellie Clark, and open your eyes, see what everyone else sees. If you could hear what the girls at Duff's say – they're having bets about which of you two soppy sods will do something about it!'

Nellie had got used to Lily's constant teasing about Sam, but she was shocked that the delusion had spread. It certainly explained why Sally in the White Feather League had felt justified in challenging her.

'If he wants to say anything to me, he can.' Nellie got abruptly to her feet. 'Where have those boys got to?' she said irritably. 'I suppose they'll be off playing bloody toy soldiers in the street, with the rest of 'em.'

'Oh, don't be cross, Nellie, they're out earning a bob or two. They're good boys.'

Nellie relented, feeling guilty for her harsh words. 'Sorry, Al, it's not their fault, or yours or anyone's fault – except the bloody politicians'.'

From nowhere came the memory of Ted's bitter voice, complaining about those very politicians, who now seemed to be deciding her fate: *War!* he'd said. *They shouldn't be worrying about the Germans. Don't they know we're already at war, with* them, *the rich bastards…* And for once she found herself agreeing with him. But Alice's voice interrupted her musings.

'Anyway, he won't go to war, so you needn't worry. He wouldn't leave Charlie and Matty, would he?'

Over the next couple of weeks Sam's misery only intensified. Nellie tried everything to lift his mood. She invited Matty over for more cookery lessons and the young girl was sent home with the fruits of her labour, basins of mutton stew and suet puddings. One day Sam accused Nellie of wanting to fatten him up so that the recruiting sergeant would reject him. To her chagrin, he had not been far from the truth. Sam and his family were now regulars at her dinner table on Sundays, but she noticed his normal gentle manner with Charlie and Matty was changing. He would be harsh with them if they misbehaved at the table, and his patience was in short supply.

Soon after the white-feather incident, Nellie confided in Lily; she simply could not contain her emotion any longer. They clocked off and, instead of turning towards Vauban Street, Nellie stayed with her friend, who now lived over the chandler's shop in Rotherhithe Street.

'What you coming this way for, ain't you got no home to go to?' Lily joked.

'They can wait for their tea for once. I want to talk to you about something.'

Lily looked intrigued. 'Ooh, have you got a bit of gossip for me?'

'No! That's the one thing it's *not*, and if I tell you about it you've got to promise me it won't get round the custard tarts!'

Lily dutifully promised and listened intently as Nellie confessed her love for Sam.

When she'd finished, Lily nodded triumphantly. 'I knew it! I *knew* it! I was only telling Jock the other night, you two was made for each other, except one of you didn't know it yet!' She circled her arm round Nellie's waist. 'So, what shall we do about it?'

'We?'

'You wouldn't have told me if you didn't want my help.'

'Oh, Lily, love, I don't think anyone can help me. I've told him I only wanted to be friends and after the Ted business he's never going to want me now.'

Lily waved away all her objections. 'There's ways round that. Don't forget I'm married to his best friend!'

'No! You mustn't, Lil, you promised you wouldn't tell—'

'You said the custard tarts! You didn't say nothing about telling me husband.'

Nellie pleaded and by the time they'd reached the river, had agreed that she could tell Jock, but he wasn't to repeat it to Sam.

'Sam told me Jock's decided he's definitely volunteering.' They'd stopped at the river wall and now looked out over the Thames, silvered with early evening light, packed with tugs and barges hurrying to make the most of the long summer days.

Lily grew sombre. 'He's going down the recruiting office next week.'

'Can't you stop him, Lil?'

'Stubborn Scotch git, he's made up his mind. He won't listen to me.'

Though Jock had been born in Bermondsey, whenever Lily was particularly exasperated with him, she brought up his

Scottish parentage. It angered him, which was the point. Lily wasn't the sort of woman to be bossed by her husband, and if she couldn't stop Jock from volunteering, then Nellie despaired of ever influencing Sam.

'Sam will take it very bad. I'm so worried about him. I've never seen him so miserable, not since the days I used to turn him down for a lift on that blasted cart, do you remember?'

Lily smiled at her friend. 'Weren't we mean to him?'

'You were worse than me!'

The two friends fell silent as they leaned on the river wall, a musky dampness wafting up from the river mud. Suddenly Lily turned to Nellie.

'Tell you what, me and Jock's going to the picture palace Saturday night. I'll get him to ask Sam. Want to come?'

Nellie hesitated.

'I'll treat you, if you haven't got the money this week.'

Nellie shook her head. The truth was that with Freddie's extra earnings they'd been able to afford a few extras lately. 'No, I'm all right this week. What's on?'

'What's on? Who cares a tuppence what's on? You'll be sitting next to Sam!'

Nellie laughed and agreed. Besides, when Lily told her it was *The Prisoner of Zenda*, she hoped it would cheer Sam up. If he couldn't actually go on his big adventure, she thought bitterly, at least he could watch it on the pictures!

They arranged to meet at the picture palace in Grange Road on Saturday night. Alice was happy to send Nellie off with good grace, but her brothers were sulking because they both wanted to see *The Prisoner of Zenda* themselves. Even Bobby refused to be excited for her until Nellie promised to take them and Alice next time.

'Come on, boys, be fair,' said Alice. 'Nell don't get no time to herself, she deserves a night out with her friends.'

Bobby sulkily handed Nellie the wide-brimmed hat she'd

brightened up with new ribbon and Freddie, declaring a truce, mumbled, 'Just make sure you pay attention, so you can tell us the story.'

Sam arrived at the picture palace wearing his best suit, collar and tie. His normal flat cap had been replaced by a smart straw boater, which she complimented him on.

'Matty made me wear it, she said you'd like it.'

Nellie smiled. Matty was sharp as a drawer full of knives.

When Lily and Jock arrived, talk turned to the coming baby and Nellie noticed that the two boys refrained from any mention of the war, which was noteworthy in itself these days. But Nellie couldn't escape it, much as she tried. Kitchener, with his droopy eyes, even droopier moustache and pointing finger, pleaded from every hoarding: *Your country needs you*. Still, tonight she was glad the boys seemed to forget Kitchener too. They were all excited to see the film and, rushing to get a good seat, Lily ensured that Nellie sat next to Sam. The lights dimmed, and as the organ in the pit started playing, Nellie relaxed, looking forward to being spirited away to a make-believe world where good triumphed over evil, where no real blood was shed and where every dead soldier got up at the end of the film and walked off the set.

In the light of the flickering screen, Nellie stole glances at Sam. He seemed enraptured, totally engrossed by the film. She was aware of his arm resting next to hers and when he shifted in his seat, she held her breath. Desperately trying to follow the plot, so she could give the boys details later, she found she could only concentrate on the point where her arm met Sam's. When the story took a romantic turn, she noticed Lily and Jock cuddling up closer and prayed fervently that Sam couldn't see her blushes in the dark.

Then came an interval, after which the organ struck up a rousing military tune. The lyrics, plastered over the screen so the audience could join in, filled Nellie with dread.

Oh we don't want to lose you, but we think you ought to go,
For your King and your Country, both need you so!

She cursed Lord Kitchener for following her into the picture palace. The lyrics faded out and were replaced by footage of young men in khaki drilling, then boarding steamers for France. Suddenly she felt Sam lurch forward. He climbed over people's legs, tripping and stumbling, in his haste to escape the theatre. Lily clutched her arm.

'Go after him, Nell,' she whispered. 'Jock's told him he's signed up.'

Nellie ran out of the picture palace, just in time to see Sam rip his straw boater from his head and begin running. As he turned the corner, she called out to him. She knew he'd heard her, but he didn't stop or turn round, he just kept running. When she got to the corner he was nowhere to be seen. The street was crowded with young men and couples, enjoying their Saturday night off. She stooped to retrieve Sam's hat, brushing off the dust.

'Oh, Sam, you soppy 'apporth,' she muttered.

Then she remembered that when his mother was very ill, there was a place he'd liked to go that comforted and calmed him. She was certain he would go there now. Sure enough, when she arrived back at Wicks's yard, the gate was unlocked. She went in, carefully swinging the gate shut behind her, and walked across to the horses' stalls. There he was, his arms round Blackie's neck, feeding him a couple of sugar lumps. She heard him speaking soothingly to the animal, but she thought it was more himself he was soothing and she longed to just walk up to him and put her arms round him. Instead she called softly to him. He slowly removed his arms from Blackie and turned to face her.

'I thought I'd find you here,' she said.

He gave Blackie a pat.

'You dropped your hat.' She held it out. He took it and shoved it back on to his head.

'Thanks, Nellie, I'm ashamed of myself, running out like that.'

He took a heaving sigh. 'It's the coward's way, ain't it?'

Looking more miserable than she'd ever seen him, he led her to the gate. 'Come on, least I can do is walk you home, even if it is only next door.'

'Sam, I don't want you to go home so upset. Come round our back yard.'

They walked, single file, through the passageway between the houses leading to the back alley. Nellie softly lifted the latch of her back-yard gate, and was relieved not to hear Alice or the boys call out. They negotiated their way round the penny-farthing and perched themselves side by side on the trailer cart.

'I've never seen you like this, Sam,' she began. 'Is it because Jock signed up today?'

He heaved a great sigh and shook his head. 'Partly, Nellie,' he said softly, 'and it didn't help that I had a visit from George Gilbie.'

'George Gilbie? What did he want?'

'I couldn't believe it when he knocked on the door. I was surprised he even remembered where we lived! Anyway, he came to tell me I'm a disgrace to the Gilbie name, reckons I should get myself round the recruiting office.'

'Well, that takes the cake! Bloody cheek, how many times did he show his face when your mum was ill?'

'Not once. But he made me feel like a piece of dirt under his shoe. I could've knocked his block off and if the kids hadn't been there I would've.'

'He didn't say it in front of the kids?'

Nellie could see that Sam was trembling now with anger and shame. He spun the boater round and round in his hands. 'I think he did it deliberately, wanted to shame me. Then he says *If you're worried about leaving the children, I've already discussed it with my wife and we'll take them in, so you can go and do your duty.*'

Sam pounded the tyre of the penny-farthing.

'Oh, Sam, you're not going to do that, are you?' Nellie knew it would be like sending the children to live with strangers.

'I don't know I've got any choice,' he said morosely. 'I daresay Katie Gilbie's a decent enough woman, though it's well known she does like her drop of drink, but it's George worries me. He wouldn't be nice to them, he'd make sure they knew their place all right.'

'What do you mean, you've got no choice?' she said. 'The kids have got to come first.'

'Don't look at me like that, Nell, I can't bear the thought of sending them there, but the fact is they've got to go somewhere. I've made up me mind …'

She was very still. The night seemed to tremble around them; the day had been warm and now a hazy smog filled the purple-tinged sky. It seemed to descend thickly, filling the little back yard with ominous shadows, muffling their voices. She felt that if she were still enough, silent enough, time would stop and he would never finish that sentence, but he did.

'… I'm going to enlist.'

She was barely aware that she let out a groan, or that she reached out to hold his hand.

And you can't do it without my help, can you, Sam? she thought, and before she could change her mind heard herself saying, 'I'll have them, Sam. They can come and live with us.'

What she had so long resisted, fulfilling her promise to Lizzie, came to her as naturally as her next breath. In the end, it was simple: however much she'd wished it otherwise, the man she loved was going to war and if taking in his family would help him get through it, then that was what she would do. She understood now that not all promises were burdens. This felt more like a comfort; at least she could do something for Sam while he was away fighting for his country. The wheel of fate groaned, turned and clicked into place. In the face of Sam's misery and distress, Nellie's pledge to Lizzie was fulfilled. He would never have asked her directly, yet she saw immediately relief flooding his face.

'Are you sure, Nellie? You know you're not obliged—'

'Don't think for one minute it's because of what I promised your mum, it's not that at all. If you must go, I'd rather your mind be easy about the kids, that's the only reason.'

'The only reason?'

She felt his hand grip hers more tightly. Though her heart felt ripped in two, she would not tell him the other reason. If she told him now that she loved him, he would feel she was asking for some emotional recompense for taking on his family.

'There's only one promise matters to me now, Sam.' She took her hand from his and placed it on the penny-farthing wheel, thrumming her fingers round the spokes.

'What's that?' he asked.

'I'll look after the old penny-farthing and I'll look after your family. You just promise to come back home for them.'

23

OH, WE DON'T WANT TO LOSE YOU

They agreed to tell the children about Sam's decision the next day, but Nellie thought that, as her sister would be shouldering half the burden with her, she had to talk it over with Alice. She deserved the chance to say no. So, after saying goodbye to Sam on Saturday night, she slipped into bed, woke Alice and told her. Alice's response was predictably generous and practical.

'Oh, the poor little mites, he's all the family they've got left; of course I don't mind them coming here! We'll have to work out where they'll sleep, though.'

The little house in Vauban Street was already bursting at the seams, with only two bedrooms, a front kitchen where the family lived and ate, and a small back scullery.

'What with all them soddin' matchboxes, we'll have to put the kids up in the shed!'

The girls laughed, but Nellie was only half joking.

'Sam says we can talk about all the details tomorrow. They're coming for dinner and we'll tell them all together. Matty'll take it bad, but he's made up his mind.'

'How do *you* feel about it, Nell?' her sister asked, turning to face her in the bed. Moonlight fell across the pillow and glinted off an obvious teardrop as it trickled down Nellie's cheek.

'Oh, Al.' She nestled her head into her sister's neck. 'That stupid song keeps going through my mind, I can't get it to stop: '*We don't want to lose you, but we think you ought to go.*' Well, I don't,' she sobbed, 'I don't think he ought to go, and I don't want him to go!'

'Does he know how you feel?' Her sister stroked her hair.

'He knows I don't want him to go, but I don't think he really knows why.'

Alice sighed. At fourteen, she was wise beyond her years. 'People have a way of knowing, don't they? But he might not feel he can say anything, not till he's back safe and sound.'

Nellie nodded and swallowed, taking her cue from sensible Alice. 'And they say it'll all be over by Christmas, don't they?'

Sam, Charlie and Matty were a cheery threesome when they arrived on Sunday morning. They had been sharing some joke on the way and when Nellie answered the door they were convulsed with laughter. She wondered how Sam could laugh, but it was the same as those men waiting outside the recruiting office – no sadness, no fear, only a seemingly heady joy.

God forgive you, Sam Gilbie, she thought. *I think you're actually happy.*

She could only suppose there must be some emotional switch men could turn on, which converted the prospect of horror into the hope of adventure; perhaps they felt it was what they were made for. To her it seemed pitiless, but if it was light-heartedness that would get him through the coming danger, she didn't begrudge him his laughter.

Well, she asked herself, *that's what you wanted, wasn't it? To see him lose all that misery? Now you've got your wish.*

All this she registered between opening the door and ushering them into the kitchen. It wasn't until dinner was over that they announced the coming change in their lives. They still sat at the table and Nellie could see the boys itching to make their escape. She interrupted the rowdy chatter. 'All right, everyone pipe down. Me and Sam's got something to tell you.'

Matty's head shot up and she clapped her hands. 'You're getting married!'

Sam blushed and the boys hooted with laughter.

'Don't you know nothing, you stupid little canary?' Charlie said. 'They're not even walking out!'

'Put a sock in it, Charlie, and don't talk to your sister like that.' Sam's voice was stern but, softening, he turned to his sister.

'It's not that, Matty, but in a way we *are* going to be one family, so you're not far wrong. The fact is I'm signing up for the army tomorrow and that means I'll have to be away from home for a bit.'

Matty's face fell and Charlie's brightened considerably. At thirteen he was mad for the war. 'You're going to fight the Bosch!' He was beaming. 'Now I can tell 'em in school to shut their mouths up about you!'

Nellie and Sam exchanged looks. So the slurs had already reached the schoolyard. Matty started crying. 'I don't want you to go, Sam. We'll have to go into the workhouse!'

He opened his arms and Matty ran round the table to him.

'Shhh, you don't think I'd let that happen, do you? What do you think of coming and living here with Nellie for a bit, eh?'

Nellie gave her an encouraging look. 'You can keep all your own things, Matty, we'll put your bed in mine and Alice's room, and we can carry on with your cookery lessons. Won't you like that?'

After some coaxing, Matty was reassured and actually began to see the positive side. 'I think it'll be more fun, living with girls than just boys all the time,' she said, after a while. 'At least I'll have someone to talk to, won't I?'

Nellie remembered the night she'd spent in Matty's bed and how the little girl had chattered all night. There were all sorts of sacrifices required in a war, she thought ruefully, and sleepless nights might be the least of hers.

Charlie needed no such persuading. He was already fast friends with her brothers, especially Freddie who, at twelve, was close to him in age and temperament. So it was settled that he would sleep in the boys' room, and by the time the dinner things were cleared away they were already hatching schemes to bring Charlie into what Freddie now called his 'roses business' of dung selling. 'Fall in shit, come up smelling of roses!' he explained to Charlie, with all the knowing pride of a successful businessman.

Sam would enlist in the Royal Field Artillery, like Jock, who'd already been assigned as a horse driver, since he'd been used to driving his father's cart. Jock urged Sam to sign up to the same regiment, as they were particularly in need of men used to working with horses. An added incentive was the extra pay offered to anyone who could drive a horse team. Sam spent a long day at the recruiting office being questioned, weighed and measured, then waiting around for forms to be filled in. Eventually he was deemed fit for service in the Royal Field Artillery and rushed back to tell Nellie.

'I've got me papers!' His hand shook with excitement as he held up the documents. 'Can you come for a walk with me, Nell? I couldn't keep still if I tried!'

She nodded and nipped back into the kitchen, where Alice was working on the matchboxes. 'Alice, Sam's back.' Nellie looked at the clock on the mantel. The boys would soon be in bed. 'Can you spare me for an hour? He wants to go for a walk.'

Alice looked up from her matchboxes. 'Take your jacket, don't rush back!' She smiled as she bent her head to her work.

The early September evening was fine and warm, and Nellie had no idea where they were walking to. She just concentrated on keeping up with Sam, who was striding ahead as though he were already in uniform.

'Hold up a minute, you're not on a route march yet!' she complained.

He slowed his pace a little as they made their way down Spa Road, towards St James's Church. Nellie looked up as they passed Pearce Duff's factory on the corner. The windows were open and the chatter of the girls on the late shift drifted down, with the golden custard powder that coated every window sill. Nellie smelled the familiar vanilla sweetness and felt strangely comforted. Some things were going on as normal at least. Just as they passed beneath the St James railway arch, a steam train thundered overhead and Nellie jumped as the tunnel reverberated like a booming kettledrum. She always scuttled through the railway arches and now she instinctively took hold of Sam's arm. He looked down and smiled at her.

'Good job you're not going out to the front. They say the sound of the guns is deafening. I'll have to get used to that, especially being in the artillery.'

This was not what she wanted to hear, but she smiled back encouragingly. 'Maybe you'll just be driving carts and not even have to go near a gun!'

'I doubt that, Nell, but anyway I wanted to talk to you about arrangements for the kids and the money side of things. Let's walk round the churchyard a bit.'

St James was an imposing 'Waterloo' church, with a front that looked like a Greek temple. Steps led up to the pillared portico and four massive doors formed the entrance. Decades of Bermondsey soot and smoke had blackened the church's honey-coloured stone, so that now it had a sombre, heavy air. It was a church born out of a historic battle and it had seen many more in its time; now here it stood awaiting another great conflict.

Sam pointed up to the bell tower. 'Did you know the bells are made of melted-down cannons from the battle of Waterloo?'

She hadn't, though the great bells of St James were a familiar part of her life. Their pealing punctuated her Sundays. Often she cursed them, as they put paid to any hope of a brief lie-in. But she had never once considered the connection between that house of prayer and the bloody carnage of a long-forgotten war. She shuddered as she peered at the bells high above them, just visible within the tower.

'So anyway,' Sam went on, 'the kids seem happy enough to come to you. I'll have to get rid of our few bits of furniture, not that there's much.'

'Except the beds,' she said, her mind turning to practicalities. 'We'll have to squeeze them in somehow and you'll want to keep mementos, your mum and dad's things. We'll find room, Sam.'

'I'm so grateful, Nellie. I can't tell you how much easier this makes it for me. Dad would never forgive me if I didn't keep the family Bible. It's big, though!' he said, indicating something about the size of the penny-farthing cart. Nellie laughed at his exaggeration.

'Now we've got to work out the money side of things, Nell. Soldier's pay's about seven bob a week, but I'll get an extra four bob for working with horses, and 'course I'll send most of it home to you. Then there's the separation allowance.'

'What's that for?' she asked

'If you've got kids depending on you, they give you five shillings a child every week, so that'll be another ten bob.'

She knew that these were practicalities they had to speak about; certainly she could barely afford to keep her own family fed and clothed, let alone another two. But the simple way that Sam put their welfare above all other considerations tugged at her heart. His own possible death in the war was not in the forefront of his mind; his main concern was simply how many extra shillings he could send home to Nellie.

'Do you think you'll be able to manage on that and what you've got coming in at the moment?' he asked.

'To be honest, I think we'll be better off,' she said a little guiltily, 'but you make sure you keep enough of your wages for what you need out there!'

'You get your food and clothes supplied, Nell, and I don't reckon I'll get much time for fancy French shopping, though I might find something nice to send home to you. Wouldn't you like a pretty French hat, blue... same as your eyes?'

She realized this was the nearest he had ever got to talking like a sweetheart. She looked up into his kind, dark brown eyes and thought she saw the old devotion still there. She waited for him to say more, but instead he hesitated and said, 'You're the best of girls, Nellie, for taking on my family, but I want you to know it doesn't mean you have to take on me as well.'

She went to speak, but he wouldn't be interrupted.

'What I mean is that I couldn't ask that of you, not now. I couldn't bear it if you were just being kind to me, because you thought I might be going out to die.'

'Sam, I wouldn't be doing anything out of kindness or pity. I've changed.' She wanted to explain, but he stopped her, taking both her hands, holding them between his palms as though in prayer. They stood facing each other in front of St James's portico.

'I know what you're saying, Nellie, and nothing would make me happier, but I can't ask it of you. If it's meant to be, then I'll come home safe and sound and we'll see how you feel then.'

'All right, Sam, if that's what you want, that's what we'll do.' Her throat closed with emotion and her breath raked her lungs; she knew she had to match his bravery with her own. She stood looking up into his eyes, wanting to fix him in her mind as he was just at this moment. Nineteen now, he was a man in body, and five years outdoor labour had given him a sinewy, hard-muscled frame, but his face, as she studied it, still showed much of that expectant boy she had so scorned as he'd waited for her patiently every day outside Pearce Duff's. Now it was she who would wait for him. They had come to an understanding.

24

THE POWER OF A PROMISE

Sam had given her the photograph just before he left for training camp in September. Nellie took it out of her bag for the tenth time that day. Sam, Jock and four other young recruits were posing beneath trees on a sun-dappled common near the RFA base. They were all wearing new khaki uniforms, with leather pouched bandoliers across their chests. Their legs were wrapped in khaki webbing, spurs adorned their boots, and each one carried a riding crop. She scrutinized Sam's face, looking for any clue as to what he might be feeling. His eyes were shaded by the cap's peak, but his full mouth was set in what seemed gritty determination, his strong chin thrust slightly forward, as if to convince the world that he was ready to fight and to prevail. The pose was carefully arranged. He lay resting on his elbow on the left of the group and Jock mirrored his position on the right. Behind them, their mates stood in suitably firm stances, crops held at their sides, hands on hips.

Nellie was not fooled for an instant. These were not warriors; they were boys playing at soldiers, who knew no more of war than she did. She sighed and put the photo away in her bag. She couldn't believe it had been three long months since Sam had enlisted. After the wrench of him leaving for training camp, she'd expected him to sail immediately for France. But it seemed that the overwhelming number of volunteers for Kitchener's Army had taken everyone by surprise and it was taking months to get them kitted out. Sam had written her tales of shortages, not just of uniforms but of guns to practise with. They were even running low on horses, so many had been mown down in the early months of the war. The weeks of waiting had turned into months and Christmas now shone like a bright light of hope for her. If his training was prolonged till then, perhaps it would all be over by the time his division was ready to embark for France.

Lily carried around that same photograph of Sam and Jock, her copy covered in creases and smudges where she had kissed it each night. She and Nellie had become even closer since Sam and Jock had left, drawn together by a need to talk endlessly of the boys' whereabouts and to tell each other the meagre scraps of news that filtered through from training camp. They shared the agonizing wait, neither feeling they could live properly until the boys came home.

Lily was now heavily pregnant and today would be her last at Duff's. Nellie and the other custard tarts had been planning a celebration for weeks and had been gathering together a layette for Lily to take home with her. Nellie left Vauban Street early, to be sure of getting to Duff's before Lily. She carried a wicker baby basket that her mother had used for all her children. With Alice's help she had re-lined it, and the plan was to meet Maggie Tyrell in the cloakroom to put together all the gifts. She hurried down to the basement and found Maggie already at work. She was folding a blanket and had a pile of handknitted baby clothes beside her.

'Look at this, Nell!' She held up a cardigan and bonnet. 'Shy Annie knitted 'em, ain't they sweet!' Nellie came over to inspect them, holding their softness to her cheek. Maggie looked up, her bony careworn face softening. 'You'll have one of your own some day, Nell. Almost makes me want another one...' Maggie paused, then shuddered. 'Perhaps not. Once they get to my Lenny's age they're terrors!'

Nellie laughed and knelt beside Maggie, glad of the warmth from the boiler room next door. The women had been as generous as they could, and though most of the baby clothes were hand-me-downs, all were spotlessly clean.

'Do you think Albert would let us give it to her on the factory floor?' Nellie laid some booties on top of the other things and began tying a length of satin ribbon round the whole basket.

'Him? Miserable git, you know what he's like where women with kids are concerned. We'll just have to do it down here after work.'

Just then Ethel came clattering down the stairs, puffing with exertion. She was carrying a crate of beer. 'Sod me if I didn't bump into Albert as I was coming in with this lot!' she gasped, dropping the crate with a crash on to the nearest bench. 'Don't know what's come over him, he never batted an eyelid!'

Nellie rushed to help Ethel with the crate, which they quickly hid under some old sacking.

'Better hide this now too.' Nellie stowed the basket in a store cupboard, and as the cloakroom began to get crowded the three women made their way up to the packing room. Nellie felt an odd mixture of joy and sadness. She was happy for Lily and looking forward to the arrival of the baby, but it would be strange not to have her friend standing next to her each day. Although real conversations were impossible at work, with all the clatter and clamour, to say nothing of the watchful eyes of Albert, they hardly needed to speak. For what made the work bearable were the sympathetic looks when one of them felt down or the muttered jokes and insults directed at Albert; these oiled the machinery of all their long days. She would miss Lily, but for her sake she kept her face bright and her banter flowing all day.

When the hooter finally sounded all the custard tarts turned off the machines and downed packets even more speedily than usual. They surrounded Lily, who looked gratifyingly surprised, and made to sweep her off to the basement. But they were all stopped in their tracks by the intervention of none other than Albert himself.

'Excuse me, ladies!' He had to shout through their chatter. 'Can I have some quiet, please!'

Nellie looked at Ethel in alarm; perhaps he had noticed the beer after all.

'If he spoils this, I swear I'll knock his block off!' Ethel muttered, and Nellie saw her push her sleeves up. Some of the women groaned, fearing the end of their festivities for the day, and Lily, seeing Nellie's disappointment, squeezed her hand.

'Never mind, Nell, we'll go to the Green Ginger later on.'

Nellie smiled weakly back.

'I've got an announcement to make,' Albert went on. 'I'm proud to tell you that I have answered the call and I will be leaving to serve King and Country tomorrow!'

There was stunned silence. Albert looked encouragingly around the room – perhaps he expected a fanfare – and Sally from the White Feather League started to clap, which resulted in desultory applause. Albert held up his hand. 'As you know, the men of Duff's have been among the first to sign up, which means we are running short and will have to rely on you women to struggle as best you can without us!' Albert smirked.

'Is he joking?' Nellie whispered to Lily.

'So I'm pleased to announce that your new foreman will, in fact, be a forelady, Ethel Brown!'

All eyes flew to Ethel.

'Sod me!' Ethel blurted out, as surprised as all the rest of them. Albert gave her a disapproving look, but said nothing other than, 'You'll find the ledgers all in order, Ethel. Good luck to you all.' And he stood at the double doors, nodding goodbye to each of them. Nellie felt she ought to salute, but instead shook his hand and wished him good luck. For all his faults, she could not send him off with bad feeling; after all, he might never be coming back.

They kept their delight under control until they reached the basement, but once in the cloakroom their celebrations were less than clandestine. There were cries of congratulations for Ethel, laughter at Albert's expense, and delight at the crate of beer sequestered beneath the sacking. Lily sat smiling on a bench, calm and radiant, with her hand on her stomach.

'Oh, Nell, you couldn't have planned a better send-off. I felt a bit guilty leaving you here on your own, but at least you'll be rid of Albert!'

It was Saturday afternoon. Lily had been gone for over a week and although it had been strange without her, Ethel soon made it clear things would run very differently in the packing room from now on. At the end of each day they had all fulfilled their quotas, without once being terrorized or humiliated. Nellie had to smile at Albert's idea of them 'struggling on' without him; in fact, they were doing very well indeed.

Nellie put on her coat and set off on the penny-farthing for her delivery round. The discounted Co-op bread and groceries were in even greater demand these days; the war had sent food prices rocketing and the Labour Institute could barely cope. They'd asked Nellie to do more hours, but with her growing family she was already stretched to the limits of her time and endurance. She pedalled determinedly through her round and with relief turned the bicycle towards Rotherhithe to make her last delivery at Jock's father's shop, above which Lily was still living.

When Nellie arrived at the chandler's shop, out of breath and chilled to the bone, she stowed the penny-farthing in the back yard and mounted an outside flight of wooden steps which led up to Lily's rooms above the shop. She knocked and called out, 'Lil, it's only me, don't rush!' She waited patiently, her breath pluming in the cold December air.

Lily, with only a month left of her pregnancy, was beginning to look as wide as she was tall. Nellie privately believed there had to be more than one baby in there, but she didn't dare mention it to her friend. Her nerves were raw enough and her once ready smile came less often since Jock had gone. She answered the door after a few minutes and threw her arms round Nellie, as though she hadn't seen her for months.

'Come in out the cold, love, you're perishing. Oh, it's so nice to see a friendly face!' She rolled her eyes dramatically. 'His mum and dad are driving me potty over this baby. Sooner Jock gets back, the better!'

The friends buoyed each other up with hopes that the boys would be home before the baby was born in January.

'What's happened now?' asked Nellie, as she began putting Lily's groceries away in her kitchen cupboard.

'They say the back stairs is too dangerous for me and they want me to live downstairs with them!' Jock's parents' home on the ground floor sprawled out behind the shop and round the yard. 'I know it's their first grandchild but, gawd, you'd think I was carrying Bonnie Prince Charlie, the way they go on!'

Nellie had been careful herself as she'd negotiated the steep back steps, coated as they were with a rime of frost. She could see the McBrides might have a point.

'I suppose they're only being kind, Lil.'

'Don't you start taking their side. I've had enough of it with Jock saying I should live with them till he gets back.'

Lily sat down heavily on the wooden kitchen chair and Nellie set about making them tea. 'Have you heard from Jock? I didn't get anything from Sam.'

'A postcard yesterday.' She seemed to hesitate. 'I expect yours'll come soon, love.' Lily pulled her shawl closer around her and shivered, in spite of the fire burning in the little grate. 'They've had their marching orders, they're shipping out next week.'

Nellie carefully put the two cups of tea on the table, but they rattled in the saucers as she tried to steady her hands. She sat down at the table next to her friend, feeling as though Lily had punched all the air out of her lungs. How could they comfort each other now? The threads that held Sam and Jock to them had just stretched as taut as an anchor chain on a full tide.

'Next week?' she said weakly. 'Why no warning?'

Lily shrugged. 'Suppose they needed to keep it hush-hush. We'll have to get used to being the last to know anything.' Lily put a protective hand on to her swollen stomach, as though shielding her child from the news. Nellie noticed the gesture and took her friend's hand.

'He'll be home soon and till then you're not on your own, love. There's your mum and dad, and you know you can call on me any time.'

'Thanks, Nell, but you've got your hands full, with that brood of yours. Anyway, how are they all getting on?'

'Oh, Charlie's fitted in fine with the boys. Freddie puts his nose out of joint sometimes, trying to boss him. You know our Fred, he's always got to be the one in charge, but Charlie can stand up to him. Bobby's so easygoing, he just lets them get on with it.'

'What about the little canary?'

The family nickname had stuck. It suited Matty's quick bright ways. She seemed like a flitting ray of sunshine about the house and her songs could always lift Nellie's spirits.

'Oh, she's missing Sam, but she can be a little madam some-times! She got used to ruling the roost, with her mum being so ill, and Sam spoils her rotten. Mind you, she's sharp as ninepence… and she's got a good heart, like Sam.'

Nellie's voice faltered at the mention of his name and then it was Lily's turn to comfort her. After they had both finished shedding tears and drinking tea, the subject turned to Lily's family. Her brother Ginger had also enlisted and their mother Betty had taken it particularly badly.

'I swear to you, Nell, if she could have tied him to the kitchen table to stop him going, she would've. She's shed enough tears over our Ted, but it's hard to lose two sons.'

The subject of Ted wasn't an awkward one for them any longer. Nellie had often tried to fathom how it was that such an inconstant, volatile man had so captivated her; in the end she settled in her mind that he was simply a painful mistake, the memory of which she preferred not to resurrect. But sometimes, as now, she would be ambushed by him and whenever that happened she was flooded with unease. Her deepest fear was that if she ever met him again, she would still feel the old draw. She didn't want to ask about Ted, didn't want to know where he was, or what he was doing, but he was, after all, Lily's brother.

'Do you know what Ted's doing about the war? Will he come back to sign up?'

Lily's face was suffused with an uncharacteristic blush. 'Gawd knows, Nell. Last we heard he was still in Russia, but he don't even write to Mum any more. Could be dead, for all we know. Sometimes I think it might be best if he was.'

'Oh, Lil, don't say that. Then your poor mum's heart really would be broken.'

'Too late, Nell, it already is.' Lily's bitterness would not be assuaged by any comforting lies.

'I don't think your mum would agree with you there. He can always come back from Russia, but last I heard, love, there's no coming back from the dead.'

When Nellie returned to Vauban Street the house was unusually silent. She had come in at the back door, after leaving the penny-farthing in the yard. She had expected to find Alice in the scullery: usually on Saturday evenings her sister was responsible for preparing the tea in time for Nellie's return from her round. She went through into the kitchen and immediately noticed the postcard propped on the mantleshelf. Matty was sitting alone at the kitchen table, slicing a loaf, and when Nellie saw her puffy eyes and red nose, she knew the postcard was from Sam.

'Hello, all on your own?' She kissed Matty's cheek. It was damp and salty.

Matty nodded and sucked in a breath. 'Alice had to go down the "Blue" for a few bits,' she said, doggedly slicing away.

'I think you've done enough there to feed an army,' said Nellie gently, immediately regretting the military reference, which tipped Matty over the edge. The young girl let the knife clatter to the table and pointed to the postcard.

'Sam's going to France!' she sobbed.

Nellie plucked the card from the shelf. There was Sam's fluent, firm handwriting, telling her what she already knew. He would take the train from Waterloo early next Friday and then a troop ship to France.

'Can we go and see him off?' Matty pleaded.

Nellie took Matty in her arms, but the girl was inconsolable. Nellie knew that somehow she must try to catch Sam in all the melee of departing troops, if not for her own sake then at least for Matty's.

'We'll be lucky to see him, there'll be thousands of them… but we'll give it a damn good try, eh, Matty?'

Nellie was rewarded with a hug and a wet kiss. She read the card again.

'He says they're marching through to Waterloo Thursday night and sleeping on the station. I'll find out the best place to see them go by. I'm sure you and Charlie can have the afternoon off school. All I've got to do is persuade Ethel to cover for me.'

Now that Ethel Brown was Nellie's new forelady, life had become much pleasanter for all the custard tarts. Not only was she rigidly fair with the overtime hours, unlike Albert, more importantly she understood that sometimes a sick child really was a valid reason for a woman's absence from work. Nellie had little doubt that Ethel would agree to an unofficial afternoon off.

At work on Monday, Maggie Tyrell was the one to tell her which was the best place to see the troops as they marched through south London on their way to Waterloo. Maggie's husband Tom would be amongst them. When Maggie first suggested her husband might sign up, Nellie had been surprised. 'Surely no one would think badly of Tom if he didn't, not with six kids to worry about!' she'd said.

'Oh, he's not worried about the white-feather brigade,' Maggie said dismissively. 'No, he says to me, *Six kids! Mag, we'll be rollin' in it, that's thirty shilling a week separation allowance!* And then he says to me, *and if I cop it you'll get the widow's pension.*'

Nellie shook her head. There it was again, just like Sam. Somehow the prospect of getting blown to smithereens was less of a consideration to these men than making things financially easier for their families.

'Anyway,' Maggie went on, with a laugh that turned into a chesty cough, 'my old man's like one of them bad pennies, he'll turn up again soon enough.'

But in spite of her bravado, Maggie Tyrell told Nellie that she wouldn't miss waving Tom off for the world. 'They're marching through Old Kent Road Thursday evening, so I'm taking the kids up there in the afternoon. You come with us, love, and we'll sort you out the best spot!'

So many of the custard tarts had men they wanted to see off that Ethel Brown went to see the boss, Old Plum Duff himself. Afterwards, she stood on a packing case at the end of the factory floor, waiting for the girls to pay attention.

'Will you shut yer traps and listen?' Ethel boomed out, in her best coal heaver's voice.

When the hubbub died down, she went on. 'He didn't bat an eyelid,' she announced triumphantly. 'Factory's shuttin' Thursday afternoon, so you can *all* go and wave 'em off.'

A cheer went up from the custard tarts and a round of hoorahs for the factory owner. Nellie reflected ruefully on how things had changed since the strike days: now, in a world where the male workforce was dwindling suddenly, the factory was only too happy to consider the women's requests. Looking round at her friends' beaming faces, she kept her cynicism to herself. Perhaps the boss was just being patriotic, but it was Maggie who leaned over to whisper to Nellie, 'Got to keep us sweet now, haven't they?'

The local schools allowed children a half-day holiday as well, so on Thursday afternoon Nellie's cuckoo's brood and Maggie's six children followed the two women, in a rag-tag band, towards the Old Kent Road. They made their way to Grange Road and cut down Pages Walk, which would lead them directly to what Maggie insisted was the best spot on the Old Kent Road. There was a holiday atmosphere as they joined a crowd of mostly women and children, all heading in the same direction. Once at the Old Kent Road, Maggie's children efficiently elbowed out a space with a good view both ways. They eagerly craned their necks for a first sight of the men, but it was the sound that came first. The deep boom, boom, boom of the marching drums and the thud of a thousand boots came echoing along the road, before ever they caught a glimpse of the soldiers. It was hard to tell how far away they were, for the sound of bugles bounced off buildings and strains of 'Tipperary' floated on the wind. Matty was jumping up and down at her side as the first Tommies came into view. Arms swinging, rifles shouldered, they all looked so alike.

'Is that him?' Matty pointed.

No, it was not him and as the first column thundered past, Nellie began to despair of picking out Sam's face amongst the thousands. Suddenly Maggie's sharp-eyed children spotted Tom and their shouts drew his attention. He blew kisses, but didn't break step. Maggie's voice broke as she called out, 'God bless, Tom, give 'em hell, you old sod, you!'

Tom gave Maggie a cheery wave and was gone. Now Nellie scanned each face. Where was Sam? Matty would be distraught if they missed him. Her eye swept the passing column of men and noticed they were all wearing spurs. Then, when she looked up, there he was, dark eyes staring straight at her, almost pulling her gaze towards him. He was only feet away! She couldn't believe it; he had just seemed to appear from nowhere.

'Sam, Sam!' She waved and jumped up and down, then he smiled, knowing she'd spotted him. Before she knew it, she was dragging Matty out into the road and they were running beside him.

'Good luck, Sam!' Matty called out above the din.

'Matty!' He was obviously overjoyed to see his sister, but he was peering at the crowd.

'Charlie's over there.' Nellie pointed to their little group, who whooped and cheered even louder once Sam had spotted them. Nellie could see Jock on the far side of the column. Reaching into the ranks, she thrust a letter into Sam's hand, panting, 'For Jock, from Lily!'

Poor Lily had gone through agonies because she had been ordered to rest and couldn't make the trek up from Rotherhithe. The column was moving swiftly forward; soon Sam would be out of sight, gone for who knew how long.

Then, perhaps because she had more reason than most to know the power of a promise, Nellie called to him. 'Sam, remember your promise…' He could not break step, so she held on to her hat and trotted to keep up. 'Your penny-farthing promise, remember… come home for it, and for us!'

He turned his head and shot her a look shining with love. 'I'll remember, Nellie, I promise. I'll remember!'

And with that, he disappeared, his cap indistinguishable from all the hundreds of others that followed after, but the echo of his voice stayed with her. It was enough; he had said he would remember and she had to believe this was one promise he would never break.

The crowd of onlookers began to disperse only after the last of the troops had passed. The boys were excited – the military band and the smart brave soldiers had captured all their imaginations, and even the peaceable Bobby joined in when Charlie organized them into a troop, marching with swinging arms, in imitation of the Tommies. Matty hung back, holding on to Nellie's hand on one side and Alice's on the other.

'Aren't we lucky we saw him, Matty?' Alice said. 'We could've missed him, in all that lot.'

Matty nodded. 'But Sam would never have let us miss him.'

And Nellie felt she was right. It had been Sam's eyes that drew her gaze to him, she was certain. In spite of her brave smile, Nellie could see that Matty still needed cheering up. Nearly thirteen, the girl was tall for her age and a recent growth spurt meant that the clothes she had brought with her were now far too short and tight. Alice had no cast-offs for her, as practically everything she wore had once belonged to Nellie anyway and was falling to pieces.

'Tell you what, why don't we make the most of our afternoon off? Me and Alice'll take you down the clothes market and get you a new dress!'

Matty's eyes lit up. Alice went to explain to the boys, who didn't want to give up their marching to join a shopping expedition. Nellie told them to go straight home, with little expectation that the order would be obeyed. They would be out playing soldiers all night, she knew.

They turned down Grange Road towards the Bermondsey 'Old Clo' market. It was packed with second-hand clothes stalls on either side of the road. Crowds round each stall were like bees around honeypots, picking over the wares and moving quickly on, jostling each other out of the way, in pursuit of a bargain. There wasn't an inch of spare pavement. People came from far and wide to get a bargain suit or dress. But there were varying degrees of age – some dresses were only second hand, others third or fourth. Nellie and Alice headed for the stall their mother used to frequent; here at least the clothes were all washed first. The Clark children had always been clean and smartly turned out. Age of clothes hadn't counted, but cleanliness was everything, as far as Nellie's mother was concerned. Alice and Nellie had always loved those trips for 'new' dresses and Nellie was surprised to see Matty hanging back, looking decidedly uncomfortable in all the jostling throng.

'Have a look at this one, Matty!' She held up a pretty striped-print dress, with a frilled bottom and puff sleeves. It had no apparent wear and was of a good cotton.

'Let me hold it up against you.'

Matty dragged her feet and it became obvious that she was near to tears. Nellie despaired. What could she do to raise the girl's spirits?

'What is it, love? If you don't like it, there's plenty more to choose from.'

Matty looked up at her with a pained expression. 'I don't like it here, Nellie. I thought I was getting a new dress.'

'Well, you are…' Realization dawned. 'What, you mean *brand* new?'

Matty nodded. Nellie was dumbfounded. Surely it wasn't possible that Matty had been brought up in Bermondsey, without ever coming to the Old Clo' market, and how could she think that 'new' meant 'brand new'? In most homes, children's clothes were either cast-offs from siblings or second hand from the 'Old Clo'; brand new was reserved for weddings and funerals. She simply couldn't imagine how the Gilbies had managed to kit Matty out in brand-new clothes all her life.

'Did your mum used to make your clothes?' she asked, but Matty shook her head.

'We used to go over the other side once a year. I thought that's where we was going.'

Nellie shot a look at Alice. Poor Matty really had been spoiled if she'd had West End clothes every year. If that was what she was used to, there would be more shocks in store for her in her new home.

'Well, love, I'm sorry, but we just can't afford *brand* new, but I promise you we'll get you something nice, no old tat!'

Matty wasn't stupid; neither was she a selfish child, and now, seeming to notice Nellie's discomfort, she threw off her own. She picked up the edge of the dress that Nellie was still holding.

'It *is* a pretty colour,' she said, and Nellie sighed with relief.

Nellie paid the stall holder, and by the time they arrived back in Vauban Street Matty seemed happy to try on the dress. Walking up and down the little kitchen, she even showed off a little, swishing the skirt as she turned for them to see the back.

'It'll need taking up a bit, but you look lovely, don't she, Al?'

Alice, already with a mouthful of pins, nodded enthusiastically as she knelt to tuck up the dress.

Later that night, when they were alone, Alice brought up the subject of Matty's dress again. She had spent the evening making alterations to sleeves and hem and had just finished ironing the dress. She held it up for Nellie's inspection. 'How could Matty's mum and dad afford West End clothes every year?' she asked Nellie.

'Well, Mr Gilbie was a foreman, but even so, they had other kids and I can't say I've ever noticed Sam in really expensive stuff. When we were kids at the Settlement club, he was the same as all of us, darns and patched-up boots, but clean. But now I come to think of it, I've never seen a darn in anything of Matty's.'

It was a puzzle and in the end they concluded Matty must have been spoiled because she was the youngest and perhaps because Lizzie knew she would not be there to see her grow up.

'Poor little thing, I did feel sorry for her in that market,' Alice said. 'She looked like a rose among the thorns, didn't she?'

Nellie could only agree, and determined that whatever she could not give to Matty in monetary terms, she'd make up for in love.

25

HOME SOIL

By the time she received the letter in December of 1914, it had travelled round the world and back. Eliza looked at the crossed-out forwarding addresses, first Mecklenburgh Square, then the villa in Melbourne, back to the NFWW headquarters in London, from where her friend Sarah had forwarded it here. She didn't know the handwriting, but something about the looping 'G' was reminiscent of her father's lovely copperplate hand: this was from a Gilbie. She ripped open the envelope and read Sam's brief note, telling of her mother's end.

'Oh, no, Mum! No!' she wailed, looking around for someone to tell, but the house was empty, except for her two-year-old son. Alone in her grief, she sat down and wept till her chest burned. The shock had set her body trembling and now she tried to understand how her mother could possibly have been dead since March – five months – without her ever knowing! Surely she should have felt something go out of the world, her mother's flame-like spirit extinguished, and all the chances of changing their damaged past gone forever. Pulling herself to her feet, she walked unsteadily upstairs, to look at her sleeping child. She'd named him William, after her grandfather and her long-dead but still beloved older brother. She could only now feel grateful that his grandmother had at least met her child. When she'd taken the three-month-old William to see Lizzie that day in 1913, her mother had seemed pleased with the name. William, the Gilbies' firstborn, had been a simple, sunny-natured boy who'd not long survived the family's move to London from Hull. Eliza, aged five at the time, remembered him only dimly, but Lizzie had always said he was like a delicate flower that didn't bear transplanting.

Looking down now at her own sturdy sleeping two-year-old, she thought how different he was from his namesake. He had Ernest's strong-boned limbs and dark hair, but Lizzie's eyes, which could turn from limpid pools to flashing fire in an instant, shone from his face. Perhaps it was those eyes, looking up at her from his crib, that had finally steeled Eliza to make her escape from Ernest. Fortunately, her William was no delicate flower; at three months old he'd transplanted with ease from halfway around the world. After introducing him to his grandmother, she'd returned to her birthplace, Hull, the one place she hoped Ernest would not think of looking. He'd go to find his 'cockney sparrer' in Bermondsey, of that she was sure.

He hadn't let her go easily. She was surprised in the end by how much she meant to him, or perhaps he just couldn't bear to lose a fight, and their battle over William had at times felt like a fight to the death. It hadn't been so much a question of many rows or arguments but more a silent clash of wills. She'd never repeated her initial pleas to keep the baby; it was not in Eliza's nature to beg. Instead she'd behaved as though she had lost, all the while knowing she had won. She'd set her will to keeping the child, whatever the consequences, and made her plans, going along with Ernest's wish for her to take the child to the country, while a suitable foster-home could be found.

'He is, after all, my son, Eliza, and even though he will be in the care of others I should, of course, want him to be brought up a gentleman,' Ernest had said.

She let herself reflect silently on the contrasting lack of interest he'd displayed in his daughter's upbringing. Her station in life seemed unimportant to him. He had provided the money to keep her fed, clothed and well looked after, but that was all. Eliza hadn't foreseen the different treatment a son would elicit from him. Still, it made no difference to her own plans; they just might need to be more subtly executed than she had imagined. So she kept her counsel and retired to the country, seemingly happy to go along with all Ernest's wishes.

They even talked of the new direction their work could take once, in Ernest's words, they were 'unencumbered'. Her position with the Australian trades unions had a stipend attached, which she began to squirrel away soon after she learned of her pregnancy. Ernest was open-handed when it came to her financial needs, she had a clothing allowance and the run of the household expenses. She silently built up the means of securing her passage to England and enough capital to establish them in a small house in a suburb of Hull. The only person she confided in was Sarah, her trusted friend in the NFWW. Sarah had found Eliza a small, affordable house in Hull and had also drummed up some paid work for her with the NFWW Hull branch: it would supplement the interest on her savings and in any case poverty didn't frighten her.

She bided her time and, bit by bit, eased herself out of the material shackles in which Ernest held her. The emotional shackles, however, proved more difficult to shed. The early years with him had been full of excitement and promise; he'd given her much. It was only as she grew older that she realized the value of what she had given up in return: home, family and in the end her child. She had thought becoming Ernest's mistress was a radical choice; instead she'd found it was a trap. Without her knowing it, she'd entered into a contract. In Bermondsey she would be known as his 'fancy woman'. She was certainly a 'kept woman' and only now that she was breaking away did she realize how much she depended on him. For the last decade, her every decision had been vetted by him, even down to the clothes she wore, the books she read. Shortly after William's birth, as she'd sat nursing her newborn, isolated in the bush country outside Melbourne, she'd reassembled memories of her childhood: the rough and tumble of Bermondsey streets and pubs; the steely determination inherited from her mother; the bookish curiosity passed on from her father. She tried to reconstruct herself. She remembered her poor brother William and asked herself, Who would Eliza Gilbie be today, if *she* had never been transplanted to Mecklenburgh Square?

Little William, her demanding, angry, bawling child, gave her the answer. She would never find strength in a vanished past, or an imaginary version of herself. She would only find it in the present. Who she *would* have been, she couldn't say; what she was today was a mother determined to keep her child. That had become her guiding light, powerful enough to get her down to the dock office, to purchase her steamer ticket in secret. It gave her the armour to fight off guilt about deceiving Ernest; it steeled her to pack up her few things and carry her six-week-old baby to the waiting cab. Only when the ship steamed out of the harbour and she held her child up to see the disappearing coast of Australia did she finally allow herself to feel anything. The emotion took her by surprise – she'd imagined she would feel relief, but she laughed when she recognized that what she felt was pure joy.

Almost two years she'd had now, of holding that joy like a secret pearl in her heart, almost two years since she'd docked in Southampton. She could scarcely believe it, but she only had to look down at her sleeping toddler to prove to herself the passing of time; his first words and his first steps were already behind him. Now, in this quiet upstairs room in a suburb of Hull, with the northern light settling over his cot, she remembered him as a babe in arms, how she'd carried him off the boat on to the waiting train. Going to Mecklenburgh Square had been unthinkable; Ernest would have wired the steward looking after the place and she'd needed to remain undetected for as long as possible. But it hadn't been so much the need to remain anonymous as the need to be known that had driven her on that day as she'd made her way like a homing pigeon straight to Bermondsey. Bundling herself and her son into the motor taxi at London Bridge Station, driving through the close clustered streets of Bermondsey, she'd had only one thought: to see her mother.

She couldn't have known it would be the last time, for now

Lizzie was gone. With Sam's crumpled letter still tightly balled in her fist, the tears came again. Letting herself sink down beside William's cot, pushing aside the grief that threatened to overwhelm her, she allowed the memories of that last meeting with her mother to wash over her.

She'd attracted the street urchins' taunts as she'd emerged from the taxi in her expensively cut travelling suit and feather-trimmed hat – 'I got an 'at, just like that old rotten 'at ...' had come the sing-song insult she remembered from her own childhood. They'd crowded curiously round her, asking, 'That's Matty's house, d'ye know her?' But when she'd opened the front door, Matty hadn't seemed to know her at all. 'Mum, there's a lady come to see you!' she'd called. Then came her mother's voice, tremulous, weaker than she'd remembered it. 'Well, ask her in, Matty, love.' Finally, in the kitchen, there was her mother, eyes widening. Eliza had felt so awkward, filling the little room with her height and her hat and her long absence, but most of all with her child. Her mother gazed for a telling moment at the baby, then suddenly held out her arms for him.

'His name is William,' Eliza said.

Then Lizzie gave her the warmest of smiles. 'I'm glad we've got another William.' Turning to Matty, her mother asked, 'Don't you remember your sister Eliza?'

Eliza recalled now, with satisfaction, the thrust of Matty's chin and her ready response. 'If she'd come more often, I might've.' And the young girl turned sulkily away. 'I'll make some tea.'

Lizzie excused her. 'She's not normally so rude, it's the shock of seeing you, I expect. I'm a bit shocked meself, to tell you the truth.'

Eliza remembered her energy draining away once she was seated opposite her mother. 'I've left him, Mum,' she said, too weak for more explanation.

Lizzie nodded. 'Good, you should have done it years ago, if you ask me. Your poor dad was right about him. He always said you'd have no life of your own while you were under his roof. Is it his child?'

Muscles held taut for all the long weeks of her voyage finally relaxing, she let her tears fall then. 'Yes, but he doesn't want to keep him... and I couldn't lose another one, Mum.' Kneeling beside her mother, she let herself be soothed.

'Shhhh, shhh, Liza, what's done is done. She's been as happy as any child could be and you know she's been loved, but it would be a cruelty now to take her from her family, you understand?'

Eliza had understood only too well: like William, her long-dead brother, Matty was a flower that would not bear transplanting.

Now she bitterly regretted not staying longer with her mother, but when Sam came home, though he made much of the baby, he barely acknowledged Eliza. He'd obviously cast her in the role of heartless daughter and feeling awkward in his disapproving presence she soon made to leave. She promised her mother she would write once she was settled and had already impressed upon her the need to keep her whereabouts a secret, even from Sam. Ernest would undoubtedly come looking for her and the fewer people he could question, the better.

Sam took her back to London Bridge Station in a taxi and their leave-taking was particularly painful. They walked together to the station entrance and, standing beneath the glow of a gas lamp, he turned a stony face to her. 'I'm not letting you take our Matty away, you know.'

Eliza was dumbfounded. 'Have you always known?'

'I didn't, for a long time,' he said. 'I came home from school one day and there was a baby laying in the bottom drawer, I just accepted she was my new sister. I loved her right off.' Sam's voice trembled.

'When did you find out?'

'Not until you turned up, during the strike. Mum had to tell me then. She was terrified you'd come to take her back. You can't come walking back into people's lives, turning everything upside down...'

'Sam—' Eliza tried to explain, but he grew angry.

'You'll ruin that little girl's life if you take her away from everything she knows—'

'Sam! I'm trying to tell you, I'm *not* taking her away!' Eliza shouted over him.

'You're not?'

'I promised Mum, when I gave her up, that I wouldn't take her away and I'll keep my promise.'

The truth was, she'd known as soon as she'd arrived at Beatson Street that it was too late for her to be anything other than Matty's sister, but she wanted to reassure him. 'Sam, I haven't come to upset Matty's life. I know you've blamed me for staying away all these years, but I hope now you understand why. It was just too hard to see her and to know…'

'You missed out on a lot, Eliza.' He didn't make it easy for her. 'She's special, our Matty.'

As he dipped his head to kiss the baby goodbye, she was overcome by sadness. 'I know, Sam. Letting her go was the biggest mistake of my life.'

Now William, stirring in his cot, reclaimed her attention. She didn't know how long she'd sat there, replaying those painful scenes, but she pulled herself up, stiff now with cold and shock. William's eyes were open – Lizzie's eyes. It was true, she'd certainly made her share of mistakes, but there were two she could never regret. William was one of them and bringing Matty into the world was the other.

Since hearing the news of her mother's death, Eliza had become paralysed by unaccustomed indecision. Should she go to Sam and explain why she hadn't replied, or gone to the funeral? He must despise her even more than before. She was tempted to just let it all go, all her ties to the past, to her family, and perhaps she would have if it hadn't been for the war. True, she'd promised her mother to leave Matty with the only family she'd ever known, but didn't the war void all promises? What would happen to her daughter if Sam was called up?

She went through the motions of her life for a whole week, mulling over the best course of action. She was proud of the life she'd made for herself here in Hull. Her house, in this respectable suburb, was worlds away from Mecklenburgh Square, but at least it was hers rather than Ernest's. She'd kept her activities with the NFWW deliberately low-key and the Hull branch had offered her a small amount of paid administrative work; that, with the interest from her own investments, gave her enough to keep herself and William comfortably. Though she still gave speeches locally and helped arrange meetings, the balance of her life had changed dramatically. Now William was the priority in her life, not her work and certainly not Ernest.

And that was the other complication she had to consider. Ernest was back in England. Her contact with him had been filtered through the NFWW offices in London: apparently his initial rage at what he called her betrayal and ingratitude had dwindled, after he found that the sisterhood at the NFWW would not break silence over her whereabouts. But the last letter had informed her that he was coming home to offer his services to the war effort. Ernest wasn't the only radical to put his beliefs on hold, to do what he saw as his patriotic duty, though her own opinions differed, and if conscription were ever introduced she would be on the side of the conscientious objector. She decided the best thing was to write to Sam. When, after several days, the letter had been returned to her with *unknown at this address* on the envelope, she panicked. She arranged for a friend to look after William, then took a train to London the next day.

It was a bitter January day when she found herself in Beatson Street once again. An icy wind whipped off the river, bringing with it the long-remembered musky, muddy smell. But the house was not as she remembered. It looked shabbier; one of the front sash windows had several broken panes stuffed up with newspaper, the front step, which Eliza knew her mother had insisted on keeping spotless, was filthy and a pile of windblown rubbish had collected around the front door, the paint of which was peeling. Eliza knocked, with a sense of foreboding. A ragged child of about four answered the door, wearing nothing but a shirt. His legs and feet were bare and his face, Eliza judged, hadn't seen soap and water in weeks.

'Is Sam Gilbie home?' she asked hopelessly, knowing he wouldn't be. He would never have allowed the place to go to ruin like this.

'If you're the tallyman, then Mum ain't in!' The little boy's voice piped out in a rehearsed sing-song voice.

'Tell your mother it's not the tallyman and that a lady's here to see her.'

The child trotted off, a none-too-clean behind visible beneath the short shirt. Eliza waited and eventually a careworn woman, holding a tiny, pale infant, came to the door. She was full of apologies. 'I'm ever so sorry, madam...' she did what looked like a curtsey '...but I've been sick and bad since the baby come and I can't get to the door quick. Reggie's always there before me!'

She drew the scantily clad boy to her skirt. Eliza guessed Reggie was always the one to open the door, the gatekeeper who kept out the tallyman.

'I'm so sorry to bother you,' said Eliza, 'but I'm looking for Sam Gilbie, he used to live here.'

'Oh, Sam! Yes, he's a lovely boy. Did you know the Gilbies? Sad about his poor mother. He took it very bad.'

'Yes, I've only just heard. I wanted to see Sam... to pay my respects.'

'Well, he's gone, madam,' the woman went on.

'Do you know where?'

The woman looked as though Eliza were an imbecile.

'Well, to France, I should think, madam,' she replied.

For a moment Eliza stood in uncomprehending silence and then the sickening realization dawned: she had come too late, for if Sam was in France, where were Charlie and Matty?

26

CUCKOO'S NEST

By January of 1915, Pearce Duff's male workforce had been so depleted by the war that Ethel Brown was able to give Nellie all the overtime she could cope with. Today she'd worked the day shift, and now, after popping home for half an hour to have a bite to eat, she was back for another three hours' overtime on the night shift. She pulled off her coat and lifted the mob cap and smock from the peg; she was sick of the sight of them. Sometimes she wondered what it would be like to have a clean job, one where you could do your work in nice clothes that still looked decent at the end of the day. As she passed the boiler room, she looked with sympathy at the girl stokers. Stoking! Nellie was glad she hadn't been commandeered to do it. Since most men in the boiler room had enlisted, the stronger girls in the factory had taken on the job. Peeking through the open doors, plumes of steam rolled towards her and the furnaces hissed like fire-breathing dragons. One girl was tottering along under a sack of coal, which she tipped on to a great pile in front of a furnace. Looking up at Nellie, eyes white in her blackened face, she asked, 'Fancy a go?'. And grinned.

'No fear!'

The place looked like hell. As soon as the piles of coal were replenished, there were other women waiting to start shovelling coal into the fiery maws. The coal dust was even worse than custard powder and Nellie hurried upstairs, counting her blessings.

She walked on to the factory floor and blinked. It was aglow.

Light, from gas lamps suspended from high ceilings bounced off cold, darkened windows, forming a golden cocoon around the packers. Nellie settled into the slightly slower, more subdued rhythm of the night shift.

She spent much of it worrying about Freddie and Charlie. Now he was thirteen, Freddie had big ideas. He was itching to leave the board school and start working full time, and he wasn't the only bird in Nellie's cuckoo's nest anxious to try their wings. Fourteen-year-old Charlie had just left school. He'd brought home a surprisingly good report, with a recommendation he try the college exam; apparently the boy was clever. Nellie had never considered him brighter than the rest of the children. Always so silent and stolid, he just seemed to move steadily through the world, towards some private destination.

When she asked him about his report, he said firmly, 'Even if there was money for college, I wouldn't go. I'm better off out earning, Nellie.'

She was relieved, grateful she wouldn't have to be the one to squash his dreams with practicalities, and he'd gone straight to Wicks as a carter's boy. Sam had already taught him everything he knew about horses and, after losing half his drivers to the war, Old Wicks was only too grateful that Charlie could take Sam's place. Wicks also promised Freddie a full-time job at the end of this school year. But, not the sort of boy to let the grass grow under his feet, Freddie had other ideas.

The overtime was certainly helping them out, but the drawback was that the family was now behind with this week's home-work delivery. After her three-hour night shift, the last thing she wanted was a late session of matchbox pasting, but she came home to find Alice still working. With a sigh, she sat down dutifully and started pasting on labels. Freddie couldn't have picked a better time to put his proposal. Before going to bed he casually announced, 'I want to expand me roses business, Nell. Thing is, what with all the parks being turned into allotments, there's people crying out for manure and they can't get hold of it!' Not realizing that she hadn't an iota of resistance in her, he pushed his case. 'An' I reckon I can make enough extra money so we can give up these matchboxes!'

This got her full attention. He didn't have to explain the economics of it. Every square inch of public space in London was being dug up for vegetable growing; people feared being starved out by the German convoys before the war was over. He stood by the kitchen mantelshelf, waiting for her answer, and as she saw him glance in the mirror above it, she noticed how tall he was getting. He was a good-looking boy, with fair hair and bright blue eyes. His growing limbs looked a little gangly now, but she knew that as he filled out he would have the imposing physique of his father. Just now, though, she was painfully aware of his wrists poking out from the too-short arms of his jacket and the trousers flapping an inch above his boots. At least she had a few months before he started work, but then he really would need new clothes.

'I can't see anything wrong in that,' she said. 'It's good *honest* work, ain't it?' she added, as sternly as she could manage. Freddie's blue eyes widened in surprise and he simply laughed at her.

'I don't 'alf-inch the horse shit, if that's what you mean!' he said indignantly.

'Well, it's about the only thing you don't!'

Freddie chose to ignore this and carried on. 'So, I can do it?'

'All right, but don't you hop the wag, you're not finished school *yet*!'

Freddie gave her a kiss goodnight, which was unusual for him, and said he would have to discuss it with his 'boys'.

'Do you think he's got something dodgy cooking up?' asked Alice, looking up curiously from her work.

'Do you know what, Al, I'm getting to the stage I'd rather not ask, but this sounds better than some of the other stuff he's been getting up to!'

Freddie was proving to be an adept businessman in all sorts of areas. Nellie had noticed a series of enigmatic boxes being stored in the yard. They never stayed for long, but they usually resulted in a few extra shillings in the housekeeping tin, which Freddie would drop in ostentatiously after each transaction. She told herself that if some of her brother's gains were through the black market, they were on a small scale and she just hoped that, once he got a regular job, the shady dealings would fall by the wayside.

'Wouldn't it be good if we didn't have to do the matchboxes any more?' Alice said wistfully.

Nellie groaned as she reached for the pot of glue. 'What I wouldn't give for a house that didn't stink of glue. And I do worry about the kids breathing it in all the time. Perhaps with Freddie's extra money and Charlie's wage, it might just be enough...' Looking over at Alice's hopeful face, she decided. 'Bugger it, once we've finished this week's, that'll be our lot, Al. I don't care how much overtime I have to do. We're packing in the matchboxes!'

Alice's normally quiet, worried face creased into a smile and she shouted, 'Hoorah! No more white slavery! Get the banner out, Nell!'

To show she meant business, Nellie gathered up a stack of labels, threw them up in the air and slumped back against the chair, laughing, as they fluttered down around them like multicoloured butterflies.

'France!' Eliza should have known he would be in the first rush of volunteers. *Sam*, she thought bitterly, *so full of your sense of what's right, no wonder you jumped to be Kitchener's cannon fodder!* The woman could give her no information on Charlie or Matty's whereabouts and, unsure what to do, Eliza walked briskly back along Rotherhithe Street, her face gradually growing numb in the icy air. She had brought an overnight bag; perhaps she should just look for a hotel and think about her search tomorrow? But the thought of Matty with strangers wrenched her heart. She had borne their separation when she knew Matty was safe with her own family, but now Sam was gone, perhaps never to return. She was her daughter's only family now. Who would be looking after her? Perhaps, if she could only find her, this was her chance to make up for past mistakes? She saw a tram heading for Southwark Park Road and ran to catch it. She would go to the Fort Road Labour Institute; there was a chance someone there might know something.

The tram was full; she huddled into a seat on the top deck, pulling up the leather apron designed to keep out the worst of the weather, but still she shivered in the freezing mist rolling off the Thames. As the tram turned past Rotherhithe Tunnel and away from the river, she hoped the damp mist might clear, but getting off at Southwark Park Road she found herself enveloped in a thick yellow fog, all the everyday traffic sounds of horses' hooves, iron-rimmed cartwheels and puttering motor engines muffled by its density. Registering only the thud of her own heart and the rasp of her own stinging breath, she started to feel herself overtaken by panic. Images of her daughter lost and alone in this fog assailed her. She quickened her pace, heedlessly colliding with startled pedestrians, each time wondering: *Do you know Matty? Have you seen my daughter?* Ignoring their puzzled looks, hurrying on through the late-afternoon streets, she found herself stumbling forward, breaking into a trot. She was dimly aware that the young girl she was frantic to find wasn't the real Matty, a child she barely knew; but there was another Matty, an imagined child, dear to her, one she'd kept in her heart through all the years of separation, and this was the child she sought. But when she'd visited she'd seen a comforting tough streak in the real Matty that was totally absent from her imaginary daughter, whom she'd always imagined as a fragile rose amongst thorns. Trying to convince herself another day wouldn't make much difference was useless – all composure had left her as she dashed on, desperate to find Matty. She darted down a side street, looking for a quicker way to the institute, but so many confused, conflicting thoughts raced through her head

271

she was soon lost in a swaddled maze of back streets.

Forcing herself to stand stock still, she faced her terror: she *would* find Matty. She just had to think! Peering through the mist in search of a landmark, she spotted the dark spire of St Anne's. This must be Thorburn Square! She knew where she was. Feeling her way forward, she followed the iron railings round the churchyard, till she came to Fort Road and the double-gabled institute. Suddenly the kindly face of Frank Morgan was staring at her from the front door of the Labour Institute.

'It's Eliza James, isn't it? Come in, come in, you're frozen!' He drew her into his office, his surprise evident. 'We haven't seen you since... what, the year of the strike? I thought you were in Australia, with Mr James!'

He drew up a chair for her in front of the office fireplace, where he had a bright blaze burning. She was shivering.

'Let me get you a cup of tea to warm you up!' he said, and immediately despatched his young assistant to bring some.

'Thank you, Mr Morgan, you're very kind, but I really can't stop.' Eliza tapped her foot on the grate, leaning forward to warm her hands at the flames. 'You see, I'm looking for a child, well, two in fact, and I'm very concerned for their welfare...'

She stopped herself short, growing aware of the irrationality of her panic. Telling herself to breathe, she accepted the tea and made herself sip it slowly. Sam loved Matty, she told herself, he would have left her safe. She took another deep breath and as the warmth of the room thawed her numbed hands, she explained her quest.

'Oh, the Gilbie children! Yes, I know the family, poor Mrs Gilbie was on our Co-op round, and of course you are... I mean, you have a connection, don't you?'

Frank Morgan was a local man, old enough to know the rumours about Eliza's parentage, but though she was grateful for his tact, she no longer had anything to hide.

'Yes, Mr Morgan, Lizzie Gilbie was my mother, but I've only just found out about her death.'

'Oh, I'm very sorry to hear that, Mrs James. Is that what brought you back from Australia?'

'I've been back for some time.' She didn't have to tell him everything. 'But not in London. Do you know where Sam sent the children, by any chance?'

Frank went to his desk and brought back a set of index cards, which he flicked through as he spoke.

'Ahh, here she is!' He looked up, having found the address. 'Nellie Clark, she does a Co-op round for us, you may remember her from the strike days, one of the custard tarts?'

Eliza cast her mind back to a time that seemed part of another world, a golden summer's day of hope and triumph, when Nellie Clark, bold as brass, had faced down a guardsman's bayonet and then surfaced from the crushing crowd worrying only about the state of her new wool jacket.

'Yes, I remember Nellie Clark very well,' she said.

Nellie knew the children would be overjoyed to see the end of the matchbox-making, for once the novelty had worn off each evening had seen them produce less and less; of late she and Alice had done most of the work. Matty and Bobby still lent a hand, but Freddie and Charlie were now exempted. Still, she wanted them all together when she told them the good news, so she'd waited till teatime the next day.

Bobby's relief was characteristically low-key. 'At least we'll be able to get into our bedroom now, them boxes take up all the space!' he grunted.

But Matty was ecstatic, for handling the glue brought her out in a rash. She held up her red hands. 'And I'll have the hands of a ladeee!' she sang out.

'But listen, kids, we've got to give it one more push, so you'll all have to muck in tonight to get them finished. I promise once I've taken this last lot to the depot, that's it!'

Even Freddie and Charlie agreed to help and they all squeezed round the table, as of old.

'Brings back memories, eh?' Bobby asked, to snorts of universal incomprehension.

He could be sentimental about anything, Nellie observed fondly.

'Yes, and *all* bad!' said Freddie. 'Stop wandering down memory lane and get workin'!'

'Let's have a sing-song, to keep us going!' Matty set up a tune and their voices were soon making such a din that at first they didn't hear the knock.

'Shhhh, shhh a minute.' Alice called for quiet. 'Was that a knock?'

They all fell suddenly silent. Nellie's heart lurched and her stomach tightened. Since Sam had left for France, every unexpected knock made her feel sick. The telegrams could come at any time and the news was never good. All the high-spirited cheer vanished from the room as she got up, white-faced, to answer the door.

A young boy that Nellie didn't recognize stood at the door, gasping for breath so much that at first he couldn't deliver his message. She felt relief flood through her, as soon as she saw he wasn't wearing the uniform of a telegram delivery boy. She relaxed her grip on the door handle; thank God Sam was safe – for now.

'Are you Nellie Clark?' the boy eventually managed to pant out.

She replied that she was and he delivered his message between heaving breaths. 'I've come from Lily at the chandler's shop. She said, can you come quick. She's fallen down the stairs and thinks the baby's coming!'

Nellie pulled the boy inside and stood him in front of the fire. All matchboxes were dropped, as the family followed his story. The boy was employed to do odd jobs around the chandler's shop. Lily's in-laws had gone out and the boy had been charged with watching the shop for the afternoon.

'I heard this almighty clatter in the yard and when I run out

274

to see what it was, Lily's gone down the stairs!' The poor boy's eyes were wide as saucers.

'Why didn't she send you to her mum's?' Nellie was throwing on her coat.

'She did. I run all the way there, but no one was home! She said to come to you next.'

Nellie took charge. 'All right now, you stay here and catch your breath, then on your way back, you knock for Mrs Bosher again, she can't have gone far. Al, give him a penny and a cup of tea. Can I trust you lot to finish the boxes?'

The little audience, squashed round the table, nodded in unison. The drama unfolding before them had for once stunned them to silence.

'I'm off – I'll take the penny-farthing, it'll be quicker. I'll be back as soon as I can, but go to bed if I'm late!' she ordered as she launched herself out of the back door. She trotted the penny-farthing out into the icy fog and flung herself on to the saddle. Sam had fitted a lamp on the front handlebars, and she was glad of it now. She couldn't afford to be run down by a hansom or a motor bus tonight!

By the time she finally turned into the chandler's back yard she was damp through with sweat and freezing fog penetrating her clothes. She removed the bicycle lamp, shining it through the thick mist. She could see no light on in Lily's upstairs rooms, the shop or the McBrides' home.

'Where the bloody hell is everyone?' she called out. 'Lily, where are you, love?'

A tremulous voice called back from the bottom of the steep flight of stairs that led up to Lily's home. Nellie rushed to her friend's side.

'Oh, Lil, don't tell me you've been stuck here all this time. Why didn't you go in the McBrides'?'

Lily raised a pale face. 'I've twisted me ankle, I can't get up!' she wailed.

'All right, shhh, love, I'm here now, we'll get you up.'

Summoning a strength she didn't know she had, she put Lily's arm over her shoulder, grasped under her other arm and heaved. Lily's little boots slipped and scraped on the slick cobbles. Nellie strained, then, taking all Lily's weight, managed to haul her upright.

'All right, love, my dad always did say us Clark women was tough as coal heavers – here we go!'

Nellie lifted her friend like a sack of coal. Bending forward, she tottered under her weight towards the McBrides' back door. Nellie kicked at it and it swung open. Using the last of her strength, she got Lily through the back scullery and into the McBrides' kitchen, where she lowered her on to a chair.

'Thank God there's some embers.' She glanced towards the grate. 'Let's get a fire going.' Nellie knelt down and pulled out the damper, adding coal from the bucket at the hearth. Then she pulled off the kitchen tablecloth, wrapping it round a frozen Lily, whose teeth were chattering with cold.

'I'm scared, Nellie. I think the baby's coming and there was no one home, I didn't know what to do. Where's me mum?' She burst into tears, sobbing and shaking.

'She was out, love, but I've sent the boy to wait for her. Where's your interfering in-laws when you need 'em, though?'

Lily managed a laugh. 'I'll never hear the last of it, will I? It was those soddin' stairs! I'd 'ave been all right if it wasn't for the mist. They was slippery as a bowl of eels. Ooohhhh!'

She clutched her stomach and Nellie remembered her mother's various labours. She knew she had a bit of time. 'Where's your midwife live? I think I'd better get her.'

Lily clutched her hand. 'Can't you wait till someone else gets home – I got so scared out there on me own, I kept thinking, what if I've killed me baby?' And she resumed her sobbing.

'Don't be such a soppy cow – your baby's fine, he just wants to come out and see what all the fuss is about! But, Lil, I don't think we can wait any longer. I'll be back in a jiff.'

Mrs Turner, the old lady who supervised all the births in

Rotherhithe Street, lived only a few doors away, so Nellie didn't have to run far. The old woman was not at all disconcerted by Nellie's story and seemed to take a delight in gathering her things at a snail's pace.

'She's been out in the freezing cold for over an hour!' Nellie tried to convey the urgency.

'You run back, dear, get some hot water on and find me some clean linen, will you? I'll be along shortly.'

Nellie, exasperated, shot off, glad to be doing something. Mrs Turner sauntered in fifteen minutes later, by which time Nellie had boiled kettles and raided the McBrides' linen cupboard.

Finally, when half an hour later the McBrides appeared, with Betty Bosher and the shop boy, Nellie faced a barrage of questions, but the parents seemed incapable of taking in the situation. The little kitchen was full to bursting and so was Lily, suddenly letting out one long howl, which finally galvanized Mrs Turner into action.

'Come on, this is like Casey's Court. Will someone help me get the poor girl to the bedroom?'

Helped by the two men, Lily was installed in the spare bedroom, next to the kitchen. Nellie followed them in, squeezing Lily's hand as she asked gently, 'You be all right now, love?'

Lily nodded. 'Thanks, Nell, you're my angel!'

'Funny sort of angel, me, on a penny-farthing!'

She left her friend in good hands and after making the two sets of parents cups of tea left them still discussing those stairs. Lily was right, she never would hear the last of it!

Frank Morgan had given Eliza directions, but once she found herself in the right vicinity, she merely followed her nose. He'd told her Vauban Street ran off Spa Road, not far from Pearce Duff's. That vanilla scent told her exactly where she was. She passed the factory gates and looked up at the glowing windows; the factory was lit up now for the night shift. Peeking in through the ground-floor windowpanes, she could see the sills thick with golden powder and beyond them rows of women bending over the powder machines. It satisfied her to know they were considerably better off for her efforts of three years ago. How she had fought for those women! She doubted any of them would recognize her now but all the same she hurried on past; she preferred her anonymity. The area looked shabbier than she'd remembered it; perhaps back then she'd viewed it through the eyes of her own triumph. On this fog-draped night it looked drear and down at heel. She passed the Salvation Army; lines of shuffling men still queued in hopes of a bed. Skirting round them, she was assaulted by the aroma of unwashed bodies. Did Matty have to walk past them every day? She passed a public house, just as the door was flung open; from inside came a fug of smoke and a flare of light. A drunk tumbled out, held up by a woman who was haranguing him.

'That's all yer good for,' she bellowed into his insensible ear, 'pissin' it all up the wall, while the kids are indoors starvin' 'ungry!'

The woman dropped the man and gave him a well-aimed kick, brushing past Eliza. Looking for somewhere to vent her anger, she shouted at her. 'And if you're one o' them Band of 'opers you can sling yer hook. He's signed the pledge hundred times and look at 'im!'

Eliza mumbled some useless words of sympathy and scurried on. At the next corner she sniffed, as the unmistakable smell of boiling bones reached her through the fog. She knew there was a glue works near by; how could she have forgotten? Bermondsey wasn't all strawberry jam and spices. The delicate Matty of her imagination wouldn't flourish here, not at all. She turned into Vauban Street, a long row of closely packed terrace houses that had seen better days. The house where Nellie Clark lived was directly next door to a carter's stable yard. The smell of horse dung wafted past her as she hesitated on the doorstep. She hadn't planned what she would say, and for the moment she just wanted to know that Matty was safe and well cared for. Her knock was answered almost immediately by a bird-boned young girl of about fifteen. Her look of surprise told Eliza she had been expecting someone else, but she was polite enough, once Eliza explained she had business with Nellie.

'Oh, I'm sorry, madam, she's not home, but I can give her a message—'

'I'm afraid I must speak to her tonight,' Eliza interrupted in her most cultured and persuasive tone. She would not be put off.

The girl hesitated, then asked her to come in. 'You'll have to excuse the mess, Nellie was called away sudden and we're in a bit of a two an' eight tonight.'

She was shown into a tiny front kitchen, filled with children, crowded round a square deal table covered in matchboxes in various states of assembly. There was a huge glue pot in the centre, containing several dripping brushes, the smell so pungent it made her light-headed. The fire in the range, coupled with the many bodies in the room, gave off a heat that was too stark a contrast to the cold outside and she staggered to one side, suddenly overcome with faintness.

The young girl hurried to her side and, with surprising strength, guided her to the only spare chair in the room. 'Bobby, get the lady a drop of water, quickly!'

She was aware of a skinny boy darting from the table to the scullery, and then of a cup being put to her lips.

'I'm so sorry,' she said between sips. 'I've had a long journey and I'm just a little chilled. I'll be all right.'

The girl introduced herself as Alice, Nellie's sister, and then, excusing the mess again, she explained they were finishing some home work. For the first time Eliza had a chance to look properly round the table. On one side sat the skinny little boy, dressed in what looked like hand-me-downs far too big for him; next to him was a well-built youth who, in contrast, had grown out of all his heavily darned clothes. At the end was her brother Charlie, wearing a collarless shirt, sleeves rolled up. He carefully replaced a glue brush into the pot and looked through her, without any sign of acknowledgement. Turned away from Eliza sat a young girl with auburn curls flowing down her back. Matty, after twisting her head briefly to see who the intruder was, quickly looked away and continued her work of glueing labels on to the box sides. All Eliza could see were Matty's small hands, covered in a raw rash, deftly dipping and pasting, dipping and pasting. She was horrified. It seemed obvious that Nellie Clark was running a sweatshop and there was her daughter, just as she had feared, a rose among thorns.

Nellie took the penny-farthing straight round to her back yard. The fog had grown even denser and her ride home had been slow and frightening. Hansom cabs and horse-drawn buses were upon her before she knew it, the warning clip-clop of horses' hooves dulled by the fog. Even motor-car lamps seemed unable to cut through the soaking yellow miasma swirling about the riverside streets. She was bone-tired and grateful to be home. She had on her father's old mackintosh, her old work boots and a flat cap covering her hair, which had frizzed up alarmingly in the fog. She dreaded finding a messy kitchen, still full of matchboxes and glue pots.

'I'm back and I hope you lot have finished that bloody home work!' she called out.

She stopped short at the doorway. The sight of Eliza James sitting in her front kitchen, being ministered to by Alice and stared at by a table full of children, was more than she could take in.

'Madam Mecklenburgh!' The nickname was out of her mouth before she knew it. 'Oh, sorry… Mrs James…'

Eliza waved away her apology, but Nellie could see she was not happy. The woman looked ill; perhaps it was the heat of the kitchen, but her face looked feverish and the cup she held in her hand shook slightly. As she tried to stand up and tottered, Alice caught her.

'Thank you, Alice, I'm not quite myself.'

Alice took Nellie's mackintosh, while Matty gave Nellie her chair, kissing her cheek as she did so and offering to make her a cup of tea.

'Thanks, Matty, love. Mrs James looks like she could do with one too.'

Matty gave Eliza a cold stare and went to the scullery to fill the kettle. Nellie remembered that night she'd first met Matty, when Nellie had been the intruding stranger and had to suffer the same mistrustful stares. Matty was fiercely protective of her family circle and, weary as she was, Nellie felt slightly irritated with Eliza for upsetting her. Apart from missing Sam, Matty had settled in happily to her new surroundings. Nellie hoped Eliza wasn't about to throw a spanner in the works. She couldn't imagine why the woman had turned up now with no warning. She certainly couldn't have picked a worse time, and looking round at the state of the kitchen she doubted Eliza had formed a good opinion of her household so far.

She decided not to apologize, but asked politely, 'What brings you back to Bermondsey, Mrs James? I thought you were in Australia.'

'Nellie, I have to speak my mind.' Eliza, seeming to gather strength, burst out, ignoring Nellie's question, 'I'm not sure if you know of my connection with Charlie and Matty, but I am their sister and I strongly object to the conditions you're keeping them in! This is sweated work! I've fought my entire life to stop this sort of slavery and I will not have my family involved in it! I don't know how Sam could think of leaving them with someone as irresponsible as you, but I won't have it!'

Nellie felt the combined intake of breath in the room, as the boys' eyes widened and grew eager, just as they did when they gathered round a street fight. Matty, who was bringing in the tea, overheard Eliza's last remark, and stood, cups in hand, hesitating in the doorway.

Alice's fear-filled eyes were locked on to Nellie's. Perhaps if she had spent an easier day, Nellie's response might have been more diplomatic, but she'd had enough. Eliza, in spite of her agitation, was an imposing figure, carrying an air of authority acquired over years of public speaking, as she sat there in her fine clothes, talking in that carefully doctored accent, but Nellie was not to be over-awed in her own kitchen. She stood up and for once in her life she was glad she'd inherited her father's strong frame, rather than the bird-like bones of her mother.

'*You* won't have it?' The scorn she felt was real as she let rip. 'Who the bloody hell d'you think you are? Coming into my house, accusing me of running a sweatshop! We're all just mucking in to keep us in house and home, if you must know, though it's none of your business!'

Eliza tried to interrupt, but Nellie's anger froze the woman in mid-flow, and she fixed Eliza with her ice-blue eyes. 'Sam's told me all about your so-called "connection" with these children, and there ain't none!'

She banged the kitchen table for emphasis and the glue pot toppled. The boys leaped to catch it, obviously not wanting anything to interrupt the show. Nellie's voice grew steelier as her indignation took hold. 'You haven't been near nor by them in years! They could've been starving in the street, for all you knew, and you've got the bloody cheek to blame Sam for putting them with me?' Eliza had no chance of interrupting; Nellie didn't pause for breath. 'Where were *you* when your mother died and the poor boy had to cope on his own? Where were *you* when he marched off to war? Well, let me tell you, even your own mother didn't trust you with these children! *She* was the one who asked me to take them in, not Sam!'

Now she could see that she had hit her mark. Eliza sat open-mouthed, all her righteousness evaporating. She seemed to shrink in size and the cup of water dropped from her hand, smashing on to the hearth as she crumpled in a heap on the floor.

'Alice, get the salts! Boys, help me get her up!' Nellie marshalled them and the kitchen exploded with activity. 'Matty, put those teacups down and stopper that glue pot!'

When Eliza came round, Nellie offered her the hot sweet tea, which she drank gratefully, surrounded by six anxious faces.

'I don't think you're the ticket, Mrs James,' Nellie said more gently, her anger paling at the thought Eliza might be truly ill. 'You've caught a chill. Where are you staying?'

Eliza gave the name of a hotel near London Bridge.

'I'll send Charlie to get you a cab,' suggested Nellie.

'No, I don't want to trouble you any more,' Eliza said weakly. 'I can walk to Spa Road Station and get a train from there.'

The small station, built into one of the railway arches at the end of Spa Road, was the halt before London Bridge, but Nellie was doubtful Eliza would be up to the walk. 'It's no trouble, you shouldn't be hanging about for trains in this weather.'

Nellie gave Charlie the eye and he shrugged on his coat, nodding once to Eliza as he left. Nellie decided it was best to send the other children to bed. 'Matty, love, come over and say goodnight to your sister.'

Matty walked sullenly over to Eliza and said dutifully, 'Goodnight, Eliza.'

Eliza grasped her hand. 'How you've grown, Matty, since I saw you last!'

Nellie could see that Matty was uncomfortable, squirming her hand until she released it from Eliza's grip. Walking up to Nellie, she reached up to kiss her goodnight and whispered, 'I ain't going with her!'

Nellie was unsure if Eliza had heard; given the woman's agitated state, she doubted it.

'Go on, Alice will take you up to bed.' Nellie put her arm round Matty's shoulders. 'Everything's all right now,' she reassured her.

Now her anger was spent, Nellie began to feel sorry for Eliza. When they were alone, she tried to explain. 'I think you might have got the wrong end of the stick, Mrs James. We had to take in home work after my dad died – but we're on our feet now and this was our last lot of matchboxes.'

Eliza nodded slowly. 'Perhaps I jumped to conclusions, but there are things we must talk about, Nellie, things that you're not aware of.'

Nellie gazed at the older woman. 'I'm sorry if it upset you... what I said about your mother, but it's the God's honest truth. She did want me to look after them when she was gone and Sam wouldn't have enlisted otherwise.'

'The war has changed everything,' Eliza said sadly, 'and with Sam gone, I'm their nearest relative.'

'Their place is with me,' Nellie replied firmly. 'I made a promise.'

27

MOTHER LOVE

Eliza insisted she must return the next day and speak to Nellie again. Nellie agreed, mostly because she wanted Eliza gone. She felt she'd been ambushed in her own home and only when she heard the disappearing cab wheels hissing down the damp cobbles of Vauban Street did she allow herself to relax. She sank into the chair lately occupied by Eliza and found that she was shaking. Alice sat opposite her and they were both silent for a long moment, then Alice voiced what she had been thinking.

'Could she take Matty and Charlie away from us?'

Nellie shook her head. 'I don't know, Al, but she'd have a bloody good fight on her hands if she tried.'

'She would know about the legal side of things, I suppose?' ventured Alice. 'What if we're breaking the law, keeping them?'

'I don't think she'd be bothered with that, I mean she hasn't cared about them up till now. No, I reckon it was just seeing them doing the home work did it, more to do with her principles than the kids, if you ask me. Sam always said she put her own work first, why would it be any different now?'

Nellie didn't want to worry Alice with her own fears, but she suspected if it came to a court of law, Eliza James would seem the most respectable guardian. She felt suddenly alone, caught in a net of bewildering responsibilities and doubtful if she were up to a battle with Eliza. If only Sam were here! But there was nothing to be done about it that night, so they extinguished the gas lamps and went upstairs to bed, being careful not to wake Matty. As they were undressing, Alice said quietly, 'Oh, Nellie,

I never even asked about Lily!'

The events of the evening had completely pushed Lily from her mind. 'Poor thing was still sitting out in the yard!' Nellie whispered. 'I ran for the midwife and by the time I left, everyone had turned up. Just think of it, she might be a mother by now!'

She felt guilty that she hadn't spared her friend a thought. She could only hope Lily's labour would be an easy one and again she felt a stirring of resentment at Eliza's intrusion. She and Lily had talked so often about the day when they'd be married and have babies of their own, yet Eliza had managed to deflect all the attention to herself. Nellie suspected that had always been the way with Eliza.

She spent a sleepless night. Waking with the dawn, she crept out of bed, leaving Alice to sleep on, and went downstairs to light the fire. She'd just got a good blaze going when there was a rather hesitant knock on the front door.

'Not again!' she said to herself, exasperated that Eliza should have returned already when they'd agreed to meet at a coffee shop during her lunch break.

She was wrapped in an old dressing gown of her mother's, and her hair hung down in a plait, but she didn't care. If the woman couldn't keep to the agreement, she couldn't expect royalty treatment. Nellie flung open the door.

'It's a boy!' Betty Bosher stood on the doorstep, beaming. 'I've just popped home for a few bits, but I had to come and tell you!' she explained.

Nellie threw her arms round Betty. 'A boy! How are they both? Come in!'

Betty came in, saying she couldn't stop long. Lily had begged her mother not to leave her alone with the fussing McBrides.

'The midwife said the fall had brought on the labour, but once she started, it was quick! He was born early hours and he's the face cut off of Jock!'

'Oh, Betty, I'm so pleased for her, I can't wait to see him! I'd

286

go up in my dinner break but I've got to see Sam's bloody sister.'

Betty was puzzled until Nellie explained which sister.

'Oh, my gawd, she's not turned up again, has she?' she gasped.

'Of course, you would know her, Betty, I forgot you were Mr Gilbie's cousin.' Nellie could see that Betty Bosher, born a Gilbie, shared the family prejudice against Eliza.

'She's the sort needs to remember where she come from, but Michael spoiled her rotten and shit was his thanks.'

Betty never minced her words. Her straightforward bluntness could sometimes wound, but Nellie knew Lily's mum saw things straight. 'Betty, I know you've got to rush, but can I ask your advice?'

'What you worried about, love?' She sat down solemnly at the kitchen table. 'Come on, I've got time for a cuppa.'

She told Betty all that had gone on with Eliza the previous night, finding it a relief to unburden herself. She waited, while Betty drained her tea.

'Lizzie Gilbie picked you for a good 'un, didn't she?'

'I suppose she did... But what should I do about Eliza? Sam didn't want the kids to go to her, nor to his Uncle George either!'

'Good job an' all. George and that wife of his 'ave got no idea where kids is concerned. He's such a miserable git, they'd 'ave had no life at all. But my advice is, you should meet Eliza and listen to what she's got to say—' Nellie went to interrupt, but Betty held up her hand. 'I'm not saying you give her the kids! No... just give her the chance to tell you...'

'Tell me what?'

Betty didn't answer; instead she got up.

'Chances are, she won't want them anyway. Her sort have got no time for kids...' Her face suddenly lit up. 'Talking of which, I'd better get back to me daughter and grandson!' Betty was again all smiles and Nellie thanked her.

'Go on, then, Nanny! And tell Lily I'll be round to see her and the baby tomorrow!'

As Betty hurried down the street, Nellie called after her, 'What's she named him?'

'John, after his dad!'

Nellie went to work in her best navy coat and skirt, nearly new from the Old Clo' market. The cut was good and the cloth a fine wool, with braided collar and cuffs. She'd taken up the skirt to a more fashionable length above the ankle and was determined that Eliza James would see not a speck of custard powder on her shoes, so she had her best small-heeled black tie-ups in a bag ready to change into at dinner break. Once at the factory she carefully tucked every inch of her abundant hair inside the white mob cap, wrapping the factory smock tightly around her. She knew she'd looked a state yesterday, with her frizzy damp hair and old mac. God knows what Eliza must have thought of her – today at least she could make a better impression.

As soon as the dinner hooter sounded, Nellie rushed to clock off, dashing down to the Jamaica Road coffee shop, where they'd agreed to meet. Eliza wasn't there when Nellie arrived, and for a brief moment Nellie hoped she might have changed her mind, that she would just disappear and leave them all in peace, but then she remembered the look of longing on Eliza's face as she'd held Matty's hand and said goodnight to the indifferent young girl. No, she didn't think Eliza would give up. Nellie chose a window seat, going over in her mind her talk with Betty. Was it true Eliza needed to remember where she'd come from? Nellie disagreed; from what she knew of her, Eliza was a woman who remembered all too well, and every remembrance came with a good dose of guilt. This wasn't someone ashamed of where she'd come from. If that was the case, why devote her life to improving conditions for those who still lived there? No, in Nellie's mind, Eliza hadn't escaped with a good riddance on her lips. Hers was more like a chosen exile, long regretted. Perhaps now she simply wanted the chance to make amends?

Nellie had a good view of the street and was surprised when

she saw Eliza stepping off a tram at the nearby stop; she'd expected her to come in a cab. Eliza paused briefly, looking around, then walked briskly towards the coffee shop. She was carrying her overnight bag, which Nellie hoped meant she would be leaving straight after their talk. She came through the door, looking a different woman from yesterday. Here was the controlled, composed figure Nellie remembered from three years earlier. Eliza smiled as she sat down, her first words an apology.

'I'm so sorry about my behaviour yesterday, Nellie. I jumped to conclusions about the home work. I of all people should know that sometimes there is no choice about how to put food on the table. I know you're a good girl and you're only doing your best.'

Eliza's warmth was in stark contrast to the stony-faced woman of last night, but Nellie knew all about Madam Mecklenburgh's reputation as a negotiator: 'Feed 'em a juicy worm, reel 'em in,' was what Ted used to say about her dealings with the bosses, 'then whack 'em over the head before they know what's hit 'em!'

Nellie knew she'd just been fed a juicy worm and waited to be reeled in. It wouldn't do to struggle, not just yet; she needed to hear Eliza out first.

'What I should have said last night was thank you.' Eliza fixed her with a look of gratitude, which seemed genuine, though it could have been the first tug of the hook. 'So let me say it now.' Eliza reached out and squeezed Nellie's hand as it rested on the table. 'Thank you for stepping in to look after my family. And the other thing I should have said was let me help.'

Eliza waited for her response. Nellie, who'd heard the clicking of a reel being turned, wondered what Eliza's 'help' might consist of. She suppressed an irritated sigh. If the woman thought she was in a boardroom with old Plum Duff, she was mistaken. She only had an hour's break and if she clocked on late, they'd dock an hour's pay. She decided to cut through Eliza's old flannel. 'What sort of help would that be, Mrs James?'

'Please call me Eliza, and Mrs James is no longer appropriate either. In fact, I should tell you that my situation has changed, Nellie. As you can see, I'm no longer in Australia, but neither am I living with Mr James... which is one of the reasons why I can offer to help.'

Ahh, so she had made her bid for freedom! Sam was wrong in his prediction that she would go back to Ernest. But Nellie didn't show her surprise; it was none of her business where Eliza lived.

'Is your child with you, then?' was all she said.

It was Eliza's turn to be surprised, but Nellie thought she made a good show of hiding it. She reached to a small heart-shaped locket at her throat and Nellie saw a dark lock of plaited baby hair caught behind the glass.

'Sam told you?'

Nellie nodded.

'You've obviously grown close; Sam's not the type to easily air the family dirty linen,' Eliza said, with a hint of bitterness.

Nellie was surprised at her honesty; she could have gone on with the pretence of being married. Perhaps she deserved some honesty in return.

'Yes, we are close. Life's brought us together, and if you want to know the truth of it I hope we always will be.'

'You love him then? Does he love you?' Eliza asked softly.

Nellie felt tears prick her eyes. *Dear God*, she thought, *don't let them fall!* 'Nothing's been settled, he wanted to wait... till after the war.'

'Now I think I understand,' Eliza said almost to herself, 'why you are so fierce about keeping your promise to my mother. It's for him, isn't it?'

'And for *them*. The poor little bleeders would've ended up with your Uncle George if not!'

Eliza surprised her with a deep laugh, which alerted Nellie. *Here comes the whack on the head!* she had just enough time to think, before Eliza interrupted her laugh suddenly.

'But now there's another choice, apart from Uncle George. Me! I'm already a mother, I have a house and the means to give them a good life. Nellie, you're very young to be the little old woman who lived in the shoe! Why not let me relieve you of some of the burden at least?'

So sensible, so reasonable, Nellie thought, and so exactly what she didn't want, wouldn't allow. 'No, Mrs... Eliza, thanks all the same. We may not have blood ties but we're a family now. Anyway, Sam's their guardian and that was his wish. I'm doing nothing without his say so.'

Eliza sat back in her seat, as did Nellie. The two women stared at each other in silence. Eliza was the first to speak. 'I'm afraid that's where you're wrong, Nellie. Sam may be Charlie's guardian, but I have a greater claim where Matty's concerned.' Her amenable manner had changed; there was steel in her tone, which set Nellie's heart thumping.

'Why is Matty any different from Charlie?'

Eliza seemed to hold her breath before landing her blow. 'Because Matty is my daughter.'

If Eliza had been swinging a two-by-four plank she couldn't have hit Nellie harder. She reeled under it, all the while trying to resolve the host of unanswered questions thrown up by this revelation. Most of all, she thought of poor Matty, who had loved her 'mother' more than life, who trusted her brother with such sweet loyalty. What would such knowledge do to her world, already ripped apart by death and war? Nellie knew she still grieved the loss of her mother. How would she survive being told all she'd known of her had been based on a lie?

'Does Sam know?' Stunned, this was the first question Nellie wanted answered.

'He didn't, not until the year of the strike. Then our mother told him.'

So he'd known, when he'd entrusted Matty to her, that she had a mother alive but, loving Matty as he did, of course he would want her shielded. And then Lizzie must have known too when she'd fixed on Nellie for a replacement mother. How bitterly she must have felt Eliza's absence then.

'She can't ever know,' Nellie said. 'You can't tell her.' Eliza had lost her own world; surely she wouldn't be so selfish as to rob Matty of hers?

'Then don't make me,' Eliza replied.

A week of sickening anxiety followed Eliza's visit. The first thing Nellie did was write to Sam. She had no idea exactly where he was; she suspected it was somewhere in Belgium but all his letters were heavily censored. The only consolation she had was that her letters got through to him eventually and she always got a reply, however brief. His letters were always cheerful; the only complaints he made were about the lice, which drove him mad with itching. Of death and terror he made no mention. The only request he ever made of her was that she should keep smiling. While Sam was suffering real bombshells in silence, she had to deal with Eliza's bombshell and she wished with all her heart that she didn't have to pass on the worry to Sam, but what could she do? She either gave Matty over to Eliza, or risked blowing the young girl's world apart. They were all of them trudging through minefields not of their own making.

But there was one light shining for her in that dark week: Lily's baby. She, Alice and Matty visited Lily the day after Nellie's talk with Eliza at the coffee shop. Nellie had told Alice Eliza's story and was relieved when her reaction was the same as her own. She'd sworn Alice to secrecy, deciding this was as far as the story should go till Sam's reply arrived. But she was determined to show nothing of her trouble to Lily. Once they were all gathered round the newborn, a weight seemed to lift from her shoulders.

'Ohhh, look, Lily, look at his round little face, it's Jock all over!'

'I know,' said the proud mother, holding the infant up and showing him round like a lot in an antique dealer's, 'but look at all this Bosher hair, he's going to be a right little ginger nut! Still,' she said, kissing the baby's pretty nose, 'at least he hasn't got me dad's squashed nose!'

Nellie took the baby into her arms and gave him a finger to grasp. She could see Matty looking on longingly.

'Can Matty have a hold?' Nellie asked Lily.

''Course she can! He loves a cuddle, doesn't mind who from.'

Nellie relinquished the baby and Matty took the child, rocking him in her arms. She walked him around the bedroom, singing a soft lullaby.

'That's a lovely tune, Matty,' Lily said, as she saw her baby's eyes droop and close.

Matty looked up from the baby, smiling. 'Mum used to sing it to me.'

Nellie felt the pity of it; she needed no other confirmation that she was doing the right thing.

'Well, I wish you'd teach it to me, looks like it's doing the trick!' said Lily.

Nellie was astonished when Sam's reply came after only six days. This was a record and she thanked God and the army post office that her wait was so soon over. She ripped open the envelope, scanning the letter first to see how long it was, then she stroked her fingers across the firm, flowing handwriting. This was the closest she could be to Sam while this damn war lasted and she allowed herself that moment. When she took in the contents she understood its speedy arrival – it was completely uncensored!

Holding the sheet of paper in a shaking hand, she read:

My dear Nellie

I am writing this quickly, before we go up the line tonight. I explained family circumstances to my CO, who is a good bloke and has allowed me to do my own censoring for speed. Firstly Nellie, I'm sorry my sister Eliza has landed this on you while I'm not there to help you. You might be asking why I didn't tell you about Matty, the truth is Nellie I grew up thinking she was my sister and that is what she will always be to me. I hope you don't think I did wrong, but I thought it best not to burden you with that secret. I want to put your mind at rest about Matty, I have it in writing from Mum in her will that I am to be Matty's guardian. You will find it in the box of policies I left with Charlie. If it comes to anything legal, this letter is proof of my wishes that Matty be brought up by you, as my mother requested. Show it to Eliza and I trust she will do the right thing by Matty. You're right, Nellie, that Matty is better off not knowing and, if Eliza truly loves her, she will say the same. I'm surprised she kept her baby boy, but when you see her again, please tell her I'm glad we have another William in the family. Write and tell me what happens and thank you, dearest Nellie, for all you've done for me and my family. Knowing you are looking after them makes it easier to do my bit out here. Give my love to Alice and the children. God bless and keep smiling!

Love, Sam

'Oh, Sam, you're going up the line,' she announced mournfully to the empty room, and in order to banish the sickening fear gathering in the pit of her stomach, she prayed, 'Please God, keep him safe and let him come home to us.'

But Nellie thanked God that Lizzie had named Sam as Matty's guardian in her will and she waited impatiently for Charlie's return. And as soon as he came home from work, she asked him for the box of policies. If Eliza forced her into a battle for Matty, she would not hesitate to produce Lizzie's will. At least now she would have some ammunition. Charlie, puzzled by her request, retrieved the box of family documents from under his bed and handed it to her.

'Is anything wrong with Sam?' he asked anxiously.

The poor boy had been no trouble to her since he came, had handed over his wages dutifully once he started work and had good-naturedly squashed Freddie's bossiness, without any help from her. Nellie felt guilty that because he made no fuss he got little attention from her. Eliza had said she was like the little old woman who lived in the shoe, and Charlie, she felt with a pang, was one of the children who had suffered in the crowd.

She hugged him. "Course not, silly, I would've told you. No, it's just some family business he wants me to sort out. He sends his love to you all and he seemed quite cheerful. Tell you what, why don't you write and tell him how you're getting on at Wicks's, he'd love to hear about that, and tell him about Blackie. He loved that horse.'

Charlie looked pleased at the idea of doing something for his brother and Nellie let him use her meagre supply of writing paper. He sat at the kitchen table, writing steadily in his careful copperplate, while she went through the box. She quickly scanned Lizzie's will, before slipping it into her pinafore pocket. It was just as Sam had said and she felt armed. Now all she had to do was wait and see what steps Eliza would take.

She didn't have long to wait. Eliza wrote that she was coming to London the following week with the idea of spending some time with Matty; she made no mention of Charlie. Again, the quiet young boy had been overlooked, but in this case, Nellie thought ruefully, it was more like a lucky escape. Nellie broached the subject at the tea table, and before she'd even finished detailing the plans, he interrupted. 'Oh, it's a work day, I can't go! Wicks just lost another driver and he's going to train me up for it.' Charlie was clearly relieved he wouldn't be included.

Matty was equally unenthusiastic about the idea of spending a day with Eliza. 'That's not fair! Why does he get let off?' she chimed in. 'And why is she coming round, upsetting things, anyway? She always used to upset Mum when she turned up and I don't see what she wants with me now!'

'She's just being kind, Matty. Perhaps she thinks now Sam's away you'd be feeling lonely.'

Nellie did not feel entirely comfortable playing Eliza's advocate but, whatever she'd done, she was still Matty's family and Nellie thought it best to tread softly for the time being.

Matty let out a snort. 'Lonely! With all you lot round me? I never get a minute on me own!' Her tinkling infectious laughter always came suddenly and brightened her sometimes sulky face. 'More likely she's feeling guilty.' A remarkably observant girl, she picked up on people's moods and motives, often seeing beneath the surface of things. 'Well, let her take me out if she wants to, won't make no difference to me.' She shrugged.

Nellie felt sick at the prospect of Eliza's visit. What she dreaded most was that she would say something to Matty. It was too risky to leave to chance, so she wrote back agreeing to Eliza's suggestion, but asking for her promise to say nothing to the girl about her parentage.

On the day of the visit, Matty put on the pretty striped print dress they'd bought at the Old Clo' market and because it was still chilly, they decided she'd borrow Alice's best winter coat. Nellie carefully brushed Matty's long auburn hair till it shone and tied it with a lilac ribbon.

'Don't you look pretty!' Nellie pushed the girl towards the small mirror hanging above the mantelpiece. 'You'll have all the boys running after you soon!'

Matty blushed, but looked up shyly at her reflection. Nellie had begun to notice her blossoming. At thirteen she was almost as tall as Charlie now, and her fine bone structure had become more evident. Her flashing eyes were reminiscent of Lizzie's but, looking at her in the mirror, Nellie was stunned by another unmistakable resemblance: Matty, emerging from childhood to womanhood, had become a reflection of Eliza.

Eliza was to collect Matty early and Nellie was nervously looking out of the front window every few minutes. When a motor taxi rolled up, it caused a stir; motor taxis were an unheard-of luxury in Vauban Street and it was soon surrounded by a crowd of excited children. Nellie quickly dropped the net curtain. Hmm, no tram for Madam Mecklenburgh today, wonder who she's trying to impress? she commented softly to herself. 'Come on, Matty, love, looks like you'll be travelling in style!' she said out loud.

Matty had never been in a motor taxi and her studied sullenness flickered into excitement at the sight of it outside their front door. Nellie hurried her out in a vain attempt to dodge the stares of several neighbours, who'd come to their doorsteps to see the show. Matty dawdled behind Nellie, her sulkiness returning at the sight of Eliza sitting in the back of the taxi.

'Who'd she think she is, the queen?' she muttered.

Nellie groaned, feeling almost sorry for Eliza. She didn't envy her the day ahead, caught as she was between a grumpy thirteen-year-old and her own desperate desire to make up for her past mistakes.

'I thought the taxi would save us time!' Eliza said brightly as Matty clambered into the motor. 'We've got a lot to pack in!'

28

LITTLE CANARY

Nellie had been looking out for the taxi's return all evening and when she heard its motor running outside the house, she dashed to the front door. They'd all been sitting round the table, debating where Eliza had taken Matty and what time they would be back. When she opened the door Nellie was surprised to see the taxi disappearing down Vauban Street and Matty already standing on the doorstep, a bag in her hand and a large flat box under her arm.

'Didn't you think to ask her in?' Nellie was annoyed that Matty had let Eliza go off before Nellie could find out what her plans were for the rest of the week. If there were to be more outings, she needed to know. She was also desperate to find out if Eliza had kept her promise to say nothing to Matty.

'She didn't want to come in.' The girl walked past her into the kitchen and almost immediately Nellie heard Charlie berating Matty.

'You should've told her to stick her presents up her—'

'Charlie!'

'Sorry, Nellie, but Mum always used to tell us you can't buy people and that's what Eliza's doing!'

The flat parcel was lying unopened on the kitchen table, surrounded by several huge bars of Nestlé's chocolate. Matty normally had a quick answer for anything her brother threw at her, but now she merely looked at him miserably and said, 'She's not all bad, she just said she wanted to give the rest of the family something nice.' She shot her brother a scathing look. 'You're the one who's always scoffing sweet things!'

'Come on, love.' Nellie drew Matty away. 'Bring your parcel up to our room to open.'

When they were alone she asked her about the day.

'We went over the other side shopping – she was all excited about getting me a new dress, she said this one was looking a bit shabby.' Matty smoothed down the print dress she was wearing. 'Anyway, it was the same shop Mum used to take me to every year for my new dress – when the club paid out. I don't know why, but Eliza got ever so upset when I told her.'

Nellie realized now how Lizzie had afforded that yearly dress for Matty: the 'club paying out' was no doubt really a money order from Eliza.

'And that's what's in the parcel? Your new dress?'

Matty nodded.

'Let's see it, then!'

Matty slowly took off the cardboard lid and drew back the layers of tissue paper. It was a beautifully cut satin dress, in a warm oyster colour, perfect for Matty's colouring. She held it up out of the box, for Nellie to see how the long sleeves had been caught up in little ruches. The draped skirt was trimmed with burgundy braid and Matty held it against her, to show off the fashionable short length. Nellie could only gasp. 'Oh, Matty, you'll look beautiful in that dress!'

Matty carefully began folding the dress back into the tissue paper. Closing the lid of the box, she said, 'She wanted me to change into it straight away, but I said no thank you, that I preferred to wear this one home.'

And again she smoothed down her print dress, the one Nellie had bought for her the day Sam marched away to war.

Nellie didn't question Matty further that night, but she did find out from her that Eliza would be staying in London for a couple of days and giving a talk at the Labour Institute the following evening. Matty seemed so miserable and confused by the day that Nellie began to suspect Eliza had told her secret. She had to find out. The following evening, saying she had to go to

Lily's, she made her way to the institute, arriving just as Eliza finished her speech. She spotted Nellie hovering at the back of the room and came over to her.

'I'm sorry I wasn't able to see you yesterday,' she explained, 'but it was a long day and I still had to prepare my speech.'

Eliza was smiling but her voice seemed forced.

'I told Matty off for not asking you in, she usually has better manners. I hope she at least said thank you for the day out?' Nellie asked.

'Yes, yes, she was very *polite*.' Eliza emphasized the word; at least Matty hadn't disgraced herself.

Eliza looked drained, Nellie thought. 'I hope you don't mind me turning up here, but I wanted to ask you—'

'If I told her?' Eliza interrupted.

Nellie flushed in spite of herself.

'No, it was just an outing, that's all. I wanted to give her something. So I took her to the West End, to buy her a new dress.'

They had sat down at the back of the room, which was now largely empty but for a few stragglers still chatting and saying goodnight. Nellie realized with alarm that Eliza's face had crumpled at the mention of the dress. The woman quickly turned her back to the room and began to sob quietly. 'It's too late, Nellie, she hates me.'

Nellie would have put her arm round the woman, but she obviously wanted to hide her distress from prying eyes. Instead Nellie said, as gently as possible, 'She doesn't hate you, Eliza, she just doesn't know you. And you don't really know her. Matty's clever, she can sniff out what people are up to and she knows you wanted something from her; please God she'll never know what.'

'She'll never hear it from me, not after yesterday. Do you know she never stopped talking about "her mum", almost as if she knew.'

Nellie shook her head. 'I'm sure she doesn't. It's just she's got an instinct, like I said.'

'Well, you know her better than I ever will.' Eliza's expression was so mournful Nellie felt compelled to say something.

'Well, even if it's too late to be her mother, there's still time to be her sister,' she said. And though it might not have been the wisest thing to say, she knew it was the kindest.

Eliza reached out and took Nellie's hand. 'Bless you for that, Nellie, I'd like to try.'

So in the end it had been Matty who'd won the war with Eliza. Nellie never learned all that had happened during her visit. All she knew was that she never had to recommence battle with Eliza; or resort to Lizzie's will. Looking back, she should have known that Matty, being after all Eliza's daughter, had a fearsome talent for getting her own way. Nellie was just thankful that in this case the young girl's wishes coincided with her own, not for her own sake but for Matty's.

The change in Eliza's attitude had eased Nellie's mind and her cuckoo's nest felt safe for now. But towards the end of 1915 both Freddie and Matty were due to leave school. Old Wicks had offered Freddie a full-time job, but he had other ideas. He insisted he would be better off staying a part-time stable lad so he could concentrate on what he grandly called his other 'operations'.

'It's me patriotic duty, Nell,' Freddie explained. 'The country's got to be fed and you can't do that without muck. Look at the poor little bleeders walking around with badges hanging round their necks sayin' *I eat less bread*. I'm just helping feed hungry children!'

His appeal to her human kindness was bolstered by the list of figures he'd prepared to illustrate the clear economic advantages of his plan. She gave in, but drew a line at his idea of using the penny-farthing and trailer to transport large quantities of manure all over London.

'You must be joking!' she said. 'The Co-op groceries would end up smelling very sweet, wouldn't they? And don't think you're storing any of that stuff in our back yard!'

'I'm not talking about *your* cart, that's too small! Me and Charlie are making a much bigger one!'

Nellie shooed him out of the kitchen. 'Just make sure I've got the bike back for Saturday afternoons, I'm not letting the Co-op down. And don't you *dare* put horse shit in my cart!'

Custard tarts were in short supply. The factory was now run almost entirely by women and Nellie had got used to the sight of girls in greasy overalls doing jobs previously reserved for men. Only this morning, when all the filling machines had come to a grinding halt, a young girl not much older than Matty was sent up from maintenance and in minutes had them all working. They were even accepting the more literate girls in the office as order clerks. But even with so many women willing to try the new jobs, there still weren't enough. Nellie had noticed, this morning, even more empty spaces in the teams, for the women were being spirited away from their regular jobs into war work. Filling shells with gunpowder was seen by the government as a better use of female labour than filling custard packets. The packing room, which had once been crammed to bursting with hundreds of women, was now beginning to have a deserted feel – so many women had migrated from Duff's to the dangerous and far more lucrative munitions factories. At break time Nellie sought out Ethel Brown. She was struggling with her ledgers, the one part of the job that she stumbled over. Nellie let her finish the calculation.

'If I could keep it all in me head I'd be fine!' she said. 'But it's the writing gets me, never got that far at school!'

Nellie looked down at the blotched ledger. Albert would have a fit, but the bosses weren't complaining. Somehow, in spite of having fewer workers, the new forelady kept the quotas up.

'Ethel, I was wondering if you could put in a word for our Matty, she'll be leaving school soon.'

''Course I will, love, she won't have no trouble getting took on and if she wants triple shifts she's welcome !'

And so, when Matty came home from her last day at school, Nellie sat her down to talk about her future. 'How do you think you'd like to work at Duff's, with me and Alice?' she asked, smiling.

Matty's face fell. 'What me? A custard tart?'

Nellie nodded, feeling a little hurt at her lack of enthusiasm. 'At least you'll know people there and Ethel says you're guaranteed a job.'

'But don't I get any choice?'

Nellie had been sure Matty would want to work with her, but now she considered the options. 'Choice? Well, you could always try Lipton's, but peeling oranges all day? Those lady's hands of yours'll soon be cut to ribbons.' She lifted one of Matty's pale hands, recovered now from the matchbox paste.

Matty looked stricken.

'What's the matter, love?' Nellie asked gently.

Matty lifted her beautiful oval face, her lower lip trembling. 'I thought I'd be a singer.'

It felt a long, long time since Nellie had been young enough to dream so impossibly. She reflected now that perhaps once, before her parents' deaths, she'd had her own fanciful ideas of a different life. But now she blamed herself for not talking to Matty earlier; she'd just assumed the young girl knew what the facts of their lives were. Nellie felt she was holding a little bird in her hand. Trying very hard not to close her fingers around those fragile bones, she went on gently. 'Well, love, I'm not saying you ain't got a beautiful singing voice, it's just I don't think you'd get enough work to make a living.'

Matty's large unblinking eyes flashed. Nellie always forgot the little bird had bones of steel.

'I've been up the Star in Abbey Street already! Bernie, the manager, remembered me from singing competitions… he says they'll give me a trial, a couple of nights a week.'

God help me, Lizzie Gilbie, didn't you teach this child anything about real life? Nellie thought in exasperation.

Nellie proceeded to give Matty a lesson in home economics, going over the costs of keeping their combined families on their pooled wages. 'So you see, love, we'll lose Sam's separation allowance once you start work and unless you're bringing in a good weekly wage, we'll have to start doing the home work again.'

'No, no,' Matty said, suddenly deflated, 'I don't want to make us do that again.' She thought for a moment and then declared, 'All right, then, I'll be a custard tart, but I don't want no night shifts!'

Nellie had to laugh; the little canary was not one to give up on her dreams easily!

At first Matty seemed happy to fall into the routine of powder packing by day and singing by night, and when she was happy, Matty could brighten everything she touched. She surprised Nellie with her toughness again and again, seeming to take the physical strain of factory work much more easily than Alice ever had. Most days she boosted her own and the other women's spirits with her beautiful voice. Ethel, unlike Albert, allowed as much chatter as they liked on the factory floor, and certainly didn't ban singing. In fact, she was often the one to shout over the rows of women, 'Start us a song, Matty, love, it's dull as ditchwater in here today!' Matty would dip into her repertoire, now full of the latest music-hall songs, and soon have the factory floor joining in.

Matty got her regular two nights at the Star Music Hall and the manager soon saw how best to use her innocent charm and sweet good looks. After the interval, they would regularly run a reel of film, showing Tommies embarking for France or marching up to the line. Afterwards Matty would come on and sing a suitably sentimental song, which left most of the audience in tears. Those who had family in the forces felt comforted to know that 'their boys' were not being forgotten.

One night, Matty got the family concession tickets for the performance. Nellie and Alice rushed home to make a quick tea, and while they put on their finery they sent the boys ahead to save a good place in the queue outside the Star. When the doors opened, all five of them dashed for the best seats in the front row, ready to cheer Matty on. The first half was taken up with a comedian, who specialized in dressing as an old woman, followed by a novelty juggling act from a pair of twins, long past their prime, and a comedienne tap dancer. After the big act, a popular lady soprano, came what they were all waiting for, Matty's big moment. The lights dimmed, the screen flickered into life, and suddenly Nellie realized she was looking at film of an artillery regiment. She leaned forward in her seat, scanning the teams of horses pulling heavy gun carriages along foreign roads lined with ruined buildings. As each team of drivers spotted the camera, they lifted their crops and smiled. Searching each face, she hoped, ridiculously, that one would be Sam's, and once or twice convinced herself, but the soldiers moved too quickly, trotting down the muddy road and on to who knew what battle or what fate. That some of them might even now be lying dead on a battlefield was too horrible to think about, and she was glad when the lights went up and Matty walked on, wearing the oyster satin dress Eliza had bought for her. The boys set up a loud cheer, and they all stood clapping, till the piano struck up 'Keep the Home Fires Burning'. Nellie didn't know how Matty could keep her own tears at bay as she sang the verse.

> 'Let no tears add to their hardships
> As the soldiers pass along,
> And although your heart is breaking
> Make it sing this cheery song.'

She must surely be thinking, as they all were, of Sam, and yet the girl sang with a steady, pure voice, never faltering. By the end of it, Matty had the audience in the palm of her hand. Nellie cast a quick look behind her, to see hundreds of faces lifted to their little canary standing in the middle of that huge stage. Some cried unashamedly, as they joined in with the chorus.

> 'Keep the Home Fires burning,
> While your hearts are a yearning,
> Though your lads are far away
> They dream of home.'

Afterwards, Nellie had to pass her handkerchief to Alice, and she noticed Bobby take it from her, surreptitiously dabbing at his own eyes. Nellie prayed the war would be long over before her soft-hearted brother need be called up – she knew he wouldn't last a week. After the show was over, Matty took them backstage, introducing them to Bernie the manager, a flamboyant man with a flashing smile, who told Nellie that Matty was a 'real trouper'. And with that she could not disagree.

But as the year dragged on and they neared their second Christmas at war, a cloud seemed to descend over Matty. Her smile was less ready and she seemed listless. Nellie worried that she had taken on too much. One afternoon, as the three girls were walking home from the factory, she broached the subject. 'You don't seem yourself, Matty. Is it a bit much for you, working all day and then singing at nights?'

Matty, who'd been walking listlessly between Alice and Nellie, suddenly came alive. Her face flushed. 'No! It's no hardship for me, singing ain't!' Matty said.

Nellie knew it wouldn't be the singing she was fed up with, so she pressed her. 'Why don't you move to jellies?' Nellie asked, thinking she'd hit upon the solution.

Matty had sometimes complained that breathing in custard powder made her so hoarse it affected her singing. But packing jelly crystals was 'clean work', powder free. Still Matty shook her head.

'Well, ain't you happy at Duff's no more?'

'It's not that I'm *unhappy* there,' Matty said finally. 'It's just…

oh, I'm so worried about our Sam!'

Nellie knew the girl pored over newspaper war reports and often talked to Charlie about their brother's whereabouts, trying to guess what battle he might be involved in.

'I'm worried too, love, but he wouldn't want us to be gloomy, not when he tries so hard to keep our spirits up.'

Matty's head drooped and she said softly, 'You know as well as I do that's all for show.'

'If Sam's putting on a show, it's only the same as you're doing at the Star!' Nellie replied heatedly. 'It's just a way of keeping people's spirits up, and that's not a bad thing. I'm not so stupid I believe he's got no more to complain about than the vermin, but he don't dwell on it, so neither should we!'

Matty took her hand. 'Sorry, Nell, you're right, but I feel so useless making custard powder and singing. I want to do my bit too and get Sam home.'

Nellie put her arm round Matty's shoulders and drew her in. 'He'll come home, love, he promised! His last letter said he was being relieved, so at least we know he's not on the front line now. Anyway, he's due some leave soon, that's a blessing, ain't it?' She knew she was speaking with just the forced cheerfulness Matty seemed to disdain.

'But he's in the artillery,' Matty persisted, 'and I read they're running out of shells. Soon he'll have nothing to shoot back at the Jerries with! Here, look at this.'

She produced from her coat pocket a folded-up newspaper article, which Nellie read aloud for Alice as they skirted the queue outside the Salvation Army hostel. The nature of the queue had changed since the war began. It now contained very few young men; three square meals and army pay seemed better than a life on the streets, even with the dangers. The newspaper reported that Mrs Pankhurst had changed tack. Now campaigning for 'A Woman's Right to Serve', she was appealing for more women munitions workers. The bold slogan at the top of the article read: *Shells made by a wife will save a husband's life!*

Nellie looked with alarm at Alice and then back to Matty. 'Matty, don't tell me you're thinking of doing that? You're too young!'

'I'm fourteen now! Anyway, what if I make a shell and it saves Sam's life, don't you think that would be worth it?'

'Yes... No... What I mean is...' Nellie shook her head vehemently and appealed to her sister. 'Sam wouldn't want it, would he, Al?'

Alice shook her head just as vehemently and said, 'No, it's too dangerous, Matty. Anyway, you'd have to go all the way to Woolwich, you'd never get back in time for the Star.'

Matty had already thought of that. 'I can get a tram all the way, forty minutes. Besides, it'll make life a lot easier for us all – I can earn thirty shillings a week! Plenty for me housekeeping *and* a new costume!'

Nellie begged Matty to wait, at least until the following year. If she could delay her until Sam's leave she believed he could talk her out of it. Nellie insisted on writing to both Sam and Eliza and it wasn't long before their objections came flooding back. But it was like holding back a racehorse after the off; Matty ignored any attempt to rein her in. She gave her notice in at Pearce Duff's and the very next week started work at the Woolwich Arsenal munitions factory.

Eliza even made the trip down from Hull and this time Nellie was grateful for her interference. Over the course of the year Eliza had made several visits to London to see Matty. At first she would just collect the girl, take her out for the day and drop her at Vauban Street in the evening, but on her third visit Nellie had asked Matty to invite Eliza in after their day out. When Eliza arrived one bright December Sunday morning shortly after Matty's announcement, Nellie was ready to invite her in again. She wasn't prepared to see her standing at the door, hand in hand with a sturdy, dark-haired three-year-old. Nellie could see this new charm offensive was likely to succeed – Matty fell in love with every baby or toddler she met.

'I thought it was time for Matty to meet her... nephew. Nellie, this is William.'

The child pushed past Nellie, trotting up the dark passage and into the front kitchen. Eliza, apologizing to Nellie, half ran after him but he increased his pace, barrelling headlong into the kitchen. Nellie and Eliza arrived just in time to see him launch himself at Matty's legs, demanding to be picked up.

'I made the mistake of telling him he'd be meeting his aunt, he's very excited,' Eliza said, shamefaced.

'He's not a bit shy, is he?' said Nellie.

'He's... forceful, shall we say.' Eliza smiled indulgently as she saw how Matty was immediately entranced.

'Oh, he's so like Sam! Don't you think so, Nellie?' asked Matty as she sat the boy on her lap, playing Ride a cock horse to Banbury Cross.

Nellie didn't think William looked like Sam, but she didn't say so. There was a photo of Ernest James hanging in the Labour Institute – this was obviously his son. William had a will to match Matty's, though, and soon dragged her out of the kitchen, through the scullery and into the back yard, as though he owned the house. Nellie left Eliza in the front kitchen and went to make tea in the scullery; through the window she watched Matty showing William the penny-farthing. Eliza followed her in. Coming to stand beside Nellie, she looked intently at her two children.

'Nellie, do you know how dangerous that work is at Woolwich?' she asked solemnly.

Nellie turned, feeling suddenly cornered by Eliza. Still in her wide-brimmed hat and travelling coat, her presence filled the tiny room. Quickly arranging the tea things on a tray, she hustled Eliza back into the front kitchen, where they could talk out of earshot.

'Of course I realize how dangerous it is,' she said, setting the tray down on the table and taking Eliza's hat and coat, 'and don't think I haven't talked to her, till I'm blue in the face. She just won't listen, says she's doing it for Sam.'

'But they could be blown up at any moment, and those women still get paid half the men's wages! It's appalling,' Eliza said fiercely, bringing the flat of her hand down on to the kitchen table so that Nellie feared for her best china.

'Nothing changes there, then,' Nellie sighed, handing her a cup of steaming tea, 'though she's getting better wages than she could ever get at Duff's.'

'But is it worth it?' Eliza demanded, ready for a fight.

Nellie tried not to feel defensive. She knew Eliza wasn't trying to blame her, but still she felt responsible for Matty's choices. Sometimes this woman could make her feel like that admiring sixteen-year-old custard tart all over again, instead of a woman bringing up her child, and Nellie resented it. She carefully put down her teacup, all the while fuming inwardly. 'Of course nothing's worth Matty being blown to smithereens!'

'Nor being poisoned, either. Do you know the nickname for these women munitions workers, Nellie?'

Nellie shot her a puzzled look and gave her the name she'd read in the newspapers – 'munitionettes'. It was what Matty called herself.

'Yes, but there's another name,' Eliza went on. 'They call them the canaries…'

Nellie's heart skipped a beat. 'Matty's nickname?'

Eliza nodded. 'Yes, ironic, isn't it? But it's not because the girls spend their days singing. No, the sulphur gets into their system, their skin turns yellow… and then their livers fail.'

The two women gave each other identical worried looks as the sound of Matty's voice, singing to William, drifted in from the back yard.

29

'NOTHING TO MAR OUR JOY'

Maggie Tyrell was running down the middle of the factory floor, screaming and waving a piece of paper in her hand. Nellie jumped away from the bench, spilling an entire packet of custard powder down her clean smock. She caught Maggie round the waist so that both women were propelled into a loaded trolley, spilling broken custard packets everywhere. Clouds of sticky yellow dust erupted like a spewing volcano and the entire row of women burst into laughter.

'Oi, oi, oi!' Ethel Brown's voice boomed from the far end of the floor. 'Behave yerselves! What's going on?' She waddled over, her forelady's green overall stretched across her ample stomach. The war shortages had somehow made little impression on Ethel's considerable bulk.

'It's Maggie,' Nellie spluttered, her mouth full of sickeningly sweet powder. 'She's got *the telegram*.' Ethel's face fell as Nellie held Maggie tight in her arms ready for the inevitable explosion of grief. The laughter died away as all eyes turned sympathetically towards Maggie, who now alarmingly started laughing hysterically. She extricated herself from Nellie's arms. It was well known that women took the news in all sorts of ways, but Nellie had never seen hilarity.

'No, you silly cow!' Maggie finally turned to Nellie. 'It's not *the telegram*! My old man's got a Blighty. He's coming home!'

Now the women's concern turned to cheers and congratulations.

'Oh, Maggie, I thought you'd gone mad with grief!' Nellie explained, brushing down her smock.

'But what's his Blighty, Mag, is it a bad 'un?' asked Ethel.

The group of women nearest craned to hear as they went back to the rhythmical filling and packing of the custard powder.

'Well, bad enough, he's got a lump of shrapnel in him size of an egg. Got to come home and get it operated on.'

'How is he taking it?' asked Nellie

'Taking it? Well, he's overjoyed. Listen to this. She read from the letter. *"My Dear Mag, you'll be pleased to hear that I have got my Blighty! I'm the luckiest of fellers, I shall be coming home with a piece of German metal in me groin, but rest assured, the Family Business is still intact!"'*

The women in earshot roared with laughter and Ethel said sympathetically, 'Well, small mercies, love, eh?'

'Small mercies?' Maggie pondered. 'To be honest, love, with six kids, it would've been a mercy if that shrapnel had gone a bit lower!'

Nellie was pleased Tom Tyrell had got his Blighty. For Maggie the war had been particularly hard, with so many small children to cope with. Nellie started imagining what sort of Blighty wound she would find acceptable for Sam, how much of him would she want damaged or missing in order to bring him home. It wasn't a game she enjoyed playing. That evening she decided to visit Lily after work. When she missed Sam badly, she would often go to Lily's, just so they could talk about 'the boys', as they still called Jock and Sam. Christmas of 1915 had come and gone and still there was no sign of the long-promised leave. She'd received a letter from Sam just before Christmas, saying that they'd been posted to another front line and were on the move. She'd made a parcel of knitted socks and thick wool underwear and some hard-to-come-by slabs of chocolate. The children had written individual messages and Nellie had cried as she'd waited in line at the post office, trying to infuse the little parcel with every ounce of love that she felt for Sam. As the year had turned, the lists of casualties reached appallingly high numbers. Perhaps, after all, a missing hand or a useless leg would indeed be worth it, if they came home alive.

When Nellie arrived at Lily's that night, her friend handed her the grizzling Johnny, instead of putting him to bed as she usually did at that time.

'Here, take him!' she said, thrusting the child at her. 'He's not stopped all day! I don't know what's the matter with him. He's driving me mad.'

Nellie looked down into Johnny's red-cheeked, screwed-up face, his little trembling chin wet with drool. Nellie had far more experience with babies than Lily, who was the youngest in her family.

'Ohh, poor little bleeder, he's just getting another tooth! You make the tea. I'll get him off to sleep.'

Nellie gave Johnny a knuckle to chew on and began marching up and down the kitchen with him, rocking him all the while. As soon as she saw his eyes beginning to droop, she laid him carefully in his crib and began rocking it with her foot.

'Oh, Nellie, you're so good with him,' Lily sighed admiringly. 'You'll be the same with your own kiddies, when they come.'

'*When* they come? Don't you think I've got enough to do, with my lot at home?'

'But they're not kids any more, are they?'

It was true. Bobby was the only one still at school, and not for much longer. Sometimes she missed the boys' raucous presence. Most evenings they were out with their friends, or working with Freddie's 'business', and Matty, too, was absent all day at Woolwich and two evenings at the Star.

'You're right, the house is getting too bloody quiet! Gives me too much time to think…'

The young women fell silent. Only the rhythmic rocking of the crib and the soft breathing of the baby intruded on their thoughts. They sat sipping their tea, until Lily went to a small kitchen cupboard. She drew out a tin and brought it with her to the chair by the fire.

'I had a letter from Jock,' she said. They were in the habit of reading their letters to each other, leaving out what Lily called 'all the lovey-dovey stuff'. Nellie grew excited; the boys were in the same battery, riding the same six-horse team that transported the heavy guns wherever they were needed. A letter from one generally meant that a letter from the other would not be far behind.

'Does he say anything about leave?' she asked eagerly.

Lily shook her head. Looking glum, she unfolded the letter and read, '"*My darling wife Lily…*"' Lily pulled a face at Nellie. 'You don't want to hear all his sweet nothings, do you, love? "*I know you'll be as happy as I am, when I tell you that I will be home and in your arms, this time next week!*"'

Nellie jumped up, wagging an accusing finger at her friend. 'You little mare, you!'

Lily laughed. 'Surprised?'

'I can't believe you kept me in the dark all this time I've been sitting here!'

'Well, I wanted you to get the baby asleep first, didn't I?' she joked.

'Oh, Lily, you always get the letters first. Do you think that means Sam's got leave too?'

''Course it does. They drive the same team. Stands to reason they'll all get a rest together, don't it?'

Nellie could hardly wait to get home to see if she too had a letter, even though she knew it was now far too late for a delivery. She was impatient all the next day, and when no letter came, she began to despair. Perhaps Lily had been wrong and the boys wouldn't be on leave together after all. If Jock's letter had taken two days to get from France, Lily could expect him as early as the end of that week. But the week dragged on and still there was no letter from Sam. Nellie's misery was obvious to the whole family.

On Friday night, Alice was going out to the Time and Talents Club with her friends. 'Why don't you come too, Nell?' she asked gently, during tea. 'It's no good sitting in worrying, is it?'

'No, love, you go and enjoy yourself with your friends. Don't worry about me.'

Soon after Alice had left, Matty came home from the Arsenal and began her usual Friday night routine, dashing to get ready for the evening performance at the Star, curling her hair, dressing, eating and practising her song all at the same time. She was like a fiery whirlwind and Nellie knew not to get in her way on 'turn' nights. She dashed through the kitchen, kissing Nellie briefly on the cheek,

'I'll be late tonight, Nell. Don't wait up,' she said breathlessly. 'Bernie says we've got an American scout in, looking for singers!' Matty's eyes shone, and she turned at the door. 'Might end up in vaudeville, you never know!'

Nellie smiled. If only Sam could see this confident, radiant young woman now, he wouldn't recognize his little Matty.

'Well, I *will* wait up, and don't make it too late!' Nellie called, but the front door had already slammed closed. Nellie stayed in the chair, letting the quiet emptiness of the house settle around her. She thought of Matty, all unquenchable youth and hope, and all she could say to her was, 'Don't make it too late!' She sounded like an old mother hen, which, she had to admit, she was. But all the same, at twenty-one, wasn't she still entitled to dream of a life full of promise, as Matty did?

The clock ticked away and the spring sunshine finally gave up the day, casting a warm orange glow through the front kitchen window and across Nellie's folded hands. Into the silence, a scraping sound intruded. It was coming from the scullery, behind her. Nellie started up. Was someone in the house after all? She darted through into the scullery, to find the back-yard door swinging wide open. The golden evening light filled the doorway and spread across the scullery's tiled floor. The sound was coming from outside. Going gingerly to the door, she saw a figure scraping his boots on the step. He must have heard her intake of breath: looking up from his task, he said, 'Hello, Nellie, you look like you've seen a ghost!'

Nellie, fearing that she had indeed seen a ghost, flung herself forward into Sam's arms and squeezed him tightly to her. He certainly felt like solid flesh! His body against hers was warm! His chest rose and fell with the breath that spoke of life and she felt it, there it was, his breath soft on her cheek. She was certain this was no phantom.

'Sam, you're really here! You're home!'

Nellie wouldn't let go and Sam didn't seem to want her to relinquish her hold on him. He tightened his arms round her and for a long time they simply rocked back and forth, reassuring each other that they were indeed both real. By the time Nellie's tears had soaked through Sam's tunic, the sun had set. Finally, he lifted her face from his chest and dipped his head to meet her lips with his own. It was their first lover's kiss and if Sam had not been holding her so tightly, she was certain her legs could not have supported her. A mutual passion, fuelled by absence and peril and long denial, came on with the night and shone brighter for Nellie than the rising moon and all the sky full of stars. How long they kissed, she didn't know. All she knew was that she loved and felt most completely and satisfyingly loved in return.

When Sam went to move away, she clasped him more tightly still. 'Not yet, Sam. Don't go away yet,' she said softly. 'I've made us wait so long… Since you've been gone, all I could think of was how much time we could've had together. I was such a fool.'

Sam chuckled gently. 'I'm going nowhere, Nellie, not now I've got you in my arms! And you mustn't blame yourself, this is perfect. Oh, Nellie, love, if you only knew how the thought of this has kept me going out there…'

He buried his face in her abundant chestnut locks. 'Ahhh, your hair…' he said. 'I've dreamed about your hair…'

A breeze began to swirl around the little back yard and she shivered. Sam eased her away gradually and looked into her eyes.

'We'll have to move some time, my sweet girl, and you're getting cold.'

Reluctantly, she let go and allowed him to pick up his pack. Once they were inside, she made him sit down in her father's old chair, while she made him tea and toast. While he ate and drank, she sat on the floor next to him and plied him with questions.

'Why didn't you let me know you'd got leave? I could have had everything ready for you!' she chided.

She looked up as she spoke, not wanting to take her eyes off him. She thought she must look very foolish, but she didn't care, nothing seemed more important to her at this moment than Sam's next word or look. All the world was reduced to the little circle that encompassed Nellie and Sam, and from the way his eyes followed hers, she was certain he inhabited that same bubble. He put down the tea on the tiled hearth and leaned forward, seeming to want to feel her lips as much as she wanted to feel his.

'Ah, Nellie...'

And then she remembered he hadn't answered her question. 'Jock sent Lily a letter.'

'Didn't you get my letter, then?' he asked, as though he'd only just registered her question.

Nellie thought it was very strange, the way they each seemed to be reacting at a dreamlike pace. She gave up trying talk sensibly about anything and allowed herself to surrender to his kisses. Words could wait.

She knew that their first few magical hours were over when Alice's key turned in the front door. They looked at each other, reluctantly letting go of each other's hands and moving apart. Sam rose to greet Nellie's sister. Alice's shock was almost as great as Nellie's own and shortly afterwards, when the boys all tumbled through the back door, poor Sam had to repeat everything over again. He'd come down from the line a fortnight ago: men and horses were in bad need of a rest, he said. Nellie read in his expression untold reasons why they needed that rest and resolved to ask him more later. He and Jock had sailed together from Boulogne the previous evening and caught the military train to Victoria. They'd been lucky enough to cadge a lift on an army truck travelling through to London Bridge and the two friends had walked from there. It was only after they'd exhausted him with their questions that he asked: 'Where's our little canary?'

Sam insisted on waiting up for her and when the others went off to bed, Nellie stayed with him. It was after midnight when Matty came home, calling from the passage, 'Oh, Nellie, I told you not to wait up!' She walked into the kitchen and her hands flew to cover her mouth.

'Sam!' She let out a cry. She was across the room before he had a chance to get up. Draping her arms round his neck, she sat herself on his lap just as she had as a little girl.

Sam laughed. 'Little canary's not so little any more! Look at you, in your finery!' He lifted her off his lap, and letting go of his hands she stood before him. She was wearing a new gown, which she'd paid for in weekly instalments. The pale green chiffon draped fashionably across her shoulders and at her throat she wore a gold and green choker.

Sam couldn't hide his pride and astonishment. 'Matty, you're beautiful!' he gasped.

She twirled round for him. 'You won't say that when you see me in my Arsenal cap and trousers. I look like a chap!'

Sam's face darkened. He was about to say something when Nellie gave the merest shake of her head. He stopped short and said instead, 'Well, we've got a lot of catching up to do in the morning. Where am I kipping down, Nellie?'

She was grateful he'd taken the hint. She didn't want this precious homecoming spoiled by a tussle with Matty. Sam might not realize it but his little sister had changed, and not only physically: her naturally strong will had grown with her. Nellie doubted that Sam would any longer have the power to tame it.

'Charlie's going on the floor, he says you deserve a bed to yourself.'

She knew how bone-tired he was when he didn't argue. He groaned, pushed up from the armchair and shouldered his pack.

'I'll stow this upstairs. Come on, then, my two beautiful girls, escort me up the wooden hill to Bedfordshire!'

They all three linked arms and squeezed up the narrow staircase, giggling and stumbling in the flickering amber gaslight. At the top Matty slipped into their bedroom, leaving Sam and Nellie just enough time for one precious goodnight kiss.

The next morning Nellie was up early: she wanted Sam to have a decent breakfast. He didn't have to tell her how badly he'd been fed, for his once-full boyish face had been chiselled away by too many hungry days, and as she'd held him tight the night before, she'd distinctly felt each rib. How they could expect men to fight when they were half-starved was beyond her. If she could do nothing else, she was determined to send him back with some flesh on him.

Before the house was awake she dashed round to Spa Bakery, keen to get there before the bread queue formed; by mid-morning it was usually snaking down Spa Road. The pre-war mounds of golden-crusted bloomers, which had always filled the bakery shelves, were in short supply now. Most of the bread was bulked out with potato flour and called 'war loaves', but she knew there were still a few of the genuine variety to be had. She'd known Big Mo, the local baker, since childhood, and when he came out of the back bakery with a tray of rolls, he smiled at her.

'Nellie, you're early, love!' He slid the tray of rolls into a basket, wiping his floury hands. She stood, holding her purse, looking up at him and hesitating, before asking for the favour.

'What can I do you for?' he asked.

'I've got Sam home on leave, Mo. I wanted to give him a proper bit of bread with his breakfast,' she said hopefully.

Mo nodded, tapped his nose and ducked back into the bakery behind the shop. Soon he came out with a wrapped loaf and a bag of rolls. 'Here's a special for the boy.' He winked, shaking his head as she dipped into her purse. 'Go on, love, tell him it's on me, will you?'

Nellie nodded and thanked poor Mo, who had lost his only son last year. As she made her way back down Vauban Street, she noticed something flapping at the upstairs window of her house.

It looked like a broom handle, stuck out like a crazy flagpole with a full set of army underwear, tunic, trousers and puttees attached, all blowing about in the breeze.

What the bloody hell's he done that for? she wondered, easing open the front door. She was surprised to see Matty already up and poking at the range.

'I thought I'd make Sam a good breakfast!' She smiled brightly.

'Beat you to it, love.' Nellie put the bread on to the kitchen table and Matty gave her an affectionate squeeze.

'You love my brother, don't you?' she said mischievously, and Nellie, too shocked to reply, playfully shoved her off.

'Leave off, Matty! Just help me get some bacon on, smell of that'll get him out the bed quick enough!'

But Matty wouldn't be put off. 'I could tell last night, you two couldn't take your eyes off each other! No sense denying it, Nellie, it's all over you!'

'You be quiet, or I'll get your brother to sort you out!' Nellie ducked her head as she sliced the lovely new bread, but she could feel the blush spreading up her neck.

'Well, before he gets up, I wanted to say thanks, Nell, for last night.'

'What do you mean?'

'You stopped him jawing at me about the munitions work.'

'I didn't want no trouble his first night home, but you know he's going to have it out with you, sooner or later.'

Matty flipped the sizzling bacon in the pan. 'I don't like him being cross with me. If you could have a word...'

Nellie pursed her lips and shook her head. 'I can't help you there, Matty. I don't want you working at the Arsenal either.'

Matty looked up at the clock – it was almost six.

'I've got to rush, the early tram's always packed for the Arsenal.' She grabbed her bag and, as she kissed Nellie, decided to give her a second. 'That one you can give my brother for me when he's up.' Her eyes twinkled mischievously, then the little canary flitted out, singing softly to herself, 'The boy I love is UP in the gallery!'

'Cheeky little cow she's getting,' Nellie muttered, but smiled all the same. She would definitely be passing that kiss on to Sam later!

She was disappointed when he didn't come down alone. All the boys had been tempted by the smell of bacon and came crowding round the little kitchen table. Alice followed soon after, to help her lay the table. Nellie heaped Sam's plate the highest, with bacon, a fresh fried egg, and slices of bread with their meagre supply of butter spread thickly. The boys were content with their own smaller portions – bacon was always a treat.

'Mmmm, Nellie, this is grand!' Sam tucked in and soon the only sounds were the boys contentedly devouring their breakfast. Sam was wearing his civvies.

'I saw you've put the flags out. What's that in aid of?' she asked.

'He's lousy,' Charlie offered, with his mouth full of bacon sandwich. 'Had to sleep starkers.'

'Sorry, Nell.' Sam looked embarrassed. 'I'm running alive. I didn't want to leave any visitors in Charlie's bed, thought the best place for the little buggers was hangin' out the window. Maybe they've all dropped off in the night!'

'A bar of carbolic soap might do a better job. I'll get the tin tub out when I get home.'

Sam scratched at his arms and ribs. 'Thanks, Nell, and I ought to get in the tub with 'em, I reckon!'

It was Saturday and they all had a morning's work to do. Nellie had the added task of her Co-op round in the afternoon, so it was late in the afternoon before she saw Sam again. Alice had already boiled up the copper and washed his kit. She came home to find the kitchen steaming, with wet khaki draped in front of the fire and hanging from a line strung across the ceiling. As she pulled aside a pair of long johns, she was confronted by Sam's soapy upper torso. He was leaning back in the tin bath, dark hair plastered down over his neat round head, eyes closed, full mouth set in a slight smile. He was beautiful! In his stillness and contentment, she felt she was seeing him for the first time totally unguarded, totally at ease. Unwilling to disturb his peace, she was about to duck back behind the long johns when she saw a jagged red scar snaking from shoulder to chest. She gasped and his eyes snapped open.

'Nellie!' He pulled up his knees and grabbed for the flannel, draping it strategically over himself.

'Cover your blushes, Sam, I'm coming through!' She sailed right up to him and planted a kiss on his wet head.

'That's from Matty and this one's from me.' Leaning down, she gave him a loving, lingering kiss that left him gasping. She ran her finger along the shiny scar, following its jagged route across his chest.

'Why didn't you tell me?' she whispered, and before he could say more, she headed for the scullery.

'I'll get you some more hot!' she called through the open door.

'No, no, I'm all right, I'm out!'

She heard water splashing about and was astonished at her own boldness. Where had it come from? She hadn't thought twice about his nakedness, or propriety. There was the wound, evidence of all he'd been going through, and she had simply been propelled forward by love. Still, she smiled secretly to herself, she strongly suspected it hadn't been an unpleasant experience for him!

That evening they'd arranged to visit Lily and Jock. Sitting on the top deck at the back of the tram, Sam slipped his arm round her waist. She looked up into his eyes and remembered the unguarded, contented figure she'd witnessed in the tub. Sam now had on what she thought of as his 'cheery face' and she knew it masked a worry. Matty's hours at the Arsenal were longer than most and she hadn't been home by the time they'd left.

'What are you going to do about Matty?' she asked, guessing the source of his anxiety.

'She's got to give it up. Do you know how dangerous that

TNT is, Nell? And God forbid a Zeppelin ever gets a direct hit on the Arsenal!'

'You'll have a hard time convincing her. You know she thinks every shell she makes is keeping you alive?'

He sighed. 'I won't say we can't do with the shells. There's been times when we just had to call it a day 'cause we had nothing left to shoot Jerry with. And that meant leaving our boys in the lurch in no man's land with half the barbed wire still there. But that's not the job for her, is it? Not Matty.'

'She's a lot tougher than you think. She's even stood up to Eliza and won, so she won't take any notice of you.'

Sam shot her a look of concern. 'What's Eliza been poking her nose in for again?'

'Don't worry! We're all on the same side this time. She's been coming down every now 'n again, to see Matty.'

His silence was disapproving.

'Listen, Sam, it's been a good thing in the end, she only had to spend one day with Matty to know she could never replace your mum. I think she just wants to make up for the past. Anyway, she even brought her little boy down to see Matty. He's a real character.'

'William?' Sam smiled. 'I'd like to see how he's growing up.'

Nellie hoped this was the first sign of a thaw between Sam and his elder sister. Nellie had ceased to think of Eliza as Madam Mecklenburgh. Through their brief meetings over the past months, a respect for her strength as a lone mother had replaced the old hero worship.

'She's kept to her word so far, Sam,' she said tentatively, 'and I think she could do with her family now. She's bringing little William up on her own.'

'Ernest didn't want the boy after all?'

'He tried to make trouble when he first got back from Australia, but, from what Eliza told me, it's more like he wanted *her* back and thought he could use William to get to her.'

Some old protective family feeling cut through the years of

resentment and Sam's face flushed with anger. 'Well, he'll have me to deal with if he tries taking that boy off her!'

When they arrived at the chandler's in Rotherhithe Street, Lily's door was open. They went in, to find Jock sitting alone, with the baby on his knee.

'She's gone to the pub for a jug of beer!' Jock said, a broad smile on his face. 'What do you think of young Johnny, then?' he asked Sam proudly, holding his son up for inspection and standing up to greet Nellie with a kiss.

'Looks like you, poor little blighter!' Sam joked.

Nellie shoved his shoulder. 'Don't let Lily hear you say that, he's her darling!'

At that moment, Lily pushed through the door, carrying the foaming beer. 'Haven't you got the glasses ready, Jock?'

Jock pulled a face. 'See, started nagging the minute I walked in the door, she did!' He handed the baby to Sam, who immediately began to make Johnny laugh and hiccup.

When the glasses were full, they raised a toast to the boys' safe return and a quick end to the war. That was the only reference they made to the fighting: both men seemed to have forgotten the war the minute they crossed the Channel. They were determined to enjoy every minute of their freedom and had soon drained the ale jug dry.

'I'll nip out and get another!' said Jock.

'I'll come too, I might need a breath of air!' said Sam.

When she heard a clatter, followed by the stifled laughs of the two friends, she realized they had both tumbled down the slippery stairs to the yard. She went to jump up when Lily stopped her.

'Leave 'em, Nell, they've been dodging German shells all this time. I reckon they can manage the stairs on their own!'

She drew her chair closer to Nellie. 'Has he kissed you yet?'

Nellie blushed and nodded.

'I knew it!' Lily was triumphant. 'He looks like the cat that got the cream.'

Nellie sighed contentedly. 'Oh, Lil, I don't mind being the cream, I can tell you!'

After a night of laughter and reminiscences, Nellie and Sam left their friends with promises to meet up again before the boys' leave was over. The April night was bright with stars and when Sam suggested a slow walk home, Nellie was pleased. Rotherhithe Street, the longest in London, meandered round the river's loop and they walked arm in arm along its length, as slowly as they could. Any time alone with Sam was precious now to her, even surrounded by the gaslit, late-night bustle of Rotherhithe. Groups of rowdy Tommies, on leave, were turning out of pubs and many shops, still glowing with light, were serving customers. In spite of the noisy crowd, Nellie felt she and Sam continued to be enclosed in a charmed bubble.

'Let's have a look at the river,' Sam suggested.

He led her away from the busy street, down an alley leading to the foreshore, where they made their way out on to a jetty. The Thames spread out before them, inky black, slick and striped with moonlight. Golden globes of light bobbed up and down, on moored vessels, strung out across the river. The stars spread out thickly above them like a silver quilt, as Sam put his arms round her. He kissed her gently at first and then more deeply. When eventually they stopped for breath, he said, 'I love you, Nellie. Will you marry me?'

Nellie looked up into his face, aware that above them in the sky myriad stars were moving slowly into their appointed places in the heavens. Without pause or hesitation, she replied, 'Yes, Sam, of course I'll marry you.'

30

'KEEP THE HOME FIRES BURNING'

That night, as Nellie slipped into bed beside Alice, she felt as though she might float away with happiness. She wanted to lie there and remember the touch of Sam's lips, the feel of his strong arms round her, and she had just repeated his proposal to herself for the third time when she felt a nudge in her back. She turned over, to see the wide, inquisitive eyes of her sister.

'You're not asleep?' Nellie whispered, not wishing to wake Matty, but then a voice came from the other bed.

'I'm not asleep either!' Matty sat up. 'Has he asked you?'

Nellie nodded, a wide smile suffusing her face: joy seemed to have robbed her of the power of speech. She sat up in bed, nodding and smiling until she burst out, 'Yes!'

She found herself being smothered in hugs from Alice and being jumped upon by Matty, who squirrelled herself into bed between the two sisters.

'Tell us all about it!' Alice sat up and through their giggles Nellie recounted the details of Sam's proposal.

'Ohhh,' said Alice, 'how romantic, under the stars by the river!'

Matty threw her arms round Nellie and whispered, 'You're already more than a sister to me, Nellie. I'm so happy for you and our Sam!'

The next morning, at breakfast, they told the boys. Charlie and Freddie each got up to shake Sam's hand in a manly way, offering their congratulations. Bobby, in his normal unaffected fashion, was unable to restrain his joy and caught Sam in a hug.

'Welcome to the family! Our Nellie deserves to be happy,' he said, casting a loving look in her direction.

Nellie looked on in contentment, thrilled that Sam had been given such a resounding thumbs-up from her brothers.

But the days flew by after that. Though they snatched every possible moment together, she found herself wishing she could hold back time and never have to say goodbye to him again.

The night before Sam's leave ended, he and Nellie went to the Star together, for Matty wanted him to see her on stage. They sat in the stalls near the front, Nellie with her arm through his, snuggled as close as she could, glancing at him from time to time to see how he reacted to Matty's performance. As she finished her first rousing chorus of, '*If you were the only boy in the world and I were the only girl!*' Sam turned to look at Nellie in astonishment.

'She's got even better! She should be up the West End!' he whispered.

Nellie nodded and squeezed his arm, glad that Sam had this magical memory of his sister to take back to France. Matty certainly put on a show for her brother that night, strolling up and down the long stage as though she owned it, getting the audience to join in the chorus. She seemed to become a different person on the stage, as though she belonged there. Afterwards they'd planned a supper at the Green Ginger so they could announce their engagement to the rest of their family and friends. Nellie was a little disappointed that no one was in the least bit surprised.

'Surprised?' Maggie Tyrell said, when she told her. 'The only surprise is why it took you so long! I tried to tell you, love, he's worth 'undred of that Ted Bosher!' She lifted her pint glass and proposed a toast to the other custard tarts sitting round the table. 'To our Nellie, who said she'd never get up on a cart with Sam Gilbie!'

'And to Sam. Now she's up there, you'd better hold on to your whip!' Ethel added, downing her pint.

'Don't be filthy, Ethel!' Maggie's retort sent the girls into fits of giggles, while Nellie moved away to hide her blushes and greet Lily and Jock, who'd left the baby with his parents for the evening.

'Couldn't you have told me before? I've been in such a suspense all week!' Lily scolded Nellie.

'We wanted it to be a surprise!'

'Dozy mare,' was Lily's loving response. 'No one's surprised but you!'

'But you're happy for me?'

For answer, Lily kissed her and asked her if they'd set a date. Nellie shook her head.

'Sam wants to wait till after the war.'

'No!' Lily's shock would be felt by most girls. It was usual for engagements to be short when the proposal came on a soldier's leave, for when marriage could be cut short so easily by a sniper's bullet, or a German shell, there seemed little point in delaying. But Sam had insisted he didn't want her to rush into marriage just because of the danger he faced. Nellie didn't want to wait, but she would, for Sam's sake.

Jock kissed her loudly on the cheek, whispering in her ear, 'If he's got you to come back to, that's the best thing to keep him going out there.' He turned to shake hands with Sam.

'Well done, mate,' he said, 'well done!'

Had she been that frightening? Nellie wondered. It was as though Sam had performed some superhuman feat of daring. Certainly, at one time, she'd tried to scare Sam off, but the boy of sixteen waiting at the factory gates had never quailed or faltered. He'd simply been quietly persistent through all her indifference and then faithfully, through their friendship, he'd persevered still, until finally she'd seen him. And seeing him, she couldn't help but love him. Nellie smiled to herself and thought, *Yes, well done, Sam… well done.*

The day she'd dreaded dawned, when their charmed time together came to an end. She'd been wakeful all night, the words of that sentimental song going round and round in her head: *Let no tears add to their hardships, as the soldiers pass along*... Yes, she was determined to be brave. She was up early to see him off, the morning grey and full of a fine drizzle. Shivering, she quickly dressed and crept downstairs. It was far too cold for spring. The others had said their goodbyes the night before, leaving Nellie and Sam to say their farewells before the rest of the house was stirring. He was already up and in his uniform and she made him sit at the kitchen table to eat a slice of bread, even though he said he wasn't hungry. She took comfort in the amount she'd fed him during his leave, and in the cleanliness of his clothes and the package of food she'd just put in his knapsack, but these were the only comforts she could find that morning. He stood in the passage, holding her, as she cried. She had so wanted to be courageous, but she cursed the words of the song in her head that mocked her: *And although your heart is breaking, Make it sing this cheery song*. It was no good, no cheery song had any place in her heart at that moment. The best she could do was tell him she loved him and make him swear, for the thousandth time, to be careful.

'Remember that promise you made on the penny-farthing, before you went away?'

'Of course I do, darling Nellie. You've kept your penny-farthing promise ten times over and don't think I won't keep mine. You've got me for life now!'

He hugged her tightly. He was bundled up in a greatcoat and webbing with a huge pack on his back, and she couldn't get her arms all the way round him. As she laid her head on his breast she remembered the image of him in the bath, the pale skin of his chest and the raw scar. She let herself feel that her head now rested on warm skin, not on the horrible scratchy khaki. In the end, he had to untwine her arms.

'Nellie, my love, I've got to go. No more tears now. What do I always say?' He lifted her chin and she said obediently:

'Keep smiling!'

'Well, give me one, then, to keep in my heart.'

Full of misery, she gave him a brave smile and then he was gone from her arms. When he reached the end of Vauban Street, he looked back. She was still there and he blew her a kiss.

'Goodbye, Nellie.'

Returning to the lonely kitchen, she sat down heavily and twined her own arms about her, trying to recall the memory of his. Then she made a decision: she knew if she allowed the tears to return, she might never stop. So instead she repeated Sam's injunction to 'keep smiling, Nellie', and decided that from now on, every smile would be for him. There would be no false cheerfulness, just heartfelt gratitude that a man like Sam could love her.

She was glad she'd made the decision before the others appeared for breakfast. They were all so morose, especially Matty. As they drank a pot of tea together and ate bread and dripping, Nellie announced, 'Sam's told me we've all got to keep our peckers up, so all you misery guts had better liven up. We'll do exactly as he wants and keep smiling! Hear me?'

Charlie gave her an approving, 'Too right, Nell!' Chewing the last of his bread, he marched out of the kitchen as if he were off to the front himself. 'I'm off to do me bit.'

Then Matty began gathering her things for work. 'Well, sitting here ain't getting the shells made, is it?' she said.

Then Bobby jumped up, always eager to please her, announcing he was off to his early morning job at the vicarage, where he did odd jobs before school.

'Won't get the vicar's boots blacked either!' he said brightly.

The rest of them dispersed one by one, leaving only Alice who walked arm in arm with Nellie to Duff's and, with her quiet delicacy, never once dared ask about her sister's parting from Sam. Nellie was determined this would be a day like any other day.

And it was an ordinary day, which made her feel proud of herself and of her family, that they could carry on as normal, even though the heart had been ripped out of them. And that

330

ordinary day was followed by a succession of others, until a month later she came home to a letter from Eliza. After enquiries about Matty's welfare, Eliza gave her apologies for being unable to come down for Sam's leave at such short notice. There had been union work she couldn't drop and a meeting of the No-Conscription Fellowship she couldn't cancel – all excuses that Nellie thought little of. If Eliza had really wanted to see her brother, she would have been on the next London train; not that Sam had missed her presence. But Nellie was surprised Eliza had mentioned the No-Conscription Fellowship, for she rarely spoke of her work with conscientious objectors. Perhaps she feared Nellie would see it as a betrayal of Sam. But that was far from the truth. When conscription had been introduced earlier that year, all Nellie could think of were her young boys, Charlie, Freddie, Bobby. The eligible age for call-up had dropped to eighteen; how soon before they started snatching boys from their classrooms?

She read on, until the news of what Eliza called 'an odd coincidence' dropped like a bomb into Nellie's day. Eliza wrote:

> At first I didn't know him. He's changed from that handsome young firebrand of five years ago. I'm sure you would remember him, Ted Bosher? I think you may have even had a soft spot for him! I was astonished to hear he's been living in Russia! I always knew he was a radical, but to exile oneself for the cause is not easy. He's come home with the very laudable intention of offering his services to the No-Conscription campaign. The upshot is that we spoke of the strike days in Bermondsey and I mentioned that my sister and brother were now living with you.

Nellie could read no more. Her stomach lurched, tightened and twisted, like a coil of snakes. All the equilibrium of ordinary days was undone with one stroke of Eliza's pen. Nellie was filled with dread at the mere thought of Ted being back in the country. She forced her limbs to stop trembling, trying to identify what it was that frightened her so much. Russia or Hull, did it make so much difference where in the world he was, when he had no interest in her, or in her life? Was she frightened she might succumb to his charms again? Or was it her newfound happiness with Sam that had made her so vulnerable? Somehow she knew, if Ted ever found out about Sam, he would see it as a challenge. Even though Ted's interest in her had been fleeting, she was sure that in his vanity he would imagine her waiting her whole life for him. Ted loved nothing more than to be adored. Still, at least for now, he was two hundred miles away in Hull and, please God, he would stay there.

However sensibly she spoke to herself, she could not settle; she decided to go to Lily's. Unable to even face waiting for a tram, she threw on her coat and jumped on the penny-farthing. The old thing was more and more of an oddity these days and now that motor cars were increasingly common, a little more dangerous to ride amongst the traffic. Still, it did for the Co-op round and the times when she couldn't afford the tram fare, and today she relished its speed and power. She wanted to be on the move, and it served her well in that respect. She dashed down Spa Road, into Jamaica Road and on towards Rotherhithe Tunnel, pedalling so fast she sometimes found it necessary to lift her feet clear of the pedals as the wheels flashed round. She wasn't sure what she was fleeing, but when she arrived at the chandler's shop, she was panting like a hunted animal. She leaped off the bike, letting it clatter to the cobbles, and she took the back stairs to Lily's two at a time. Lily answered her knocks almost immediately, holding the baby tight to her. The immediate look of panic on Lily's face finally calmed Nellie down. She had frightened her friend, and she knew why.

'No, no, everything's all right with Sam,' she said, before Lily had a chance to speak.

'What the bloody hell's up, then? I thought you'd got a telegram for sure! You look like a whirling dervish. Look at the state of ya!' Lily pushed her angrily towards the mirror, where Nellie hardly recognized herself. Her hair was a tangled frizz, her face a sheen of sweat, and there was a wild-eyed look about her that frightened even herself.

'Oh, I'm sorry to frighten you, love,' she said repentantly. 'I don't know what got into me… well, I do. Here, let me take him, you read this.'

She reached out for the baby, who, sensing her own agitation, began to whine.

'No, he's hungry.' said Lily. 'You just get your breath back a minute.'

As Lily began to nurse Johnny, Nellie forced herself to concentrate on the calming ritual of making them tea. Soon the baby's contented nuzzling noises gave Lily her opportunity to take the letter from Nellie. After a few minutes she looked up, her eyes wide with astonishment.

'So he never let you know?' Nellie asked.

'Not a dickie bird, the bastard!'

Lily's vehemence caused Johnny to protest. She went on in a hushed, angry voice. 'Heartless git hasn't told Mum, or no one. Not that I give a monkey's whether he's home or not… but Mum…' She shook her head sorrowfully. 'But why's it got you in such a two 'n' eight? You're surely not telling me you think anything of him—'

'No! It's not that, Lil. To be honest, since that business—' she dropped her voice '—with the bomb… I'm scared of having anything to do with him.'

'Look, if he's not told me mum he's back, I reckon he's still lying low in Hull. You probably won't hear nothing more about him.'

Nellie was not convinced, but instead she asked, 'Will you tell your mum?'

Lily shook her head and the sadness of her expression told Nellie just how deeply Ted Bosher had managed to break his mother's heart. But Ted was a man who held hearts far too lightly, and Nellie knew it was quite possible for him to turn up on her own or the Boshers' doorstep, expecting all to be forgiven and to be loved, as he had once been.

Eliza thought it an odd coincidence. She was in Sculcoates, visiting her old Aunt Annie, one of the few remaining Hull relatives she had contact with. When she'd first returned to Hull she'd made a courtesy call, not expecting a warm welcome as she hadn't seen the old lady for over twenty years. But Aunt Annie had an old lady's vision – the past was more in focus than the present – and she saw Eliza as the little girl who'd lived in a back-to-back in Dock Road. After hearing she was bringing up her boy alone, Aunt Annie insisted on seeing him. Her aunt had no children of her own; instead she'd lavished her attention on Eliza and her brother. Now, as her own little William played in the cosy kitchen, Eliza remembered days when she and his namesake, her simple brother William, would do the same. Sometimes it felt more like coming home than her return to Bermondsey had.

On this particular day, she didn't really have the time or inclination to visit, but the old lady was now all alone and she had been kind. Eliza's work with the No-Conscription Fellowship had become much more demanding. She was now being called upon to speak at rallies of the local branch, which had expanded since the introduction of conscription in January that year. More and more young conscientious objectors were coming to them, in need of aid and advice. Sometimes a desperate young man, on the run from the military police, would need a safe house. But she largely left this dangerous side of the work to other members: William's safety came first and she could not be a mother to him from prison.

On the day she visited her aunt, her thoughts were full of a nervous young boy who'd arrived in a state of near collapse the night before, begging for their help. He had declared himself an Absolutist, who would undertake no war work at all, not even in ambulances or on the land. If he were caught, he could be shot or sentenced to years of hard labour. She needed someone reliable she could pass him on to. When she'd walked into her Aunt Annie's parlour and seen the dimly remembered Ted Bosher sitting at his ease, drinking tea out of her aunt's best china, she was astonished and, at first, bewildered. He stood up to shake her hand, answering her questioning look.

'Ted Bosher, Bermondsey? Nineteen-eleven strike?'

Now she remembered him, but he was changed. A rough life seemed to have scuffed those youthful good looks. His rather long red-gold hair still fell across his forehead, but now it was carefully arranged to hide a burn scar running from his forehead across his cheek. His face was quite gaunt and his good suit hung loosely on a rather emaciated frame. Whatever he had been doing in the intervening years, life had obviously not been kind. But his eyes were the same: they had a sea-green phosphorescence that burned with a slow intensity, reminding her why she'd been wary of him all those years ago.

'Oh, yes, of course. You did marvellous work, supporting the factory girls! I do remember you had a way with them,' Eliza said, thinking specifically of Nellie Clark. 'But how do you come to be here, of all places?'

'Aunt Annie's a relative of my mother. She was a Gilbie,' he explained.

'His mother, Betty, was your father's cousin!' Aunt Annie chimed in as she brought another cup for Eliza. 'You two chat about your Bolshevism,' she said benignly, 'while I take this little fellow out to the back yard. He wants to help feed my chickens.' She took William by the hand and left them alone.

Then Ted told her about his years in Russia, his involvement with the Bolshevik cause, and the reasons he had decided England needed him more.

'What bigger oppression is there than for a government to tell men what they must die for? That's the sort of dictatorship I want to fight!' he said passionately.

His green eyes flashed, and he stood up, pacing the little parlour like a caged animal.

'If you ever wanted to do something nearer to home,' she suggested, 'I hear the Bermondsey No-Conscription Fellowship could do with some help.'

This got his attention.

'Could you recommend me to them? I shall declare myself an Absolutist... though it might bring trouble.'

She didn't doubt Ted Bosher would bring trouble, wherever or whatever he was involved in, but the NCF was growing and it was a fact that many of their members would do nothing at all to aid the war effort.

'I'll recommend you, Ted, but first I wonder if you can help with a little problem we have in the Hull branch?' She explained the arrival of the young man the previous evening.

He nodded decisively. 'I think I can help. I know people I can pass him on to.'

She thanked him and decided to ask no more questions. The quivering young man who'd arrived at their branch meeting would never survive hard labour, let alone the Western Front. She would take any help she could get.

'And I'll be in Hull for a few more weeks,' Ted added, 'so any more waifs and strays, send 'em my way!'

They talked for another hour. Ted never left off in his railing against the war government; the generals; the profiteers. As she listened to his stream of condemnation and resentments, she was reminded of Ernest's unyielding focus.

'There's only one war to be fighting at the moment and that's the class war. Any other just benefits the profiteers. Look at the way the munitionettes are being exploited now!'

She mentioned that her sister was a munitionette at Woolwich and he became attentive.

'Your sister!' His tone was rather accusing, which Eliza didn't appreciate. 'A lot of the girls are fed up being on half the men's wages,' he went on. 'If you're blown sky high, doesn't matter what sex you are, does it?'

His words chilled her: she had tried everything to dissuade Matty from munitions work, but the girl had an even stronger will than her own.

She shook her head. 'I've got very little influence over my sister. But she wouldn't listen to me, or my brother Sam, or even your old friend Nellie Clark, and that young lady can be persuasive when she wants to be!'

When she told him that Matty was now living with Nellie, he sat down again, elbows on the arms of the chair, his long fingers steepled under his chin, as though he were trying to recall Nellie to mind. Eliza noticed then his rather elegant wrists, too fine for a docker, she thought. She tried to picture Ted dock-labouring. It was like imagining a highly strung thoroughbred doing the work of a carthorse. No wonder he chafed and railed so.

'Nellie Clark?' He sat back and smiled. 'Yes, I do remember her persuasive ways now.'

The other thing that hadn't changed about him was his smile, which, in spite of the puckering scar, was still charming. She said goodbye, wondering if she'd been wise to confide in him so much. Still, they were on the same side in this conflict – the opposite side to the warmongers – and she judged that a common enemy must make him a friend.

Several weeks later Eliza received a letter from Ernest, forwarded by her loyal friend Sarah at the NFWW. He wanted to see William. Since his return from Australia last year, she'd met him only once. Although she believed his bitterness against her outweighed his concern for the boy, he seemed intent on pursuing his son. She knew that sooner or later she must face him, so she'd agreed to a meeting in London earlier this year, on one of her trips to see Matty. His letters had hinted at legal action; she hoped if she met him that their contact could at least remain civilized. Unwilling to return to Mecklenburgh Square, she'd suggested the more neutral territory of the NFWW headquarters.

Sarah was to serve them tea in a small parlour on the top floor, a dusty room crammed with an assortment of odd bits of furniture and filing cabinets. Ernest strode in with a businesslike air, pausing to give her a long stare.

'Eliza,' was all he said by way of greeting. Taking the chair she offered him, he put his despatch case carefully at his feet as though he suspected she might run off with that, as she had run off with his son. It exasperated Eliza, more than anything else he could have done, and she launched in on the attack.

'Ernest, why on earth do you care that William is with me? You wanted to send him away!'

'I see we're to have none of the niceties of polite society.' Ernest flushed. 'Not that I'm surprised.'

'Reverted to the gutter, you mean?' She would let him get away with nothing, not now that she'd broken the shackles.

'You left me, without warning or explanation, taking our son halfway round the world. I haven't seen you for over two years. I would think that deserves at least some humility and explanation on your part!'

How haughty he was! She'd forgotten just how different his public persona was from his behaviour with her. A man of the people, he had been called, and once she'd believed it too.

'You threatened to take my child away! I don't need to give any other explanation for why I chose to escape with him, rather than give him up to strangers.'

'And yet you did exactly that with our firstborn?' he asked in the open-ended way he had, laying a trap for her to fall into. But she had already decided she would never divulge to him Matty's whereabouts.

'I was much younger then, and I was in awe of you.'

'And you are no longer?'

She sighed; she had no desire to talk about their relationship. The only thing that interested her was how best to keep William with her. 'I'm very grateful to you.'

'Grateful!' He slammed his fist on to the tea table, rattling the fine-bone china teacups and saucers. 'Next you'll be bobbing me a curtsey! It's *you*, Eliza, who could never escape your ridiculous ingrained ideas of class. Don't try to cast me as that particular villain!'

That would be too easy for him and she wouldn't allow it. 'I'm not talking about our class differences, Ernest. What I know is that as a man you wanted to own me and I found that I didn't want to be owned!'

He appeared stunned. 'But I gave you every freedom!'

'For a woman who used to be your housekeeper, perhaps, but never the freedom of an equal.' She tried to slow her breathing, wishing the struggle over. Still she dug deeper into her stubborn reserves of emotional stamina. 'What is it that you want, Ernest?'

'Want? What I want is a say in how my son is raised. As I told you in Australia when he was born, I wish him brought up a gentleman.'

'And there you have it. *I* can't bring him up as a gentleman, can I?'

'Eliza!' His exasperation erupted. 'You were *never* maternal!'

'And you were never *paternal*!' She knew now that she would win. When she'd asked him what he wanted, she knew he hadn't been completely truthful. No doubt he did want William brought up a gentleman, but she suspected a deeper motive; she'd seen through his bluster. He wanted her back. If he'd answered, 'What I want is you,' she might have relented and lost, but he hadn't.

'I *will* bring up our son, Ernest.' She was implacable now. 'If you wish to ensure he's given the education of a gentleman, then pay the fees of a good day school; I won't have him sent away! If you like, I will bring him to see you.'

That was her offer, her bluff. She couldn't go back to him, but she would be part of his life again. At least she'd allowed him his pride; let them both pretend it was only William he was interested in seeing.

He looked at her, letting fall the wounded veil of haughtiness.

His dark eyes glowed with a softened light. She had hurt him, but he still loved her. Abruptly, he rose, picked up his despatch case and turned to her. In the dusty light of the long sash window, she noticed the grey flecks in his dark hair, the sagginess around his eyes. She felt pity, but wouldn't relent.

'Very well, Eliza, we'll do as you suggest... How is the child?'

'He's thriving, he's determined and clever... and he has a temper... like you.' She got up and went to him, putting out her hand. 'I'm sorry, Ernest, that I hurt you.'

He nodded. 'I didn't realize you felt so caged, I wish I had known...'

Then he turned briskly away. 'Perhaps you'd care to visit me in Mecklenburgh Square, next time you're in London... and bring the boy?'

She'd told him she would write; the weeks had passed and she'd delayed. She'd wanted to keep William to herself for as long as possible, but she had offered Ernest the compromise and now she must honour it.

Nellie was sitting up alone, late one warm Wednesday night, towards the end of May. She'd thrown up the sash window and opened the front and back doors to let some air blow through. The draught brought with it fetid odours from the Neckinger tannery. After a month of cold, grey days, summer had arrived today, with a sudden oppressive heat. She'd sweltered all day in the packing room and then come home to a steamy kitchen. Even though it was not laundry day, Alice had seized the opportunity to get it done and dried in the sunshine. The boiling copper's humid heat still hung about the house. Now Nellie simply wanted to enjoy a few minutes' peace in the cool breeze wafting through the house. These days she prized her moments alone, when she allowed herself to reread Sam's letters and to send him her silent thoughts and prayers. Perhaps it was superstition, but she believed, wherever he was, he heard those unspoken words of her heart. After she'd read them all through,

Nellie tidied his letters back into a bundle and she was about to extinguish the table lamp when her attention was caught by a shadow flickering past the open window. She went to pull down the sash, but a hand shot out to grab the window before she could fully close it. The face on the other side of the window broke into a grin, one that she'd once found charming but that now filled her with shock and dread.

'Ted!' Nellie gripped the window frame even tighter, trying to push it down, while he resisted. Eventually he said, 'Ain't you pleased to see me, Nellie?'

She stood rigid, but eventually his grip proved the stronger. Forcing the sash up, he coiled his long frame and slipped through the open window. He closed it softly behind him, turned and dipped forward, quickly snatching a kiss.

'You could've used the front door, it's wide open,' she said, with a coolness that belied her racing heart. Pulling back, she deliberately wiped the kiss from her mouth. Every inch of her was trembling, but she was determined not to show it. 'I'd best close it.'

She went to the front door, desperately trying to work out the best way to deal with Ted. She forced herself to stay calm, looking carefully up and down the street to check for nosy neighbours before closing the door. When she returned, Ted had untied the bundle and was reading one of Sam's letters. All her studied calm vanished. Furious that he should touch something so precious, she dived to snatch it from him but he pulled it away, tearing the thin blue paper.

'Give that to me, Ted Bosher,' she hissed.

He tossed it back on to the table. 'You must've been bloody desperate after I left if he's the best you could do.'

'You was glad enough of him the night you blew yourself up!' she shot back, gathering up Sam's precious letters.

Ted snorted. 'He never did it for me!'

'Don't matter why he did it. He ended up in Tower Bridge nick because of you!'

'Well, it wasn't me shopped him.'

Nellie was stunned, not by his ingratitude but that he didn't seem surprised. She'd always been suspicious about the mysterious informer who'd seen Sam at the arches.

'If you *did*, you're a selfish, ungrateful bastard and you can get out!'

'I just said it *wasn't* me! I swear to you, Nell. But I couldn't help it if one my pals decided to steer the Old Bill in the wrong direction, could I?'

Once Nellie might have doubted Ted was capable of such a betrayal, but not now. 'I don't believe it was your pal,' she said coldly. 'Just go, Ted, and don't come near me again.'

Ted threw himself down in her father's chair and turned the scarred side of his face towards her. She hadn't seen, in the dim light, just how bad it was. Now she gasped. He drew a long finger down it.

'I didn't get away scot-free, Nellie,' he said quietly.

'I'm sorry, Ted, but you did it to yourself. I've got no sympathy.'

He grinned at her. 'Same old no-nonsense Nellie, eh? How long did it take Gilbie to step into my shoes, then?'

'Don't tell me you're jealous, Ted. It won't wash, not after five years and not a word out of you. What did you expect me to do, sit indoors and cry myself to sleep every night? And not that it's any of your business. I've found the man I'm going to marry, and it ain't you! Me and Sam's engaged.'

This seemed to genuinely shock him. 'You know I was nuts about you, Nell, the only reason I never come back is *this*.' He jabbed at his face. 'I was scared you wouldn't want an ugly git like me on your arm.' His voice had taken on that resentful, childish tone she remembered. He really did expect her sympathy.

'The only ugly thing about you now is what's on the inside.'

'I don't give a tinker's whether you believe me or not! The truth is, I wouldn't have come to see you if it wasn't for our old friend, Madam Mecklenburgh.' Light from the gas lamp picked out the gold flecks in his eyes and she was aware of him studying her reaction.

'Eliza told me she'd met you in Hull,' she said calmly.

Ted pulled an impressed face. 'First-name terms with the great lady!'

'She's a Bermondsey girl, same as me.'

'Was once, but I know where her loyalties lie and it's not with her brother in France, you can be sure of that.'

'I know all about the conchie work she does. Anyway, I never wanted Sam, or any of them, to go. It was their choice.'

'When they *had* a choice!' he flung at her. 'So long as donkeys like him were lining up to get slaughtered, they let 'em choose. Different now they're running out of cannon fodder, ain't it? Did he think he'd be protecting you and the kids from the evil Hun? Idiot. The only ones he's protecting are the profiteering bastards, getting rich off munitions.' His vitriol seemed to sap him and he sank back. She observed his laboured breath and noticed how thin he was. Hardship had etched his face with lines she didn't remember. The fire of his spirit seemed to be burning him up from the inside out. She hated him, yet she couldn't forget that once she had loved him.

'I'll get you a drink and something to eat, then you can be on your way, Ted.'

As she passed his chair, he caught her hand. 'I was hoping you could put me up, just for the night, till I get some digs?'

She had to give him that, the old unquenchable bravado was still there. 'Well, you can't stay here.' She pulled her hand away. 'Try showing your face at your mum's, before you disappear again. She might take pity on you,' she said tartly, as she disappeared into the scullery. She quickly brought him some bread, cheese and a bottle of beer, desperately wanting him to be gone. But he chewed the food slowly and after gulping the beer he seemed revived, sitting back easily in her father's chair.

'I've already been to see Mum and Dad today. Didn't get a warm welcome from the old man.'

'Can you blame him? Lily told me you stopped writing to your mum. You could've been dead! Do you know what that

343

does to a mother? It'll take a lot before your family trusts you again, Ted.'

He shrugged sullenly. 'Well, whether you believe me or not, I'm back to stay. I've got war work of my own to do. I've joined the Bermondsey No-Conscription Fellowship and if the police come for me I'll declare myself an Absolutist!'

'Ted, for God's sake, what's the matter with you? They could shoot you! Why didn't you just stay in Russia?' It was obvious to her that Ted was not a coward, but why he would deliberately come home, to put himself in front of a firing squad, was beyond her. He seemed so careless of his own life, and of other people's. He was silent, looking at her intently.

'The fact is, Nell, I'd rather face an English bullet than a Russian one. I got myself on the wrong side of some dangerous people out there.'

Why he would tell her the truth, she didn't know, other than that he had so few others he could confide in. She noticed a slight tremor in his hand as he picked up the beer and drained it.

'Besides, Bermondsey is where my fight is. And I'm going to take on the munitions profiteers over at Woolwich, too. Now the bastard union's sold us out to the government, they can't even go on strike!' He looked at her quizzically. 'Eliza James says her sister's a canary at the Arsenal?'

Looking into Ted's dangerous sea-green eyes, a memory flashed before her of that day on Goodwin Sands when he'd almost got her killed. She saw the two bright claws of water closing round her, cutting her off from everything safe; she heard again the incoming rush of the tide as it swirled around her, threatening all she held dear.

31

A DARK MOON

Another sound had been drowned out by the echo of that rushing tide: the click of the latch as a key turned in the front door. Nellie was standing in the middle of the room with her back to the open kitchen door. She saw Ted's gaze shift, suddenly, to the passageway behind her and his expression change, in an instant, from bitter to sweet. Like a spring slowly uncoiling, he stood up, all geniality, to greet Matty.

'Ah, this must be the canary herself. We were just talking about you, weren't we, Nellie?'

Nellie whirled round, to see Matty framed in the doorway. She wore her stage dress, with a fine chiffon stole of pale gold around her shoulders. Her height, and the elegant coil of her auburn hair, made her look much older than her fifteen years. Her hair shone like spun copper as she stepped forward into the pool of light cast by the gas lamp. Nellie could tell, from the confident way she strode across the room, that this was still 'Matty on the stage'. Normally, as soon as she walked in after a night at the Star, that persona was dropped, along with her hat and coat. Nellie usually stayed up to make sure she had something to eat before going to bed, and Matty would always greet Nellie with a kiss and a scolding for waiting up. Stepping over the threshold of her home invariably restored Matty to their loving, contrary little canary once more. But tonight she kept her stage armour firmly around her.

'How d'you know me nickname?' she asked, with a wide bold smile, as though he was one of the audience.

'Yours and a few thousand other lovely girls!' Ted replied, falling in with the banter.

Matty shot a look at Nellie. Beneath the veneer there was little Matty, unsure of this stranger in their cosy kitchen.

Nellie jumped to the rescue. 'This is Ted, Lily's brother. He means the canary girls at the Arsenal.'

'Oh, hello, Ted, pleased to meet you,' Matty said, dropping the stole over the back of the kitchen chair and sitting down with studied poise. 'Why were you talking about me?' She looked brightly at Ted and back to Nellie.

'I was asking Nellie if she thinks it's right that your life's worth half a man's?'

'Oh,' Matty said, 'that's right, you're a *Bolshevik*, ain't you? Have you come to stir us all up?' Her voice was mocking. But then she went on more seriously. 'I know some of the women complain about the wages, but I'm really not sure my life's worth twice my brother's, when you come to think about it like that. Seems to me, if I walk out with thirty shillings a week and Sam's fighting over there for eleven, then I'm paid too much. Anyway,' she said with finality, 'we're not allowed to strike.'

'Who cares?' Ted said, standing up now, ready for a debate.

'They'll all care if they end up in Holloway,' Nellie cut in. She needed to get Ted out. 'Anyway, Matty, I'll get you a bite to eat and then you'd best get on up to bed, love. You're on earlies tomorrow.'

Nellie turned to Ted with a look that brooked no argument. 'Ted was just going, weren't you, Ted?'

He didn't reply. Instead he picked up his cap and moved to the door. As he passed Matty, he extended his hand. 'Pleased to meet you, Matty, I've heard you do a great turn at the Star, maybe I'll come and see you one night.'

Matty gave him her stage smile and inclined her head.

''Night, Nellie. I'll see yer when I see yer.'

He brushed past her and she followed him down the passage.

'Not if I see you first,' she whispered to herself, as she shut the door behind him.

But his visit had shaken her. She feared this wasn't the last she'd be seeing of Ted Bosher and that night she slept badly.

The next day dawned grey, cold and damp again. Yesterday had been a single day of summer and now it had vanished, taking Nellie's peace of mind with it. Ted's reappearance had left her unsettled and preoccupied. She was grateful that, at least, it was Thursday. Since Lily had left Duff's, she and Nellie were in the habit of meeting up in the Green Ginger every Thursday night: it was a comforting ritual they allowed themselves. Little Johnny was left with Mrs McBride and Alice took over at home, while they shared news of Sam and Jock, and Nellie entertained Lily with the latest custard tart news. They considered it well worth the five pence a pint of Russian Stout, their favourite tipple.

Tonight, Nellie was first to arrive in the pub. Once, she would have felt shy of sitting there on her own, but since the war it was a common sight to see women drinking alone. *And why not?* thought Nellie. They were doing the work of men; surely they should have some of their privileges. Which brought her back to Ted; her thoughts hadn't strayed far from him all day and she resented it. Still, she couldn't deny he had a point about the munitionettes' wages. If only he weren't so extreme and careless of consequences. She smiled to herself, remembering Matty's retort about soldiers' pay. The young girl had stopped him in his tracks, a sight Nellie had rarely seen. She'd so often tried to best him in an argument herself, and failed.

The red velvet curtain round the pub door was pulled aside and in walked Lily. She was a little more buxom since the birth of Johnny, but she had lost the frazzled look of her early motherhood and now her bright prettiness had returned. She came over eagerly and kissed Nellie on the cheek.

'Oh, good, you've got the stouts in!' she said, undoing her coat. 'I need this. Johnny's been such a little bugger today I almost chucked him at Grandma McBride tonight!' She took a long sip of the dark creamy stout and ended up with a frothy lip, which Nellie leaned over to brush away. She hated to spoil her friend's good humour, but she was bursting with the news.

'I had a visit last night. Guess who from?'

Lily paused mid-sip and shook her head.

'Your brother!'

Lily put down the pint glass and groaned. 'Oh, Nell, that's trouble. What's he doing back? He's got a cheek, turning up on your doorstep! What did he have to say for himself?'

Nellie told her Ted's excuse for not coming to see her and his plans for working with the No-Conscription Fellowship.

'Typical Ted! *Poor me! I'm scarred for life, so I can't pick up a pen and write a letter to me girl, nor me family!* I'm sorry, Nell, but he's always got to be the centre of attention. That's the only reason he's working with the conchies. He wants to play the martyr, that's all.'

Her friend's dismissive analysis allowed Nellie a little more perspective, she thought gratefully. On her own, she could never seem to get the correct distance between herself and Ted, to be able to see him clearly. 'He said he'd gone round your mum's and your dad told him to piss off!'

Lily sighed. 'Dad's got no time for him, but Mum'll find a way to bail him out.'

'He tried it on with me,' Nellie whispered.

'Never!' Lily's eyes widened. 'I hope you told him to sod off.'

''Course I did! But then Matty came home, and I tell you, Lil, I'd swear he was eyeing *her* up!'

'Matty's got more sense.'

'More than me, you mean?'

Lily laughed. 'I didn't mean that!'

'Well, I did. You can't see it, 'cause he's your brother, but there's definitely something about Ted.' She thought it over, trying to find the key to his attraction. 'Even though he looks a bit rough now, he can still turn on the charm when he wants to... Oh, I'm probably being silly, it's just put me all up the wall.'

'Well, Matty's got other things on her mind, what with the

singing at night and then all day at the Arsenal, she's too busy for fellers!'

'That's the other thing that put the wind up me, though. He's trying to organize an unofficial strike at the Arsenal.'

'Just tell Matty to stay well clear. You're talking about prison for that!' Lily now looked as concerned as Nellie, and the two girls sipped silently until Nellie decided to change the subject to sixteen-month-old Johnny, which soon had Lily in full flow about her son's latest exploits.

The so-called summer months of 1916 dragged on, the coldest, greyest and wettest that Nellie could remember, the only sunny day marred by Ted's return. Still, she had more important things on her mind than Ted. Day-to-day life was becoming much harder as the German blockade took hold, and basic foodstuffs were in short supply. The factory had been badly affected as their sugar had always been imported from Germany. Added to that, half the fruit growers of England were on the Western Front, so the jelly department was working at half-strength. Nellie got used to seeing new faces as women from jellies were moved to powder packing. One day Ethel came in with a basket full of jellies.

'Free samples, girls!' She went along the line, handing them out. 'We've got to try 'em out and let jellies know if we like 'em!' she announced.

'Oooh, look at lady bountiful!' Maggie Tyrell took one, then dipped her hand in the basket for another.

'Oi, one each!' Ethel slapped Maggie's hand.

'I've got six kids, Ethel. It's no good me taking home one jelly, there'll be murders.'

'Oh, all right, then, here y'are!' Ethel's massive hands scooped up a handful, dumping them into Maggie's lap.

Nellie looked at the packet, it was branded as 'War Jelly'.

'Listen to this, Mag,' she read. 'It's made from rhubarb and beets! Do you think your kids will eat it?'

'My kids'll eat anything,' Maggie assured her. But next day

she told Ethel to report back to jellies that 'War Jelly' was vile and that even her perpetually hungry brood wouldn't touch it.

Bread, potatoes, milk, butter, all had doubled in price, and now a government soup kitchen had opened next door to the Salvation Army. Spa Road was constantly packed with shuffling humanity: there was a queue of tramps outside the Sally Army, a queue of women and children for the soup kitchen, and still the long line of recruits snaking down the steps of the town hall. This was the queue that Nellie saw most of, for she would walk to the town hall every day during her dinner break to check the casualty lists posted there. It was a harrowing ritual, for there was never a day when some poor woman didn't find the name she'd been hoping not to see. Some would merely collapse into the arms of the nearest woman; others would have to voice their grief. The wail would start so pitifully, a feeble moan, building to an unbearable keening that grew louder, till it pierced Nellie's heart. God only knew what sort of effect it had on the eager recruits, lining up to become statistics on such a list.

Food shortages meant she'd long ago abandoned any scruples about Freddie's odd contribution to the household. In fact, she blessed every tin of corned beef or sack of potatoes he came home with. But even he could do nothing when the government started watering down her beloved Russian Stout. 'It's like a glass of gnat's piss!' was Lily's gloomy opinion of the brew now being served up at the Green Ginger.

In spite of her fears, Ted hadn't crossed her path again. But a month or so after his visit Matty told her Ted had been frequenting the Star. He'd taken to waiting at the stage door for her.

'He's started bringing me flowers, walks me home, and we sometimes go for a drink in the Golden Fleece,' Matty said, seeming a little embarrassed. 'I've been seeing a bit of him over at the Arsenal too, he still thinks he can organize a strike... I thought you'd want to know, Nellie.'

Nellie felt fear catch in her throat. The thought of Ted's

attention being directed towards Matty was horrifying, like witnessing a bird being fondled by a green-eyed cat, and Nellie's instinct was to snatch the little canary from his grasp. She didn't know how much the girl knew of her past with Ted and she wasn't certain how much to tell her. Matty's revelation filled her with a sense of failure too. She'd promised Lizzie Gilbie she'd look after the children, hadn't she? How would letting Matty fall into Ted's dangerous hands be protecting her? She was about to forbid Matty from seeing him again when she remembered her own father, sitting in his chair, picking away at his pipe, ordering her to have nothing to do with 'that Bosher boy'. It was ironic to find herself in the same position, and she wouldn't let panic at her own impotence lead her into the same mistakes her father had made. All the warnings or beatings in the world hadn't prevented her from doing exactly as she'd wanted. Giving Matty a direct order generally tended to bring out her stubborn streak, and usually prompted her to do the opposite. Perhaps she should just gently warn Matty off Ted.

'We used to walk out, me and Ted,' she explained, 'but he didn't treat me well and my advice is steer clear, love. He might be handsome enough, but he's a wrong 'un.'

Matty gave her a long look. 'I do think he's handsome, Nell, and he'd make a lovely hero on the stage, but he's not *that* good an actor.'

Nellie should never have doubted that Matty would see beyond the veneer of Ted's charm. 'No? Well, he took me in, love, and I paid for it. I don't want you doing the same.'

'Oh, Nellie, I know he's just a charmer, but don't blame yourself. It's just I've had a lot more stage experience!' She laughed. 'The thing is, Nell, all the young boys are at the front and it's just nice to have a bit of attention.'

Matty really was growing up and Nellie would just have to trust her judgement and rely on the little canary's native intuition. After all, she'd always had that uncanny ability to sniff out the smell of gas.

So, over the following months, Nellie allowed herself to relax and tried to forget Ted's presence in Bermondsey. It was towards the end of September before he came up again in conversation. This time it was Eliza James who mentioned him, in one of her letters to Nellie. Eliza's visits to London were now longer and more frequent. She often spoke at the Fort Road Labour Institute and since the moratorium on strikes she'd been called in to help arbitrate many local disputes. During her extended London visits, she usually rented a couple of rooms in the Morgans' house. Frank Morgan was now driving an ambulance in France and his wife had taken over as manager of the Co-op. She often put up visiting speakers, or union officials, in their pleasant terraced house in Reverdy Road, one of the more respectable Bermondsey streets, where doctors and professional people chose to live. Eliza wrote that she was coming to Bermondsey the following week to give a speech for the No-Conscription Fellowship and went on to mention Ted.

I hear he has become one of their most committed workers. Though he risks arrest, he's trumpeting the Absolutist cause now! Sadly, I've come to realize he is rather a heedless young man, and stories are filtering back to me that suggest he's a little cavalier with his own and other people's safety. The Bermondsey NCF has always been staunchly pacifist, but I hear Ted's militant ways have put the cat amongst the pigeons. I wonder if I did right to put him in their way... or yours. Has he been in touch with you?

It had the air of an apology. It sounded like Ted was making his true reckless colours known. Nellie didn't send a reply; she thought it best to save the news about Ted and Matty till Eliza came down. She was glad her initial mistrust of Eliza's motives had been overcome, and since her engagement to Sam she'd certainly felt more at ease with Eliza, more on an equal footing. It meant that they could be friends – of a sort – and it made it easier for Matty. For the young girl's loyalties were so hard won and so fiercely held she would never have been able to be friends with Eliza, if Nellie had not. And for that reason alone, Nellie was glad she'd made the effort to befriend Eliza.

When Eliza arrived in Reverdy Road with her son, she blessed the bright remnant of the waning moon. It was no more than a fingernail, but she judged there would be no Zeppelin raid tonight: they only attacked when the moon was dark, so for the moment they were safe. Her journey had been full of delays and she was exhausted. The train timetable had been suspended while a horde of Tommies entrained at Hull Station. Only after the troop train pulled out was she able to board the London train. After hours in a cramped, smelly carriage, the motor taxi had been a necessity, not a luxury – she simply couldn't face a tram ride from London Bridge Station with her tired child. She scooped a sleeping William out of the taxi and picked up her bag with the other hand. Ruth Morgan, Frank's wife, was already at the front door and came hurrying to take her bag. The woman was a stalwart type, who could turn her hand to anything. She'd taken over the organization of the Co-op seamlessly and had even been known to do delivery rounds in an emergency. Now she was all domestic bustle and welcome, and the house was cosy with supper already laid out in the dining room. Today, like all the others this summer, had been chilly and the fire in the grate was welcome. After William was settled into bed, Mrs Morgan served her a light supper and began her cheerful chatter: for all her qualities, the woman was a notorious gossip. She knew details of all the political in-fighting at the institute, and the Co-op gave her contact with half of Bermondsey, so her gossip coffers were full tonight. 'When is your No-Conscription speech?' she asked.

'Not until Monday. I'm visiting my family tomorrow.'

'There's been murders at the NCF. It's that young feller Bosher that you sent down.'

Eliza felt a pang of guilt. She had suspected something of the sort, but knew no details.

'What's he been up to? He's not the only Absolutist in the ranks, surely?'

Ruth Morgan shook her head and pulled up a chair, while Eliza ate. 'Of course, there are others, but you know most of the COs there are happy to do land work, or drive an ambulance, like my Frank – which is dangerous enough, I can tell you.'

Eliza reached out to squeeze her hand – just because the woman was calm and capable, it didn't mean she could escape that ubiquitous fear for loved ones at the front.

'Anyway, the Absolutists are totally against the war. But young Ted's stirring 'em up to fight another war... at home! All I will say is that I've heard some of his ideas just don't fit with the pacifists.' She leaned forward and mouthed, 'Anarchist ideas!'

Eliza shivered: the fire in the grate was dying down and she felt as though a chill wind had blown through the room. Ruth Morgan noticed. 'I'm sorry it's a bit chilly, but you just can't get the coal...'

'I'm not cold, just a long day,' Eliza excused herself.

Mrs Morgan took the plates out and called from the scullery, 'Will you be at Nellie Clarke's tomorrow, then?'

'Yes, visiting Charlie and Matty.'

'Matty's turned into a lovely girl. I saw her at the Star the other night. She was marvellous, better than Vesta Tilley! I suppose you know she's been walking out with that Bosher feller?'

It hit her like a blow in the stomach; she barely had wind to answer the woman.

'Is there anything more you'll need tonight?' Mrs Morgan asked as she came back in, drying her hands on her pinafore.

'No, thank you, Mrs Morgan, I'll go up to bed, I think. I know where everything is.'

Ruth Morgan gave her a gas lamp to take to her room. It was connected to William's by a double door, which she eased open.

Her son was sleeping soundly and she softly retreated. Eliza was glad to be alone. Ruth's news had totally stunned her. Matty at fifteen had indeed blossomed into a beautiful young woman, and it was inevitable she would attract attention, especially from the stage-door johnnies, but Ted must be more than ten years older and totally unsuitable. He was the last person she'd want Matty involved with. What was Nellie thinking, letting it go on?

The next morning was a Sunday and Eliza dressed three-year-old William carefully in his newest sailor suit, his dark hair curling out from beneath the straw hat. She gave him his toy boat and asked, 'Would you like to sail your boat on the pond today, William?'

'Yes! Sail the boat!' The little boy spun round with the boat, ploughing it through imaginary waves. 'Now!'

She planned to visit Vauban Street that afternoon, but this morning she took a tram to Greenwich Park. Fortunately, the rain had held off and huge clouds scudded across Blackheath, moving swiftly enough to allow patches of sunshine to warm her and William. She walked hand in hand with him to the boating lake and sat down on a bench. She saw Ernest from a long way off, dressed in a tailored tweed jacket, with a brown trilby, and a cane swinging with every step. He strode purposefully towards her, shook her hand and turned to shake William's.

'I am Mr James,' he said formally, 'a friend of your mother's.'

William shoved the sailing boat into Ernest's extended hand and ordered, 'Sail the boat, now!' Then he grabbed Ernest's other hand and began dragging him towards the pond.

Ernest looked at her with a raised eyebrow, and she was just about to defend her son's ungentlemanly behaviour when Ernest remarked, 'I have been commanded by the admiral. Will you join us?'

She followed them to the pond edge, watching in wonder as her bossy toddler took charge of the man she'd once cast in the role of gaoler. She smiled secretly to herself. Ahhh, she thought with satisfaction, the biter bit!

There followed tea and cakes in a café in Greenwich, during which Eliza was thankful William chose to mind his table manners. Towards the end of their visit, Ernest concluded, 'He seems a remarkably intelligent young fellow, and strong-willed! You must put him down for a good day school and let me have the details.'

She breathed a sigh of relief. She needed no formal arrangement. Ernest would keep his word, she was sure of it, and she would keep William.

'How could *I* let it happen?' Nellie was incensed with Eliza. 'When you're the one who sent him back down here!'

'And in case you hadn't noticed, I've got a tongue in my head. I could tell him where to go if I wanted to!' Matty was equally angry. 'But I don't want to... not yet, anyway!' she said provocatively.

Matty and Nellie were facing Eliza across the kitchen table. The boys had taken William out to play and were now running him up and down Vauban Street on the penny-farthing. Every now and then they would run past the front window, whooping as the little boy bounced up out of the saddle.

'All I said was that his anarchist talk has got everyone worried at the NCF and if Matty's connected in any way,' Eliza shot a meaningful glance at Matty, 'then she could be implicated!'

Nellie had decided not to go into the details of Ted's past activities. Eliza was already nervous enough about him.

'He's drawing so much attention to himself, giving out Absolutist leaflets, stirring things up at the Arsenal, it's almost like he wants to be arrested,' Eliza went on. 'And I dread to think what he got up to in Russia.'

Nellie could tell her a thing or two about his bomb-making skills but now wasn't the time. The annoying thing was that she agreed with her wholeheartedly; she just knew this wasn't the way to convince Matty.

'All we can do is *advise* Matty,' Nellie said pointedly. 'She's old enough now to earn her living and make her own decisions, and she's not so stupid as to put herself – or her family – in danger because of a bloke!'

Matty responded with a warm smile for Nellie and a scowl for Eliza. At that moment Alice came in with a tray of tea things, which effectively ended the conversation. They called the boys in and squeezed round the table, for what Nellie hoped passed for a splendid tea in these austere days. It consisted of a loaf of Mo the baker's 'real bread', a tiny amount of butter, two pots of fish paste from a cache that Freddie had 'found' in a bombed-out shop, a tin of corned beef, from the same source, and a pink blancmange, courtesy of Pearce Duff's. The allotment owners often paid Freddie in kind and this week he'd brought home a bag of tomatoes and a cucumber. Nellie surveyed the table and thought they hadn't done a bad job between them.

Charlie turned the conversation to Sam, arguing with the other boys about his brother's actual whereabouts, always difficult to guess from Sam's censored letters.

'He's been in the thick of it, the Somme, I'm telling you!' said Freddie.

'Yes, but their division's moved on by now!' Charlie countered.

The boys regularly plotted Sam's movements on a map pinned to their bedroom wall, but Charlie was the most avid follower of the war. Patiently gathering every piece of information, he scoured newspaper reports and gleaned stories from soldiers on leave till he could predict the next battle with surprising accuracy.

After tea, Nellie read the shareable parts of Sam's letters to Eliza. He always sent his love to the whole family and this now included Eliza and William, which Nellie could see pleased her.

'Is he due more leave?' Eliza asked.

'I shouldn't think we'll see him this side of Christmas,' said Nellie sadly. 'Please God, it'll be over by then!'

'Not the way things are going, it won't,' Charlie said, then added, 'but he might get a Blighty.'

'How can you say that?' Matty shoved her brother.

'They all want one!'

Alice, ever the peacemaker, intervened. 'Don't squabble, you two, there's enough fighting in the world without bringing it home. What about a song, Matty?'

This was a request the little canary could never resist and the evening ended with them all joining in to the chorus of 'Pack Up Your troubles in Your Old Kit Bag'. When they came to the last line, Nellie thought of Sam and defiantly sang the loudest, 'Smile, Smile, Smile!'

Nellie was pleased the evening had ended on a good note, but the next day brought some worrying news. That Monday afternoon, Matty came home looking troubled. After tea, she and Nellie were washing up the dinner things in the scullery when Matty suddenly blurted out, 'Nellie, I think Ted's up to something really bad at the Arsenal.'

Nellie studied the girl's strained white face – she looked almost nauseous. Nellie immediately thought of the young, impressionable munitionettes: if anyone could persuade them to break the moratorium on strikes, Ted could. Most of them probably wouldn't understand that they could be arrested for it.

'Has he got them to agree to a strike?' Nellie asked fearfully.

Matty put down the teacloth and looked nervously back towards the kitchen, where the others still sat round the table chatting. She pulled Nellie out into the back yard. 'No, it's much worse!' she whispered.

Matty hung on to her hand and Nellie felt her strive to control her trembling. Now Nellie began to panic. The girl seemed badly frightened, but what could be so bad that she was frightened the others might hear?

'What is it? Tell me.' Nellie was dreading the answer.

'I think they're planning to blow it up!'

'Blow up the Arsenal?'

Matty nodded, squeezing Nellie's hand till it hurt. Nellie felt sick. She should have known Ted would be up to his old tricks, and if it didn't go wrong this time, half of south London would be blown to pieces, to say nothing of her own dear Matty.

'I couldn't believe anybody would be so wicked,' Matty said, ashen-faced.

'That bastard would be.' Nellie shook her head grimly. 'He's tried something like it before. Oh, I blame myself, Matty. I should have shopped him years ago.'

Now Matty wanted to know exactly what Ted had done and Nellie told her the whole truth this time.

'Well, then, it's true. I didn't want to believe it; I thought it was his fantasy,' Matty said, when Nellie had finished.

Nellie sat down on the penny-farthing trailer, pulling Matty in close next to her. She put her arm round the shivering girl. 'But when did he tell you? Did he give you the details?'

'No, it was about a week ago. He just asked me not to work night shifts, especially not Zeppelin nights. And I said we didn't get to pick and choose our shifts, and he told me he didn't want me getting hurt and to make an excuse not to be there. Anyway, one of the girls got ill and today they asked me if I could stay on for the night shift tonight. I met him in the pub at dinner time and he went nuts when I told him. He grabbed me, look!' Matty rolled up her sleeve to show Nellie a red weal, encircling her arm. 'Then he went pale as a ghost and said that because he thinks a lot of me he had to warn me, but I wasn't to breathe a word or we'd both end up dead!' Matty's trembling was now uncontrollable and Nellie soothed her till her limbs were still.

'Go on, what did he say next?' she asked, trying to keep the urgency out of her voice.

'He said there's a group want to smash the profiteers and tomorrow there'd be nowhere left for me to work, because tonight they're going to get into the Arsenal and blow it sky high. He said he wasn't going in himself, but they'd made him get the information for them. Then he called me a stupid little cow and hadn't he told me not to work Zeppelin nights and it was going to be one tonight. He wouldn't let me go till I promised not to stay for the night shift.'

On moonless nights, Nellie, like everyone else, would listen out for the Zeppelins' sickening hum, their pale cigar shapes heralding an explosion of flame along the Thames as they bombed the docks. She was used to the raids and the anxiety, but not inured to them; any one of those bombs could miss their target and land on nearby Vauban Street. But Woolwich Arsenal was another matter altogether: a direct hit on it would ignite hundreds of tons of TNT. Nothing would survive for miles around. But a bomb, strategically placed there, might well have the same effect. And now Nellie began to realize why Ted's friends had chosen a Zeppelin night. An air raid would be the perfect cover, and what's more, the explosion might lure in the Zeppelins to finish off the job.

'Matty, you said Ted had given them information. Did *you* ever tell him anything he could use?' she asked gently.

The young girl paused to think and then put her head in her hands. 'Oh, God.' Her voice was small, strangulated, not Matty's voice at all.

'What sort of things?' asked Nellie.

'He used to ask me in such a natural way, Nell, like he was worried about my safety. I didn't know. He asked about where I worked, where the exits were, how many coppers guarding the TNT store... Oh, Nellie, what are we going to do? If we don't do something, think of all the people that could die!' Matty began rocking back and forth, repeating over and over, 'What can we do?'

They were both almost paralysed with fear, but Nellie had been in this position before and was determined not to make the same mistake again. This time there would be no covering up for Ted, no misplaced loyalty or excuses. He had to be stopped.

'Come on, Matty, we need some help.'

When they got to the house in Reverdy Road, Ruth Morgan answered the door. 'Oh, I'm sorry, Nellie, Eliza's not in. She's giving a speech at the NCF.'

'Did she say what time she'd be home?'

'Soon, I hope. She said she wouldn't be late, she's left the little one with me.' Just then there was a piercing cry from inside the house. Mrs Morgan looked anxiously behind her. She looked frazzled. 'That's little William, he hasn't settled since Eliza went out. Poor mite, I'm a bit of a stranger to him.'

'He knows us,' offered Nellie.

Ruth Morgan smiled gratefully. 'Follow me!'

William's screams had grown frantic.

'He's in a right two an' eight,' said Matty. 'I better see to him.' Mrs Morgan led her upstairs, while Nellie went to wait in the front parlour. Soon the sweet strains of Matty singing a lullaby floated downstairs, and William's cries ceased almost immediately. Mrs Morgan came back into the parlour, smiling at Nellie. 'Thank God you two arrived, he was set to go on for hours!'

Nellie smiled. 'He'll never give in, that one.'

Mrs Morgan cocked her head, listening. 'Well, Matty's certainly got the touch. I'll make you some tea, you might as well wait here for Eliza. She won't be long now. Besides,' she said, 'if he wakes up and Matty's not here, there'll be hell to pay!'

Nellie was glad of the distraction; it had calmed Matty down and given her time to think what she would say to Eliza. She was still shocked to the core that Ted could even think of putting Matty in danger. True, he'd warned the girl, but what about all the other innocent canaries who might be working tonight, to say nothing of the families who lived around the Arsenal? No doubt Ted would class them as casualties of the class war, and the arms manufacturers a legitimate target.

Soon Matty joined her and Ruth Morgan, and Nellie tried to keep up chatter to distract Matty, who looked anxiously at the mantelpiece clock every few minutes. They both started up when Eliza's knock came. As she walked into the parlour, Eliza's first worried question was: 'Is it Sam?'

They put her at her ease and Mrs Morgan praised Matty's

lullaby skills. 'I'll take myself off upstairs now and leave you three, if you don't mind,' she said tactfully.

Eliza thanked the woman and apologized for her son's tantrums. When they were alone she turned a worried face to Nellie. 'If it's not Sam, it's got to be something serious to bring you here. What's happened?'

She listened intently as Matty repeated her story, then Nellie added what she knew of Ted's past activities. It felt unreal to Nellie to be sitting in this respectable room, full of heavy furniture, antimacassars and dainty ornaments, discussing anarchist plots.

'The only thing I don't understand,' Eliza said eventually, 'is the timing. Why choose a Zeppelin night, when security is highest?'

'Where will everyone be looking?' asked Nellie.

Matty and Eliza replied as one. 'At the sky!'

'And I reckon the bombers will try to slip into the Arsenal while everyone's distracted by the Zeppelins! We've *got* to tell the police. He's not getting away with it this time,' Nellie said, with finality.

'I'm responsible for this,' Eliza said hollowly, looking up at Matty. 'I put you in harm's way. I sent him here.'

Nellie knew how she felt. 'It's not your fault, Eliza. If it's anybody's, it's mine. I should've given him up five years ago. Sam would've done, if it weren't for me.'

Matty looked impatiently from one to the other. 'Oh, stop wallowing, you two,' she said fiercely. 'I could say the same. I was the silly cow give him all that information! It's nobody's fault but Ted's, and all that matters is how we stop this!'

Eliza got up. 'It's ironic, I've seen him tonight. I've just been talking to a room full of gentle Quakers and pacifists, who wouldn't hurt a fly, and there he was sitting in the front row, smiling at me and no doubt despising the lot of us. At least he has his alibi. I'll telephone the police, but I don't want Matty involved.'

Nellie agreed.

362

'And I don't want Nellie involved,' Matty quickly jumped in.

'None of us need be involved,' Eliza said firmly.

She walked determinedly to the telephone on the side table and pulled aside the heavy curtain. She peered out.

'It's a dark moon,' she said.

Nellie and Matty listened in silence as Eliza got through, after many attempts, to the right police officer.

'Yes, I believe it will happen tonight. They plan to get in under cover of a Zeppelin raid... No, I don't know how many bombs... no, I don't have more details, but I do know that unless you take this seriously, Officer, the Arsenal and everyone in it will be blown up... No, I don't wish to give my name.'

The telephone clicked as she rested it back in its cradle. The three women looked silently at each other. It was left to Matty to voice their remaining concern.

'What shall we do about Ted?'

'I have an idea,' Eliza said. 'He'll be handing out anti-conscription leaflets in Bermondsey Square tomorrow evening. It only needs for the police to come along at the right time and...' Eliza shrugged.

'Can they arrest him for that?' asked Nellie.

'Oh, yes,' said Eliza, 'and once they find out he's an Absolutist, he'll be drafted...'

'But Ted's not going to serve,' Nellie added, following Eliza's reasoning, 'so what happens then?

'He'll go to prison... for a long time,' said Eliza. 'Hard labour, it won't be pleasant.'

'Give me that phone,' Nellie said.

32

TILL THE BOYS COME HOME

Nellie stood, shielded by an old square tomb of pale stone. The curly inscription, eroded by time, was picked out by lumps of grey lichen. The tomb was almost as tall as she was and she had to stand on tiptoe, peering over it towards Bermondsey Square. Behind her, the squat form of Old Bermondsey Church stood comfortingly ancient, solid and reassuring. She had chosen the churchyard as the perfect vantage point; she needed to witness this, but did not necessarily want to be seen. A small crowd had already begun to gather in the square, some holding placards, others handfuls of leaflets. Then she saw him, flinging himself through the crowd, his striking tall figure standing out above the others, his smile flashing. He leaped up on to a soapbox and began brandishing one of the leaflets. He'd just begun his speech when Nellie caught sight of the Black Maria careering round the corner of Tower Bridge Road, screeching to a halt in the square. Ted was immediately surrounded by policemen, grabbing his arms and pulling him down off the soapbox. She crept forward to the churchyard's black iron railings. He was struggling, but not so fiercely as to get away. He threw back his head, bright hair flying from his forehead. He was shouting something about 'oppression' and 'freedom', but she only heard snatches. She stood very still as he was bundled towards the Black Maria, studying his face. He was enjoying it, playing up to his dwindling audience. She almost felt sorry that she'd handed him the stage to play upon, but to have him safely locked up was worth the trade. Just before they pushed him into the van, he looked up and their eyes met between the black iron bars of the railings. Nellie nodded once, just to let him know, and she was satisfied. Behind bars, that was the only place for Ted Bosher.

The evening before had been a nightmare of waiting. She and Matty had left Reverdy Road straight after her phone call to the police. They didn't want to be caught in the Zeppelin raid themselves. They hurried through the darkening streets and, as soon as they arrived home, insisted that Alice and Bobby join them in the brick shed in the back yard. Nellie would be taking no chances tonight. The boys had already packed sandbags round the brick shed as soon as the air raids began, but it was only on these dark, clear nights that they ever bothered to shelter there. Mostly, they chanced to luck. Charlie and Freddie were both still out, but at least she could gather the rest of the family around her in safety. They kept up their spirits, joining in with Matty's songs until the dreaded drone announced the Zeppelin's arrival – it would be making its way up the Thames. Nellie could only pray that the police were already in position at Woolwich.

The explosion, when it came, was massive; they all started violently, clinging to each other in terror.

'But that's too close, isn't it?' Matty asked Nellie.

'Too close for comfort, I'd say!' Bobby said.

But Nellie knew what Matty meant. It had been too loud. The ground beneath them shook; even the shed roof rattled. No, that wasn't at Woolwich. Nellie shook her head at Matty.

'Sounded like it was over by Butler's Wharf,' Alice said.

They gripped each other's hands, their eyes lifted to the roof of the shed, as if they could see through it. After what seemed like hours of silence, they heard a rumbling and a rat-a-tat, very close, almost as though it were in the street.

'Strafing?' whispered Bobby. Sometimes the Zeppelin would come so low it was able to strafe the streets with gunfire. They held their breath until the clattering got so close it seemed to burst through right into their back yard.

'Oh, my gawd!' shouted Alice. 'The Germans are in the yard!'

But it didn't sound like strafing to Nellie. She crept to the door, fearing Ted and anarchists coming for Matty more than she feared Germans. Easing the door open, for a moment she couldn't believe her ears. Was that giggling she could hear? Yes, someone was giggling uncontrollably and someone else was snorting with laughter, in their back yard! She flung open the door.

'Who's there?' she said, more boldly than she felt, and was greeted by the sight of Freddie and Charlie collapsed over an enormous barrel.

They both looked up, and Freddie smiled inanely at her. 'Hullo, Nell, fancy a stout?'

It took a while to get the story out of them, but between periods of prolonged giggling she was able to piece together their evening, which had been almost as eventful as her own.

'We wash over b'river an' a bloody great bomb 'it Courage's! Beer ev'where, streets runnin' wiv it, sloshin about in it, wasn't we, Chas?'

Charlie nodded, eyes unfocused, a smile fixed to his face. 'Sloshin',' he repeated.

'Barrels flyin', floatin' in river, we reshcued 'em, didn't we, Chas?'

Charlie nodded.

'From the stink of you, I reckon you must've been swimming in it. Sounds like you sampled a barrel on the way home too!' Nellie said.

The giggling resumed. 'We brung y'ome some, Nell.' He pointed to the name stamped on the barrel: *Imperial Russian Stout*. '"S'yer favrit, pre-war strengf, innit, Chas?' Charlie had collapsed across the barrel while Freddie staggered across the yard. He clung to the back gate and slipped down it slowly. 'Gonna get 'nuvver one, c'mon, Chas...' he said, before collapsing on to the cobbles.

'You're not going nowhere,' Nellie said. 'Come on, Bobby, help me get 'em up to bed, they're pissed as puddins.'

By the time they'd dragged the two insensible figures up the stairs and tipped them into bed, Nellie was exhausted.

'I'm not going back in that shed. I don't care if a hundred Zeppelins come over, don't wake me up till the morning!' she said to Alice, and collapsed fully clothed into bed.

The next morning's newspapers contained more about the raid on the brewery than the one on the Arsenal. The report condemned the behaviour of those who'd 'profited in an unpatriotic way', by making off with barrels of beer shot into the Thames by the explosion. The real target was thought to have been Butler's Wharf next to the brewery. There was only a small paragraph about a 'failed' Zeppelin raid on Woolwich, which mentioned that two men had been apprehended, trying to get into the Arsenal during the raid. There was no suggestion of anarchists, or bombs, but Nellie took the paper home to show Matty.

'They got them,' Nellie whispered, 'thanks to you, Matty.' She hugged her. 'Now all I want is to see Ted put away.'

That was when she'd decided to go to Bermondsey Square, to make sure for herself. Now, after witnessing his arrest, she walked home, feeling safer than she had since Ted's return. She realized she would have to tell Lily, before anyone else did. She went home first, to pick up a present she hoped might make the news easier for Lily to take, and then took the tram to Rotherhithe Street, making her way carefully up the wooden stairs behind the chandler's. Lily was surprised to see her.

'This couldn't wait till Thursday!' was all Nellie would say, and then produced a stoppered earthenware jar from her bag. 'Get the glasses out, Lil,' she said grimly, 'you're going to need this.'

Lily was looking alarmed now; the perennial question on everyone's mind hardly needed articulating. 'No telegram, love, but I've got some bad news and some good news.'

'You'd better give me the bad news, then.' Lily went white as Nellie quickly told her everything that had gone on the night before and about Ted's arrest.

'Oh, God, no! He may be my brother, but he's a wicked bastard. What am I going to say to me mother?'

'You don't tell her nothing, except he's a conscientious objector! There's only the four of us know about the Arsenal now, and that's the way we'll keep it, all right?'

Lily nodded meekly. 'And you saw him put away, with your own eyes? Did he see you?'

'Oh, yes, he saw me all right.'

'I'm shaking, Nell, look at me.'

'All right, love, you need some of the good news...' She uncorked the jar and poured two creamy-topped glasses of Russian Stout.

Lily sat down and took a long draught of the thick black stout and looked up in amazement. 'Full strength!' she exclaimed.

Nellie nodded. 'I give those boys merry hell when they woke up this morning, but I reckon you'll be coming to my house of a Thursday now!' she said with a smile.

The barrel of Russian Stout lasted them well into Christmas and on into the New Year of 1917. They used some of it to celebrate little Johnny's second birthday in January and Nellie fervently hoped there would be some left for Sam's next leave. When the anniversary of their engagement came round in April, they drank the last of the stout and toasted Sam, but she began to despair of seeing him now before the war's end. His letters were continually hopeful, however, talking of all the things they would do together when the longed-for leave arrived.

When, that summer, she wrote, *Surely you're entitled to a few days' leave now?*, he replied that everyone was in the same boat; they simply couldn't be spared from the front, not now there was a big push on. Charlie told her that the 'big push' was taking place at Ypres, in Belgium. She asked him to point it out on the map, so she could imagine Sam there in Flanders. It looked tantalizingly close; she knew it would only take him a few days to get home, and yet the distance between them seemed infinite. One morning, in July, the hundred odd miles between them suddenly disappeared, when, on her dinner break, making the short walk along Spa Road from Pearce Duff's to Vauban Street, a great booming thunder rolled in from the east. Nellie knew, though, that it couldn't be thunder, for by the time she'd turned the key in the lock of her house the booming hadn't stopped for an instant. Bobby was at home, standing in their little kitchen, keeping very still, as they tried to make out the cause of the rumbling.

'Could it be a Zeppelin raid?' she asked

Bobby shook his head. 'What, in broad daylight? That'd be suicide!'

Boom, boom – another round reverberated through the house, as suddenly Charlie came rushing in.

'Can you hear it?' he asked, his eyes on fire with excitement.

''Course we can hear it, it's everywhere,' she answered. 'But what is it?'

'It's Sam!' he cried exultantly. 'It's the guns at Ypres, the battle's starting!'

Sam? How could Sam, her beloved gentle Sam, be in any way connected to that awful, hellish sound? If she could hear it here, hundreds of miles away in her cosy Bermondsey kitchen, how must it be for him? It must sound like the end of the world, she thought.

'Oh, Sam, my poor Sam,' she said, horrified.

'Poor Sam?' Charlie said scathingly. 'He's driving the gun teams, right in the thick of it! I wish I was out there!'

Nellie couldn't believe her ears. 'You stupid little sod,' she said.

But the sound of the guns thundered on all through that July of 1917. Nellie grew to hate their ominous rumbling, though for Charlie they exercised a pull, like a drumming tattoo. For her they were a nightmare, but she could see that for him they were a call to arms. It didn't help that he was now out of a job. The army had come calling and requisitioned every last one of Wicks's horses; even poor old Thumper had not escaped.

'It's not fair,' Charlie had objected. 'Thumper's too old to be any use to the army, he'll end up in some French git's stew!'

But the army had not been impressed by his argument and in the end Old Wicks had been forced to close.

'I'm going to enlist, Nell,' Charlie announced bluntly, one evening towards the end of July.

At first she laughed at him. 'Don't be ridiculous, Charlie, you're too young, you're only sixteen!' Looking at him, Nellie had to admit he looked much older, but they would only have to look at his birth certificate to see otherwise.

'They don't ask your age, Nell.'

'Oh, please don't do it, Charlie,' she begged. 'I promised your poor mother I'd look after you!'

She could hear herself moaning, for the young boy who wanted to follow in his brother's footsteps, and for Sam, who, she was convinced, would come home in a heartbeat now if he could. Charlie rushed round the table to where she stood and threw his arms round her.

'And you *have* looked after me,' he said. To her astonishment, the normally impassive Charlie was almost sobbing now. 'You've kept your promise, Nell, but I'm old enough to look after meself now, and I want to go and help Sam.'

Perhaps it shouldn't have surprised her. Of all the children, he'd been the least reliant on her. Of course he'd be able to look after himself; perhaps he always had. And certainly, ever since the war had started, he'd single-mindedly followed every campaign. He always knew what he was going to do; she just hadn't wanted to see it. So Charlie joined the seemingly inexhaustible line of recruits snaking its way down Spa Road to the town hall. He signed up for the Royal Field Artillery and was overjoyed to be posted to Sam's brigade, though in a different battery. Unlike Sam, who'd waited three months to be posted, Charlie was out in Belgium within weeks. His first letter home was that of an excited schoolboy:

I've even seen Sam! He was coming down the line to a little town called Poperinghe, as I was going up the line! We didn't have long, Nellie, but I nearly fell behind my battery, trying to give him all the home news. He was well and sends his love and a special message just for you, 'Keep Smiling!'

That was the last they heard from Charlie, or Sam, for many weeks. Lily hadn't heard from Jock either. They tried to reassure each other that the boys must be on the move, with no opportunity for letter writing. Nellie stopped going to the town hall. The casualty lists were simply too long to get through in her dinner hour and, besides, when she looked at the endless names, her imagination quailed at the broken humanity they represented. Then one early morning, in November, a sharp knock on the door caught her by surprise. She was dashing to get ready for work, the boys were getting in her way and Alice was nagging at her to hurry.

'Who the bloody hell's that at this time o' the morning?' She dashed to the front door to be confronted by a boy in a blue uniform; he had a bicycle with him and a piece of paper in his hand.

Nellie took the piece of paper, the world went silent and a cold sweat enveloped her. A darkness closed in around her; she was aware of a loud booming, coming from somewhere inside her own head, throbbing with the pulse of her own blood. She placed her hand flat on to the distempered wall of the passage, seeking for purchase, for a solid grasp on something, but there was nothing she could physically do to keep upright. Her sweating hand slipped down the wall and she sank slowly to the cold linoleum floor. And that was where Alice found her, crumpled like some wilted flower, crushing in her hand the still unopened telegram.

'Come on, Nellie, come and sit in the kitchen,' Alice coaxed.

Nellie was rigid, shaking her head, refusing to move. If she didn't move, if she didn't open the telegram, everything would be all right, she knew that. What was Alice fussing about, trying to get her up for? Couldn't she see that she had to stay put?

'No!' she said through clenched teeth. 'No! I'm all right here, I'll just stay here a bit.'

But then Freddie and Bobby gathered round and gently, as though Nellie were the tiniest child, lifted her between them and half carried her to her father's old chair. Alice got brandy and forced it through her lips, which were as grey as her face. Then she prised open Nellie's fist and gave the telegram to Freddie.

'You read it, Fred… to yourself.'

Tears were pooling in the boy's eyes, and he swallowed hard before opening the telegram. He nodded, then mouthed to Alice: 'Missing in Action.'

Alice mouthed back, 'Who?'

Nellie looked up just as Freddie whispered, 'Sam.'

Then came the days when Nellie's world turned to dust and ashes. No matter how much Alice and the boys explained the difference between 'Missing in Action' and 'Dead', she could not see it. How could anyone have survived that horrendous clamour of guns, or the drowning mud that was the battlefield? The news had come back from Ypres, tales of men fighting up to their armpits in ooze, and even the heavy howitzers that Sam's team pulled had sunk in the quagmire. Still they told her she must 'keep her pecker up', but such injunctions were as meaningless as Sam's last message to her. What did she have to do with smiles now? Her face would simply not remember how to form one and, in any case, her breaking heart would not want it to.

The boys moved gently and quietly through the house; at times Nellie had a remembrance of their clamour and wondered where it had gone. Then she would get unaccountably angry and shout at them, 'For God sake, don't creep around me like ghosts, I'm not an invalid!' But in reality her anger was all for herself, that she was not stronger, braver, that she did not have enough faith to believe that 'Missing' did not mean 'Dead'.

Freddie's response was to bring her even more contraband. Piles of vegetables appeared in the kitchen, gifts from the allotments he visited; a whole pound of butter turned up in the safe one day, from God knew where; a crate of condensed milk was suddenly spirited into the brick shed. It felt as though he were trying to feed her back to happiness. Lily was the only one who knew how to comfort her, for shortly after the telegram arrived at Vauban Street, an identical one had been handed to Lily. Jock was missing too.

Eliza had stepped in to help, writing letters to Sam's brigade commanders, seeking out any surviving Tommies from his battery. She had even pressed Ernest James into using his family connections to make enquiries, but the story was always the same. Both men had last been seen in the dying stages of the disastrous battle for the Passchendaele Ridge. None of the field-dressing stations or base hospitals could shed any light on their whereabouts. Then finally, after weeks of searching for his brother, Charlie had written to her in that schoolboy copperplate he'd once been so proud of:

> My dear Nellie, I am sad to say that all my searches have turned up nothing and I'm afraid we must accept the loss of our Sam and Lily's Jock. I wish there was better news I could write, but I wouldn't want to give you false hope, Nellie. The losses have been beyond belief, Sam's battery lost so many men, it's been merged with another. My battery was down the line at the final push and that's the only reason I'm still here, I reckon. Nellie, you've been like a mother to me and I just wish I could be there to help you now. Pray God, we'll get this job done quickly and I will be home with you soon.
>
> Your loving Charlie.

It seemed Nellie must accept that Sam was almost certainly one of the many thousands of men engulfed by that vast swamp of mud surrounding Ypres. But, in her darkest hour, she learned the strength of the cuckoo's-nest family she had raised. They allowed her to pretend to be carrying on as normal, all the while knowing that she was far away in spirit. Though custard powder was still packed, laundry still done, meals still made, they might have been the actions of an automaton. Her thoughts were ensnared in the life-sapping exercise of denying Sam's death and the only time she could be honest was on a Thursday evening when she met with Lily, who was doing exactly the same thing. On those nights, the two friends mostly sipped their stouts in silence.

Into the miasma of her grief sometimes came bright spots of light, which she did not question. Matty would drag her along to the Star and she would sit in the womb-like darkness of the old theatre, staring at the stage where Matty sang brightly on, then she would suddenly finding her foot tapping. Or Alice would lead her to the Old Clo' market and she would come home, miraculously, with a 'new' red coat to keep out the winter chill, for suddenly there was deep snow on the ground and it was Christmas. She had begun to measure her life in two periods, before the telegram and after.

Then there was Bobby, who never seemed to leave her side. At fourteen, he was still the same old loving Bobby and now he became her shadow. He'd been taken on full time at the vicarage, as a handy boy, but he offered to take over her Co-op round, which she'd insisted on keeping up. But she refused. Strangely, it was only when flying through the Bermondsey streets on the old contraption that she felt anything remotely like hope. The wheels would sing to her of a promise, the promise of her sixteen-year-old self to a dying woman, the promise of Sam to return to her, but the thrumming of the spokes in the wind spoke to her of another promise, the promise of hope.

Shortly after Sam's disappearance, the house in Reverdy Road became Eliza's permanent residence. She now rented the top floor of Mrs Morgan's house for herself and William. Her speaking engagements and union work were mostly carried on in London, and Ernest, with his new softly, softly approach, had suggested a London day school might be better for William. She knew, too, that he wished to see more of the boy, to say nothing of herself. But mostly she had come to Bermondsey for Nellie. After Sam's 'disappearance' – she insisted on not calling it death – Nellie's spirit seemed to have dispersed to the four winds, her solid, bold, cheerful self stretched as thin as a veil of mist, and Eliza was worried, as were all her family. Eliza could truly say that now she felt like one of Nellie's family. She had, after all, helped raise her own daughter and been engaged to her brother, but more than that, her mother had trusted Nellie Clark with all that was precious to her. Now it was Eliza's turn to help Nellie, and she judged the best thing she could do was to continue trying to find out what had happened to Sam. That search was best conducted from London and with the help of Ernest James. Ernest had disappointed his largely military family by going into politics, but he still had the necessary clout to contact a colonel-in-chief or a general.

An unexpected bonus for Eliza was that Matty became a regular visitor to Reverdy Road. She was able to share with her some of the leads Ernest was feeding back to her; even if they were ultimately dead ends, Matty was still keen to hear them. But Eliza would pass nothing on to Nellie unless she knew it had been verified.

Shortly before Christmas, Matty arrived at Reverdy Road looking flushed and excited. She was wrapped in a turquoise woollen coat with a huge shawl collar, and had a fur hat like a Cossack's pulled over her auburn hair. Mrs Morgan showed her upstairs and she carried in with her the fresh smell of snow. She shivered, drawing near the fire, which was blazing in the grate. It was nice to see the girl with a spark in her eyes again – for months they'd been like dull pools. Nellie wasn't the only one Eliza worried about; she knew how grief-stricken Matty was, but she also knew the lengths to which she went to hide that from Nellie.

'You look excited!' Eliza exclaimed.

Matty pulled off the hat and her cheeks began to flush in the heat. She dropped the coat with a flourish and twirled round.

'Bernie's American scout's offered me a job in a musical!'

'Matty, that's marvellous news!' Eliza exclaimed, before realizing what this meant. '*American* scout?'

Matty nodded, jumping up and down, hugging herself. Eliza hadn't the heart to squash her joy; she forced a smile to her face. 'You'd have to go to America?'

Matty flopped down into a chair by the fire and her face turned serious. '*Would* have to,' she emphasized, 'if I was to accept it, which I'm not.'

'You're not?'

She smiled ruefully. 'I would never leave Nellie, not now.'

Eliza's emotions fought silently as she looked on at her daughter. She felt nothing but relief that Matty wasn't going abroad, but still there was a strain of sadness that tugged at her. For Nellie, the girl would abandon all her hopes, something Eliza was sure she would never do for her.

'Do you think Nellie would want you to give up your chance, Matty?' she forced herself to say.

'No, but I'm not telling her, and neither must you! I was so bursting with pride that I had to tell *someone* about it, though!'

At least Eliza could be grateful Matty considered her a confidante now. 'Well, I'm proud of you, Matty, and if the rest of the family knew, they would be too!' she said, smiling. 'But listen, I have my own confidences to share. You know Ernest's brother's a major in the RFA? Well, he's uncovered something that gives me a *glimmer* of hope about Sam!'

Matty went white, all the flushed excitement draining from her in an instant.

'But this is something else we mustn't tell Nellie, not until we're sure!' Eliza went on.

'What have you found out?' Matty asked, wide-eyed.

'Well, apparently there's *another* Samuel Gilbie in the RFA, who enlisted on the same day as our Sam, and their army numbers differ by one digit...'

Matty looked like she was about to burst. 'And where is this other Sam, is he alive?'

'Breathe, Matty dear, please.'

The girl took a huge gulp of air.

'Yes, he's alive, in a hospital in Belgium, but badly injured, and Ernest's brother thinks it could possibly be a case of mistaken identity... Oh, Matty, it might be *our* Sam!'

'But if it's our Sam, why hasn't he told them who he is, or even sent word?'

'Major James says he was brought in from a field-dressing station, unconscious, and he's been that way for weeks, but now the doctors say he's more lucid. The major's stationed not far from the hospital and he's going out to see for himself!'

She was swept off her feet by a hug from Matty, whom she had to beg to settle down. As she saw her off, Eliza again warned her.

'It may not be our Sam, Matty – don't get your hopes up too high. And you've got to keep it quiet until Ernest gets confirmation one way or the other. We can't afford to give Nellie false hope either. You'll need to stay calm and make use of all those acting skills of yours!'

It was Christmas Eve and snow was falling in great fat flakes outside the high windows. The custard tarts, who were finishing early, were in high spirits. They had been paying into the Christmas Club all year: tonight, in spite of the watered-down government beer and the curtailed pub hours, they intended to enjoy themselves in the Green Ginger. Those women who'd lost sons or husbands or had someone 'missing' wouldn't put a damper on the other girls' good humour. They would either quietly absent themselves or, like Nellie, would go along and 'put a brave face on'.

She looked at the thick white swirl outside and imagined snow falling in Flanders, the once glutinous mud now crusted into frozen peaks and the flooded shell holes turned to frozen ponds. No matter where she was, her mind seemed lodged in Belgium, as though her thoughts were searchlights and one day they might light upon Sam. She looked through the pale golden haze of custard powder and saw, instead, mustard gas creeping over barbed wire, nestling into trenches.

'Nellie! Nellie! Wake up, duck!' Ethel Brown's voice brought her back reluctantly to the factory floor. 'You're wanted on the top floor!'

'Top floor! Why?' Nellie panicked. She had never been called to the offices on the top floor: that was reserved for firings or disciplinary interviews. 'What have I done wrong?' Perhaps her absent-mindedness had reached the notice of the bosses?

'I'm sure you ain't done nothing, love,' Ethel said unconvincingly.

Nellie slipped off her work smock and cap and went slowly upstairs to the offices. These rooms, where management worked and Duff had his office, were like another country to Nellie. A young secretary spotted her and led her to a wood-panelled, carpeted room with a massive walnut desk in the centre. Behind the desk, sitting in a leather chair, was the rotund figure of 'Old Plum Duff' himself. He got up and gestured her to come forward.

'Come and sit down, Miss Clark,' he said, in a chesty voice. She could hear him wheezing from across the room as she went to sit on the edge of the leather chair, on the opposite side of the desk. She gripped her hands together tightly. Why he had to sack her himself, she couldn't imagine. Perhaps there had been, after all, some black mark on her record, since the strike days. Suddenly the door opened and another person was shown in.

'Eliza!' Nellie almost started out of her chair. Surely Eliza was the last person that Duff would have invited here willingly! But he was greeting her politely and then he looked towards Nellie. His chesty voice softened.

'Mrs James telephoned me with some news, Miss Clark, that she wanted you to hear straight away.'

Nellie prepared herself for what she knew must come and, now, fixing her eyes on the green patterns swirled into the ruby-red carpet, she saw only mud and blood and the broken body of her beloved Sam. She looked up at Eliza, who had walked over to her, reaching down to grip Nellie's trembling hands.

'Nellie, we've found him. Sam's alive!'

'Alive? My Sam alive?' She was shaking, struggling to take it in. 'Are you sure?' She didn't dare believe it was true. 'But where's he been all this time?'

Nellie tried hard to concentrate as Eliza explained that Sam had been in a Belgian hospital, unconscious, for over a month and mistaken for another soldier. Her brain seemed to be working overtime to comprehend these simplest of phrases.

'But how do we know it really is Sam?' Hope was edging its way into her heart but tinged with a sickening fear that it might prove false. Old Duff's secretary walked softly into the room and whispered in the old man's ear. The telephone rang and he picked it up.

'We have some evidence that might convince you, young lady. Here!' He pushed the telephone across the desk and Eliza handed it to Nellie. The line crackled, a man's brisk voice asked if he was speaking to Miss Nellie Clark, she said yes, and her heart wanted to break through her chest. She was aware of the eager eyes of Duff and Eliza looking at her; then she heard another voice on the line, weak, far away, but, oh, so familiar.

'Hello, Nellie?'

'Yes,' she said in a small voice.

'It's Sam.'

'*My* Sam?'

'Yes, Nellie, your Sam.'

Hearing his familiar, warm voice drew him close enough for her to feel his breath brushing her cheek.

'Oh, Sam, I thought I'd lost you!'

'No, darling Nellie, never,' he said, and his breath sounded laboured. 'Didn't I promise to come home to you?'

'You did!' she whispered. 'I should've believed you. Come home soon, Sam, I love you!'

Afterwards, Nellie learned that the phone call had been Eliza's idea – she knew Nellie would simply not accept the truth unless she had the solid form of Sam in front of her, or at least his voice, to verify it. She'd got Major James to pull strings and Old Duff had been only too pleased to help. That night in the Green Ginger, the celebrations were bitter-sweet. All Nellie and Sam's family were there, even Eliza, but when Lily came in, Nellie had to take her off into the saloon bar. Lily collapsed into her arms. 'Oh, Nell, I'm so happy for you!' And Nellie knew, more than anyone, how Lily's tears of happiness were mingled with bitter grief for Jock.

'If they've found Sam, they could still find Jock,' she whispered to Lily.

Her friend wiped tears from her cheeks. Hugging Nellie and forcing a smile, she said, 'Please God, they do, love, please God, they do. Now let's go and drink to Sam… and my Jock, with some of that gnat's piss they're calling stout, shall we?'

33

TURN THE DARK CLOUDS INSIDE OUT

Nellie could hardly believe almost a year had passed since that miraculous telephone conversation with Sam, in Duff's office. What a Christmas that had been, not just for her but for all of the family. Who cared what privations they suffered? They'd known Sam was alive and they'd celebrated with what they'd had. Nellie felt that she had been given back her life and had firmly believed she would have Sam in her arms by New Year. But it was to be many months before Nellie saw Sam again, for as soon as he was declared fit for duty, he was sent back up the line, to fight on. She wouldn't allow herself to think of the dreadful possibility he might be snatched from her again, so through the whole of the last year she had tended the flame of hope, keeping it alive until today, 11 November 1918, when her faith in Sam's penny-farthing 'promise' was finally vindicated, for the war was over and he would be coming home!

Although the long agony of waiting to see Sam again was almost over, the end of the war seemed somehow to take her by surprise and she found she didn't know quite how to greet it, her deep relief tinged with grief and overshadowed by too much loss. Lily wouldn't be celebrating, not with Jock still missing, and Nellie suspected that her friend had given up hope. In the end, it was her fellow custard tarts who helped her celebrate Armistice Day properly. After clocking on that morning she found the packing room in uproar, the girls surrounding a red-faced Ethel Brown, who looked as though she were about to start another war.

'Pipe down, you lot,' Ethel roared. 'I said I'm going to see about it!'

'What's going on?' Nellie asked Maggie Tyrell, as she pushed through the circle of angry women.

'Old Plum Duff's got a bloody cheek. He's not letting us have no time off to celebrate! Ethel's going up there!' Maggie jabbed her thumb at the ceiling as Ethel marched down the factory floor, the girls cheering her on. 'Go and tell the mean old git, he'll have another strike on his hands if we don't get today off!' Maggie shouted after her.

Nellie didn't think much of Duff's chances today. The women were so fired up it seemed to unlock the floodgates in her too. She finally allowed joy to bubble up in her own heart; the war was over, Sam was coming home! Letting it sink in, she suddenly found herself caught up in Maggie Tyrell's skinny arms.

'Come on, Nellie, give us a smile! It's over!' she said, swinging Nellie clear off the floor. They both toppled over, laughing, just as Ethel burst through the swing doors.

'Come on, girls!' Ethel bellowed. 'Poor old Duff's in tears up there. It was a mistake, he was gonna let us off anyway. The mayor's up the town hall at ten, let's go and have a party!'

Nellie joined the custard tarts streaming out of the factory, hundreds of them, singing, dancing, holding up the traffic in Spa Road, some jumping aboard vans and car running boards, pulling the whole street into their celebration. On the way, they gathered with them the women and children queuing outside the soup kitchen; then the tramps, outside the Sally Army, peeled away to join them too. It seemed the whole of Bermondsey had stopped work to converge on Spa Road, till, like a raggle-taggle army, they all reached the town hall. There, bunting had been hastily looped around the entrance and the Salvation Army band was playing 'Tipperary'. Nellie joined the others, singing herself hoarse, until the mayor came out on to the town hall steps and there was a hush. After his speech, the bells of St James rang out, peal after deafening peal, and she allowed herself a moment to look around. How different the steps of the town hall looked today, revellers instead of eager-faced recruits, unbridled joy instead of anxious faces peering at the names of dead and wounded. The casualty list was still posted there, but Nellie's heart was overflowing with happiness; tears of joy streamed down her face as she realized she need never search for a name on that list again.

It was the Friday before Christmas and she'd taken the day off work. Sam was due to arrive at Waterloo Station this very morning, and she wanted everything to be perfect, including herself. Nellie took the mirror off the kitchen wall, propping it up on a chair. It was the only way she could see herself full length. She smoothed her hands down the bodice of the midnight-blue dress she'd been saving for Sam's homecoming. She tightened the broad, pleated sash, which emphasized her small waist, then pointed her foot; the shorter length showed off her ankles, which thankfully, were shapely. Satisfied, she hung the mirror back in its place above the kitchen fireplace and sat down to wait. Tonight the whole family would celebrate Sam's safe return. Matty and Alice had spent all week cleaning the house. Nellie had baked a cake, with black-market butter and flour, and Freddie had 'found' a crate of beer outside Courage's. They would all have their chance to welcome Sam home but now, just for an hour, she wanted him to herself.

It was no good; she couldn't sit still. Was that footsteps? She went to the door, peering the length of Vauban Street. No, it was only a neighbour, bashing a rug against her front wall. She went back to the kitchen mirror, checking the back of her hair, which was caught up softly at the nape of her neck. Walking to the window, she twitched the net curtain. If he'd been lucky enough to get a lift on an army lorry, he might be turning the corner any minute. Resisting the urge to check the front door yet again, she sat there, willing him to hurry up, her imagination clearing his way through the weekday traffic, speeding his feet along the crowded pavements. What was taking him so long? What was there to keep him? She imagined farewells to his mates at the station; had he stopped for a beer? But, no, surely he wanted her arms round him, as much as she wanted his.

She'd almost given up, thinking perhaps his troopship had been delayed, when she heard it – the sound of boots ringing on cobbles. She flew to the door, flinging it open, and in a moment was in his arms, kissing him unashamedly in full view of the neighbours.

'Oh, Sam, thank God, thank God, you're home!' she said, pulling him into the passage. He kicked the door shut behind them, taking her in his arms, squeezing her so she could barely breathe.

'Ohhh, Nellie.' His voice was thick with an emotion that seemed more like pain than joy. 'Ohhh, Nellie.' He kept repeating her name till she pulled away from him and looked him full in the face for the first time.

He was gaunt, grey, his chin dark with stubble. She searched his eyes. Their dark depths had always been lit by a gentle, welcoming warmth, so often revealing his feelings when his words could not. But not now. With a shock that made her take a step back, she realized there was no answering look in those eyes, which before had always sought her own. They told her nothing.

He noticed her recoil and, heaving the pack off his back, looked down at himself, shamefaced. 'Look at the state of me, and I've made your new dress dirty.' She began to protest, but he went on, 'It's been a long old haul, I must stink to high heaven and I've not slept all night...'

Putting her fingers to his lips, Nellie said softly, 'Sleeping can wait...' And, grabbing his hand, she led him into the kitchen.

Heedless of his filthy tunic, she twined her arms around his neck till he dipped his head, kissing her with a probing hunger she'd never experienced with him. His kisses were fierce but, after four years surrounded by death, had she really expected

384

gentleness? She found herself matching the depth of his kisses. He still smelled of the battlefield, but she clung to him, her own mouth searching for that old answering tenderness. But with each kiss he felt further away and instead of finding him, she succeeded only in losing herself.

Nellie's relief that Sam was back, and in one piece, carried her through the rest of the day. She filled the tin bath for him with boiling water from the copper, she fed him mounds of toasted 'real' bread, with the black-market butter, and put all his muted reactions down to his tiredness.

But when the others came home and still no spark returned to those dull, bruised eyes, Nellie had to admit that something was very wrong.

There had been a case of mistaken identity; it had robbed her of Sam for many months, but then he'd been restored to her, or so she'd believed. But identities are fluid things, she now realized, and in the furnace of a war, such as Sam had experienced, how could his have stayed intact? Surely the metal of any soldier's character would melt and re-form every time they faced death, or saw a pal blown to pieces in front of them? Her foolishness shamed her. She'd believed she was getting back 'her Sam' from the war, but from the first time he'd held her in his arms, his uniform still caked with mud, still smelling of blood and sulphur, she felt this was not her Sam.

The signs were there to see, from the start. Their reunion had left her feeling anxious; she was hoping for a word from him, that he was overjoyed to be back, even that he loved her. But she'd got neither. In the evening, during the family celebration, he sat like the silent centre, around which all their emotions of relief and happiness swirled. Matty, dressed in her stage finery, sitting next to him, her arm through his, sometimes leaned her head on his shoulder. Nellie wondered if the young girl had noticed Sam's odd remoteness too. Looking across the table at Sam picking at his food as the chatter got louder, Nellie thought he looked uncomfortable, cornered almost, and her heart sank as she realized he would rather not be the centre of all this loving attention.

Then, halfway through the meal, Freddie stupidly asked if there had been any more news of Jock. Nellie kicked him under the table, but it was too late. Sam, his already ashen face turning white, pushed his chair back and stumbled round the crowded table, out into the yard.

'You idiot, Fred!' Bobby hissed. 'Why d'ye go an upset him?'

Matty went to follow Sam, but Nellie stopped her. 'I'll go,' she said, glaring over at Freddie. 'Alice, will you cut the cake while I get him back in?'

Sam was smoking, leaning up against the brick shed. She put her arm through his, leaning in close to him. 'I know it's hard, with Jock not coming home,' she said softly.

He took another deep drag on the cigarette and blew smoke in the air while she waited for him to answer. Shaking his head, he threw down the cigarette, grinding it with his boot.

'It's cold out here, best get in, duck,' he said.

Nellie went to bed, full of misery at the change in Sam. For so long she had looked forward to his homecoming and now it felt as if she had lost him anyway. Waking next morning with a sick feeling in her heart, she told herself she must simply wait patiently for him to learn to trust her, with all those dark tales she knew must be locked up inside him, along with what he knew of Jock's fate. She hadn't seen him for over two years and she was beginning to realize how little she knew about his war. Still, she wouldn't push him; she told herself to be grateful they both had the rest of their lives to get to know each other again.

It was barely dawn and Alice still slept quietly on. As Nellie forced herself to get out of the bed, she thought she could smell burning. Hurrying across the cold lino to the window, she looked out over the back yard to see smoke billowing up. 'That bloody Freddie!' she muttered, thinking some of his contraband must have contained combustibles. She pulled on her shoes and dashed downstairs. Grabbing her coat from the passage, she sprinted through the scullery and out into the back yard, where she pulled up short in front of Sam.

'What are you doing?' she panted. 'I thought the place was on fire!'

He looked up at her through flames, his gaunt face lit by their false ruddiness. He was in his civvies, which only served to emphasize how emaciated he'd become. A thin neck stuck out of his collarless shirt; his trousers were baggy and cinched in tight around his waist. It seemed to Nellie as though the war had pared him down to the bone. There was nothing left of him.

'I'm burning my uniform,' he said flatly.

Then she saw that he'd stuffed his uniform into the old dustbin. It was full of khaki, now crackling into flame, blackening and turning to ashes. Only his greatcoat had been spared, laid over the penny-farthing trailer, along with his spurs. He saw her looking at it.

'I might as well hand back the greatcoat – up the army depot at London Bridge. They'll give me a few bob for it,' he said, turning away from her to poke the flames to life again.

'Sam,' she said hesitantly, 'I think we ought to go and see Lily, don't you?'

'I don't know anything, Nell,' he said, and his reluctance was painful to watch. 'I've got no good news for her.'

'But still, she'll want to hear whatever you can tell her. It's the not knowing that eats away at you, I had it for long enough with you. She'll be happy you're home...'

Although Sam didn't looked convinced about that, he finally agreed, and later that day they took the tram up to Rotherhithe to see Lily. It was heartbreaking for Nellie to see how brave her friend was in the face of Sam's return, her joy unfeigned. As they sat round the kitchen table, Lily took Johnny on to her knee, listening, while Sam stitched together all her dark imaginings, with a few threads of fact about Jock. He told how they'd both been driving their team when it was hit with shrapnel. Jock had fallen, along with the other team driver, and Sam had been forced to go on alone. They'd been separated on the battlefield and Sam hadn't seen Jock again. The battle of Ypres had dragged on another week or so, their battery decimated and Sam himself wounded.

'After that, I didn't know nothing till I woke up in that Belgian hospital,' he said flatly. He'd forced out these bald facts in short, emotionless sentences and when he saw Lily's tears begin to fall he simply got up and walked out. Nellie gathered Lily and Johnny into her arms. 'I'm so sorry, Lil,' was all she could say. 'He's not the same.'

The year turned and it was January of 1919 before Charlie came home, still only seventeen but now a manly, seasoned soldier. She hoped he might be able to reach Sam, but although the brothers greeted each other warmly enough, they never mentioned the war in her hearing. Wicks's yard had closed during the war, so neither of them had a job to return to. They both sat, every day, scanning the newspaper advertisements for jobs, exchanging the odd complaint about the scarcity of work for returning soldiers. Charlie, always self-sufficient, one day announced, to everyone's surprise, that he'd decided to stay in the army. Nellie waited for Sam's protest, but he greeted the news with uncharacteristic indifference.

In the weeks since Sam's return Nellie had been forced to admit that she hadn't grown to know this new Sam at all. She began to ask herself how she could marry a man who was now a complete mystery to her. It was a cruel irony. For all she knew, this Sam might as well be that other soldier he'd been mistaken for in the Belgian hospital. He had come back older, sadder, harder, but worse than all this, Sam wouldn't talk to her. She wanted to take the burden of some of his awful memories, but from the moment he'd stepped off the boat from France he hadn't said a word about it. Perhaps he never had been a great talker, but she could always tell what he was feeling. Now she didn't even know if he was happy to have survived. He was impenetrable.

And she wasn't the only one hurt by his indifference. Even Matty couldn't penetrate Sam's new rock-hard exterior. It was a bitter sadness to Nellie, seeing how the little canary hovered around her once adoring brother. When she hugged him, he would slowly disentangle himself with a cutting, 'You're not a little girl any more, Matty.' Nellie almost felt that those who loved him most were being punished, or perhaps he was punishing himself, by pushing them away. But what had he done wrong, except fight in a war not of his making?

One night, early in the new year, Nellie and Sam were sitting up late, waiting for Matty to return from the Star. She came in with a troubled look on her face.

'Want something to eat, love?' Nellie asked, but Matty shook her head, glancing at Sam. 'Actually, I've got some news!' She waited for Sam's response and when it didn't come, sighed.

'Good news, we hope! Don't we, Sam?' Nellie said, rather too brightly.

'Well,' Matty went on, 'that American agent's been after me again. I'm thinking of taking him up on his offer.' Again the young girl looked hesitantly at her brother. Stirring in his seat, he looked at her blankly. 'Well, it's your life, Matty, you must do as you like.'

Matty's face crumpled. Turning away, so Sam couldn't see the tears on her face, she left them alone together. Nellie couldn't believe what she'd witnessed. She guessed Matty had no intention of going to America but merely wanted Sam to protest, as he once would have done. Nellie decided enough was enough. She screwed up her courage.

'Sam, I want to know what happened to you out there...' She paused as the fire crackled and wind soughed down the chimney, filling the little kitchen with a burst of smoke. He poked the fire.

'Needs sweeping,' he said.

'For God's sake, Sam.' She was getting angry. 'I can't pretend any more! You're a different feller. Look at the way you've treated Matty and you've hardly said two words to Charlie since that boy came home. If you'd seen the hell he went through looking for you, you could at least show some interest in him! I know it's the war but I think if you could just talk to me—'

He cut her off. 'Well, you should know me by now, Nellie. I'm a quiet old stick at the best of times. Anyway, there's things I don't want to put in your mind, you're better off not knowing. '

He wasn't angry; in fact, she would have welcomed some anger. Any feeling would have been better than this impenetrable shell. But what did she expect? He'd been away for most of the time they'd been courting. Perhaps she was now as much a stranger to him as he was to her. She remembered him as a soft boy, certainly far too soft on her and how she'd scorned him for so long. In the end she knew that what had attracted her was his goodness. He was a good man, one she knew would always do the right thing. She'd taken to studying that old photograph of him she'd carried all through the war. She could see in it now, the beginnings of the change, his face set and grim, trying to look like a hard man, but under the man's uniform there had still been her Sam. As she bent down to kiss him goodnight, he turned his cheek to her. Standing up, she felt her heart shrivel a little.

'Goodnight, love,' she said, and, wishing she believed it more, 'We've got all the time in the world for talking.'

But it was to be weeks before Nellie eventually found out that it had happened at Ypres. 'Wipers', Sam pronounced it, not because he didn't know better but just because to give it a silly name might somehow diminish its horror. Like calling the devil 'old nick'. But whatever it was called, it was at Ypres she'd been robbed of her Sam, the good man she'd grown to love. Oh, he had come back all right in body, the head wound that had left him unconscious for weeks all healed up. He still had all his limbs attached, eyes seeing, ears hearing, though he had grown deaf in the clamour of firing off a million shells a day. But however grateful she was to have him back, through the long winter weeks of 1918 she had become convinced it was a different Sam who'd returned from Flanders. His coldness, she was sure, wasn't intended to wound, yet for her it bordered on cruelty. He hadn't once told her he loved her since he'd got back. Now it was she who hung about him, waiting for a smile. And still he wouldn't talk.

Then one sad day, towards the end of January, she made her decision. 'The wedding's off, Sam,' she said.

He was sitting by the fire, reading the job adverts in the *South London Press*. He looked up sombrely and began slowly folding the newspaper, while she stood in front of him, waiting. The old Sam would have pleaded, perhaps even cried, at least asked for an explanation. Instead, he looked at her fixedly and said, 'If you think that's best, you must do what you want.'

'How can you be so cold about it?' she blurted out. 'You're not the same, Sam! I always liked you to be strong, but not hard. I know it's the war's done it. If you'd only tell me about it, maybe I could help you get back your old self.'

Sam shook his head. 'Leave it, Nell!' he shouted, flinging the paper aside. 'I've told you there's things happen in war that a woman's got no business knowing. Now leave it alone, will you, for Christ sake!'

He'd never raised his voice to her before, and she recoiled. Although Nellie had learned early to stand up for herself and had carried her whole family through the war, what she loved about being with Sam was that she didn't have to be the strong one all the time. He'd always had his soft side to others as well as her, but where she was concerned, he'd been unfailingly protective. This new, silent Sam now revealed a coldness she'd never imagined his warm heart could contain. He simply didn't seem to care.

'I'll find lodgings somewhere else. I don't want it to be awkward for you, Nell.'

He walked out, without another word, and she didn't follow. He'd left his army greatcoat hanging over the back of the kitchen chair and as she picked it up, a small book fell out of the pocket. It was his army service book; it had a buff cover with *Royal Field*

Artillery. 'C' Battery Camberwell Howitzers printed on the front. With it was a voucher for the return of his greatcoat, promising a pound if he took it to the receiving office at London Bridge Station. She put the voucher on the mantelpiece, then, sitting down by the fire with the coat over her knees, she opened the book. The light from the gas lamp revealed brown stains on the cover… blood? Was it Sam's? Or maybe it was just from the mud at Ypres. Here, perhaps, was a speck of that slimy sea of clay and ooze into which her poor boy had vanished.

She knew she shouldn't read it, but the temptation was overwhelming. If he hadn't been such a closed book himself since he'd come back, maybe she would not have opened it. She angled the book up to the lamp. She read all the official entries, his enlistment date, his boyish signature. It was a sparse record of his four years. Training, posting to France, where in France? Just 'in the field', which field? A muddy, bloody one, with no name. Wounded early in 1916, he'd been sent to hospital and then back to the fighting. She remembered the day she'd come upon him in the bath. How sick she'd felt, seeing that scar snaking across his chest. Here it was recorded, so matter-of-factly. Then came the record of that leave in April 1916, when he'd been so passionate and asked her to marry him. Nellie smiled, remembering the excitement of walking out with her handsome soldier beau. She turned to the conduct sheet, all signed off as exemplary, until she reached October 1917; then came something that shocked her to the core. The model soldier had been charged with neglect of duty and locked up in an army prison.

She had to read it twice. Sam? Neglect his duty? Never! Desertion? No, she knew they shot them for that. But something had happened. Was this what was stopping him from talking? Was it guilt? What had her Sam done that warranted imprisonment? She had to know.

That evening, before she left for the Star, Nellie took Matty into her confidence. 'Matty, I've called off the wedding.'

'Oh, no, Nell, you can't! He still loves you, I know he does!'

'Well, I wish he'd tell me that himself. You wouldn't know it, to hear him.'

'I know he's not been himself, but you could bring him back… don't give up on him, Nellie, not after all you two have been through.'

Matty had more faith in her ability to get through to Sam than she had herself. But the girl was right: she couldn't give up on him. She waited up for him, and when he came home, he looked more weary and sad than she'd ever seen him.

'I've found a room with one of my old mates from Wicks's,' he said. 'Can Charlie and Matty still stay here for a bit till they're settled?' he asked dully. Nellie's heart twisted at the thought of breaking up her adopted family.

'Don't talk like that, Sam. This is their home.'

Sam sat himself in her father's old chair. With one leg crossed over the other, foot swinging gently, he began rolling a cigarette. That was another thing he'd picked up out there: he'd come back a chain smoker. He stared blankly into the fire. Quietly, she sat down opposite him and placed the book on the arm of the chair.

'I'm sorry, I read it. About you being locked up. What happened, Sam? Did you do something bad? Tell me. I won't think none the worse of you. What does it mean, neglect of duty? You're not one for breaking the rules.'

Sam looked into her eyes for a long moment, then he shook his head, as though he could shake away the memories held there. She took it as a dismissal.

'All right, Sam,' she said, getting up to leave. 'I won't trouble you no more with it. I always thought you was a good man, but if you can't even tell me, it must have been pretty bad, whatever you did. Goodnight.'

As she turned away, suddenly Sam started to talk. 'I'll leave you to decide if it was a bad thing I did, Nell.' His words were slow and heavy, as if he was struggling to get them out. 'Bad and good got all topsy-turvy out there. It was hard to know, sometimes, which was which.'

Nellie watched as he took out his tobacco pouch and rolled yet another cigarette. He pinched the end, pulling out loose strands of tobacco, struck a match and watched the tip glow as he inhaled. She studied his beloved face, noticing again how its boyish smoothness had been etched by the sorrow of war. He no longer needed to play at being the hard man: the war had made him into one. Staring into the fire, he seemed to forget Nellie was there and his story began to pour out.

'I think I *was* a good soldier, Nell, or as good as any. I did my duty, and I *wasn't* a coward. I didn't get locked up for desertion, they would have shot me for that! No, it was the horse. I did it for the horse.'

'The horse?' She couldn't have been more surprised. 'What happened with the horse, love?'

'I called him Dandy Grey Russet. It wasn't his army name, but we all gave our horses pet names. It was from one of those sayings me mum had, she'd call me in from the streets. "Let me wash that neck of yours, it's dandy grey russet", and she'd scrub till my skin was red raw, or she'd say, "That shirt needs a bloody good wash, it's dandy grey russet!" Where it came from, I couldn't tell you… it just meant that shade of grey, you know, when things need a wash.'

Nell smiled, her face softening. 'Your mum couldn't abide dirt, could she?'

Sam carried on. 'As soon as I saw that horse, I thought, I know what I'll call you! He was a Yankee horse, shipped over from America to France, poor beast had no choice. See, by 1915 we'd run so short of our own horses, all dead or worn out, we had to buy up American horses. But they was a sorry sight, after months swilling about in a boat on the Atlantic. Shaggy coats, no shoes. Mustangs they called 'em, meant to be tough, and they never once disappointed us. Anyway we fed 'em up, clipped their manes, put shoes on 'em, and by the time I first saw him, my Yankee was such a beautiful sight! Light grey, black eyes, charcoal mane and tail. So being a Yankee Doodle Dandy and a grey, I couldn't call him anything else but Dandy Grey Russet!'

'That was a lovely name to give him, Sam, he sounds beautiful.'

Sam looked up, remembering she was there. She held her breath, hoping she hadn't broken the spell, praying he would carry on.

'Soon it was just Dandy. We learned the ropes together. At first I think I was on the floor more than I was on his back, but we soon got to know each other's ways. I was driving a six-horse team, pulling a big old howitzer. We had three drivers on each team. I was the front rider on Dandy, farthest from the limber. All our team were Yankees, tough as you like. By the end of training, we weren't six horses and three men, we were like one animal. We lived and breathed together and sometimes, when it was cold enough with the snow on the ground, we even slept together. We'd take our blankets down to the picket line and sleep with our horses for the warmth.'

'Oh, did you ever get the socks?' She bit her tongue, it sounded so pathetic, but for the first time Sam smiled.

'Thanks, Nell, I got them, they fitted a treat.'

'So, how was it you got into trouble for the horse?'

'I got to love Dandy. He had a lovely nature – brave, clever, heart of gold. He always set the pace, always eager, would do anything you asked, go anywhere. He was special. We had to pull that gun over rocks and streams, through woods, up hills, and when it got bad, we pulled it through battlefields, bumping across dead and dying men, through sucking, stinking mud, always the mud. Dandy would fly through the shelling and I'd just about stay on his back.'

Sam threw his cigarette end on to the fire and immediately started to roll another. He inhaled deeply.

'I remember, once, we came up to a shell hole too quickly and I thought we'd tumble in and have the gun roll on top of us, but I swear he turned into a Pegasus and flew! Where he went the other five followed, we was like some flying chariot. How the gun didn't pull us back to earth, I don't know, but it bounced behind us till we got to the line, with it still in one piece. And then came the day when we both got wounded. Do you remember, Nell, that day I was in the bath, you saw my scar?'

'Do I remember? I couldn't sleep for worrying how you got it, and you never did tell me.'

'In the records, it says I was wounded by my horse falling on me. But it was nothing of the kind. Dandy saved my life that day. We'd just unhitched the gun when Jerry starts their bombardment, we fire back and the whole field explodes with shells. Dandy could take the noise, didn't shy and bolt like some of them. But he was trembling. I speak in his ear and he stays with me solid as a rock. I'm looking for a way through the fire and smoke when all of a sudden Dandy's pushing me back towards our guns, where I don't want to go. "No, yer stupid beast," I shouts at him, "not that way!"' I'd just unhooked him, and normally he'd know it was time for us to get behind the lines till our guns needed to be moved on again. But he just wouldn't budge and I got angry.'

Sam leaned forward, staring into the fire; he seemed to be following the battle in the flickering flames. 'I could see a way out of Jerry's firing range and I was damned well going that way. But Dandy keeps shoving me with his flanks and edging me back towards our guns, there was no way I could get him to turn. Suddenly his legs buckle and he falls ever so slowly on to his knees and then over on to his side, with me pinned underneath. That's when I hears the whine. They say you don't hear the whizz bang that kills you. Well, I heard this one, and it *would* have killed me if I'd carried on going the way I wanted. It landed just in front of us and Dandy got sliced with the shrapnel, down his left flank, and I got sliced down mine. But I tell you, Nell, that shell would've blown me to bits if I'd been up front, leading Dandy where I wanted him to go. I swear that horse knew what was coming, and he saved me.'

'Thank God for the horse,' Nellie gasped. 'I love him too now!'

'We went to the hospital together. I got strapped up and he

had a couple of days' peace in a field far away from the shelling. I fed him up with warm bran mash, the way he liked it. Looked after him like a baby, I did. Dandy thought he was back on the prairie. It was lovely to see him kicking out in that field. But peace didn't last very long in that place.'

Just then Nellie heard the front door; it was Matty back from the Star. She opened the kitchen door, but Sam didn't even look up. He was oblivious, lost in the memories that had begun to pour out. Nell simply nodded at Matty, who crossed quietly to the scullery. Nellie heard her making tea. Sam carried on.

'After a few days we had to hitch up our team and get back up the line. But that wasn't the last scrape old Dandy got me out of. A whole year I didn't get a scratch, it seemed like nothing could touch us. Then we got to Ypres.' Sam took in a great heaving breath and shook his head. 'We should never have pushed on. The rain, you never saw nothing like it, solid from July to November, turned the place to a swamp. It wasn't the right time to push forward, but the bloody generals had to stick to their plan, didn't they? It was all for a ridge. Passchendaele; I don't know what it means, but I know what it felt like. It felt like hell, rain and thunder, shells pounding and mud churning. We had to ride our horses into that, moving the guns further up the line. Our own bloody shells had broken up all the drainage, the rain had nowhere to go, just turned the earth into yellow soup. It was awful, stank of blood and guts and sulphur and gas. We put down duckboards, but either side the mud was treacherous. The standing order was that if the horses went into the mud, they had to be left or shot, on no account was we to stop for the horses, we had to push on... for the ridge, for Passchendaele.'

Matty crept in, put two cups of tea on the table, and silently took her own tea up to bed. Nellie heard the creak of the stairs, and when all was quiet, she asked Sam to carry on. She felt spellbound, carried back to the thick of that battle she had so long tried to imagine. Only now was she realizing how far away Sam had really been from her during all those years of fighting.

'Our team was nipping along when two wheels of the gun carriage edged off the duckboards and started to sink. We whipped our poor old beasts on till they couldn't pull them through that sludge any longer. First the back driver, Tom, got hit and he fell off, with his head half blown off, and then the shrapnel hit Jock behind me, he hung on for a bit, then he fell off.' Here his voice broke. 'I couldn't stop for him! Me and Dandy pressed on, we had to, Nell. If we'd stopped, the gun would've sunk, we had to get them to the line. I heard Jock, yelling at me to push on and get the gun out. And we did! Those brave beasts broke their hearts, pulling that gun, and when we got to the new line the bodies were lying two deep. It was carnage, what was mixed into that mud, I can't tell you. All sorts, arms, legs, bits of flesh…'

Sam started shaking, the cigarette fell to the hearthrug, and Nellie threw it on the fire. She handed him the cup of hot, sweet tea, cupping it for him with her hands; as he drank it down, the shaking subsided, but Nellie was frightened she might have pushed Sam too far.

'Oh, my poor love, you don't have to go on, not if it's too hard.'

'It's getting late, duck. I wanted to tell you, but it's getting late and…'

Nellie knew that, for now, she would have to be patient. Sam's silence had cracked, but she had to have faith that eventually the truth would pour out, and she would have her Sam back. He still hadn't told her he loved her, but for that, too, she would have to wait.

Two days passed, and though Sam didn't move out into lodgings, neither did he open his heart to her again. It was early in the morning and they were all rushing to get ready for work. Sam had already left for London Bridge; he was going to hand in his greatcoat and collect his de-mob suit. It was to have been his wedding suit. A knock on the door came shortly after he'd left and, thinking he'd forgotten something, Nellie dashed to open the door. She was instead met by a round-faced young man, with curly fair hair and an eye patch, still dressed in khaki. Nellie started back in shock. Expecting Sam, she had instead come face to face with a ghost.

'Jock!' He caught her as she stumbled forward into his arms.

'Sorry to give you such a shock, Nell. I only got back last night. Lily told me to get round here first thing and tell you and Sam before any one else!'

Alice came running in when she heard Nellie's cry, then the boys careered down the stairs, till the little kitchen was full to bursting. Tears of joy were followed by a barrage of questions. Alice plied him with tea and toast, while the family gathered round to hear Jock's story. That day at Ypres, when Sam had had to leave him, the shrapnel wound hadn't killed him. Instead, he'd been left half-blinded and insensible. Somehow, he had crawled to a shell hole. When he'd regained consciousness, the battle had moved on and the shell hole had filled up with water.

'I kept slipping down, couldn't see, couldn't climb out. I thought that was me lot, I'd drown there, for sure. Then I see this head peering over the shell hole. Sodding Bosch! They had me out of there in a jiff, decent enough fellers, bandaged me eye and makes me join a line of prisoners. Put me on a train to a prison camp in Munster and that's where I've been ever since! Couldn't believe it when they tipped us all out. The Jerries told us the war was over, just downed their rifles and walked out the camp. Left us to our own devices, so I started walking home!'

By now, Nellie and Alice were late for work, so Jock offered to walk down to Duff's with them.

'I really wanted to see Sam, where is he?' Jock asked as they turned into Spa Road.

'He's gone to hand his greatcoat in.'

Jock nodded and said, anxiously, 'Lily told me the wedding's off. She says he's a different bloke and I've got to talk some sense into him.'

'Well, I wish you would, Jock. I've tried, God knows,' Nellie said, shaking her head.

'I don't know what's happened to him, Nell, but it was only the thought of marrying you kept him going out there!'

'Well, he's told me it was his horse kept him going! He started to talk about what happened out there, then he clammed up again.'

'It changes you, Nell. We've all come back different. It's not you he's shutting out, it's himself. Some of us just shut ourselves down out there... had to. I reckon, right now, he's scared stiff of losing you, but he wouldn't say.'

Alice put a comforting arm round Nellie's shoulder and smiled gratefully at Jock.

'Jock, do you know what happened with that horse of his?' Nellie asked. 'Something bad enough to get him locked up?'

Jock shook his head. 'Locked up? I didn't know nothing about that! Probably already in the prison camp by then. Listen, I'll see if I can catch him on the way back from London Bridge, try and get it out of him.'

They had just reached Pearce Duff's and stood on the corner opposite St James's railway arch. Jock gave them both a hug and was about to leave them when Nellie noticed something, almost a bundle, halfway through the arch. She put her hand on Jock's arm and pointed. The arch, one of hundreds in the viaduct, was more a deep tunnel – cavernous, echoing, dripping with moisture, encrusted with soot and thick grime. It boomed with the noise of steam trains thundering overhead every few minutes. Sam had always laughed at her when she'd hurried him through one of these arches. He hardly even registered he was walking beneath twelve railway tracks and could never understand why they made her so jumpy.

'You go and clock in, Alice,' she said, ushering her sister towards the factory gates. 'You're late enough already. I just need a word with Jock.'

Alice dashed off as Nellie steered a puzzled Jock towards the arch entrance.

'What is it, Nellie? What's in there?'

'Sam would have gone through this arch on his way to London Bridge,' she said, her throat like sandpaper. She and Jock walked cautiously about three feet into the tunnel, when the first train passed overhead. It was like being locked inside a vast drum, with a giant pounding on it over and over again. Then she saw the bundle move, a huddled figure swamped in an army greatcoat, his hands clamped to his ears to shut out the reverberating memories, and she knew it was Sam. As the second and the third trains clattered over in quick succession, she could see his whole body trembling: he was back at Ypres. She could imagine him, holding the horses steady as the guns fired and fired for hours on end, till his poor ears became instruments of torture.

Now Sam was on all fours, crawling back towards them and the light of day. His progress was agonizing, as though he were crawling through sucking mud; he strained every muscle to move forward an inch. Nellie went to run to him, but suddenly there were twelve trains overhead and then the clattering, shuddering, hissing and thudding were magnified to an ear-splitting level. Billowing, choking drifts of dirty smoke filled the arch and, to Sam, it must have felt as if he had entered the mouth of hell once more.

Jock held her back. 'No, let me go, Nellie. I know what to do.'

Jock walked quickly forward into the darkness of the tunnel, wreathed in smoke and silhouetted against the filtering sunlight of the entrance. As she followed, more slowly, she could see Sam looking up, his face, through the clearing smoke, ghastly white and bathed in sweat.

'Jock?' he croaked, and shook his head. 'No, you never got up! Jock, is that you? Get your head down, man!'

Then Sam screwed himself up into a ball, until Jock bent down and put a firm hand on his shoulder. 'It's over, Sam, it's over. You're home, we're both home. Come on, I'll take you through.' And, raising his friend up gently, Jock led Sam to the other side and into Nellie's arms.

Nellie allowed Jock to take him home. It seemed that only someone who'd been in the same hell as Sam could get through to him. She wasn't in the same world as those two, couldn't hope to be. She joined Alice on the factory floor and though she'd been docked an hour's pay, she didn't care. She worked in a dream, praying that, somehow, Jock would now be able to reach Sam through the crumbling shell he'd built around himself.

When she clocked off that afternoon, it was already getting dark. The lamps weren't yet lit so she didn't notice the figure waiting for her outside the gates. It was only when he called out to her that she realized it was Sam.

She spun round. His voice sounded so youthful, she could almost believe it was the young Sam who'd once hung about for her outside the factory gates. Perhaps it was a trick of the twilight, but in the gentle blue shadows his face seemed younger, too, the lines softer.

'Jock got you home,' she said quietly.

He nodded, tears in his eyes. 'He got me home.'

Silently, she linked her arm through his and they began walking back to Vauban Street.

That evening, at Alice's urging, the family made themselves scarce. They all trooped off to see Matty at the Star, leaving Nellie and Sam sitting alone by the fire. They talked, first about Jock's miraculous return and then, as the night drew in around them, Sam was finally able to tell her how a horse had got him imprisoned.

'You deserve to know the rest, Nell,' he said, as she rose to light the gas lamps. 'Where did I get to?'

She sat down opposite him again and saw his brow furrow. 'That day at Ypres.'

'That's right. I'd got the gun to the new line and the gunners helped pull it out of the mud. That's when I saw Dandy, struggling. His forelegs was sunk in yellow slime. His wind was like a bellows and his eyes rolling, poor devil. He couldn't get to his feet. I was begging him, he didn't have no strength left in him.

Pretty soon his back legs got stuck too. His lovely grey coat was all crusted with blood and yellow ooze. I laid down in the mud and looked him in the eyes and I swear, Nell, I was crying like a baby. I didn't cry for Tom, or Jock, or any of the other lads, not even for me bloody self. I was crying for a horse. I says, "Come on, Dandy, my old son, don't let me down now, get up, old mate."

That's when Captain Carstairs comes up, starts pulling at me. "Get up, man, we've got to push on," he says. "We'll have to shoot the horse, he's done for. Here!" And he hands me his revolver to shoot the dear old lad who'd saved my life, and that's when I did it, Nell, that bad thing they locked me up for. I said, "No" to an officer on the battlefield. He could have shot me on the spot, but he wasn't a bad man. I told you good and bad got all mixed up. There we were blowing up men and calling it a good thing, and I wouldn't shoot my old friend, Dandy, and that was a bad thing. But old Dandy was the only thing kept me believing I was still human. The only thing that kept any warmth or kindness alive in me. He was all I cared about. And the terrible thing is, if I could have traded Dandy for one of my pals, I would have.'

Nell tried to protest, but Sam just shook his head.

'It *was* a bad thing – to disobey that order. I put all my mates in danger, holding up the line, for a horse. So in the end I was clinging to Dandy's neck when Captain Carstairs pulls me off and he puts a bullet in Dandy's head. He was decent enough to let me say goodbye. I kissed my old friend and thanked him for my life; then we moved on to take the ridge.'

He paused, taking a deep breath, then went on. 'I don't want you to know the terrible sights, Nell, thousands dead, screams, hell, it was. And after the battle, when they put me in the army lock-up to do my week's sentence, all I could think about was my dear old pal, Dandy Grey Russet. I got it all wrong, didn't I? How can you care for a horse more than for thousands of men? After I'd served me time, I didn't care whether I come home or not. They sent me back, with a different horse, and we got blown up near enough straight away, ended up in that Belgian hospital, out of it for a month.

'The war did something to me, Nell, and that's why I couldn't talk. I came back not knowing who I was, or what was good or bad any more. And there's the guilt I can't shake. Whenever I try to sleep at night, I see Dandy struggling to get out of that mud, looking at me as if I could save him, the way he'd saved me. But I couldn't, I couldn't save him and I couldn't save Jock, or any of them. I couldn't even save myself. Nellie, Sam Gilbie died in the mud, with his horse. So I understand why you'd want to call off the wedding. Why would you marry a stranger?'

There was a long silence. The banked-up coals on the fire were still glowing, but the flames had died to a weak flicker. Sam knelt and, with the tongs, lifted a few pieces of coal on to the fire, which sputtered and crackled into life. When he looked up, Nellie was silently weeping into her handkerchief.

'Oh, Sam,' she said, 'it wasn't a bad thing you did. I think that horse saved more than your life.'

Still kneeling, Sam reached over to lay his head on her lap. He wept too, great sobs of grief, his tears making dark patches on her skirt. She stroked his hair.

'I thought I'd lost you forever, but you *did* come back to me, Sam, just like you promised.'

'I love, you, Nell, and I'm still your Sam.' He paused. 'Will you marry me?'

Nellie kissed the tears from his face and answered, 'Yes, of course I will.'

Now the wedding was back on, they needed to start saving and Sam desperately needed to find a job. Old Wicks had died during the war, but the nephew who'd inherited the disused yard wanted to make a go of the business again. The next day, Sam went to see him at the newly reopened yard. Young Wicks was only too happy to take Sam on. He'd already begun replacing the horses taken during the war, he said, and now he needed drivers. He showed Sam into the familiar old stables to see the new stock of horses.

'There wasn't a lot of choice, they took nearly every sound horse in the country, but you can take your pick of this lot.'

Sam walked slowly along the stable block, carefully inspecting each horse, till he stopped at the corner stall. Striding past Young Wicks, he headed straight for the horse and put his arms round his neck. The beautiful grey with the charcoal mane didn't seem to mind at all, but nuzzled Sam's pocket, as though he knew he would find a treat there.

'He's taken to you right away!' said Young Wicks. 'Almost like he knew you. I reckon you two'll do fine together.'

Sam patted the grey's smooth neck and said, 'Yes, we'll do fine.'

So it was settled that he would start back at Wicks's the very next day and when Nellie went out to see Sam off, she waited on the doorstep, wanting to see him safely back in his old familiar place, up on the driver's seat, reins in hand. As the cart rattled out of Wicks's yard, she had her first glimpse of his new horse, the handsome dappled grey he'd told her was the image of Dandy Grey Russet. She waved and called out: 'He's beautiful!'

Sam smiled and his eyes met hers with that loving warmth she had so missed since his return. Her Sam was finally home.

Nellie and Sam were married at St James's Church, on a bright, crisp day in February 1919. Lily was her bridesmaid and Jock Sam's best man. After they'd exchanged vows, the newly married couple stood beneath the portico of the church while the photographer gamely tried to establish order among the rowdy, chattering guests. Eventually, they were all ranged in tiers on the steps below the portico. Sam drew her closer and his dark eyes looked into hers with undisguised adoration and happiness, while her bright blue eyes brimmed with love and joy, that this day had finally arrived. The photographer was in position and called for attention. Nellie waited patiently as the jostling subsided and, in the moment's silence, as they posed obediently, she drank in the sight of all her cuckoo's-nest family gathered around her. Alice, with her new young chap, stood beside Lily; Bobby and Freddie, both now taller than her, stood next. Next to Jock was Charlie, looking smart in his new uniform, and Matty, elegant, in her finest stage dress. Beside her stood Eliza James, a woman who'd once been Madam Mecklenburgh but was now Nellie's sister, holding fast to the wriggling hand of little William, in his sailor suit. Further down the steps were the Boshers and young Johnny, and from the bottom step she could hear the booming voice of Ethel Brown, trying to keep Maggie and the other custard tarts in order.

It was a day when all that Nellie had ever dreamed of came true and, looking back now over the years, she remembered all the people whose lives had intertwined with hers since that fateful strike of 1911. Some had made choices which were not always wise, and others had made mistakes that were often regretted, but she had made a promise. A promise to Lizzie, which, in the keeping, had proved not a burden after all but instead the source of all the happiness her heart could ever hold.

ACKNOWLEDGEMENTS

Grateful thanks are due to my agent Anne Williams at Kate Hordern Literary Agency for her faith in this story and for her many insightful suggestions, also to Rosie de Courcy, my editor at Head of Zeus for taking on the Custard Tarts with such enthusiasm and delight. My thanks to all the excellent team at Head of Zeus for guiding it so professionally to publication.

Thanks to my tutors and writing friends at Bexley Adult Education College for their unstinting encouragement; to Stephen Potter at the Southwark Local Studies Library; to Violet Henderson, who shared her vivid memories of working at Pearce Duff's as a teenager in the thirties and to the marvellous website www.bermondseyboy.net.

Many thanks to all my family and friends for their staunch support, and my special thanks to Daniel Bartholomew for long term, enthusiastic interest in my writing, lastly to Josie Bartholomew, without whom this book could not have been written.

340